The Secret
of the
Lost Pearls

Darcie Wilde is the author of:

The Secret of the Lost Pearls

A Counterfeit Suitor

A Lady Compromised

And Dangerous to Know

A Purely Private Matter

A Useful Woman

The Secret
of the
Lost Pearls

DARCIE
WILDE

KENSINGTON
PUBLISHING CORP.

www.kensingtonbooks.com

KENSINGTON BOOKS are published by

Kensington Publishing Corp.
119 West 40th Street
New York, NY 10018

All Kensington titles, imprints, and distributed lines are available at special quantity discounts for bulk purchases for sales promotion, premiums, fund-raising, educational, or institutional use. Special book excerpts or customized printings can also be created to fit specific needs. For details, write or phone the office of the Kensington Special Sales Manager: Attn. Special Sales Department. Kensington Publishing Corp, 119 West 40th Street, New York, NY 10018. Phone: 1-800-221-2647.

The K with book logo Reg. U.S. Pat. & TM. Off.

Library of Congress Card Catalogue Number: 2022943474

ISBN: 978-1-4967-3801-1
First Kensington Hardcover Edition: January 2023

ISBN: 978-1-4967-3802-8 (e-book)

10 9 8 7 6 5 4 3 2 1

Printed in the United States of America

CHAPTER 1

Chance Encounters

*. . . his flight was rendered necessary by distress
of circumstances; and if that were the case, he was
not the young man to resist an opportunity of
having a companion.*

Jane Austen, *Pride and Prejudice*

February 1820

"Campbell!" Asherton hailed Campbell from where he
stood with his pretty, young companions. "There
you are! We were afraid you weren't coming!"

Campbell smiled and strode over to his friend. It was a
raw gray day, and everyone was bundled up snugly. They
made a nice little grouping at the public gate of Langford
House—Asherton in his greatcoat, muffled practically to his
ears and flanked by the two delectable girls with shawls and
muffs. The girls were cousins. *Emma and, and . . .* Hang if he
could remember the other one. Campbell's attention, and
ambition, were fixed on Emma, or, more specifically, on her
future fortunes. According to her chaperone, Emma's guar-

dians planned to settle five thousand pounds a year on her dainty shoulders just as soon as she married.

Naturally, Campbell would have preferred a more manly way of making his living, but even the manliest must eat, dress, and pay his debts of honor.

Thankfully, little Emma was pretty enough to turn necessity into a pleasure. She had a wealth of pale gold hair, bright pink cheeks, pale skin, and wide blue eyes. In Campbell's experience, dark girls were bound to be obstinate. The fair, frail ones were generally of much sweeter and malleable temperament.

"I'm so sorry!" Campbell bowed deeply to Emma and to Mrs. Rutledge, the girls' chaperone. "A chance meeting with a man who had some business. It could not be helped. Emma, my darling, do you forgive me?"

The truth was, he'd needed an extra glass of brandy to help him muster the smiles that would be required during this afternoon's tedium. However, none of the party needed that particular detail.

"I most certainly do not forgive you." Emma lifted her delicately pointed chin. She shouldn't call such attention to that dainty feature. Any man with blood in his veins would be sore tempted to nibble on it. "Not yet, anyway."

You little coquette. Campbell's grin broadened. *We will see just how quickly you forgive.*

"If you two are *quite* finished," piped up the cousin hanging off Asherton's arm. What *was* her name? "I want to see the exhibition."

"Of course, of course." Campbell slid his arm through Emma's. "If you'll allow me?"

Emma's giggle signaled her full agreement, and they set off up the path, with Mrs. Rutledge determinedly bringing up the rear.

* * *

Lord Langford, the owner of Langford House, was a dedicated art collector. He'd built an entire wing onto his family's London mansion to hold his acquisitions. Every so often, he would magnanimously throw open the doors to show off his latest trophies. These public days provided a fine opportunity for the lesser gentry to see and be seen. And, of course, they had the advantage of being entirely free, and therefore well within Campbell's means, even after another bad night at cards.

Not that an afternoon at a gallery viewing was Campbell's idea of rousing entertainment. Emma, however, had expressed a desire to attend, and ladies must be indulged.

All of them.

Campbell patted Emma's hand, tipped her a knowing wink, and then slipped back to walk beside Mrs. Rutledge, who followed after them like a fat old crow, all clad in black. Shortly after he'd fixed his attentions on Emma, Campbell had discovered that Mrs. Rutledge was not immune to charm, or bribery, or gin. Since then, he had made certain to supply the old woman regularly with all three.

"Mrs. Rutledge, how are your bunions today?"

"Oh, I can't complain, Mr. Campbell." Which meant she would start grumbling as soon as she could draw another breath.

"Well, why don't you take your ease while we wander the gallery? Look here, they've provided a very fine couch for the relief of such troubles as yours. If you'll permit me?" Campbell took Mrs. Rutledge's hand and walked her to the brocade settee as if she were a girl he was leading onto the dance floor.

"Oh, well, I'm sure I shouldn't," she said as she sat. "The girls . . ."

"Will be perfectly safe with Asherton and me in attendance," said Campbell. "After all, what could possibly happen to them in such a very public place? Besides . . ." He gave her a wink and his very finest smile. His hand also just happened to press a coin into her gloved palm. "Who's going to say a word?"

Behind him, the girls burst into a flurry of giggles. Campbell took Emma's arm and steered her into the crowd.

The walls were fairly covered in paintings. All the gathering seemed to be enraptured by what they saw. To Campbell's eye, though, they were nothing but an endless line of sentimental landscapes, stiff portraits, and scenes of normal, dull people in normal, dull postures.

He let himself be deaf to Emma's assertion that they should purchase a catalog. Fortunately, Asherton gave in to the urgings of his girl—dash it all, what was her name?—and bought one of the shilling volumes that listed the paintings, praised Lord Langford as a patron of the arts, and gave some account of the artist's life.

"Remind me again what's so special about this particular chap?" Campbell allowed some of his ennui to creep into his voice.

Emma gasped and swatted at his arm with her gloved hand, just as he knew she would. "Oh, Campbell, you are tiresome! I told you all about it, and you *clearly* haven't listened to a word."

Which was true. Not that he didn't try, but a man with as many concerns as he had couldn't be expected to remember every detail of every conversation he held with a pretty featherhead.

"Whatever am I to do with him, Claire?" Emma sighed dramatically to her cousin.

Claire! Campbell vowed this time to commit the name to memory.

"You'll soon take him in hand, Emma, I'm sure," said Claire archly.

Campbell crooked his brows at Asherton, who returned a tight grin.

Emma took the catalog from Claire and assumed the air of a prim governess. "Jacob Mayne," she read, "was born in Hertfordshire, the son of a respectable landholder . . ."

"Respectable, maybe," put in Claire, her eyes shining delightedly. "But they do say the father was given to drink and cruelty."

"His mother used her entire portion to send him to the Continent to get him out of his father's way," added Emma. She didn't even need to glance at the catalog.

"He fell in love with a French girl whose family had run afoul of Napoleon," Claire went on. That was the one problem with the pair of them. They couldn't carry on a conversation singly but had to bat it back and forth like a shuttlecock. It made a man dizzy.

"He tried to bring her back to England, but while they were crossing the Channel, a storm came up unexpectedly, and she fell overboard and drowned," supplied Emma dreamily. "The other passengers had to hold him back to keep him from jumping into the water after her."

"Oh, look! That must be her!" Claire dragged Asherton over to a portrait hung dead center on the wall. It showed a delicate dark woman dressed in peasant clothing. Her loose blouse slipped clean off one white shoulder.

"So beautiful!" Emma sighed. "No wonder he tried to kill himself! Can you imagine how his heart must have broken to lose her?"

That was hardly what Campbell imagined as he looked at that tasty bit of shoulder.

"Quite lovely," he murmured. "But not as lovely as some." He pulled Emma just the tiniest bit closer. The girl smiled and preened.

"So what happened to our young hero after this tragic bereavement?" asked Asherton.

"He returned home, entirely devastated," announced Claire. "When he got there, he found his father had died and left behind nothing for his family but a load of debts. He tried to support his mother and sister with his painting, but no one would pay any attention to him. He had to go to work, but he couldn't stop painting. His grief turned to frenzy . . ."

"They say he'd stay awake for days at a time," put in Emma. "He would not sleep. He would not eat. All he would do was paint."

"And in the end he died of exhaustion and heartbreak. His family was forced to sell his work for whatever they could get." Claire shook her head. "It's all so awful!"

Campbell found himself staring into the painted eyes of the French peasant girl. The oddest sensation overcame him. It was not quite a sense of recognition, but it was close. And there was something else. Something closer, and more familiar . . .

It was as if he was being watched.

"You've gone quiet all of a sudden, Campbell," said Emma.

"There's a man staring at you." He nodded vaguely into the crowd. He used the opportunity to look about him, but mostly he saw the backs of hats and bonnets, men's coats, and ladies' embroidered shawls. There was nothing to explain the feeling of someone's attention fixed on him.

"Silly!" Emma cried delightedly. "No one's staring at me. How would they dare when I've such a fine, strong fellow on my arm to protect me from any impudence?"

"I must be imagining things," said Campbell ruefully. "I'm sorry. It's just all this . . ." He waved at the paintings. "To see so much accomplishment from such a young fellow. I can't help thinking how much of my life I've wasted." Campbell schooled his features into an expression of melancholy. It wasn't hard. Much of his life had been wasted or stolen from him. How much bad luck could a man endure and remain standing?

"Oh, Campbell." Emma laid her hand over his where it

rested on her sleeve. "You mustn't talk like that. Things will get better. You'll have your inheritance soon, and then you'll *make* them better."

Her faith was genuinely touching. Surely such faith, such love, could change the fate of any man.

"Oh, my dear, if only I'd met you first." He smiled with all the tenderness he felt in that moment. "You would have saved me from those other false loves and kept me on the straight path."

"You talk as if it was too late."

"For me, it is. I had potential once. I had dreams once. Now what am I? Old and ruined."

"You're not so very old."

"Then young and ruined, dependent on a fortune which may never arrive—"

"But it will," said Emma. "I know you will win your suit! I believe in you entirely!" Emma snuggled up closer. She really was quite lucky they were in public.

They wandered about the gallery, nodding politely to the gentlemen and ladies as they passed. Campbell kept a sharp eye out for any familiar face but saw no one. Asherton obligingly steered his little Claire to the opposite side of the room, giving Campbell the opportunity to enjoy dainty Emma's company alone for a bit.

But as Emma exclaimed at this painting and that, Campbell found he was hard-pressed to keep his thoughts focused. That feeling of being watched had not diminished at all. Campbell was almost ready to swear it was coming from the paintings themselves, especially the one of the French chit.

"Campbell! Campbell!" Asherton's shout cut across the polite murmurs of the crowd. "You must come see this!"

Campbell quick-marched the giggling Emma into the little alcove where Claire and Asherton stood. Claire has flushed quite pink with excitement, and even Asherton looked positively energized.

"What's the to-do?" asked Campbell.

"There!" Asherton pointed at one of the paintings.

The canvas was unfinished. Most of the figures were still only rude charcoal sketches. It showed a soldier from the late wars. He slouched in a sagging tent. His tattered uniform hung off his emaciated frame. Even his boots were torn. His face turned toward the viewer, and his attitude was one of utter exhaustion.

"Oh my!" breathed Emma. "Campbell! It's you!"

"Why, so it is," Campbell murmured, and understanding bloomed inside him. He should have recognized what hand had painted these pictures that were credited to some un-known Hertfordshire boy. After all, he'd once known that hand almost as well as he knew his own. "I wonder how this could have happened?"

As he spoke, Campbell felt the first genuine smile he'd known all day spread across his face.

CHAPTER 2

A Spirited Disagreement

*. . . a wonderful instance of advice being given on
such a point, without being resented.*

Jane Austen, *Pride and Prejudice*

Rosalind Thorne would not have said she began her morning by quarreling with Alice Littlefield. There was, however, a rather spirited disagreement.

"Alice, we cannot think about leasing a new house at present," said Rosalind calmly. "It would be entirely too expensive."

"It is not too expensive," said Alice. "With what my novel will bring in . . ."

"Might bring in," Rosalind corrected her. "The first volume is not even printed yet, and your Mr. Colburn said he can make no guarantees."

"But over two dozen people have subscribed all ready," Alice countered. "And you are doing very well all on your own. You told me you have seven ladies waiting on your—"

"Six," Rosalind said, cutting her off.

"Six," repeated Alice. "All of them women of good families who can afford to—*do* forgive me mentioning it!—pay your expenses."

Rosalind's hesitancy about money was a source of amusement and exasperation for Alice. Like Rosalind, Alice had been born into a gentleman's family. They'd both been raised with the expectation that their futures would begin and end with an advantageous marriage. But those expectations had gone very far astray indeed. Now Alice worked as a gossip writer, a translator and, most recently, a novelist. She felt no bashfulness whatsoever about the fees she received for her writing.

Rosalind, on the other hand, had managed to create an ad hoc sort of living by helping the ladies of London with their difficulties—whether that meant arranging a social event or, in some startling instances, assisting with a case of blackmail or even murder.

The problem was that as a lady of gentle birth, Rosalind was forbidden by society to ask directly for money, no matter what task had been performed. To do so would instantly turn her into a workingwoman. Her claims of gentility would be immediately erased, and with them, the social standing she had fought for years to maintain.

"I have only had time to consult with three of them," Rosalind reminded her. "And I cannot even be sure they will agree to the new terms my man of business is suggesting."

"You're just being difficult, Rosalind."

"I am being practical, Alice," she countered. "We must think of the future."

"I *am* thinking of the future, and that is why we cannot stay as we are." Alice spread her arms to indicate the small and, Rosalind was forced to admit, rather crowded parlor.

Rosalind had lived in the rented house in Little Russell Street for several years. It had, for the most part, answered very well—until Alice had moved in with her. Now, in addition to Rosalind's desk, the tea table, and the chairs, the front room held Alice's writing table, not to mention her many books and periodicals, which had begun to spill over into their equally tiny dining room.

There was no denying the house now felt very full.

Alice, as if sensing a moment's doubt, pressed her advantage.

"I cannot write if I have to give up the parlor every time one of your ladies comes to call," she said. "And you cannot possibly hope to meet the habitués of the *haut ton* if you have to sit practically in their laps! You know even better than I do how much appearance matters. Our current appearance is of poverty."

"It is not poverty." Rosalind was ashamed at how peevish she sounded. But she had scrimped and made do for years to maintain her genteel facade.

"For the Marlboroughs and the Jerseys of this world, it might as well be," countered Alice. "Come, Rosalind, I'm not suggesting we lease Kensington Palace. Just come see this house on Orchard Street with me. It's perfect, I promise, and the rent is not too very much more . . ."

"It's more than just the rent," said Rosalind. "A larger house means we will need more servants, not to mention new linens and curtains and the other furnishings—"

"This is a furnished house, and—"

Whatever Alice was about to add was cut off by a soft knocking at the parlor door.

Both women turned in time to see the door open and a tall, fair man step into the parlor.

"Mr. Harkness!" exclaimed Rosalind.

"Am I interrupting?" he asked. "Amelia said I should just show myself in."

"And there's another reason," said Alice triumphantly. "You really cannot expect to properly entertain your gentlemen callers when you've nowhere to put them!"

Adam Harkness knew Alice well, and her indignation served only to make him smile.

"Callers?" he said to Rosalind, with a gentle lift of his brows. "You have more than one, Miss Thorne?"

Rosalind refused to blush. Unfortunately, her cheeks refused to obey her. "Please forgive us, Mr. Harkness," she said. "Alice and I have been having a discussion."

"Rosalind and I have been having an argument," Alice corrected her. "Mr. Harkness, you will please tell her it is imperative that we find a larger house."

Adam sighed regretfully. "If I had time, I would stay to discuss the matter. But I came only to make my farewells."

"Oh, yes. I didn't realize it was so late . . ." Rosalind glanced at Alice. "Perhaps we should take a walk?" she ventured. Alice was her best friend in the world, this morning's disagreements notwithstanding. There were, however, some things for which Rosalind needed her privacy. Saying farewell to Adam Harkness was one of them.

Alice gave a theatrical sigh, complete with a great rolling of her brown eyes. "No, no, it's freezing. You'd both catch your deaths of cold, and then I should have to dream of your sad ghosts for the rest of my life. I'll be in my room." She breezed out, or rather, she tried to, but her skirt caught on the edge of the footstool, and she had to stop to work it free.

This done, she did breeze. She also glowered meaningfully over her shoulder at Rosalind.

Rosalind shut the parlor door and turned to Adam. He was smiling.

It was Adam's smile that had undone her from the first. Even more than his quiet bearing, or his strong, weathered face and sharp blue eyes. That small, knowing smile had taken up residence in her usually very calm and practical heart and absolutely refused to leave.

And she had long since gotten past wishing it would.

"Well, I wish you good luck in Manchester," she said to him. Adam was a principal officer of the famous Bow Street Police Station. A consortium of merchants had written to the magistrates requesting an officer be sent to deal with a recent rash of burglaries. "I will miss you."

"I'm sorry that I have to leave you just now," Adam told her. "If anything comes up that you might need, I've asked Sam Tauton to look out for you." Samuel Tauton was another of the Bow Street officers. "And you will write?"

"Of course I will," said Rosalind.

"Especially to let me know when you've changed your address." Adam's grin turned cheeky.

Rosalind resolutely ignored this. "I don't think we will need to worry about that just yet."

"You might," he said. "For what it's worth, I think Alice makes a good point. The house is too small for you both."

"I know," she admitted with a sigh. "I just . . ." She fumbled for the correct words.

Since her mother had died, Rosalind had feared for her future, counted every ha'penny that came into her hands, and tried to brace herself against the day when her fragile existence would come tumbling down. It was difficult to believe that she could have finally succeeded in becoming independent.

Or secure.

Adam, as usual, understood much of what she did not say. "The world will not fall apart because you give yourself something you want."

Rosalind felt the tiniest smile form. "Do you promise?"

"I do." He spoke with deep solemnity, but a light shone in his deep blue eyes. "And you know that I am to be entirely trusted in all such matters."

"I do." Rosalind sighed. Habit made her glance over her shoulder to make sure no one was listening. "It's just . . . It feels like everything is changing. All the letters, the new house, Alice turning novelist . . . I cannot make myself trust any of it."

"You don't have to trust the change," said Adam. "Trust yourself instead. And Alice."

"And you?" suggested Rosalind.

"Always."

Rosalind laid her hand on his cheek. She savored the rough warmth of his skin against her palm and delighted in the tender mischief that shone in his eyes.

The parlor door opened. Rosalind jerked her hand away as if she'd been burned.

"I beg your pardon, miss."

Amelia McGowan was plump, round faced, and ginger haired, with a spray of freckles across her nose and a light in her green eyes that warned all comers that here was a person who brooked no nonsense.

"There's a lady in the foyer, Miss Thorne," Amelia said. "I told her you were not home, but she insisted that I bring her card."

Rosalind took it and read, "Mrs. Gerald Douglas."

From the quality of the card and the raised engraving, Rosalind could see her caller was a woman of means and taste. Something else tapped at the back of Rosalind's mind—a memory that she could not quite identify.

"Thank you, Amelia. Will you make us some tea please?"

"Already brewing," she replied. "I thought you and Mr. Harkness might be wanting a cup."

"Unfortunately, I cannot stay," said Adam, and the regret was genuine. "You may tell the lady Miss Thorne will be available shortly."

"Yes, sir." Amelia bobbed her curtsy and shut the door.

"Giving orders to my maid?" Rosalind arched her brows. "You overstep yourself, sir."

Adam simply took her hand and bowed low over it. Rosalind felt his warm breath on the back of her knuckles. The soft sensation gave life to all manner of fancies she'd thought she'd put away years ago.

He straightened again, smiled again—which made her heart turn over again.

"I don't expect to be away too long," he told her. "And never fear, I'll leave through the back, so we don't shock your new client."

He put on his hat, touched the brim in salute, and took himself out through the door that led to the dining room, and then to the kitchen and the scullery, and from there to the garden.

Rosalind stayed where she was. *Good-bye*, she thought to the place where he had been. *Good luck. Come home to me.*

Then she turned and opened the door to the lady waiting there, and to whatever her problems might be.

CHAPTER 3

An Old Friend and New Troubles

*Yet, indeed, I am in earnest. I speak nothing but
the truth*

Jane Austen, *Pride and Prejudice*

Rosalind expected a stranger to be waiting for her, but to her surprise, she recognized the other woman immediately.

"Bethany!" Rosalind cried. "Goodness! This is a surprise!"

Rosalind had met Bethany Hodgeson during one long summer when they were both girls. A school chum had invited Rosalind down to the country for a house party. Bethany had been there, as well. The daughter of a local squire, Bethany had been a quiet girl, and very aware she was something of the country cousin among the wealthier young ladies. Still, she and Rosalind had become friends and for some years had carried on a lively correspondence. But when Rosalind's father had vanished and their family had broken apart, that correspondence had fallen away, along with so much else.

"I hope you will forgive my intruding without writing first," said Bethany.

"I'm delighted to see you," Rosalind assured her, and she meant it. "I'm only sorry you've had to wait. Do, please, come in."

Bethany had been a pretty girl, and she had grown to be a lovely woman. She had a clear, pale complexion and luminous brown eyes. Her dark hair had been simply dressed by an expert hand. She wore a gray wool dress trimmed with antique lace, well suited both for the raw February weather and the fact that it was barely a month since King George III had died. All of fashionable London was still expected to show at least some restraint of feeling.

Her dress said that prosperity had come to Bethany. But her manner still spoke of the hesitancy that had haunted her as the country girl.

"And how are you?" Rosalind asked Bethany.

"Quite well, thank you." The reply felt reflexive. Bethany was clearly tired and more than a little ill at ease. "I am married, of course. My oldest son has just turned two and keeps the whole household on its toes."

"You have my congratulations."

Before either of them could make another remark, Amelia entered the parlor, bearing the tea tray. The tea set had been a Christmas present from the Littlefields—lovely Staffordshire pottery with roses and violets decorating the delicate cups and the pot.

Rosalind went through the rituals of pouring out, fixing the cup to her guest's liking and inquiring if she'd prefer a slice of bread and butter or a biscuit.

Once they were settled, Rosalind asked, "What brings you to London?"

"The season, of course. It is our hope that my sister-in-law Penelope will be properly introduced into society."

"Well, the season may be somewhat subdued this year," said Rosalind. "Nonetheless, I hope you will all be able to enjoy yourselves."

"Yes, the king's funeral brought us to town early. Douglas's grandfather was to attend and wanted Douglas with him. Since Douglas was named his heir, Sir Jasper has become very dependent on him."

"You make it sound like a recent development."

Bethany blushed and took a hasty swallow of tea to cover it. "It is. We received the news only two years ago. The fortune is . . . It's considerable. As you might imagine, it has changed the prospects for our entire family, and now that Penelope is old enough, Douglas wants her to make a sound match."

Rosalind sipped her tea and waited.

Bethany set cup and saucer down.

"Rosalind, you must forgive me. The reason I'm here is that I was talking to Lucinda Harding. She's Mrs. Robert Nicholls now, but I think you know that."

"Yes, indeed. I had a letter from her just last week." In fact, Rosalind had been helping Lucinda deal with a rather complex matter of her own. Lucinda's mother was being robbed of her monthly income by an unscrupulous banker. To make matters worse, the man had been sharing his takings with Lucinda's uncle.

If it was Lucinda who had sent Bethany here, then that explained some of her unease. This was not to be a social call.

"I cannot think why I am having such a problem speaking plainly," said Bethany.

"It is never easy to consult a stranger," said Rosalind. Bethany's expression said that she expected better of herself. "You may be sure that I hold whatever you tell me in the strictest confidence."

"Thank you. I believe I've told you about my youngest sister? Leonora?"

"Yes, of course." Bethany had two sisters—Leonora and Mariah. They'd still been little girls when she and Rosalind met.

"Leonora was always a pretty girl, lively and, well, more than a little silly. It's not entirely her fault," Bethany added quickly. "Our mother was unwell for much of our childhood. She did not have the strength or attention to give over to raising three girls, and my father has always found observation more to his taste than exertion. It eventually happened that Nora—that's what we call her—eloped with a . . . friend of my husband's. She was barely sixteen at the time."

"I see." Rosalind was careful to keep any trace of sympathy out of her tone. Bethany did not seem the sort who would welcome it.

"Yes." Bethany flushed. "You see, Mr. Cantrell expected to be paid for either Nora's return or their marriage. Douglas declined." She spoke the words flatly, but her pain showed clearly in her expressive eyes. "He and Cantrell had been friends. In fact, they'd planned on going into business together. Douglas took Cantrell's . . . behavior as a personal betrayal."

"That must have been very hard for you."

Bethany drew a deep, shuddering breath. "Yes, it was. Nora was gone for three years."

"But she did return?"

"She quite literally turned up on our doorstep, with a valise in one hand and a ruined bonnet in the other. She told us that Cantrell had died and left her destitute, and there was nowhere else for her to go."

"That must have been a shock."

Bethany's smile was wry and fleeting. "Mother took to her bed for three days. It was one of the few times in my life I have truly been tempted to emulate her. Douglas was furious, but, well, of course we could not turn Nora away." Rosalind could not help noticing how Bethany spoke these words a little too quickly. "My husband is a good man, Miss Thorne," she went on. "But he is also a proud man. He'd brought Cantrell into our house and trusted him absolutely. Cantrell's behavior, and Nora's—it wounded him gravely, and he is finding it very difficult to forgive."

Rosalind made a quick guess. "May I take it this all happened after your husband came into his inheritance?"

"You would think that would be the case, but it was not. Douglas did not learn that his position within the family had changed until fully a year after Cantrell and Nora left."

That was surprising. "Were they in love, then?"

"I am ashamed to say I don't know," said Bethany. "I didn't see any sign of lovesickness in Nora before they vanished. Mariah—she's my other sister—said she never suspected anything, and Mariah and Nora have always been very close."

"I see." Rosalind nodded. "But as you are here now, I take it something new has occurred?"

Bethany glanced toward the door, and her face settled into harder lines than she had shown yet. "A necklace has gone missing. A valuable string of matched black and white pearls that was a wedding present from Sir Jasper. Usually, it's kept in our box at the bank, but I had it brought out to wear to the king's funeral. The next morning, I meant to return the necklace to the bank, but it was gone. We searched everywhere, inquired of the entire household, but so far have discovered nothing."

Rosalind was silent for a moment, considering what she had just been told. "Does Mr. Douglas believe that Nora stole the necklace?"

"He does, and she knows it, which makes matters even more difficult than usual between them." Bethany's voice caught. "He is talking of sending her away."

"That might be the best solution, at least temporarily. If . . ."

This was too much for Bethany. "I will not send my sister away from all her family and friends," she declared. "Especially not when she'll have Douglas's name to draw on for credit. Nora would certainly not conduct herself in accordance with Douglas's wishes, and he'd be forced to cut her off. Then what would become of her?"

Rosalind refreshed her cup, using the time to consider her next question. "Do you want me to find the necklace?" she asked.

"If possible, but what is most important is to know what really happened to it."

So that suspicion can be removed from your sister.

"I understand," said Rosalind aloud. "Have you told Mr. Douglas you were going to consult me on the matter?"

"No," Bethany admitted. "I . . . He . . . would not approve of airing the family business in this way. I did tell him I was renewing my acquaintance with you. I . . . well, I have not exactly made a success of my new social opportunities." These words were heavy, edging on bitterness. "I told Douglas I intended to speak with you about how best to ensure a successful season for Penelope. I may have mentioned that you are on visiting terms with the lady patronesses at Almack's."

Which was the truth, but Rosalind felt her brows rise.

Bethany's blush deepened. "You see, I am a canny customer." Bethany tried to put a knowing tone into her words. "I presume on our old acquaintance in the hope that you can solve two separate problems for me. We never expected Penelope to become an heiress, but she is. Now, country bred I may be, but even I know that attempting to conduct a young girl through a season without the correct connections invites disaster and fortune hunters."

Rosalind drank her tea and tried to picture the household Bethany found herself in. A proud husband coming into possibilities he had never dreamt of. At least one child in the nursery. A lovely young sister-in-law, struggling with her turn of fortune as well as the weight of the new expectations on her. Added to this, there was a sister who had already lashed out against her situation in a highly dramatic and destructive fashion.

Rosalind found she very much wanted to help Bethany. She had watched her own family crumble apart without being able to do anything. This gave her a swift and natural sympathy for anyone trapped in a troubled home.

And yet, and yet . . .

"What if Nora really did steal the necklace?"

"Then she has taken me in, and I need to know that." Bethany dropped her gaze to her empty cup. "I sympathize with her frustrations, but at some point, even the most selfish person must acknowledge the effect of her actions on others. If she has not learned better, if she cannot learn better . . ." Bethany bit her lip. "I must know for certain."

"I understand," Rosalind told her. "And I believe I may be able to help."

The relief on Bethany's face was as palpable as her anger had been earlier. "Thank you."

"However, if I am to come to look into matters," said Rosalind, "you must also agree that we engage an officer from Bow Street to help with the inquiries." Bethany opened her mouth, but Rosalind did not give her room to protest. "No one wants their private concerns made public, and I will make certain it is done with absolute discretion. However, if the necklace has already been sold, the buyer might be able to provide some useful information. It might very well be the quickest way to prove that the thief was *not* your sister."

Bethany clearly had not considered this before. "Very well, if that's what you think best."

Rosalind let her thoughts run over the letters she had already entered into her correspondence book. There were two matters that could be dealt with through an exchange of letters, another that would not become urgent until much later in the season, and two others that must be refused. At last, she nodded.

"If there are any discoveries to be made in the house, it will be easier for me to undertake that work if I am your guest," she said. It would also help provide her a respite from Alice's ongoing campaign to find a larger house. "Will that pose any problem?"

"Not at all. It will sort well with the story that you are there to help with Penelope's season. I will let my husband know we are to expect you . . . ?"

"Before the week is out," supplied Rosalind. "Where are you staying?" she asked.

"We have taken a house in Portsmouth Square. My parents are with us."

Rosalind had never met Mr. and Mrs. Hodgeson, but the way Bethany held herself now suggested that having them in London had added to her domestic difficulties.

Rosalind straightened her shoulders minutely and hoped that her composure would not falter. "There may be some expenses and other particulars that will have to be addressed," she said. "If you like, my man of business can write to you about the details."

"Yes, of course," said Bethany, and Rosalind let herself breathe again.

"I am sure once Penelope and I have become acquainted, we will be able to arrange a program that will bring her into contact with a number of suitable young persons from good families."

"Thank you so much, Rosalind," said Bethany earnestly. "I cannot tell you how glad I will be to have you with us."

I wonder if you will still be so welcoming in a week's time? Because it is very clear you are not telling me all there is to know about your sisters, your husband or, indeed, yourself.

CHAPTER 4

The Trials of Sisterhood

. . . they parted at last with mutual civility, and possibly a mutual desire of never meeting again.

Jane Austen, *Pride and Prejudice*

"What have you done!" Mariah slammed into Nora's bedroom. Startled, Nora jerked her hand, smearing a broad black line across her sketch of a tired milkmaid.

"What have I done?" Nora swung her feet off the window seat, where she had been curled up. "You've just ruined the entire picture!" She held up the sketchbook to show Mariah the dark slash across the milkmaid's face.

Instead of answering, Mariah ripped the sketchbook out of her hands and threw it across the room.

"You little . . . you vile . . . you *liar!*"

It took everything Nora had not to shrink away. Experience had left her used to tirades, but this was a shock. Mariah might be bland, bitter, and occasionally sly, but Mariah was never furious. Now, though, her watery eyes blazed behind her spectacles, and her whole body quivered with anger. For a moment, Nora wasn't sure whether she should laugh or scramble backward to put some distance between them.

"Mariah, what are you talking about?" Nora tried to keep her voice even.

"I saw him! At the exhibition!"

"Who?" Nora got to her feet and went to retrieve her sketchbook. *I hope she hasn't wrinkled the pages. This was expensive.*

"Cantrell!"

The name sounded like thunder in Nora's ears. "That's not possible."

"I stood there and watched him parading about Lord Langford's gallery with some little chit on his arm."

Nora's breath seized up. The room darkened at the edges.

I will be calm, she told herself, even as she swayed on her feet. *I will think clearly.*

But calm would not return immediately. To buy time, Nora carefully closed her book. She went to the door and closed that, as well. It would never do to have the household hear this conversation.

"Did he see you?" Nora asked. She was still facing the door. *Why can't I turn around?*

"Of course he didn't!" Mariah sneered. "And if he did, why on earth would he remember *my* face? Not that it matters. You told us he was dead!"

"Well, I had to say something, didn't I? Douglas would never have let me in the house otherwise."

"Never mind what you told Douglas!" cried Mariah. "You should have told me the truth!"

A pounding on the door made them both jump.

"Mariah! Nora!" came Bethany's voice from the other side. "What is going on?"

Of course she'd come home now.

Mariah was glowering, her eyes narrowed to slits. Nora

bit her lip. Nora had never been afraid of her middle sister. But now Mariah knew too much. She could ruin everything in the next minute, if she chose to.

"Nora!" Bethany called.

Nora took a deep breath and opened the door.

Bethany stood in the corridor, her cheeks flushed and her face tight with annoyance and concern.

"What was all this shouting about?" Bethany demanded.

"Mariah thought I took a book of hers." Nora strolled back to her window seat and threw herself down on the cushions. "As if I'd be interested in any stuffy lecture about minerals or prisms or any such."

Bethany had always been reckoned to be the prettiest and steadiest of the Hodgeson sisters. To Nora, however, that steadiness betrayed a lack of imagination. For instance, Bethany seemed unable to grasp that her younger sisters could change, and had changed, as they grew up, or even that they grew up at all. Bethany still believed her and Mariah to be what their father had labeled them as children—silly, ignorant, and vain.

On occasion, Nora had found this limited vision extremely useful. Now, for instance. Bethany's barely concealed impatience said that she was perfectly ready to dismiss this incident between her sisters as just one more petty argument.

As long as Mariah keeps her mouth shut . . .

Mariah drew herself up. Nora turned her face toward the window, attempting to appear bored.

"I'm sure it's nothing to worry you, Bethany," said Mariah. "You have so many more important things to do."

Nora was glad to be sitting down. Otherwise, she might have staggered from pure relief.

Bethany sighed sharply. "Have either of you seen Penelope?"

Nora shrugged. "I believe she was going out for a drive with Mama. Isn't that what she said, Mariah?" Finally, she was able to turn her head.

"It may have been," Mariah replied. "I do not recall. So, sister . . ." She turned to Bethany. "May I take it you were successful in your errand?"

"Successful?" Bethany looked startled. *Odd.* "If you mean, was I able to call on my friend? Yes, I was."

"How pleasant that must have been for you," said Mariah. "Excuse me."

With that, Mariah brushed past Bethany and left the room.

Bethany stared after her. "What is the matter with you two?"

"Who can ever tell what's the matter with Mariah?" Nora propped her sketchbook against her knees. "Was there something else you wanted?"

"Yes. If you see Penelope before I do, please tell her I need to speak with her. It's about plans for her season."

"We're going through with that?" Nora folded back her page and selected a fresh stick of charcoal. "I thought you said you'd rather go through a storm at sea."

"Yes, well, fortunately, my friend has agreed to play ship's pilot and help us navigate the waters. She'll be coming to stay in a few days. I wanted to let Penelope know."

Nora kept her eyes on the page. "What does our Mr. Douglas say about this turn of events?" she asked.

"He's already agreed to the plan."

"Well, then, it's settled." Nora contemplated her page for a moment. The line made her think of a road. A country lane. That would be good. With hedges and sheep. Very rustic. Very sentimental. Maybe that milkmaid who had been so troublesome in her own sketch could be asleep under the hedges. She would have dark curls escaping from her headscarf. Her blouse would slip off one shoulder. "The rest of us shall doubtlessly receive our orders in due course."

Nora hoped that remark would convince Bethany to leave. She was not one to stand by while others pointed out any deficiency in her husband's rule.

Unfortunately, instead of leaving, Bethany stepped closer. Nora forced her fingers to loosen their grip on her charcoal. It was going to snap.

I am going to snap.

"Nora . . . ," began Bethany.

"Yes?" She drew a second line, more carefully this time, mindful of perspective.

"You owe Douglas a great deal."

Can't you please just go away? "You may be sure I remain devastatingly aware of the fact. I swear to you that as soon as I have marshaled the resources to leave, I will relieve him of the burden of my care."

"No one wants to see you go." She was trying to be gentle. She wanted things to be right, at least as far as she could see what was right. Bethany had always been that way.

Nora's heart stung, and she suddenly felt all the black, aching loneliness she had known since she first ran away. *Bethany must not see this. No one can see this.*

"No one wants to see me go?" Nora echoed her sister lightly. "That, Bethany, is a shocking falsehood, even from you." She lifted her head. "Is that the door? Perhaps Penelope has returned."

Of course, she had heard nothing, because there had been nothing to hear. Bethany knew that, as well, and she surely knew Nora wanted to be rid of her. After this last exchange, however, she would think that Nora was just being rude and ungrateful, as usual.

"I'd help, if you let me," said Bethany.

Bethany met her gaze. Nora made herself look bored.

"Would you? Really? No matter what Douglas thought?"

Bethany's pretty face hardened. But rather than give any voice to that anger, she turned on her heel and sailed out of the room. The door swung shut behind her.

Alone, Nora bowed her head and pressed her sleeve across

her eyes. She held it there until the urge to rage and weep subsided.

Cantrell was in London. Mariah had seen him. She would not be mistaken. He was here, and he had been . . . he had seen . . .

Nora gritted her teeth to stop the scream.

Once she had regained control of herself, Nora set paper and charcoal aside and got to her feet. Thankfully, the hallway was empty.

She knocked softly at Mariah's door.

There was no answer. Nora tried the handle, and when it gave, she pushed her way into her sister's room.

The boudoir was airy and well furnished. Being Mariah's room, it was also filled with books and papers. The writing desk was stacked with scrapbooks and diaries. Mariah's great hobby was making extracts from her various readings. A variety of pens and brushes had all been laid out and were ready for use, along with colored paper and several different sizes of scissors.

Mariah sat bolt upright in her wingback chair by the window. She held her book rigidly in front of her. She might even have been reading it.

"Mariah . . ." Nora slipped up to her sister's side.

"I have nothing to say to you."

Nora crouched at her feet, trying to catch her eye. "Mariah, I'm sorry."

Mariah turned the page.

"Mariah, will you listen?" Nora laid a hand on her wrist. "I was wrong not to tell you I knew Cantrell was alive. I should have trusted you. But at first, I didn't see the need. I never thought he'd risk returning to England. The whole country is crawling with his creditors. And later . . . well, later, I was already trusting you with so much, I didn't dare."

Mariah kept her gaze on her book and turned another page.

"*Please*, Mariah!"

"How do I know you two don't have some new scheme brewing?" she said to the book.

"What?" Nora sat back on her heels.

Mariah's sigh sounded exactly like Bethany at her very worst. "How do I know you and your beloved have not cooked up some new scheme to fleece our dear brother Douglas and escape with the money? Leaving me quite in the lurch. Again," she added, and that single word overflowed with bitterness.

Nora wanted to scream. She wanted to shake Mariah and force her to pay attention.

And if she did any of that, she would lose everything she had worked for since she returned to England.

"Please, Mariah. I swear, I've nothing to do with Cantrell. Not anymore. I came back only because I needed time to gather my own resources. You know that. Nothing's changed. As soon as Mr. Sommerton forwards me the money we've realized, I'll be leaving for the Continent, and you are coming with me. We will be free!"

Mariah shifted in her seat. She settled her gaze back on her book. She turned her page.

"So, you see, you can't give me away." Nora hated pleading, but what choice did she have? "Will you promise?"

"I shall have to see," said Mariah, but the worst of the anger had faded from her round face. "But I'm not your real problem. You need to worry about this woman Bethany has acquired."

"What are you talking about?"

Mariah sighed again and laid the book aside. Nora took it as a good sign. Mariah lecturing was Mariah in charge, just as she liked to be. "This person—this so-called friend our sister went to visit—is a woman named Rosalind Thorne. She is . . . Well, she deals in other people's problems."

"What do you know about it?"

Mariah looked down her nose at her sister. "I heard Bethany talking with Douglas a week ago, saying she intended to renew her friendship with Miss Thorne. And then I heard Betsy talking about it with Mrs. Hare. They were both quite excited. Apparently, this Thorne woman is some sort of lady thief-taker."

Surprise drew a laugh from Nora. "A *lady* thief-taker? That's nonsense. There isn't such a thing." She stopped. "The necklace. This is about that blasted necklace."

"If you're lucky," said Mariah.

"No. I don't believe it," said Nora firmly. "Bethany would never . . . She doesn't *know* anything."

"She knows you're up to something," said Mariah. "I've seen the way she watches you."

Nora was silent for a minute. What Mariah said could not be true. It must not be.

It doesn't matter if it is. I can't stop.

"Mariah, all I need is a few more days," said Nora. "A fortnight at the very most. Then I'll be able to keep every one of my promises to you."

Mariah was silent for a long time.

"I shall consider it," Mariah said finally. She also took up her book and found her page.

Nora loosened her fists and made herself breathe again. "Then I suppose I must be content with that."

Mariah made no answer. Nora turned and quickly walked out of the room before she could be tempted to give vent to the fear and anger boiling inside her.

She did not look back to see the tear trickling down her sister's cheek.

CHAPTER 5

Some Polite Introductions

How humiliating is this discovery!
Jane Austen, *Pride and Prejudice*

Just as soon as Bethany Douglas took her leave, Rosalind went to her desk and wrote a carefully casual letter to their mutual friend Lucinda Nicholls.

The reply arrived three days later, on the very morning Rosalind was set to leave for the Douglases' house in Portsmouth Square. She read it over in the warm and well-sprung carriage Bethany had sent for her. Bethany had written, as well, of course, to thank Rosalind and confirm that she had agreed to the terms Mr. Prescott outlined. That letter was in Rosalind's reticule, as well, but she could refer to it later if necessary. Lucinda had the news she needed right now.

After the comfortable details of Lucinda's domestic life, and several paragraphs about her precocious, beautiful, and unusually gifted daughter, Lucinda settled into the heart of the matter.

I am glad Bethany was able to call, she wrote. I was sure you'd be able to help her with her present difficul-

ties. You should not have been so surprised at her not coming to you before. Hers is quite the country family. I can scarce recall them going to London above one or two times while we were growing up. This may have been due to lack of funds. It is the unfortunate truth that the estate was shockingly mismanaged. Indeed, shortly after Bethany married, her husband insisted that the house be put up to let and a new manager hired for the rest of the estate. Although, I suspect Mr. Douglas regrets this decision. It has meant that all that family now abide with him and Bethany. That would be a heavy burden for anyone to bear. I know this sounds unforgivably catty, but I think you'll soon see what I mean.

As to the Douglases themselves, I'm afraid we never met the London branch of the family. We know that the present Mr. Douglas's father was a younger brother. He came out to the country to practice law. The older brother remained in the city. Bethany's husband, Mr. Gerald Douglas, developed a passion for engineering and apprenticed in that line.

The older, London-dwelling brother was, of course, supposed to inherit, but he moved to the Continent and died there. You should know, Mother always thought there was something behind his sudden removal, and she is almost as good at ferreting out that sort of thing as you are.

But as to our local branch of the clan. You tell me you have already been informed about Nora Hodgeson's ill-considered elopement with Bryan Cantrell. Be sure I remember that incident very well. Nora was a particular pet of my mother's and was often at our house. She spent hours in the gallery, practicing her sketching and her painting. Our acquaintance universally believed her to be a most accomplished young lady and sure to turn out well, despite her hectic mother and careless father. Alas! We were sadly mistaken there.

Her elopement, however, is not the whole story of Mr. Cantrell's predations on the neighborhood. The true scandal is known only to a few. You see, Cantrell was a friend of Mr. Douglas's, and the two were thick as thieves for quite some time. The two talked of entering into business together. All the while, however, Cantrell was constructing much different schemes in his head. Because although he eloped with Nora, he was courting Penelope Douglas, right under the family's noses! When the poor girl was not more than sixteen! The same age as Nora!

Can you imagine the wickedness of such a man?

Unfortunately, I can, thought Rosalind sadly.

There was a great deal more to Lucinda's letter, but the carriage slowed to a halt. Amelia, who had come along to act as Rosalind's lady's maid, hopped out and at once began admonishing the nearest footman to be careful with the luggage. Rosalind could not make out what the man replied, but the tone was sharp. Amelia, Rosalind was sure, would return a few cutting remarks of her own.

The Douglases' house in Portsmouth Square was a new white terraced residence at the end of its row. Like most town houses, it was built high, long, and narrow. Once Rosalind was inside the tiled foyer, a lively, pink-faced maid with wide blue eyes helped her off with her outdoor things.

"Mr. and Mrs. Douglas are in the morning room," the maid told her. "They have asked if you will please join them?"

"Yes, of course," said Rosalind. "And you are?" In Rosalind's experience, it was at least as important to get to know the servants in a household as it was to know the principals.

"Betsy, miss. If you'll follow me?"

Betsy led Rosalind down a paneled corridor. Then, quite

suddenly, a door to the left was flung open, and Rosalind abruptly found herself face-to-face with a frowning, bespectacled young woman who clutched a book in her folded arms.

Startled, Rosalind said, "I do beg your pardon."

The girl looked Rosalind up and down, her dark eyes narrowed in an attitude of sour suspicion. Without a word, she retreated into the room and closed the door firmly behind herself.

Rosalind turned to the maid, her brows raised.

"That was Miss Mariah Hodgeson, Mrs. Douglas's next to youngest sister." said Betsy. "You mustn't be offended," she added softly. "She's that way with everyone."

The maid walked on, and Rosalind followed, but not without a glance over her shoulder. The door behind her remained firmly shut.

The moss-green morning room was airy and pleasant. Three bowed windows overlooked a walled garden that was surely splendid in summer. Now, however, burlap shrouded every shrub. The latest sprinkling of snow had turned neat flower beds into a dreary study in gray and white.

Inside, however, a good fire burned in the hearth and a beautiful Limoges tea set graced a marquetry table, making a cosy scene to greet her. Bethany stood as soon as Rosalind entered. So did the tall, squarely built man beside her.

"Rosalind," said Bethany. "We're so delighted you could come. Allow me to introduce my husband, Mr. Gerald Douglas."

Rosalind curtsied and received Mr. Douglas's grave bow in return.

Every inch of Mr. Gerald Douglas proclaimed that this was a serious, prosperous, cautious man. He still quite young, probably no more than five years older than Bethany. But where Bethany was pale, his skin had a honey-gold tint and was slightly weathered. His dark hair had been slicked back, and his sideburns were ruthlessly barbered. His solemn eyes were an arresting shade of warm amber. He dressed with taste. His coat and stovepipe trousers had been precisely tailored, and his waistcoat was subtly patterned silk, with a gold watch chain stretched across the front and gold buttons up the front.

Rosalind could not help noticing how carefully Mr. Douglas looked her over. In a moment of self-doubt, she wondered if he knew about the letter her man of business had addressed to Bethany, and if his severe expression came from the most ungenteel discussion of payment.

"Won't you sit down, Miss Thorne?" Mr. Douglas indicated a round-backed chair drawn up beside the fire. "I trust you will forgive me for sticking my foot into your ladies' tea. But when Bethany told me she planned to ask your advice for Penelope's season, I wished to know you better. I'm sure you understand."

"Yes, of course."

They all took their various seats, and Bethany began the business of pouring out the tea.

"I'm sorry Penelope isn't here to greet you, as well." Bethany handed Rosalind a cup of tea with lemon and a shortbread biscuit. "But my mother wanted company for her visit to the apothecary."

"I understand you are a friend of Mrs. Nicholls," said Douglas.

"Yes. She and my sister became acquainted when we were at school."

"A good family, the Nichollses," allowed Douglas. "My father . . . visited them frequently." Rosalind caught the small hesitation. Lucinda had said Mr. Douglas's father had been an attorney. She guessed that he'd been about to remark that his father had done work for the Nichollses, but he had re-collected himself. Like many men of independent means, it seemed, Gerald Douglas did not want to remind anyone how recently he'd come into his fortune.

"So what do you propose for my sister, Miss Thorne?" asked Mr. Douglas.

Rosalind was taken aback by this abrupt question. "I can hardly say yet, Mr. Douglas. Until I meet Penelope, I can have no knowledge of her tastes and personality."

"You will forgive my husband." The tiniest hint of a smile touched the corners of Mr. Douglas's mouth. "He believes we should be able to hire a reliable husband for Penelope, the way one might hire a new building foreman."

"Hardly," drawled Mr. Douglas. "But I do believe I mentioned that it would be easier if all this fuss and flurry were replaced with some more streamlined system. Our grandparents had their marriages rationally arranged by their families. I cannot see any reason to change."

"And what, Mr. Douglas, do you consider the qualities of a reliable husband?" Rosalind asked.

"A man of energy, imagination, and sound heritage. Someone who has demonstrated he is a credit to his position and family." Douglas leaned back, warming to his theme. "Penelope needs an establishment of her own, but her husband must also provide stability and security. Those come from family, Miss Thorne. Sound, solid family with long history."

"Then you do not approve of our self-made men?" inquired Rosalind.

"On the contrary," said Douglas. "I hold them in high esteem. If properly channeled and guided, industry and ingenuity will be the making of this kingdom. But that demands men take risks, and dedicate themselves fully to their work. This is at odds with a stable establishment. It would be irresponsible of me to allow my sister to be married into an environment where she may not be secure and well cared for."

Bethany was looking out the window, her face grave and weary. Rosalind wondered how many times she'd heard this speech before.

But before any of them could make another remark, an importuning voice penetrated the room.

"No, no, Penelope! You cannot mean to leave me! You know I can never be easy while there is a stranger in the house! I *must* meet her, and I need you to support me."

The morning room doors opened wide. A bone-thin woman dressed in acres of blue superfine wool trimmed in white and pink flounces stepped unsteadily into the room. She leaned heavily on the arm of a younger companion—presumably Penelope—who was much more sedately dressed in green and white. A stout, olive-skinned maid slipped into the room behind them and stationed herself beside the doors.

Rosalind stood, ready to be introduced.

"Ah, my dear Bethany!" The older woman separated herself from Penelope so she could press her cheek tightly against Bethany's. This then must be Bethany's mother, Mrs. Hodgeson. Rosalind noted Mrs. Hodgeson's hair had been dyed an improbable shade of butter yellow. From this angle, she could also see that the bundle of curls at the nape of her neck was entirely artificial.

"Dear Douglas!" Mrs. Hodgeson pressed her powdered cheek against her son-in-law's. Douglas extricated himself as quickly as he could and crossed the room to give Penelope an affectionate kiss on the cheek.

"I do trust we are not interrupting?" said Mrs. Hodgeson faintly as she turned to regard Rosalind with her pale, watery eyes.

"Of course not, Mother. How could you be?" said Bethany. "Mother, Penelope, please meet Miss Rosalind Thorne. Rosalind, my mother, Mrs. Hodgeson, and my sister-in-law, Miss Penelope Douglas."

Mrs. Hodgeson beamed, but it was a brittle expression.

"How do you do, Miss Thorne?" Penelope made a perfect curtsy. Delicate rose-and-gold Penelope did not much resemble her sturdy, dark brother, but they did share the same sharp cheekbones and the same unusual amber eyes.

"I'm delighted to meet you," said Rosalind.

"Have some tea, Penelope," prompted Bethany, pouring a fresh cup. "I'm sure you must be quite cold."

Penelope sat in a tapestry chair farthest from the fire. Rosalind felt a twinge of sympathetic memory as she watched the girl's careful motions—the way she kept her gaze modestly downcast and held her spine rigidly straight and the prescribed inch from the chair's back. She knew from years of experience what it was like to wear correct deportment as both shield and disguise.

"I shall take none," announced Mrs. Hodgeson. She sank slowly onto the nearest sofa. Her maid, her long face set in an expression of severe disapproval, bustled forward to arrange the pillows. Mrs. Hodgeson leaned back at an angle that allowed her to contemplate Rosalind without the bother of turning her head. "You will forgive my reclining so, won't you, Miss Thorne? My health is very poor, very poor."

"Then we must hope you shall be restored to yourself as soon as may be," replied Rosalind.

"Oh, well, hope we may . . ." Mrs. Hodgeson drew an enormous lawn handkerchief out of her sleeve and pressed it to her brow. Her nose was long, narrow, pointed, and red tipped, Rosalind noted. So were her fingers. Her skin hung loosely about her bones. She did not look as though she should have had the energy for anything at all, but despite this, she examined Rosalind alertly and spoke with firm decision.

"How was your excursion, Penelope?" Bethany asked. "Did you see anything interesting?"

"Well, no," Penelope murmured. "It was very short."

"In this weather, what else could it be?" snapped Mrs.

Hodgeson. "And you should thank me, my girl. This winter air is the bane of all such fine complexions as yours. The poor thing has no mother to look after her," added Mrs. Hodgeson to Rosalind. "So I must take her under my wing."

"I see no harm in Pen's being outdoors in this neighborhood," remarked Douglas. "Fresh air is quite healthful, even when it is a bit cold."

"Well, far be it from me to override a *brother's* opinion," Mrs. Hodgeson sniffed. "What would I know, having only raised three daughters myself?"

Having delivered what she clearly considered a devastating set-down, Mrs. Hodgeson immediately turned her attention back to Rosalind. "Well, I must say, Miss Thorne, that the house has been on pins and needles expecting your visit."

"I should be sorry to leave anyone in such a state of suspense," said Rosalind. "I'm sure I can't think—"

"Now, none of that, if you please!" Mrs. Hodgeson waved one hand languidly. "Whatever my daughter has said, *I* have heard all about your particular exploits."

"Exploits?" echoed Douglas.

"Mother," said Bethany breathlessly. "You'll recall I told you—"

"Bethany," said Mrs. Hodgeson, interrupting her. "You will recall *I* told *you*. Miss Thorne is quite notorious! I *tried* to tell Douglas at breakfast the other day, but he was in such a rush to be gone." Mrs. Hodgeson gazed mournfully at her son-in-law before turning back to Rosalind. "Had you, or your lord and master listened, Bethany, I could have told you that everyone knows that when Miss Thorne arrives in a house, there is surely to be some deplorable problem to be solved." She waved her handkerchief in the air between them. "So, you are here about the necklace? Have you found it?"

CHAPTER 6

The Consequences of Discovery

This is a wretched beginning indeed!

Jane Austen, *Pride and Prejudice*

Rosalind froze. She had never been unmasked so quickly and bluntly. Before this, she had always been able to rely on being more or less overlooked. A spinster woman in reduced circumstances was likely to be underestimated in any well-to-do household. This was extremely helpful when dealing with any delicate family issue. People tended to converse more freely when they believed you were powerless.

Thankfully, a lifetime's social training saved her from any undignified sputtering. There was no safe reply to Mrs. Hodgeson's exclamation. Therefore, none would be made.

"Mother, you are quite mistaken!" said Bethany quickly. "Miss Thorne is here to help plan Penelope's season."

"Penelope shall have no season at all if we are murdered by housebreakers!" snapped Mrs. Hodgeson.

Penelope's cheeks blushed red, but Rosalind could not tell whether the color came from anger or embarrassment. Douglas got to his feet and went to her, then laid a hand on her shoulder.

"Penelope, perhaps you should go to your rooms?"

Penelope set her cup down. Without once glancing up, she curtsied and walked carefully to the doors, as if she was afraid a heavy footfall might crack the brittle atmosphere open.

As soon as she closed the doors, Douglas turned to his wife. "Bethany, is it true? Is this . . . Miss Thorne's presence here to do with the necklace?"

"Yes," said Bethany. "Sit down, Douglas, would you please?"

"None of you know what I have suffered this past week!" wailed Mrs. Hodgeson. "Did they tell you, Miss Thorne, that I could not so much as leave my room for three days after it happened? I subsisted on nothing but gruel and barley water that whole time! And have I rested since? I have not! I know the thief is still here. I know it! He's lurking in the cellars or the attics, waiting for the moment—"

"Bethany?" Douglas interrupted. "Did you impose on Miss Thorne with our private business?"

Bethany didn't answer him. "You must forgive my mother, Rosalind. She feels it her responsibility to keep us informed of all the . . . news."

"And who else should, may I ask?" Mrs. Hodgeson snapped. "Since you will never stir a foot out of doors, it is left to me to care for this family. No matter what the consequences to my health!" She pressed her handkerchief against brow and temple. "Now, Miss Thorne, as my daughter has seen fit to engage you without consulting me, we must all make the best of it. I may gather you have not yet properly begun your inquiries. You will want to hear all about the circumstances of this horrid robbery. Where shall I begin? Oh, when I think what could have happened, I positively shudder! We could have all been murdered in our beds! And then poor little Gerry and our dear baby Evelyn would be left all alone in the world!"

But even as she made this pronouncement, Mrs. Hodgeson glanced to her waiting woman. The maid nodded toward the mantel clock, and Mrs. Hodgeson's hand flew to her mouth. "Oh dear! I am growing neglectful. You must understand, Miss Thorne, that although this house may be ruled by my son-in-law, *I* remain at the mercy of my health. If I do not take my tincture—my own recipe, you will understand—and rest for a full hour afterward, the consequences . . . the return of the most dire of symptoms . . . it is not to be thought of! So I beg you to excuse me. Come, Gilpin. We must return to my rooms at once."

Gilpin strode forward to help her mistress to her feet. Mrs. Hodgeson, despite seeming to have plentiful energy while quizzing Rosalind, sagged against her maid, as if she was about to faint, and let herself be supported from the room.

The door closed. Rosalind took a hasty swallow of tea to loosen her throat.

Douglas remained standing beside the chair Penelope had occupied. "You should have told me about this, Bethany."

"Yes," Bethany agreed, with a sharp sigh of exasperation. "I admit it. I played the coward's part, and I can only ask you to forgive me. And you, Rosalind," she added. "I am sorry you were subjected to such a disquisition."

"It is certainly not your fault," said Rosalind. "I agreed to come because I believed that my experience would allow me to help, and I still do. But perhaps it would be better to postpone my visit?" Which was a polite way of asking if she should leave.

Bethany looked to Douglas, defiance brimming in her tired eyes. "Would it be better?"

Douglas ignored the question. "We know what happened to the necklace, Bethany. We have known for weeks. We do not need a stranger—"

"No, we do not know what happened," Bethany shot back, interrupting him. "We suspect. We fear, but we do not *know.* And Miss Thorne is not a stranger. She is a friend of mine, of Lucinda's, and of a dozen of the finest families among the *haut ton.* Your grandfather may even have heard her name."

Douglas waved one broad hand peremptorily. "I am out of patience with this, ma'am. Of course, you wish to remain loyal to your sister, but . . ."

"But what?" demanded Bethany. "But I must cut her off without proof? You would never do such a thing to Penelope."

Bethany's challenge struck home. Douglas let his head fall back until he gazed at the ceiling. His fist tightened and loosened and tightened and loosened. When he raised his head again, it was to level a cutting gaze directly at Rosalind.

"Well, Miss Thorne? What have you to say for yourself?"

"I regret that my presence has caused this discomfort," Rosalind said. This polite reply had the virtue of also being true. "If you wish, I will leave at once, and naturally, anything I may have heard will be held in the strictest confidence." She paused long enough for Mr. Douglas to absorb these words. "I would assure you, however, that Mrs. Douglas's only reason for asking me here was to assist the family. She understands very clearly that the truth will heal any breach more quickly than holding on to secrets."

"Is that what you think we are doing?" inquired Douglas frostily. "Keeping secrets?"

"I think it's what any family would do to spare those they love from scandal," said Rosalind. "But I ask you to consider that so far, whoever has taken the pearls has resisted all attempts to find them out. I am, as you say, a stranger. My presence must necessarily disrupt the rhythm of the house. Whether the thief came from inside or outside, it is possible that disruption may be more than they planned for and led to mistakes." She paused. "Assuming you wish for the thief to be uncovered. If the return of the pearls will be enough, then other methods will suffice, and my presence will not be required. I shall leave a list of my suggestions with Mrs. Douglas. You will not be troubled any further."

Bethany got to her feet. She walked to her husband and looked up into his eyes. They stood like that for a long time—watching, waiting, regretting, and hoping—for and with each other. Rosalind found herself holding her breath.

Softly, Douglas touched his wife's hand and her shoulder. It seemed to Rosalind he was reminding himself of her reality, and the reality of the feeling between them.

"Bethany," he said softly, sadly. "You must swear to me, if it is found that Nora did do this thing, it is over. She leaves this house. She leaves this family. I am Penelope's sole guardian. I haven't . . . I cannot put *anything* above my responsibility to her."

Bethany looked her husband squarely in the eye. "If there is proof of Nora's guilt, I will turn her out myself." She spoke the words firmly, but her face had gone taut and pale with the effort.

Douglas touched Bethany's shoulder one more time and then stepped aside so he could face Rosalind. "My wife has decided to trust you, Miss Thorne. Therefore, we shall proceed."

"I hope to soon be able to demonstrate that this trust is not misplaced," said Rosalind. "If you wish, we can set aside a time and place to discuss how I mean to proceed, both in the matter of the necklace and your sister's season."

"Bethany will see to it," said Douglas. "I must go. There is business to attend to."

"May we expect you for dinner?" Bethany asked.

"My grandfather asked that I dine with him."

"Well," said Bethany brightly, "Sir Jasper must not be disappointed."

Rosalind turned back to them in time to see how Bethany folded both her hands together, as if she felt suddenly cold. Douglas hesitated. He wanted to speak or to reach out again.

He did neither. He bowed to his wife, and he left them there.

CHAPTER 7

The Scene of the Crime

*. . I came here with the determined resolution
of carrying my purpose; nor will I be dissuaded
from it.*

Jane Austen, *Pride and Prejudice*

"I do apologize," said Bethany as soon as the door closed behind her husband. "Truly. I didn't realize . . . I didn't even consider that Mother might hear such gossip, let alone pounce on you the minute you arrived. I would not blame you if you left us at once."

"Do you want me to?" asked Rosalind calmly.

"No, not at all."

"What do you want?"

The question seemed to startle Bethany. She gazed silently at her winter garden for a moment. When she faced Rosalind again, her eyes shone with unshed tears and her cheeks burned bright red.

"I want the same as when I came to you," Bethany said. "I want to know what is going on, and what I must do to mend what has been broken."

It was clear to Rosalind that Bethany spoke of her heart as well as her marriage.

That is more than I can promise to mend. But aloud, all Rosalind said was, "In that case, my being publicly discovered provides us an advantage. Since we have no more need for secrecy, we may move more quickly. May I see where the pearls were taken from?"

The prospect of action seemed to lift Bethany's mood immediately. "Yes, of course."

Bethany took Rosalind up to her apartments on the second floor and through to the pretty little dressing room. Bethany clearly relished her warmth and comfort. The place was well carpeted, and a healthy fire burned in the grate. However, it was the dressing table that dominated the space, with its tall triple-paned mirror, not to mention the array of bottles, jars, brushes, and combs neatly arranged on its surface.

Rosalind found herself looking about the room, trying to imagine how Adam would view the chamber. Would he note the large window framed by velvet curtains? It was high up, but not so high as to make a climb impossible. Would he wonder where the key to Bethany's door was kept and whether that door was ever locked? Or was it customarily kept open, which meant anyone might slip inside?

Thinking of Adam brought something else to mind.

"Bethany," said Rosalind, "I should warn you that the delay in beginning inquiries may make recovering the necklace difficult. I am told speed is vital in such matters as this."

"It doesn't matter if we get it back," Bethany told her. "Not to me, at least. I just want to know what happened in the first place."

Rosalind nodded. "I understand."

"Do you?" Bethany murmured.

"Yes," she said. "Your family's status has changed. That means its problems and possibilities have also changed.

Questions that could be ignored now become pressing. As mistress of the house, it's your responsibility to keep the things in order and the family together. If there's a secret in the middle of the household, how can you know for certain that what you're doing is right?"

Bethany looked at her mutely. "I have tried," she said finally. "I know I should be delighted with this new fortune. But every time I turn, there seems to be some new triviality I was supposed to have managed but did not." She gazed around her lovely room. "Like leaving a box on the table for one night."

"Is that what happened?"

"Ridiculous, isn't it?" Bethany opened a burled maple cabinet to reveal a series of drawers. "This is the case for the everyday things." Bethany drew the bottom drawer open. "The most valuable jewels are kept in the butler's pantry or at the bank." She pulled out a slim box of carved sandalwood. "After the funeral, I had meant to give the pearls to my maid, Morgan, to lock away. But Mother had one of her spells, and she kept me with her so late that I simply forgot. In the morning, I gave the box to Morgan to lock up, but . . . I don't know. I felt something was wrong. Perhaps the box felt light in my hands. I opened the lid, and the pearls were gone."

Bethany opened the box now. A scarlet velvet lining showed faint imprints where the jewels had lain.

"Where was the box while you were with your mother?" Rosalind asked.

"I suppose I must have left it on the dressing table. That was where it was when I woke up in the morning."

"Did you ask Morgan if anyone came into the room?"

"She said she did not think so, but she wasn't here for much of the time. She was downstairs, with the mending." Rosalind nodded. A household such as this might bring in a girl for regular needlework, but the lady's maid would be responsible for maintaining the fine laces, beads, and trimming on Bethany's gowns.

So, anyone who came into the room and saw the box could have simply helped themselves. No stranger or professional housebreaker was needed. It would not be necessary to so much as cleverly make off with a key or bribe a servant. All it would take was some person who decided to seize their chance.

Bethany was watching her anxiously now. Rosalind pulled herself out of her musings. "What did Mr. Douglas's grandfather say about the theft?" she asked.

"We haven't told him," replied Bethany.

Rosalind raised her brows.

"It was Douglas's decision. He . . . he was sure he knew what had happened, as you heard, and he feared that news of the loss would harm Sir Jasper's opinion of him and jeopardize his . . . standing."

What is it that made Sir Jasper's opinion so fragile? Rosalind remembered the assertion in Lucinda's letter. *Mother always thought there was something more to it. . . .*

Rosalind was inclined to believe Lucinda's mother must be correct.

"Was that why you didn't bring in anyone to help with the search? So Sir Jasper wouldn't hear about it?"

"Douglas was afraid the news might be published in the papers."

"The newspapers do love a robbery," agreed Rosalind. "And if it occurred during the king's funeral, they would be able to make much of that."

"You sound quite familiar with the habits of the popular press."

Rosalind smiled. "Some good friends of mine write for the papers. They have a great deal to say about the habits of their fellow scriveners." Which led to another consideration. "If we are to bring in a man from Bow Street, I will need a description of the necklace for him."

"I can do better," said Bethany. "I can show you the copy."

"Excellent." Many ladies had copies made of their most valuable jewels so that they could wear them out in public without having to worry about the irreplaceable original being stolen.

Bethany reached back into her cabinet and drew out a heavy chain of pearls.

"There they are." Bethany laid the necklace out on the dressing table.

During her years among the *haut ton*, Rosalind had seen a great deal of brilliant jewelry, but nothing like this. It was entirely appropriate for a funeral and yet richly magnificent. It had three strands—two were strings of brilliant white pearls. The third had the deep gray spheres known as "black" pearls. There must have been two dozen of them, and each was the size of Rosalind's little fingernail. A single pear-shaped black pearl had been set in gold and surrounded by tiny diamonds to hang from the center as a pendant.

Even though she had been told it was a copy, the necklace drew her like a magnet. Rosalind could not stop from reaching out to touch the beads, from rolling one of the faux pearls through her fingers. It was only the unnatural smoothness that told her she held a tinted bead and not a genuine pearl.

"Do you know who made the original?" Rosalind asked.

"Sterne and Fiske," replied Bethany. "But that was over a hundred years ago."

"Who made the copy?"

"Also Sterne and Fiske. I'm not sure when that was, but probably around the same time. I was given the copy with the necklace."

"Is the firm still in business?" asked Rosalind.

"I don't know. Is that important?"

"Possibly. Those who set and string jewels know those who buy and sell loose gems." It was only a few months ago that Adam had been involved in investigating the robbery of a wealthy widow. Much of his work on the matter had seemed to involve going from jeweler to jeweler, trying to find out if any stranger had been asking where loose diamonds could be sold. "I'm sorry to say that such a lovely and distinctive necklace probably would not be kept whole. It would be taken apart, and the pearls sold individually."

"I never thought of that." Bethany sighed. "But I suppose it does make sense. Even just one of these"—she touched a bead—"if genuine, would be worth a great deal." Due to their rarity, pearls were considered the most precious gemstones.

"May I make a drawing of this?" Rosalind gently spread the necklace out on the table's surface. "If it happens that someone did try to sell the entire piece, a drawing will be of more use than a written description."

"Certainly." Bethany went to the writing desk beside the window and brought Rosalind paper and pencil.

Rosalind had, of course, learned drawing as a young girl. Her progress had been hobbled by the fact that her tutors had never stayed for long, usually because of her father's failure to pay their fees. Now, however, she did her utmost to recall those long-ago lessons. After a few minutes, she had a passable sketch of the necklace, including the maker's mark, which she'd found on the bottom of the gold clasp.

"Thank you." Rosalind folded the drawing and tucked it into her sleeve. "But is there anything else you can tell me about the time the pearls went missing?"

"That is all I know." Bethany picked up the necklace. The beads clicked as she coiled it restlessly around her hands.

"Who was in the house that night? Besides the servants?" Rosalind did not bother to ask if the servants had been questioned. Of course they had. Probably some of them now feared for their positions.

"We were all here," said Bethany. "Douglas was late because he had to escort his grandfather home. But my parents, my sisters, and myself were home."

Which led to another question. Rosalind did not really want to ask it, but she could not in conscience avoid it, either.

"Bethany . . . why didn't you tell Douglas I was coming to help discover what happened to your pearls?"

"I hardly know." She looked at her hand, all but invisible under the coils of artificial pearls. "It's been so difficult, all these changes . . . these past weeks especially."

"Because of the inheritance?"

She nodded. "At first, it seemed impossibly wonderful, something like out of a novel. Everything had been so bleak and confused since Nora's elopement. This was . . . It was like everything was finally back on the right road. Douglas had such *plans*. But he couldn't seem to trust that his luck, our luck, would hold. Right now, our income is dependent on Sir Jasper. He's made a settlement on Douglas and gives him an allowance, but . . . well, that could change if he decides he disapproves of . . . us."

"I see," said Rosalind.

"Douglas and I quarreled," Bethany said, but then she stopped. With an effort, she corrected herself. "We do quarrel. All his time has become absorbed in attending to his grandfather. You see, Sir Jasper has made it clear that should Douglas disappoint him, he will put the whole of the estate into the hands of executors, to be distributed to charity. He is gone so much and comes home with these odd speeches—about the importance of family and blood, and of living up to one's heritage. Some days I cannot keep my temper." She paused and then said softly, "He is disappointed in me."

Rosalind did not attempt to contradict or correct her. "Why?"

Bethany's gaze strayed to the door. It remained firmly shut.

"Before we took this house for the season, I told him in no uncertain terms I would not grovel to Sir Jasper for the sake of the money. He . . . he has not entirely forgiven me it. In fact, he has gone so far as to declare that he cannot introduce my relations to Sir Jasper, because they could not possibly live up to his standards. He nags at me because I have not managed to make any sort of entrée into society, and he says that I also must be excluded from the great man's presence until I can . . . 'Present a better figure,' is, I believe, how he put it. So, he goes, and I stay, and . . ." Her voice broke. "I fear I have ruined everything because I could not more gracefully bend my knee."

Rosalind thought of something Mrs. Hodgeson had said. "Is it true you do not go out?"

Bethany blushed. "Well, it is true I do not go to where I might see and be seen. I call on what friends I have, but they are hardly aristocratic connections. I take the little ones driving or to the park. But I have not sought out tickets for the opera or tried to find my way into the visiting books of our more prominent ladies. It's a feeble sort of protest, but it's the only one I have." Then Bethany shook herself. She slipped her hand out of the false necklace she had coiled up so tightly, and laid it in its drawer.

When she turned back to Rosalind, she had a smile on her face. "But this is awful. I'm now neglecting my duties as hostess. Here you stand, puzzling over our family's behavior, and you've had no chance to change or rest. Let me take you to your room."

"Thank you," said Rosalind. But as Bethany moved toward the door, Rosalind let her gaze sweep across the room one more time.

If the pearls had indeed sat out all night in their distinctive box, and if the door had been left unlocked, anyone in the household could have taken them.

No, she corrected herself. *Not just anyone.* The thief would have to have recognized the box. They would have needed to come into this room deliberately and recognize the chance they had been given.

That eliminated the lower servants but left the family attendants.

And the family themselves, including the disgraced Nora Cantrell.

CHAPTER 8

Introductions Over Dinner

My real purpose was to see you.

Jane Austen, *Pride and Prejudice*

The first thing Rosalind did after Bethany showed her to the simple white and claret-red boudoir was to sit down with her new writing desk. The inlaid desk with its green-leather writing surface was another recent indulgence, but one she justified because of her frequent stays in other homes. She needed to be sure of her supply of paper, pens, and ink.

After composing her mind to the task in front of her, Rosalind wrote three letters in rapid succession.

The first was to Alice, saying she had arrived and was fully installed, and letting her know the details of the Douglas house and family. She outlined what Bethany had told her of the theft. Alice had a quick and perceptive mind. She might well see some point Rosalind had overlooked.

The second letter was to Samuel Tauton, a principal officer at Bow Street, informing him that the Douglases wished to engage his professional services and requesting an appointment to call on him.

The third was to her friend Sanderson Faulks, saying she

had a problem that required his assistance and asking that he meet her at Mr. Clements's Circulating Library at one o'clock tomorrow. Mr. Clements's establishment was closer to Portsmouth Square than Little Russell Street, so it made sense to meet him there. It was not, Rosalind told herself, because she wished to avoid the possibility of Alice trying to recruit Mr. Faulks to her cause regarding a change of living arrangements.

It was certainly not because Rosalind could easily imagine Mr. Faulks agreeing with Alice.

Rosalind folded and sealed her letters firmly. She very much wanted to write to Adam, as well. She wanted to get his advice on the matter of the missing pearls, to tell him her suspicions and hear his thoughts.

But it was more than that. She wanted to feel that he was near. She wanted to know what he was doing, that he was well, and that he would be with her again soon.

One day, Rosalind told herself as she closed and locked her desk, she would be able to think of Adam without her heart beating in such a frustrating and irregular rhythm.

"Time to dress, miss," announced Amelia.

Somewhat hastily, Rosalind collected her finished letters into a pile before she rose to be helped out of her day dress and into a garment that would be appropriate for dinner.

While the number of changes rolling through her life might unnerve Rosalind, she allowed herself to fully enjoy one point—her new wardrobe. George Littlefield, Alice's brother, had married a dressmaker. In turn, the new Mrs. Littlefield had introduced Rosalind to an entire cadre of clothiers who were able to work miracles with secondhand gowns—trimming, tucking, and refashioning, such as by adding ribbons, net, lace, and even embroidered panels, until the castoffs were turned into creations that could credibly pass in any company.

Rosalind's dress for dinner was a simple coffee-colored

gown of a slightly older cut. But since she was more stat-
uesque than the current fashions were designed to flatter, it
suited her well. The warm brown wool complemented her
golden complexion. Decorations were limited to just two
rows of delicate tucks around the hems and cuffs.

"Well, Amelia." Rosalind sat down at the dressing table so
her maid could attend to her hair. "What do you think of the
house?"

"Mmph," was Amelia's initial answer. The girl wielded
her brush like she was going to war as she wrestled Rosalind's mane of unruly gold hair into the simple twist she preferred.

Rosalind took the hint and held herself still. But her
thoughts ran on ahead.

Bethany had said the pearls were stolen because they had
been left on her dressing table. But why would they have
been left out? Bethany had a lady's maid, Morgan. Any maid,
seeing that her mistress had been careless with such valuable
jewels, would have simply taken the box away to be locked
up. So, why had Morgan allowed the box to sit on the dressing table?

Perhaps Morgan didn't. Perhaps someone stole the pearls
from the pantry and put the box on Bethany's table to cover
their tracks.

They might take the risk if the reward was great enough.
And if they knew they could sell the pearls, the reward would
be large indeed.

Finally, Amelia stuck two pins into the twist. "As to what
I think, miss, I think it's early days yet." She stuck in another
pin. "Stay put, you devil."

Rosalind assumed this last was to her hair. Three more pins
followed. Then a most uncivilized oath. Then a fourth pin.

"Talking to that Betsy, I'd say there's a good bit of discontent belowstairs." Amelia lifted her hands away from Ros-

alind's head. They held their breaths, but the twist stayed in place. Both sighed in relief.

"Any idea what the cause might be?"

"I couldn't say for certain." Amelia fastened Rosalind's best coral beads around her throat. "But some of the staff are come up from the country with the family, but some are on loan from this Sir Jasper person, and it seems the two sets don't much care for each other."

Rosalind nodded. "Has anyone said anything about the missing necklace?" If Mrs. Hodgeson knew about Rosalind's mission, it was certain the staff did, as well.

"Not yet, but I'll have them all talking soon enough." Amelia paused. "Except maybe that butler, Dowdeswell. You ask me, if there's a thief belowstairs, he's the one."

"Is he one of Sir Jasper's people?"

"That he is, miss, and he means trouble. He's got that look." Amelia squinted and thrust her face forward, presumably in imitation of *that look* the butler possessed.

"Well, be careful you don't make enemies where you don't have to," said Rosalind.

"What? Me?" Amelia sounded less shocked than she perhaps should have. "Good Lord, miss, I'm mild as a newborn lamb."

When Rosalind had told her about the reason for the visit, Amelia had been excited to come along. The fact that Amelia was willing to assist in her inquiries was bound to be useful.

At the same time, if Amelia pressed the other servants too hard on any subject, especially a theft, it could make trouble for them both.

Amelia adjusted the shoulders of Rosalind's gown and stepped back. "There. I daresay you'll not disgrace us."

Rosalind stood and examined herself in the mirror.

"Thank you, Amelia," she said. "Please add those new letters to the household post before it leaves tonight."

"Yes, miss," said Amelia. "And . . . miss?"

"Yes?"

"It is all right I should write to Miss Alice, too? Just to say we've arrived and so on. I've not got the fist yet for much more. But I thought, you see, that she might like to hear . . ." Amelia blushed furiously.

"I'm sure Alice will be glad to hear from you."

Amelia and Alice were forming an affectionate bond that went beyond their relationship as employer and maid, and beyond the fact that Alice was teaching Amelia to read.

"Thank you, miss." Amelia wiped her hands on her apron and quickly crossed the room. "I'll just ring for that Betsy, shall I? She'll get you down to dinner, as I'm still learning my way about."

But as she was about to tug on the bellpull, a knock sounded on the door. Amelia smoothed her apron and opened the door to admit Bethany.

"Hello, Rosalind. I was on my way up to the nursery to say good night to the children. I thought you might like to meet them."

"Very much," said Rosalind.

Bethany led Rosalind up the stairs to the bright, spotless nursery rooms. As soon as she pushed open the door to the children's room, a healthy, boisterous toddler in a white nightgown heaved himself off the floor and galloped over to her.

"Mama!" he screamed delightedly. Bethany scooped him up into her arms and planted a kiss on his pudgy cheek.

"Hello, Gerry!" She hugged him. "How is my boy?"

The nursemaid was a big, capable-looking woman. "He had a healthy appetite at dinner, ma'am, and was just about to be put to bed. Weren't you, sir?"

"No!" pouted the boy.

Bethany laughed. "But you must mind Mrs. Dwyer, Gerry. You must sleep so you can grow into a big, strong man."

"No!"

Bethany kissed his cheek again. "Yes," she said firmly and handed him back to Mrs. Dwyer. "Go along now."

A second, much younger nursemaid came out of the sleeping room with an infant in her arms.

"And here is our Evie." Bethany held the baby close for Rosalind's inspection.

The child cracked her eyes open, waved a small pink fist randomly toward Rosalind, and blew a milk-scented bubble.

Rosalind smiled politely at this show of infant bravado. Children remained mysterious beings to her. She approved of them in the abstract and even liked some individually. But she could not yet envision a time when she looked at such a tiny, unfinished thing with the love and amazement she saw on Bethany's face.

Bethany kissed the infant and handed her back to her nurse. "Thank you, Margery," she said, and turned to Rosalind. "Now you have seen my real treasures. Shall we go down to dinner?"

"Yes, of course."

But as Bethany's gaze swept the room, Rosalind was struck by the other woman's sense of reluctance. Bethany wanted to stay in this place, where everything was rooted in the small, comfortable reality of her children. But then she shook herself, flashed Rosalind her hostess's smile, and led the way down the long flights of stairs.

They had just passed the third floor when Bethany paused and turned to Rosalind.

"I should perhaps tell you, Miss Thorne, my father can take a bit of getting used to. He is proud of his wit, and some of the things he says may sound harsher than he means them to. I'm sure I can count on you not to take offense."

"I'm sure I shall not," Rosalind answered. At the same time, she could not miss the relief that flitted across Bethany's face. Rosalind found herself wondering just what she had to look forward to.

*   *   *

All the Hodgesons and the Douglases had gathered in the foyer outside the dining room to wait for the doors to be opened. Or almost all of them. Mr. Douglas, of course, was not there. Neither was Mrs. Hodgeson. Penelope was. She stood close to Mariah Hodgeson, as if she thought Mariah might be able to shield her from something unpleasant. Mariah, for her part, glowered at Rosalind as she descended the last of the stairs. The only man present stood nearest the doors. He was stout, stooped, and balding. His smile as he looked up at Bethany was genuine, but it was not, to Rosalind's mind, entirely pleasant.

When they reached the foyer, Bethany took her directly to the smiling gentleman. "Rosalind, let me introduce you to my father, William Hodgeson."

Mr. Hodgeson watched keenly as Rosalind made her curtsy. His general appearance was cheerful—with cherry-red cheeks, mottled pink and brown skin, and steel-rimmed spectacles perched on a high-bridged nose. He dressed in the expected black and white clothes for dinner, and his clothes were unadorned and unassuming. His cravat was simply arranged, and his thinning hair was tied back in an old-fashioned queue. The broken veins in his nose and bright cheeks, however, hinted at a history of drink.

"Delighted to meet you, Miss Thorne." Mr. Hodgeson bowed. "You will forgive my wife's absence. Her attention for her health is such that she must remain sequestered with—she assures me—a bowl of nourishing broth prepared to her own recipe."

"I'm sorry to hear she is ill," said Rosalind. "I hope she recovers soon."

"You do, do you?" murmured Mr. Hodgeson. "Well, you are new to this household." The remark was quick and cutting. Bethany, however, appeared not to notice.

"I don't believe—" Bethany turned Rosalind toward Mariah, but whatever she was about to say was interrupted by the sound of footsteps pattering down the staircase.

A slim, dark-haired young woman hurried down the stairs with a carelessness that would have gotten Rosalind severely scolded as a girl. She landed right in front of Bethany and flashed her a cheeky grin, as if daring her to make some remark.

The new arrival did not wait for that remark, however, but instead turned to Rosalind.

"I take it you are Miss Thorne?" Like her descent, the young woman's curtsy was quick and careless. "How do you do? I'm Leonora Hodgeson, the wicked sister."

CHAPTER 9

A Quiet Family Dinner

*. . . in her air altogether there is a self-sufficiency
without fashion, which is intolerable.*

Jane Austen, *Pride and Prejudice*

Rosalind kept her countenance and made her own, more decorous curtsy to Nora.

"How do you do, Miss Hodgeson?"

Leonora Hodgeson wore a simple forest-green dress that strained a little at the seams, indicating it had been made for a slimmer, younger girl. She strongly resembled both Bethany and Mariah—they all possessed dark hair, pale skin, and bright, intelligent eyes. But Nora clearly looked on the world with more cynicism than Bethany, and underneath her breezy air, her manner held more wariness than even Mariah's. The skin on her long, fine hands was rough and faintly stained, a sign that her life had been harder than either of her sisters'.

Nora seemed quite disappointed at Rosalind's calm. "I trust my family has informed you about me?" she pressed.

"Nora, we are about to go in to dinner," said Bethany. It was a plea and a warning. Nora ignored both.

"I have heard your name," admitted Rosalind.

"What?" Nora said merrily. "My name and nothing else?"
"What else should I have heard?" Rosalind inquired.

Nora's gaze slid from Rosalind to Bethany and back again. "Nothing at all, of course," she answered lightly. "Only that I'm quite willful, that I have a marked disdain for proprieties, and that I caused my family a great deal of despair with an importunate elopement."

"Well, such candor speaks very much in your favor," said Rosalind.

Mariah let out a single hard laugh. "You're going to have to try harder with this one, Nora."

Nora tilted her head to the side, examining Rosalind with her dark, intelligent gaze. "Do you know, I think perhaps I am."

"My daughter likes to shock people, Miss Thorne," cut in Mr. Hodgeson. "It's her finest accomplishment."

"And yours is publishing our faults, Papa," remarked Mariah.

"I wish I had to publish them," he answered placidly. "But I am denied that occupation since my girls are so quick to put them on daily display."

"I wish . . . ," began Penelope, but when her sisters-in-law all turned to her, she blushed and looked deeply confused. "I wish that the doors might open soon," she said. "I'm famished."

"That is the first sensible thing anyone's said yet this evening," declared Mr. Hodgeson. "And who would have thought it would come from our Penelope? Bethany, my dear, you're ceding your responsibilities as our pillar of conventionality."

"And you are giving our guest quite the mistaken impression of our family," replied Bethany.

Fortunately, Rosalind was saved from having to answer by the footman opening the dining room doors.

Since Mr. Douglas was away dining with Sir Jasper, Mr.

Hodgeson became the senior male of the household. Therefore, etiquette assigned him the seat at the head of the table,
while Bethany took her place at its foot. Rosalind, as the
guest, was seated at Mr. Hodgeson's right hand. Nora and
Mariah sat across from her, with Penelope next to her.

The dinner was excellent. Clearly, the Douglases employed
a skilled cook. There was a potato bisque garnished with
hothouse cucumbers and parsley, followed by a fish course of
John Dory dressed in cream sauce. The joint was a loin of
beef and was accompanied by a selection of sauces, a fricas-
see of root vegetables and cabbage, and stewed fruits with
custard.

"So, Miss Thorne," said Mr. Hodgeson as he carved the
beautifully roasted beef. "I am told you are here to shepherd
our little Penelope through that elaborate nonsense we call
the season."

"I hope to introduce her to some new acquaintance," said
Rosalind carefully. She did not quite like the gleam in Mr.
Hodgeson's eye.

"Well, you must take great care of her, you know." Mr.
Hodgeson handed the platter of sliced beef to the footman to
pass around so the ladies might help themselves. "She is
enormously shy. I should think she may faint dead away if
asked to speak in company."

At the moment, Penelope was staring hard at her plate.
Mariah slumped in her chair, ignoring the elbow Nora dug
into her ribs.

All of them grown women, thought Rosalind. *All still acting the part of girls.*

"Not her fault, of course," Mr. Hodgeson went on, ignoring Bethany's quelling glance as completely as he did Penelope's discomfort. "Sheltered and cosseted as she has been.
She probably has not even given a thought to what sort of
husband would best suit. What shall he be, Pen? What kind
of sweetheart do you dream of at night?"

"Papa! You cannot expect a young lady to confess such a thing at dinner," cried Bethany.

"Oh, nonsense. Come, come, girl, let's have it." He tapped his hand against the table. "Are you after a title? A fortune? Or will you be satisfied with a pretty face?"

Penelope kept her gaze on her plate. Her cheeks glowed bright pink.

"Really, Papa," said Bethany. "If your aim is to distress poor Penelope, you have succeeded admirably. Now we may change the subject."

"Oh, now, she knows I mean no harm." He waved one knobby hand.

"No, of course you don't," muttered Nora.

"I'm sorry?" said Mr. Hodgeson. "Nora, did you say something?"

"Would it matter if I did?"

Mr. Hodgeson seemed to consider this. "Well, that would depend, now, wouldn't it? If it was sensible, or at least amusing, then it would matter very much indeed."

Nora ignored him and instead turned to Rosalind. "So, tell us, Miss Thorne, what progress do you make in the matter of my sister's missing necklace?"

"I'm afraid there has been no chance to make much progress as of yet," Rosalind replied.

"What's this?" cried Mr. Hodgeson "The necklace? The famous necklace that Bethany so carelessly mislaid?"

Now it was Bethany's turn to blush.

"Perhaps she did not mislay it," said Nora. "Perhaps the house goblins spirited it away. What do you think, Father? Was it goblins? Do you think they stopped to consider how a necklace like that would compensate for a great deal of lost rent?"

The canny mischief drained away from Mr. Hodgeson face.

"It is quite obvious that the one who took it needed

money," Nora went on serenely. "Since pearls are the most valuable of jewels, the thief would now be very well fixed indeed, and no longer beholden to anyone, not even to their close kindred. Such a temptation." She gave an exaggerated sigh.

Bethany looked close to panic. From the way Mariah's shoulders tensed, Rosalind suspected she was either clutching her napkin or getting ready to kick Nora under the table. Perhaps she already had. If so, Nora took no notice.

"Nora," said Mr. Hodgeson sternly. "You might want to guard your tongue before you say too much. There is more than one person in this family who might be tired of their dependency."

"Oh?" The syllable broke slightly. Yes, Mariah had definitely kicked her, and she had just as definitely ignored it. "And who would that be? Aside from yourself?"

Which, it seemed, was all Mariah was prepared to countenance.

"I have something to say," she announced.

Nora Hodgeson turned dead white. For a moment, Rosalind actually thought she might faint.

"So much for a peaceable meal," drawled Mr. Hodgeson, apparently unconscious of his part in the general disruption.

"Well, don't leave us in suspense, Mariah," said Bethany. "What is it?"

"I wanted . . . I have changed my mind. I also want to take part in the season."

Silence fell thick and startled.

"You, Mariah?" exclaimed Bethany at last.

"I should have thought you above such frivolity," said Mr. Hodgeson cheerfully. "Welladay, such are the temptations of London."

Mariah regarded them all defiantly.

"I think it's a splendid idea," announced Nora. "Why shouldn't Mariah have some fun? It's not right that she should have to sit home. She's not the one disgraced the family. That's my role."

Slowly, heavily, Penelope lifted her gaze. "But, Mariah, you forget, we are not to have a season," she said. Her voice was hoarse, as if she had been crying or screaming. "Bethany has declined to take our part with my brother, and Miss Thorne is here only to find the lost necklace."

Mariah arched her brows. "But Bethany promised you should have a season. She'd never go back on her word."

"Please, both of you," said Bethany. "We will discuss this somewhere other than at the table."

"Will you?" cried Mr. Hodgeson. "I expect it will not go any better for you then, Bethany, knowing these three." He swept his fork out to indicate the younger women.

"What interests you about the season, Mariah?" asked Rosalind.

Mariah started, as if amazed that someone would ask her such a question. "Things have changed for us as a family," she said. "I have as much right to consider the future as anyone else. How am I to make any rational decision if all I have done is sit in my room?"

"Well, Papa?" said Nora. "How will you declare that statement to be silly?"

"No, I must admit, it is very good, as far as it goes," Mr. Hodgeson replied. "Well, well. Why not? With the dowry our good Douglas can confer, who is to say that even Mariah might not roust herself a beau from the shrubbery?"

"Is this really what you want, Mariah?" asked Bethany.

"Yes." Mariah's entire attitude radiated defiant dignity. Nora, on the other hand, looked at her sister like she'd just decided to run barefoot through the winter streets.

"Very well," said Rosalind calmly. "Provided your family agrees, there is no reason why you should not have an excellent season."

"You are a miracle worker, then, Miss Thorne?" inquired

Mr. Hodgeson. "Or do you have that much faith in the raw power of money?"

"Neither, sir," replied Rosalind. "It happens that the *haut ton* is neither quite so small nor so narrow as it appears from the outside. There are many possible entrées. What is required is to know the correct doors."

"And you do, do you?" Mr. Hodgeson grinned.

"Yes," replied Rosalind calmly.

Bethany took a gulp of her wine. "Well, of course, we must confer with Mother."

"As long as you take care of her delicate health," said Mr. Hodgeson solemnly. "Hearing that our intellectual Mariah wishes to be somewhere other than the library may bring on one of her fits."

"I'll be sure and break it to her gently." Bethany tried to match his satirical drawl.

"Do you say you mean to keep your word? About the season?" asked Penelope. "Or are you simply drawing things out before you say no?"

"You're very keen to leave us, Penelope," remarked Mr. Hodgeson. "Should we be worried that there's someone out there waiting for you?"

Penelope's hand curled tightly around her fork. For a moment, it looked as though the girl might shout or possibly try to run Mr. Hodgeson through. Given Penelope's history with the rogue Bryan Cantrell, Rosalind wouldn't have entirely blamed her for doing so, either.

"Papa!" cried Bethany desperately. "Surely you have something more amusing to speculate on than the concerns of young girls. Let us find some more engaging topic. Perhaps Miss Thorne can give us some new intelligence she has heard about the capitol."

Rosalind took the opening. As Mr. Hodgeson clearly fancied himself a student of the absurd, she tried out a few bits of public gossip she'd heard from Alice's theatrical friends.

Thankfully, this proved a good idea. Mr. Hodgeson found himself able to enlarge and speculate on the follies of strangers, while the young women were allowed to finish the meal in relative peace.

Finally, when the cheese and fruit course was cleared away, Bethany rose from the table to suggest the ladies repair to the blue sitting room for tea.

"Leaving me to enjoy your husband's port in solitary state." Mr. Hodgeson did not sound as if he regretted this particular circumstance in the least. "Bethany, I concede to you the management of the silliness committee. Be sure to leave plenty of time to visit your mother before you retire. You know she cannot sleep without having unburdened herself of today's list of complaints."

As it happened, Bethany did not have to go to her mother. When they all reached the blue salon, Mrs. Hodgeson was already there, carefully propped up on the sofa cushions, with no fewer than four shawls wrapped around her bony shoulders.

"Oh, Mama," said Bethany. "I was not sure we'd see you this evening."

"I was not sure myself, but I felt I must rally my strength for the sake of our guest." Her smile was dramatically pained. "Now, Miss Thorne, you have had a chance to know us a little. How do you find us?"

"Really, Mama," said Bethany. "You cannot expect Miss Thorne to own opinions she's hardly had time to form."

Mrs. Hodgeson waved this away. "Miss Thorne's business is to observe the house and its members. Of course we have the right to ask what progress she makes." She turned expectantly toward Rosalind.

Nora gave a loud and exaggerated yawn. "Oh! Forgive me, do. It's just that we were subjected to so many of Papa's observations at dinner that the idea that we now must listen to Miss Thorne's leaves me quite fatigued."

Mrs. Hodgeson reared back, obviously ready to reprove her daughter.

Nora didn't wait. "If we're looking for entertainment, why doesn't Penelope play us something?"

"Perhaps because Penelope remembers her manners," said Mrs. Hodgeson icily.

Nora looked to Penelope. "Please, Pen? Otherwise, I shall fall asleep right here, facedown in my tea."

"Yes, yes, of course," said Penelope hastily. "Mariah? Shall we have a duet?"

Mariah sighed and set her cup down. "Very well."

Mariah stood and followed Penelope to the pianoforte. Rosalind felt her eyebrows trying to inch up. Penelope took her seat at the grand instrument and touched the keys, sending up a rippling arpeggio that proved it was well tuned. Mariah ruffled through the music sheets and showed a pair of selections to Penelope, who chose one.

Mrs. Hodgeson, reluctantly resigned, fussed with her shawls and fussed again as her maid tried to adjust her pillows.

Mariah sat to Penelope's right and nodded the time.

The girls began to play. The music was smooth, mellow, and light. Rosalind didn't recognize the piece, but it was something for an evening's proper entertainment, calculated to show the girls' polish and practice. It was the girls themselves who held Rosalind's attention. Concentrating on their playing, they made a study in contrasts. For Mariah, the music came as relaxation. Confidence replaced the defensiveness she had displayed through dinner. She was secure behind the music she made.

Penelope, on the other hand, played with a fierce determination, as if willing the music to say what she could not. Her slim hands fell heavily on the keys, causing the bass line to thump insistently underneath Mariah's rippling melody.

The quiet, polite golden girl was desperate to be heard.

Some slight movement made Rosalind turn her head. She saw Mr. Hodgeson slouched against the doorframe. One hand held a decanter. The other cupped a snifter of port. He did not notice Rosalind's regard. He just stared at the feminine scene in front of him. Slowly, his bored, cynical face colored and shifted.

In that moment, Rosalind saw that whatever else he might be, Mr. Hodgeson was deeply, coldly angry.

CHAPTER 10

Some Private Conversation

*Through letters, whatever of good or bad was to
be told would be communicated, and every suc-
ceeding day was expected to bring some news of
importance.*

Jane Austen, *Pride and Prejudice*

At long last, the evening ended.

After Mariah and Penelope's duet, Rosalind endured
Mrs. Hodgeson's quizzing about what she had so far observed, which quickly dissolved into a tirade against her servants' inadequacies, and how it was only her own dear, loyal
Gilpin and her own continual watchfulness that kept her
alive at all.

Nora escaped first. Then Mariah pulled Penelope away by
remaking some vague promise to show her a new piece of
music that had just arrived. After that, Bethany offered to
take her mother upstairs and get her settled.

"It's getting late," said Bethany. "I do so worry you might
risk catching cold."

The mention of cold proved a strong motivator, and suddenly Mrs. Hodgeson could not leave fast enough. This left Rosalind free to return to her own rooms.

Usually, Rosalind liked to sit up of an evening, reflecting on the day. Tonight she found herself too tired and disconcerted for the comforts of the fireside and a last cup of tea. She asked Amelia to help get her ready for bed.

Bundled up in shawls and quilts, her hair braided, her cap firmly settled and tied, Rosalind was at her most homely and private. It was in this character that she opened her writing desk back up and took out the letter she had been saving, the one that had arrived just this morning, from Adam.

> *My Dear Miss Thorne:*
>
> *We have arrived in Manchester in good order. For the time of year, the roads were not too bad. We did have to hole up for an extra night at a posting inn because of the rain, and spent an interesting night watching young Prentice fleece a would-be card sharp down to his socks. I think I'll make sure that he spends more time with Tauton when we return. Such initiative needs to be channeled, or it ends up making more work for us, rather than less.*

Rosalind felt herself smiling. Adam was a lively correspondent who wrote exactly as he spoke. She could hear his voice inside her mind, and the warmth of his imagined presence filled her.

> *We've met with our society of Manchester merchants. It seems that we have on our hands an old-style burglary racket. Doors are forced, windows broken, the shop or workshop is looted, and the thieves depart the way they came in. No one seems to hear or see anything, which is more normal than not. Manchester's*

watch is even more lax than ours in London, and what
police and militia they have seem mostly concerned
with keeping the factory workers from congregating in
groups of more than three, lest the forces of revolution
be unleashed. The city is still reeling from the recent
events at St. Peter's Field, and there is a great deal of
tension in the air.

A shiver of disquiet ran down Rosalind's spine. Just a few
months before, a disastrous public demonstration had taken
place in the heart of Manchester. It had begun as a meeting to
call for change in the franchise laws and to decry the existence of the rotten and pocket boroughs. It had ended with
the death of fifteen persons after the cavalry was called in to
break up the mob.

In fact, Adam wrote, *the watch and militia captains*
I've talked to are unanimous in their opinion that our
thieves must be a gang of disgruntled workers, although
one or two also suspect the band of tinkers who have
camped on riverside. They have all made it clear we are
not particularly welcome. That the merchants decided
to bring in outsiders is being taken personally by the
local men. This is going to be a long stay, I'm afraid.
I miss you, Rosalind. I miss your good sense and
steadiness, and the chance to talk this set of problems
over with you.

Her heart skipped, and she allowed herself the entirely
ridiculous and bittersweet indulgence of reading the sentence
over several times.

My greetings and good wishes to Mr. Faulks and all
the Littlefields. Write and tell me of your latest adven-

*tures. It will help me remember you are not so very far
away, after all.*
   Yours always,
   Adam

Rosalind closed her eyes and held the letter close to her
face. She was not so lost in romance that she kissed the mis-
sive, but she did breathe deeply and let herself imagine for a
moment that she caught Adam's scent mingled with the work-
aday smells of paper and ink.

Then she took out her own piece of paper.

First, she dealt with the commonplace inquiries after his
health and said that she was very well. After that, she wrote
about her arrival at the Douglases' house and all that she had
been tasked with here.

   I recognize Bethany Douglas's nature all too well, she
wrote. *She has taken it on herself to keep peace in the
family and to fix what is broken. I believe she married
Douglas as much with this end in view as she did from
any affection.*

   *The three younger girls present a complex picture.
Penelope is, I think, more restless than her brother and
sister-in-law realize. Mariah is an intelligent girl, but unconventional, and is marooned in a house that does not
appreciate the unique. This has bred in her a form of
stagnated rebellion, which is very much in need of an
outlet if it is not to fester.*

   *Nora is hiding something and using her bluster to
cover it over. But what is that thing? Is it the theft? She
had reason to take the pearls. She wants to be free of
her dependence on her family. Selling those pearls
would certainly provide the means. Despite all this, she
is supportive of both Mariah and Penelope. Is she sin-*

cere in her sisterly affection? Or is she simply looking to use the girls as allies? But if that is so, to what end?

The mother is an invalid, and only too happy to dwell on the theft. As for the father . . . Rosalind paused, remembering Mr. Hodgeson in the doorway and the bitter anger on his face.

He also is profoundly discontent in his dependency. This wars with a natural complacency, which makes me believe he also has something he fears. There is some suggestion of serious money trouble. I am told Douglas took over the management of the estate and put the house up to let. But is it possible Mr. Hodgeson has additional difficulty that even these drastic measures will not relieve?

Rosalind paused again, took a deep breath, and began a new paragraph.

I do not like the feeling of this house. Every family has secrets. But here everyone seems to be trying desperately to protect themselves from . . . *something.*

I wish that you were here to speak with. My own mind is an unsettled and lonely place tonight. If all goes well, I will see Alice and Mr. Faulks and your colleague Mr. Tauton as soon as tomorrow. Perhaps they will help draw my thoughts out into more orderly lines.

I miss—

Out in the sitting room, Rosalind heard Amelia open the door. A woman's voice spoke, soft and indistinct.

"I'm very sorry, miss," answered Amelia. "Miss Thorne has already gone to bed."

"No, it's all right, Amelia," called Rosalind. She placed her unfinished letter into her writing desk. "I'll be right there."

She climbed out of the bed, donned slippers and her warm wrapper. In the little sitting room, Mariah—in all her frosty dignity—stood beside the banked fireplace.

"Mariah," said Rosalind, surprised. "What can I do for you?"

"I do apologize," Mariah said without an ounce of sincerity. "I had a question for you."

Rosalind pulled her wrapper closer around her. "What is it?"

"Did you mean what you said at dinner? Do you truly believe you could find me a husband?"

Mariah's expression dared Rosalind to try to deceive or placate her.

"I believe what I said was that you could have an excellent season," said Rosalind. "Do you want to get married?"

For a moment Mariah looked like she hadn't understood. "Why else would I put myself through the mill of the London season?"

"A season is one of the few times when a young woman may call attention to herself. That can be quite gratifying. However, I suspect your candor would not allow you to enjoy having suitors dancing attendance on you for your dowry. I expect you are looking for more sincere sorts of attachment."

"I suppose you will try to tell me you can make me a beauty?" sneered Mariah. "If only I remove my spectacles and dress my hair in a more becoming fashion?"

"Probably not," answered Rosalind. "But I think you can be a success."

"You're trying to flatter me," said Mariah, and the words were low and dangerous.

"I do not flatter," answered Rosalind. "It seldom works."

"You truly think you can make *me* a social success?" Mariah pressed her. "With this face? With this . . . ?" She gestured at her thick body.

Rosalind felt a wave of sympathy for the girl. It was evident she had been told, probably frequently, that she was unmarriageable. Unfortunately, even Bethany seemed to lack the imagination to see any viable opportunity for her.

"I've seen it done," said Rosalind. "You have the most important attributes."

"What's that?"

"A first-rate intelligence and a desire to triumph."

Mariah fell silent. Rosalind could see the wheels of her mind turning furiously. She did not want to believe. She wanted Rosalind to be lying.

Because it would be less painful than hope.

Mariah Hodgeson would certainly not be the first plain girl to grow a protective shell. Given what Rosalind had seen of Mariah's parents, she imagined that burying her feelings had become a means of survival.

"You cannot mean it," said Mariah finally.

"But I do. You can have what you want. If you are willing to work for it."

"How?" demanded Mariah.

"I believe when I first saw you, you had the book *Conversations in Chemistry*." Rosalind had noted the title when she almost ran into Mariah in the hallway. "Have you read it?"

Mariah drew back, startled. "I have."

"Would you be interested in meeting its author?"

Mariah's jaw dropped. She closed it immediately. "And how would that be accomplished?"

"She is a member of the Royal Institution," said Rosalind. "She and her husband have recently taken a house in Grosvenor Square, so she attends the lectures regularly. I have a friend whom I can importune for tickets and, possibly, an introduction."

Mariah regarded her fiercely, coldly, steadily. Rosalind let her have her long look. The young woman was hoping Rosalind would wilt or speak to fill the silence. Rosalind recognized the tactic. She had employed it many times herself.

Finally, Mariah pulled back. "Very well, Miss Thorne," she said coolly. "I agree to your trial."

"Thank you," said Rosalind gravely. "If you are willing, we will discuss details more fully in the morning."

Mariah nodded.

"Then I wish you good night."

Mariah said good night and took her leave.

"Well!" began Amelia, but Rosalind held up her hand. She hurried to the door and cracked it open.

Through the opening, Rosalind saw that Mariah was standing at another door on the hall. That door opened, and Rosalind was just able to see Nora standing on the threshold. Rosalind closed her own door and shook her head. Probably it was of no significance that Mariah had gone straight to Nora.

Then she recalled what she had written to Adam. *Everyone in this family seems to be protecting themselves from . . . something.*

Probably it is of no significance. But then again, perhaps it is.

CHAPTER 11

A Morning Caller

Lydia was Lydia still—untamed, unabashed, wild,
noisy, and fearless.

Jane Austen, *Pride and Prejudice*

Rosalind was a habitually early riser, and today was sure to be busy. She had her appointment to speak with Mariah. She had to stop at Little Russell Street to see if replies to her various letters had arrived and then go to her arranged meetings. There were more letters to write after that, and at least one call to make.

"Will you be needing me to come with you, miss?" asked Amelia.

"No, I'm counting on you to keep an eye on the house for me while I'm out," Rosalind told her. "I am particularly hoping you can contrive to speak with Morgan. How do matters stand with the butler and his look?" Rosalind asked.

Amelia pulled a face. "Gets no better for knowing him more. He lurks, too, always behind the door or around the corner, like he thinks he's going to catch the girls . . . Well, never mind that. Gives me the creeps." She shuddered.

"If he gives you more than 'the creeps,' you will tell me?"

"If he gives me more than the creeps, I'll give him more than he can swallow," replied Amelia darkly.

Of this, Rosalind had no doubt at all.

Amelia informed Rosalind that Mr. Douglas was reported to be an early riser. As a result, a hot breakfast was laid out on a daily basis. As Rosalind ventured downstairs, she found herself hoping that she would have a private word or two with the head of this troubled household. She wanted to know more about Sir Jasper, who seemed to loom like a shadow over the household. She also hoped to learn how Mr. Douglas personally regarded his benefactor and, of course, anything that Mr. Douglas might know or believe about the lost necklace.

But to Rosalind's surprise, when she walked into the breakfast room, it was Nora who sat alone at the long table.

"Good morning, Miss Thorne!" Nora raised her coffee cup to Rosalind in salute.

"Good morning . . ." To her embarrassment, Rosalind hesitated, uncertain which surname this young woman used.

Nora saw this and laughed. "Nora will do very well, thank you. I shall call you Rosalind, and we will be quite cozy together." This was the same brassy cheer she had used with her family the night before. To Rosalind, Nora's confidence seemed very like Mariah's diffidence—a way to conceal any glimpse of true feeling.

"Very well," agreed Rosalind. "How are you this morning . . . Nora?"

Nora shrugged. "Impertinent, disinclined to small talk, and too hungry to confine myself to those portions my mother insists are ladylike." She waved her toast at her breakfast plate, which contained fish in butter sauce, hashed potatoes, and ham. "I will give my brother-in-law his due. Since his rise in the world, he has always kept an excellent table." She crunched her piece of toast.

"Well, we must endeavor to do it justice." Rosalind helped herself to coddled eggs and a toasted muffin with orange marmalade. She sat at the table beside Nora and poured herself a cup of tea from the pot.

"So, do you really mean to do it?" asked Nora.

"What is that?"

"Do you really mean to try to find Penelope a husband?"

Rosalind added a slice of lemon to her tea. "I mean to help her grow accustomed to London society and make some acquaintance here that will hopefully grow into friendship. What else may happen is not under my control."

Nora took another bite of toast. "She's spineless."

Sensing this was another attempt to shock her, Rosalind allowed one brow to arch. "Is she?"

"She is. Pretty girls are. Their faces are their fortune, so they never have to cultivate anything else."

Rosalind thought of some of the beautiful women she knew perched at the very top of London society, and privately disagreed. "But you yourself may be considered pretty."

Nora smiled crookedly. "But not on the same level as Pen. No, my main feature is that I'm infamous."

"And do you enjoy your infamy?"

This gave Nora a moment's pause. "I have no choice," she said finally. "What I did is unforgivable. Therefore, I do not seek forgiveness. It saves time and effort."

"What do you do instead?"

"Write letters to friends to beg for money. Scheme for ways to leave my brother-in-law's house." She paused again, just long enough to smile sunnily. "Pick up small but valuable items to sell." She glanced slyly at Rosalind as she said it.

Rosalind smiled and drank her tea.

Nora sighed in elaborate disappointment. "Mariah was right. You will simply not be shocked."

Rosalind ate her eggs. Nora watched thoughtfully and dragged a bit of fish through the sauce, as if it would help her think.

"Tell me," said Nora, "is it true you found a dead man in Almack's ballroom?"

"It is."

"And another in the courtyard of Lady Melborne's house?"

"That was a dead woman," said Rosalind. "And I did not find her."

"You're in earnest."

"Unfortunately." Rosalind took a swallow of tea. "May I ask you a direct question, Nora?"

"It is the kind I prefer," Nora replied. "You may have noticed, we are not generally encouraged to speak at all, let alone share our honest opinions, lest we commit the cardinal sin of silliness." She looked at Rosalind over the rim of her coffee cup in an excellent imitation of her father looking over the rims of his spectacles.

Rosalind let this remark pass. Instead, she asked, "What do you think happened to the pearls?"

For a moment, Nora's expression was unguarded, and Rosalind saw that underneath the cheeky exterior was a mind every bit as sharp as Mariah's.

"Do you know, you are the first person to ask me that? What are you about?" Nora lowered her voice in mock suspicion. "Are you trying to trap me?"

"I'm trying to understand your point of view," said Rosalind.

Nora regarded her steadily for a long time. "I should not like to play at cards with you, Rosalind," she said. "I imagine you do not often lose."

"I do not play cards."

That earned her a laugh. "The better for the rest of us. So. You want to know what I think, do you?" Nora put down her cup, planted both elbows on the table, laced her fingers together, and rested her chin on them. It gave her an attitude that was both childish and flirtatious. Rosalind's mother would have howled had Rosalind made any such gesture, even during the informalities of breakfast.

"Have you asked this question of Bethany?" Nora mused. "No, of course you have. Mariah?"

"I have not yet had the opportunity to ask Mariah."

"Penelope?"

"Are you wondering if I have stories to compare with yours?"

Nora laughed again. "Perhaps I am. Well." She flopped backward, slouching in her chair—another careless, childish pose. "What do I think happened? Do you know, Miss Thorne, I'm not sure I've really considered it. I've been too busy trying to fend off the sharp looks from my brother-in-law, not to mention all of Bethany's sad, patient disappointment." Nora's voice had tightened. She quickly covered emotion with movement. She plucked another piece of toast from the rack, dug her knife into the butter pot, and scraped it across her bread. "If I was to venture a theory," she said at last, "I'd say Douglas took the pearls."

Rosalind felt surprise tighten her expression, and Nora clapped her hands delightedly. "Don't tell me I've finally shocked you?"

"Congratulations," replied Rosalind dryly. "Do you mean it?"

Nora touched her forehead, a salute signaling, *Touché.* "I do mean it. He's the one person who can go anywhere and do anything without a single person in the whole house questioning him. Even if someone saw him with the necklace in his hands, who would think anything of it? And if they did think something, none of the servants would risk their positions by pointing a finger at their employer, and none of the family would risk the blow to their pocketbooks." Nora bit into her toast and stared at the wall over Rosalind's shoulder.

"And it would be rather perfect, wouldn't it? Douglas takes the pearls, and I take the blame. If I am proved to be a thief, even Bethany can't argue with him throwing me out."

"But Bethany doesn't believe you took the necklace," Rosalind reminded her.

Nora shrugged. "That would be easy enough to change. All that has to be done is for the pearls to be left somewhere in my room. In fact, I'm rather surprised that hasn't already happened."

"So perhaps it wasn't Mr. Douglas who took them."

"But then who? One of the servants?" Nora gestured toward the doors. "They're not so stupid. They know they'd be the first ones suspected. Besides, if they're interested in lining their pockets, there are a thousand easier ways, and a thousand less conspicuous things they could take. Could it be a housebreaker? There was no sign."

"What of Mariah?" asked Rosalind. "Or Penelope?"

"Pen?" Nora choked on her toast. "I almost wish it was her. It would mean she has some spirit left to her. But Mariah?" Nora paused, and that sharper, warier self showed in her eyes.

"Mariah could do it," said Nora, but without any of her usual mocking confidence. "But she'd need a good reason."

"Perhaps she wants to leave this house, as well."

"Oh, she does. Of that, you may be sure. But would she steal to get the chance?" Nora frowned. "No. Mariah doesn't think that way. She is too direct."

Nora clearly believed this, but Rosalind wasn't entirely sure. It suddenly occurred to Rosalind that the oddest part of this conversation was her certainty that Nora was telling her the truth.

"Last night you seemed to think the thief was your father."

"I didn't mean it," said Nora. "At least, when I first said it, I didn't. Since then, well"—she shrugged—"I have to admit, it's possible. Although, Papa's talent for ridiculing others is not matched by a talent for self-exertion."

"But why would he steal them? I understand that Mr. Douglas has taken over the management of the estate and that your parents are now living in his house. What need does he have for more money?"

Nora looked at her in a slightly pitying fashion. "Have you never done anything just to prove you can?" she asked. "Just to demonstrate to yourself that you are not wholly useless? My father failed to secure his estate, failed to make a good marriage, failed to produce a son, and finally failed to ridicule his daughters into becoming the sort of women he believes he could approve of. If he can steal from Douglas, and keep the secret of it, he will have succeeded at one small thing."

It was a stinging appraisal, delivered with cold certainty. As Rosalind reflected on it, she also remembered her glimpse of Mr. Hodgeson slumped in the doorway, already drunk on Douglas's port and watching his daughters. She remembered how struck she had been that so much anger burned in his blurred eyes.

"Was that why you eloped?" she asked.

"I'm sorry?" said Nora stiffly.

"Did you elope with Cantrell to prove that you could?"

Nora's face hardened. "My elopement is no part of your business here, Miss Thorne."

"I beg your pardon."

But Nora was not ready to grant any such pardon. "You are to find the necklace, and any such husbands as may be lying by the wayside. Beyond that, you will kindly leave us all alone."

Before Rosalind could find a suitable reply, the footman drew back the doors to the breakfast room so Mr. Douglas could enter. Douglas was already dressed to go out for the day, in dark wool coat, patterned waistcoat, and straight trousers.

He stopped when he saw Nora. Nora raised her coffee cup in salute to him.

Mr. Douglas turned and bowed to Rosalind. "Good morning, Miss Thorne," he said. Then he added more slowly, "Good morning, Nora."

"Good morning, Douglas," answered Nora, all her cheerfulness firmly back in place. "How does your grandfather?"

"He is well, thank you." Douglas began helping himself from the sideboard—fish and kedgeree and a cup of black coffee. "You will excuse me if I seem in a hurry, Miss Thorne," he said as he sat himself down. "I have an early appointment, but you may expect my wife to be down shortly. It is her habit to breakfast with the children in the nursery before she starts her day."

"Of course," said Rosalind.

"I do wonder that you find the energy for it all," Nora drawled. "So much business during the day and so many nights being sole company of such a demanding . . . gentle man. You must be exhausted."

Douglas glanced balefully at Nora. Rosalind decided it would do no one any good to continue this particular conversation.

"I understand, Mr. Douglas, that you are interested in the recent trends in industry."

"That's right, Miss Thorne," he mumbled around his mouthful of kedgeree. "It may not be a topic of society gossip, but it is industry, and science, not the landed interest, that will shape the future of the kingdom."

"Many men fear change," said Nora. "But Douglas relishes it. Indeed, he courts it. Why, one could suggest we came to London specifically in search of it."

Douglas colored. "That's quite enough, Nora."

"Why, what have I said?" Nora's surprise was so theatrical, Rosalind began to wonder if this performance was for her sake. "I only remarked that you are so busy, you are often from home day and night."

"You would do well to remember you are here on sufferance," Douglas growled.

"How could I forget?" Nora replied.

"Nora," said Rosalind, "I was planning an outing to the modiste for Penelope and Mariah tomorrow." This was invented on the spot, but it might distract Nora from teasing her brother-in-law. "Shall we include you in the group?"

"I'm afraid not, Miss Thorne," Nora replied. "I will have several errands to complete."

"You?" barked Douglas. "What errands do you have?"

"My own," said Nora.

The doors open then, and Bethany entered. "Oh . . . good morning, Rosalind. Good morning, Nora. Douglas, were you expecting a caller this morning?"

"No." Douglas blotted his mouth with his napkin.

"I just passed the front hall and heard Smart talking with someone—"

She was not able to finish. Smart, the footman, entered and hurried to Mr. Douglas's side to whisper in his ear. Douglas glowered at him and murmured something back. From her position, Rosalind could make out nothing of what was said.

"Do you know," said a man's voice, "I've decided not to wait, after all."

The entire room turned.

A tall man strolled casually through the open doors. Nora stared, her face as white as a ghost.

"Cantrell," she breathed.

He was a lean man with a long face and curling dark hair. His pale skin had been roughened by much exposure to the elements. His clothes were good quality, but they did not fit well. His top boots were well polished but much creased.

Without pausing a moment, Bryan Cantrell sauntered across the room to Nora's chair. She shrank back, but if he noticed, he gave no sign.

"Hello, my dear." He kissed her mouth quickly and roughly, then grinned as he pulled away. "I've come to fetch you home."

CHAPTER 12

An Unexpected Reunion

. . . with such an husband, her misery was considered certain.

Jane Austen, *Pride and Prejudice*

"What are you doing here?" Douglas shot to his feet. Bethany rushed to her husband's side, but whether to support him or hold him back, Rosalind could not tell.

"As I said, I've come for my wife," Cantrell replied easily. "And I do apologize for bursting in like this, Douglas. But my love and I have been separated for so long that when I heard she was at last in town again, I found myself overcome with impatience to see her."

"You told us he was dead!" roared Douglas to Nora.

"She did what?" cried Cantrell merrily. "Oh, well, I can explain." He stationed himself beside Nora's chair and laid one long hand on her shoulder. Nora slapped him away. He shrugged, not in the least discomforted, and tucked the offending limb into his pocket.

"Times were a little hard for us," Cantrell told him. "And I took a job up in Scotland, working on a bridge site. There had been a heavy rain and the bank collapsed and a number of us were washed downstream. I was laid up for several weeks, insensible. The word spread around the work camp that we had all been killed. Poor Nora heard it and took it to heart, so that by the time I did return, she had already packed up and gone."

It was a flimsy lie, and Cantrell surely knew that. Nonetheless, he told the tale smoothly, as if he expected it would be believed as a matter of course. Rosalind instantly thought of her father, who had been as charming and as plausible.

Nora was glaring at Cantrell, as if she wished him dead again on the spot. Cantrell ignored her. Instead, he looked curiously around the room.

"We seem to be missing Mama," he drawled. "I was so looking forward to her welcome. I know she would be very glad to see me." His gaze paused on Rosalind. "But here's someone I don't recognize."

Cantrell gifted Rosalind with a smile clearly intended to dazzle. His teeth were surprisingly even and very white, Rosalind noticed. His eyes were a brilliant green and surrounded by long lashes. It was a face to stop a woman's heart, and Cantrell clearly had no qualms about wielding that advantage. "Introduce us, won't you, Nora?" he said.

Before Nora could make any sound, a blur of movement in the doorway caught Rosalind's eye. Penelope—pale and breathless, her hair still unpinned—ran up to the threshold of the breakfast room. She saw Cantrell and stopped in her tracks.

Mariah followed behind her, a dark guardian spirit. In contrast to Penelope's flushed agitation, Mariah's face was still as stone, but her eyes darted around the room, taking note of every person in it. Her attention rested briefly on Rosalind, and Rosalind saw her anger burn.

"Cantrell," gasped Penelope.

"Penelope, go back to your room," barked her brother.

Penelope did not seem to have heard. Neither did Cantrell.

He just gazed at the girl, his expression delighted, wolfish, and supremely arrogant.

"My dear Pen!" he cried. "How wonderful to find you here, too. Come, let me kiss your hand!"

He was doing this to outrage, Rosalind realized. He relished the sway he held here. She could see it in the smooth, eager way he started toward Penelope.

Bethany moved. So did Douglas, but Penelope was faster than either of them. She strode to meet the intruder and delivered a hard, ringing slap to his face with the back of her hand.

A spot of blood appeared on Cantrell's lip. He touched it gently.

"I rather expected that," he murmured. "Just not from you, my dear. You've changed."

"You have not," shot back Penelope.

"It's all right, Pen," said Nora. "You can leave us. Mariah, take her upstairs."

Mariah looked nothing so much as affronted.

"I will not be shunted aside!" shouted Pen. "I was wounded by him as much as any of you!"

"And I will deal with it," said Douglas.

"Oh dear, I seem to have caused some small inconvenience," said Cantrell easily. "Nora, let's leave the family to their business."

Nora turned her back. Rosalind suspected she needed a moment to regain her nerve. Even from here, Rosalind could see how Nora's hands shook. Pen saw it, too, and instead of leaving, she raised her chin. In open defiance, she crossed the room to stand beside Nora. Mariah followed after her. The three young women crowded close together—Pen and Nora held hands, while Mariah took up her station beside them, as if placing herself on guard.

It was an extraordinary tableau. Even Cantrell looked disconcerted.

"Come, come, Nora!" he said, but now his conviviality showed signs of strain. "I don't want to have to remind you, but it's not as if you have any real choice. You are my wife."

Rosalind's gaze flicked from Cantrell to Nora. It was obvious that Cantrell gambled that no one would, or could, defend Nora. The claim of a husband on his wife's body was absolute.

That meant there was one possible way to extricate Nora from this painful scene. Unfortunately, it would mean wounding her pride, and damaging what little position she still had among the family.

But Rosalind found she could not permit Nora to be carried off unwillingly by this person in front of them.

She faced Cantrell.

"Then the two of you really are married?"

Cantrell raised his brows. "I beg your pardon?"

"You are legally married to Nora Hodgeson?" she said. "The banns were published? The license was obtained? Or was the ceremony accomplished overseas? In what church was the wedding performed?"

Bethany's agitated face turned an odd shade of green. Douglas laid a hand on her arm, his own expression grim and cold as ice.

Penelope jerked away from Nora, as if she'd been burned, and pressed her hand against her mouth. Only Mariah appeared unmoved by the question. Rosalind wondered if she already knew the answer.

Cantrell managed to keep his composure, but it was a near-run thing.

"Well, Nora?" he drawled. "Shall I answer this legalizing female, or shall you?"

All attention turned to Nora. Her face was drawn tight. Anger and pride blazed in her brown eyes. Rosalind waited with the rest and hoped she had not mistaken the younger woman's nerve.

If Nora said yes, Cantrell could bundle her away, and there would be precious little any of them could do. But if Nora said no, she would be confessing to the greatest sin a girl of her class and kind could engage in.

Nora drew her shoulders back. She glanced once at Mariah before she turned to face Cantrell.

"No." Nora spoke the word clearly and evenly. "We are not married. We never were."

"Nora, you *told* us . . . ," Bethany blurted out.

"She told us he was dead, too," Douglas reminded her. "Look how that has turned out."

"Now, now, my dear, you stop this nonsense," said Cantrell, but it was through gritted teeth. "Speak the truth."

Nora drew herself up to her full height and did not answer. But Rosalind saw in Nora's eyes what the proud gesture cost. Up to this point, she had maintained at least a shred of dignity. Her family had believed she had made the worst possible marriage, but at least it had been a marriage. That had allowed Bethany's heart to soften and adjust. Even Douglas had been willing to extend some grudging grant of forgiveness.

Now softness and forgiveness crumbled. Bethany looked sick to her heart. Penelope, plainly shocked, looked from Nora to Cantrell, searching for some sign of what to believe.

Cantrell simply looked befuddled. It was plain he had underestimated Nora's courage.

Rosalind folded her hands and spoke calmly. "A claim of matrimony is easy enough to prove," she said. "Mr. Cantrell, can you provide a note from the officiant or a page from the registrar? An announcement from the paper would also suffice."

Cantrell pivoted slowly. He took two steps toward Rosalind.

"Who exactly are you?" he demanded

He towered over her, but not so much as he did the other

women. She had only to tilt her chin slightly to meet his furious gaze. Rosalind also had the advantage that she had witnessed this species of anger before and been closer to violence than she was now. This man might make her feel any number of unpleasant things, but fear was not among them.

"I am Rosalind Thorne," she answered. He waited for her to go on, to add a title, a relationship, a purpose. She chose not to fill this silence.

"What right have you to interfere?" he demanded.

"Never mind that," snapped Douglas. "Is what Nora says true? You did *not* marry her?"

Even as he turned away, the gleam in Cantrell's eye left behind a knife-edged promise—he would remember Rosalind and deal with her in due course. He faced Douglas and laughed.

"Of course we are married!" he said easily. "We married almost immediately after we left you. The coach ride to Gretna Green was hideous, and after that we decamped to Paris, and to Frankfurt and Florence. You may recall a letter or two we sent you, hoping for assistance, which you, of course, denied. But foreign parts did not suit, and so we returned. The little chit is simply trying to get out of doing her duty toward her lawfully wedded husband! Come, Douglas," he said, and his smile turned knowing. "You can't tell me you actually *want* her here?"

Douglas hesitated. Bethany wavered, anguish overtaking resolve. Did Douglas notice? Rosalind was uncertain. His attention was entirely on Cantrell.

"Get out," Douglas croaked.

Cantrell smiled at this, or tried to. "Now, look. I do understand your feeling, but she—"

"Get out, or my man will throw you out."

Cantrell might have been taller, but Douglas was broader and heavier. He stood in his own house. The footman by the doors was waiting for his orders. Rosalind also saw how

Nora looked ready to grab the teapot and hurl it at Cantrell's head. He would be lucky if it was not followed by a knife blow. It would just be a question of whether it came from Nora or Mariah.

Or Penelope.

It was evident that Cantrell saw all this as clearly as Rosalind did. In response, he smiled, and he bowed to Douglas.

"I see the time is not convenient for this discussion. We will have to continue it at a later date." He looked over Douglas's shoulder at Nora. "I'd advise you to begin packing your things, my dear."

He gave Bethany and Rosalind a final bow, and as the footman took a step forward, he strolled out the door.

CHAPTER 13

After the Storm

. . . sick of this folly, took refuge in her own room,
that she might think with freedom.

Jane Austen, *Pride and Prejudice*

As soon as the door closed behind Cantrell, Nora gripped the back of her chair. She stood stock-still, as if she was just trying to remember how to breathe. Mariah drew closer. Rosalind saw her fingers knotting in her skirt and thought Mariah wanted to reach out to her sister but, for some reason, did not quite dare.

Penelope collapsed outright. She dropped into the nearest chair and buried her face in her hands.

"Pen." Douglas was beside her at once. "Oh, Pen, I am so sorry."

He rested his sturdy hands on her shoulders. Penelope shook her head but did not lift her face.

Douglas swung around. Anger turned his face a pure, burning scarlet. He stalked around the corner of the table and planted himself in front of Nora, almost exactly where Cantrell had stood.

"You little . . . ," he snapped. "How could you do this to your sister? To your *family?*"

"Gerald." Penelope forced herself to lift her face. "It's all right. I'm all right."

But her brother wasn't listening. "Your lies have threatened us all with disgrace—"

"Yes, how awful it is," interrupted Mariah, her voice as bland as that of any bored society matron. "So much worse than what Cantrell did to her."

"He only did what she allowed!" shouted Douglas. "Allowed and encouraged!"

"And what he would have done to Penelope, given no other option," said Mariah. "Has it perhaps occurred to you that Nora saved Pen?"

Douglas could not have looked more stunned if Mariah had slapped him. "Pen would *never* abscond with that . . . man!"

Rosalind watched Penelope bite down on her lower lip.

"Oh, yes, of course." Mariah's voice was dragging and bland. "You're right. It does not matter that *your* friend Cantrell is a liar, a libertine, and an accomplished seducer. What matters is that Pen is a good girl and Nora is not. I had forgotten. I do apologize."

"Mariah, you're not helping," breathed Bethany.

But she was. Douglas's anger was slowly bleeding away into shock, and perhaps even shame.

Mariah sighed. "Yes, well, I suppose I am saying all the wrong things, as usual. I'll take myself elsewhere. Pen?"

Pen looked from Mariah to Douglas, pleading, angry, and sick at heart. Then, shaking, she got to her feet.

"It will be all right, Pen," said Douglas. "I promise. He will not come back. You have nothing more to worry about."

Pen opened her mouth, but nothing came out. Instead, she rushed from the room, brushing right past Mariah. Rosalind suspected there would soon be a fresh storm of tears, and wished that she could follow the distressed girl. More than that, she wished that Douglas would.

But Douglas stayed where he was.

Mariah noticed this, as well, but her face remained studiously blank.

Nora finally released her hold on the chair. "I think I will go, as well," she said. "It seems I will have to sooner or later, doesn't it?"

She stepped carefully out of the room, as if the floor had turned to ice and she feared it would soon crack. Her heel caught on the edge of the carpet, and she stumbled.

"I'm sorry," she said to no one and to everyone. "I'm sorry."

Mariah gave Douglas and Bethany one last look and left, following Nora closely, as if she meant to make sure no one could creep up behind her.

It was Bethany who moved next. She closed the breakfast room doors, firmly. Rosalind wished she had not. She wanted to leave with the others. There were things that needed to be done, immediately, but she was now trapped. She wondered if Bethany had done so on purpose. Was it possible she did not want to be alone with Douglas just yet? Perhaps she thought Rosalind's presence would blunt her husband's anger.

Unfortunately, to judge by his face, her plan was doomed.

Douglas and I have quarreled, Bethany had said to her. *We do quarrel.*

"Nora has to leave," said Douglas to Bethany. "I will not have her in this house. Not with Penelope."

"She has been with Penelope for three years now, and Pen has taken no harm from it," Bethany reminded him.

Douglas waved this away. "That was before."

"Before you knew she was unmarried?"

"Yes! Of course!"

"But you said yourself, Pen is a good girl," Bethany reminded him. "At *sixteen*, you assured us, Pen could discern that Cantrell was a villain, and that her essential nature recoiled from him. Now she is nineteen, and she has had ample opportunity to judge the consequences of Nora's sort of behavior. Why would she be any more likely to go along with him?"

Douglas openly gawked at her. "You cannot pretend you don't understand the difference between a genuine elopement and . . . what Nora did."

"I understand it perfectly," replied Bethany. "But much to my dismay, I find myself siding with Mariah. I do not agree it is the important thing."

"How can you say that!"

"I don't know," admitted Bethany. "But it would seem that I have."

Husband and wife faced each other. Rosalind fought to quell the uneasiness rising in her. She had witnessed too many strained domestic moments between her father and her mother to truly believe that all this anger would simply pass away. As a girl, in her own home, she had run to get the tea or adjusted the drapes, or any other thing she could think of, as if changing the room could change what was happening between her parents—her mother's tears, her father's building discontent at the fact that his charm was failing to win his wife's graceful, and immediate, acquiescence.

Sometimes it had even worked.

But nothing Rosalind did now could change the fact that fear as well as anger were building between Bethany and Douglas. Because there was reason for that fear. Too many unknowns had already crowded under this roof.

"Why now?" Rosalind murmured.

Douglas heard and turned. "I beg your pardon?"

"I understand Nora returned over a year ago. Since then,

she has hardly been hiding herself in some obscure retreat. She lives with her family under her own name. If Cantrell wanted to find her, he could have done so at any time. Why did he wait this long?"

Douglas appeared nonplussed. "What does it matter? He is here now."

"But if we know why he is here, then we will know what he really wants."

"Well, it's obvious, isn't it?" growled Douglas. "He heard about my inheritance, and he's come to get his share."

"If he wants money, why is he trying so hard to take Nora away?" asked Rosalind. "He knows she has no money of her own, and if you would not pay her ransom when she was abducted as a girl, how can you be expected to pay it now that she is supposed to be his legal wife?"

"Perhaps he counted on my intervention," suggested Bethany.

"But that did not work before, when it would have had much more reason to."

"Perhaps he thinks I'm afraid of what Sir Jasper will do when the scandal breaks," said Douglas.

"Or that you fear what that scandal will do to Penelope's chances in society," Rosalind added. "It is my understanding that Nora's elopement is not yet general knowledge in town. But when Penelope begins to circulate, her background will be discussed, and the story must come out."

"And a present, active scandal is always much more interesting than one that was resolved years ago," said Bethany. "But how would he know Penelope was to have her season now? She is not of such social standing for her debut to be talked about."

"Perhaps he went to your country home first and heard the gossip there," said Rosalind.

"No, he never would," said Douglas. "He was much

known in the county. If he'd been seen, someone would have written me."

"Well, now that he has failed with Nora once more, he will surely leave us alone," said Bethany, but there was more hope than conviction in the words.

"I'm afraid you cannot count on that," said Rosalind. "He wants something in this house—whether it is money or Nora or just to know that he has disrupted the family again. Whatever it may be, he will be back for it. Next time he may not be so rash as to walk through the front door."

"I cannot permit this." Douglas's fist tightened and loosened in the same unconscious rhythm Rosalind had witnessed before. "I cannot, I will not, allow this man to endanger my sister, my . . . my family, my *life*."

"Rosalind?" said Bethany. "What should be done?"

Douglas winced, as if he'd been insulted. Rosalind pretended not to notice.

"Cantrell almost certainly has some plan in mind. If he was tracked to his regular home and haunts, he might be convinced to reveal what it is."

"Tracked!" snorted Douglas. "How are we even to find him in all of London?"

"I had planned to meet with one of the principal officers of Bow Street today, to discuss the matter of the pearls," said Rosalind. "This may be of somewhat greater urgency."

"Oh, yes, those damned pearls." Douglas raked one hand through his hair. "I'd almost forgotten. Cantrell always did have the most remarkable timing."

Remarkable indeed. An unpleasant idea settled down into Rosalind's mind. But Douglas was watching her. Rosalind forced her attention back to the breakfast room and the people in front of her.

"Douglas?" said Bethany. "Shall Miss Thorne make the arrangements?"

What Bethany really meant was, "Do you still trust me?" And the slow way Douglas turned toward Rosalind said that he understood this unspoken question.

"Can you do it?" Douglas asked her. "Can you have Cantrell found? Quietly?"

"I believe so," answered Rosalind. "But I must begin at once."

"Very well," he said. "Since you seem to have the requisite experience and connections, we would be foolish not to take advantage of your being here." He took a deep breath and turned to Bethany. "I am supposed to attend Sir Jasper today, but I will stay with you, if you wish it."

Bethany mustered a smile that reached her eyes, but only just. "I will be all right. You should go see to Penelope."

This small exchange was agreement, apology, and promise all at once. It spoke to a relationship that was being tested but was holding. So far. Rosalind suddenly felt she wanted to cross her fingers like children did, to bring them luck.

Douglas bent and swiftly kissed Bethany's hand; then he pulled open the doors and nearly ran into Mrs. Hodgeson. He staggered backward, but not quickly enough.

"Is it true, Douglas?" Mrs. Hodgeson grasped his sleeve. "Has he returned? Where is he?"

Douglas disengaged her hand from his arm. "If you mean Cantrell, ma'am, he's gone."

"But he is back! He is alive!" She pressed both palms against her mouth. Gilpin came up behind her employer and stood close, in case she should be in need of immediate support. "Oh! My poor dear Nora! She must be prostrate with terror! And you"—she glowered at Douglas—"I'm sure you did nothing to help her!"

Any equanimity Douglas had achieved had now clearly dissolved. "I will not stay and listen to this," he growled, and stalked out the door.

"Well! Has he no understanding of a mother's feeling for her dearest daughters?" Mrs. Hodgeson staggered forward to clasp Bethany's hands. "Again, I must do all! Yes! It is on *my* shoulders. I must go to Nora at once!"

"Oh, no, Mama," said Bethany gently. "Let her have some time to . . . recover herself."

"Yes, indeed," agreed Rosalind. "She returned to her room. It would be most injurious for her to be disturbed when she has had such a shock."

"Yes, yes, of course. You are right, I'm sure. Even her beloved mother . . ." She pressed her hand against her breast. "I must be calm. My heart! My nerves! Oh dear."

With this, Bethany seemed on more familiar ground. "Mama, you must not agitate yourself," she said. "Why do you not return to your room?"

"Yes, yes," Mrs. Hodgeson gasped. "A draft, yes. I must have . . . I must be calm . . . And you must send Nora to me as soon as she is recovered!"

Bethany murmured her reassurances. Mrs. Hodgeson wimpered once and allowed Gilpin to support her from the room.

This time, it was Rosalind who closed the doors. She turned around in time to see Bethany crumple into a chair. Rosalind hurried to the table, poured a cup of tea from the pot, and pressed it into Bethany's hands. Bethany drank it all in a gulp. Rosalind set the cup aside.

"Thank you," breathed Bethany.

"Do you want to go upstairs? You've had as great a shock as anyone."

"How can I?" Bethany gazed at the closed doors, her expression a mix of despair and anger. "I have to look after . . . everyone. I can't—" She swallowed and did not finish the sentence. "Do you need me to do anything?"

Rosalind considered. "I'll need the carriage, if it can be spared."

"Yes, of course. I'll give orders at once." Bethany pushed herself to her feet. But instead of turning to the bell, she grasped Rosalind's hands. "You have to find Cantrell, Rosalind. You have to find him and find some way to convince him to keep away from us. Douglas will not stand for much more of this, not after the pearls and . . . and everything. Cantrell has to be convinced to leave us alone. Nora's life depends on it."

CHAPTER 14

All in Readiness

*I am sure nobody else will believe me, if you
do not.*

Jane Austen, *Pride and Prejudice*

"Miss Thorne!" cried Amelia as soon as Rosalind
barged, rather indecorously, into her rooms. "I was
just coming to find you. Downstairs is in an uproar! Half the
staff is in hysterics over this man Cantrell—"

"I have no doubt," Rosalind said, cutting her off in mid-
outrage. "Amelia, you must fetch your cloak and bonnet at
once."

"What's to do, miss?"

"I want you to walk outside as if you were going on an errand. We need to know if anyone is watching the house. Especially a tall, thin man with a long nose, weathered skin,
and bright green eyes. He will be wearing tan breeches and
creased top boots." She had seen neither his hat nor coat,
which was a frustration.

Amelia's eyes lit up. "Is that this Cantrell?"

Rosalind nodded. "But he may not be working alone and

instead left behind a confederate. So, you will need to keep your eyes sharp."

"You leave it to me, miss." Amelia snatched up her hems and all but skipped out the door.

Rosalind tugged the bell. Then she sank into the over-stuffed chair beside the hearth. She wanted to sit here and give her limbs a moment to stop their trembling.

There is no time, she told herself sternly, and then, *What have I gotten myself into?* She wiped her hands against her skirt.

There was a soft knock at the door, after which Betsy entered. "Yes, miss?"

Her manner was properly diffident, but there was a hesitant curiosity in her expression. Amelia was right. All the staff knew something had happened.

"The carriage is being readied," said Rosalind. "Please run and tell the driver he should have it brought around to the mews. I will meet him from there."

Rosalind could tell the maid desperately wanted to ask why, but she issued the girl what was, for her, an unusually curt gesture of dismissal. There was no more time for explanations than there was for emotional dramatics.

Rosalind took another deep breath and climbed back to her feet. Out in the corridor, she turned to the right and tapped on Nora's door.

"Who is it?" called Nora.

"Rosalind."

There was a long pause. Rosalind's heart thumped. *There's no time, there's no time. . . .*

"Come in."

Rosalind opened the door.

This was her first glimpse of Nora's private rooms. Like the rest of the house, everything was pleasant, clean, and airy. But it was bare. There were no books, no trinkets or knickknacks. The two paintings on the walls were quiet land-scapes, but the only personal items seemed to be a sketch-book and a stack of papers on the marquetry table, and a wooden box like those used to hold an artist's pastels and charcoal.

A scattering of sketches lay on the desk, mostly pastoral scenes, including one in progress of a milkmaid asleep under the hedgerows.

Nora sat on the window seat, her knees hugged against her chest and her arms wrapped around them. Again, it struck Rosalind how appallingly young the sisters were. Even Nora, who had seen the harsh side of the world, looked like noth-ing so much as a little girl after a scolding.

"Did Bethany send you?" she asked dully.

"No," Rosalind answered. "I am in need of a favor."

"From me?" Nora wiped at her cheeks. She was trying to muster some of her usual flippancy. "Goodness. I'd have thought you were the last person to trust me after Cantrell's little display."

Rosalind ignored this. "I need you to be seen at a front window."

"What?" Surprise caused Nora to unfold herself. "Why?"

"Because it is possible Cantrell is watching the house."

Nora's face went blank. She pressed her fingers against her brow. "Yes, of course, he would be. I should have thought . . . damn the man!" she cried. "He's driven me past reason!"

Rosalind had a thousand questions, but now was not the time for any of them. "If he's watching, he is probably wait-ing for you . . ."

"To leave, so he can corner me in the street," Nora cut her off. "But if I am seen in the windows . . ."

"We can hope he will continue to wait and watch," said Rosalind. "Perhaps even long enough for me to set a runner from Bow Street on his heels."

Nora's jaw did not drop, but Rosalind felt that this was from a great deal of self-control.

"Miss Thorne, I'm beginning to understand why Bethany sent for you." Nora got up and picked up her sketch pad and drawing box. "I'll plant myself in the front parlor. It will provide the best view."

Nora started down the front stairs. Rosalind returned to her rooms to pull her stout coat and felt-lined bonnet from the closet. She buttoned, tied, adjusted, and fussed with her outer clothing, and her own thoughts, until Betsy returned.

"Coachman is waiting in the mews, as instructed, miss," she said.

"Excellent."

Betsy guided Rosalind to the back stairs. She was grateful for her stout half boots as she hurried through the snow to the garden's back gate and the mews.

The muffled coachman had just finished helping Rosalind into the enclosed carriage when Amelia dashed around the corner, her market basket on her arm, and her face flush with discovery. She leaned in through the carriage window.

"He's there, miss!" she exclaimed eagerly. "Just as you thought! On the corner, right by the high street. Even had the cheek to beg my pardon and ask which house I was from. Said he was looking for a friend of his."

Rosalind knotted her hands under the carriage rug. "What did you tell him?"

"That I didn't talk to strangers, no matter who they were waiting for."

"Thank you, Amelia. I'll be back as quick as I can. Until then, keep a sharp lookout, especially for Miss Nora."

"You can rely on me, miss."

Amelia stood back, and Rosalind signaled to the coachman that he should drive on. She settled back on the bench and at last gave free rein to her unsettled thoughts.

While Bethany and Douglas were distracted by the past, a question much closer to the present had infiltrated Rosalind's thoughts.

Was the scene between Nora and Cantrell genuine? Or had it in some way been staged?

Because if Nora had stolen the pearls, this would be a perfect way to get them—and her—out of the house in a hurry, without the family ever following after her.

No. I cannot believe it. The shock Nora had evidenced could not have been feigned, nor could the way she had stood so quiet and pale while Douglas raged at her. The Nora whom Rosalind had seen at breakfast would have mounted a spirited rebuttal. This Nora had been so shattered, Mariah had been forced to defend her. And she'd hardly hesitated a moment when Rosalind had recruited her to the effort to keep Cantrell watching the house.

She had in fact done so in order to prove to Nora that she trusted her. Hopefully, that trust would be returned when she again tried to ask about the elopement and about Cantrell himself. And there were so many questions. How had they managed without any money to smooth their way? Why did they part? Rosalind did not for a minute believe Cantrell's breezy description of a building accident and a tragic misconception. She had seen his smooth, unmarked hands. That was not a man who had ever done a hard day's work.

So how did they live? What skills did Cantrell teach her? And with her brother-in-law so ready to turn her out of doors, which ones would she resort to now?

CHAPTER 15

Bow Street Business

*If you do not tell me in an honorable manner, I
shall certainly be reduced to tricks and stratagems
to find it out.*

Jane Austen, *Pride and Prejudice*

Perhaps there were times when the Bow Street Police Station was a calm and well-ordered place. Rosalind had never seen them.

A single broad lobby served both the police station and the magistrate's court. Clerks sat at their desks, surrounded by persons of every kind and class, most of them angry or impatient, many shouting to be heard.

As Rosalind made her way inside, Essington, the porter at the door, touched his hat brim to her. Mr. Bevan, the harried junior clerk at the leftmost desk, looked up and nodded to her in acknowledgment as she waded into the rambunctious crowd.

When Rosalind had embarked on life as "a useful woman," she had quickly become aware how vital it was to be in the good graces of those who organized the lives of the *haut ton*.

That meant knowing not only the ladies' maids and valets but also the shop and building managers, head clerks and their assistants, not to mention various confidential secretaries. But she had never expected to be required to understand the intricacies of the famed Bow Street Police Office, much less appreciate the differences in duty and function between a principal officer, a patrol captain, and a runner. Or to be on visiting terms with the wife of the coroner of London. Or to know that the chief clerk of Bow Street was one Mr. John Stafford, a married man and father of three sons.

Just now, Mr. Stafford hunched on his high stool behind a wall of people three deep, all clamoring for his attention. Despite this, when he saw Rosalind among the crowd, he immediately hailed her.

"Miss Thorne! How can I help you?"

"I'm hoping Mr. Tauton is here!" she called, because raising her voice was the only way to be heard over the dozens of other urgent demands for attention.

"So happens that he is. At least, he was less than an hour ago. Here! Toby!" Mr Stafford bellowed for a bony young man lounging nearby. "Run and fetch out Mr. Tauton."

A stout woman caught at Mr. Stafford's sleeve, and he yanked his arm away. "Now, you just wait one minute, missus, and I'll—"

"I've been waiting over an hour!" roared the woman. "What about my donkey!"

Rosalind moved to the side so that Mr. Stafford could give his full attention to the woman and presumably instruct her on what might be done regarding the problematic animal.

In a matter of minutes, Mr. Tauton strolled through the crowd like it wasn't even there.

"Miss Thorne!" he cried. "I didn't expect to see you here today."

Samuel Hercules Tauton was one of the principal officers at Bow Street. He was a canny fox of a man, with gray hair and an ample paunch and a memory for faces that was second to none. Adam had always credited Mr. Tauton with teaching him much of what he knew.

"I got your letter, of course." Tauton patted his coat pocket. "I was just about to pen a reply. I take it something new's happened?"

"It has, Mr. Tauton. Can we talk somewhere?"

"Of course, of course. Come now. Let's get you out of this mob." He surveyed the crowd and rubbed one thick finger over his lip. "I normally would not suggest this to a lady of your standing, Miss Thorne, but would you care to join me at the pub?"

Normally, this was not an invitation Rosalind would accept, but she knew the Brown Bear public house functioned as a kind of unofficial annex for the police station. Witnesses were questioned there; complaints and evidence could be heard over pints of beer. Prisoners were held in the rooms upstairs, and sometimes bodies were stored in the cellar, along with the kegs of beer.

Mr. Tauton escorted Rosalind solicitously across the street. Once inside the Brown Bear, it did not take long for him to catch the landlord's eye and request a private room, along with a glass of toddy for himself and a negus—a blend of hot sherry, lemon, and sugar—for Rosalind.

The parlor the landlord opened for them was dim, and more than a little dingy, but the fire was burning, and it was far quieter than either the Bow Street lobby or the pub's common room. Mr. Tauton left the door ajar, as much to keep an eye on the room beyond as he did for propriety's sake, and took the chair in the corner. Like Adam, Mr. Tauton did not care to put himself in a position where he might be surprised.

"Ah!" he sighed as he lowered himself into the chair. "Old bones, Miss Thorne, old bones. These winter days are gettin' to be too much for me. I've promised Mrs. Tauton we'll be off for the country soon. She's her heart set on the seaside. I'll miss London, but not the cobbles and the bricks, you may be sure!"

"We shall miss you. Tell me, how does Mr. Goutier?" Sampson Goutier was a patrol captain who had worked with Rosalind on several delicate and complex matters.

"He's captain on the day patrol now," declared Mr. Tauton. "I'd have brought him along, but they're over at Covent Garden, seeing about . . . Well, that's neither here nor there. But he's quite hardy, and proud as a peacock over his new son. And—now, say nothing—he's most likely to take my place as principal officer once I'm gone." Mr. Tauton touched the side of his nose before settling back and folding both hands over his paunch. "Now, what can I do for you? Is this about those missing pearls? For the Douglas family, you said it was?"

"It is, or rather, it was. A more pressing matter has arisen just this morning."

"More pressing than pearls?" Mr. Tauton raised his shaggy brows.

"A man came to the house this morning. His name is Bryan Cantrell, and he was once . . . closely linked with one of the daughters of the house." Mr. Tauton wagged his head solemnly, indicating that he understood her meaning. "He tried to presume on the relationship and take the woman—Leonora Hodgeson—away with him. He claims she is his legal wife."

"Is she?"

"Miss Hodgeson says she is not, and I am inclined to believe her."

"Well, well, that's most upsetting to the family, I'm sure. But I'm afraid as far as Bow Street's lookout, it's nothing but a private matter."

The landlord shouldered his way through the open door with their drinks. Rosalind wrapped her chilled hands gratefully around the pewter tankard of negus.

As soon as Mr. Tauton had dismissed the landlord, Rosalind said, "I am here under instructions from Mrs. Douglas. The family want this man, Mr. Cantrell, traced so that it can be determined what he really wants."

"Beyond money, I suppose?"

"He has no reason to expect the family would advance him any sum."

"Really?" Mr. Tauton slurped his toddy thoughtfully. "Well, well, that is unusual. Most families will pay whatever they have to for peace and quiet. However, you know your business, Miss Thorne. And finding such persons is part of our business, assuming the family will pay the runners' fees?"

"Yes."

He nodded. "I'm sure you realize that finding one man in London is no small task. Have you any information to tell me where we should start looking?"

"When I left, he was on the corner of the Portsmouth high street, watching the house."

"You don't say so?" Tauton drawled. "Well, well, that will be a help and no mistake. But what of this other matter? The pearls? What's he to do with them?"

"As far as I currently know, he has nothing at all to do with them."

"Mmm." Mr. Tauton rubbed his lip again. "Just some bad timing all round, then?"

That was remarkably close to something Douglas had said. "I don't know. Yet," replied Rosalind. "I hope to find out more in the coming days."

Mr. Tauton downed an impressive gulp of the toddy. "Very well, Miss Thorne. You take the inside of the house, and we'll take the outside, and together I very much like our chances." He smiled. "But both of us best get a move on. Neither your thief nor your scoundrel can be counted on to stay put for long. I'll send word as soon as we have results. Was there anything else?"

"No, thank you." Rosalind stood.

Mr. Tauton's eyes gleamed. "Not even going to ask when we expect to see young Mr. Harkness again?"

Rosalind remained cool in the face of this teasing question. "Would you be able to answer me if I did?"

Tauton laughed. "As it happens, we had word of him this morning. We expect him in two days' time."

Two days! Rosalind told herself it was absurd that this news should quicken her heart, but it did. "He was successful in Manchester, then?"

"That's more than I can say, but as he's coming home, it's more likely than not." Mr. Tauton got to his feet. "Here's luck, Miss Thorne." He drained the last of his toddy. "If this Mr. Cantrell is of a mind for mischief, I reckon we shall be able to make him wish he'd chosen another house."

CHAPTER 16

To Set the Wheels Turning

He *shall be mercenary and* she *shall be foolish*.

Jane Austen, *Pride and Prejudice*

Outside the police station, Rosalind took a deep breath of the frigid air. The clouds hung low and yellow over the city, and the long, ragged, rolling toll of the church bells told her it was already noon.

Part of her wanted to return at once to Portsmouth Square to see how matters stood at the house. But what good would that do? Amelia was there, and Mr. Tauton, or the man he sent, would be soon. There were other places to be, and other possibilities to be set into motion.

The Douglases' driver was still in view, standing beside the carriage, calming the restless horses. Rosalind asked him to take her to Little Russell Street.

"You need not wait after that," she said. "I will find my own way back."

"As you please, miss," the driver agreed. Probably he was just as happy not to have to keep his horses, and himself, out in the cold.

After all the tension and intricacies of the Douglases'

house, Rosalind was frankly looking forward to a few moments' peace in her familiar tiny parlor. When the driver let her down, she mounted the stairs and used her key to enter the house.

"It's me, Alice!" she called as she stepped into the familiar foyer.

"I saw!" came Alice's voice from the parlor. "You're late, you know!"

Rosalind paused in the act of hanging up her bonnet and coat on the pegs by the door. "Yes, I know. I am sorry."

Alice threw open the parlor door. Her answer to the chill of the day was to bundle herself up in an old pink wrapper over her woolen housedress and don a ruffled cap and knitted fingerless gloves. "I even had a breakfast brought in." Rosalind's brow furrowed, and Alice sighed sharply. "Don't worry. It did not go to waste. George stopped by on his way to the paper. I should have ordered another dish of kedgeree, and it still wouldn't have been enough. I'm not sure Hannah's feeding him properly."

Alice had been living on her own for only one day, but the parlor already bore signs of her informality. The coffeepot sat on the hearth. A partial loaf of bread and a jam pot waited on the footstool. Three new books, all novels, had been piled on Rosalind's usual chair.

Rosalind picked up the books and held them out for Alice. Alice blushed and put them on top of a stack of papers on her writing table.

"But truly, Rosalind," she said, "I was getting a little worried."

"That I had been swallowed by the wilds of Portsmouth Square?" said Rosalind.

"That you'd decided you weren't speaking to me, after all."

"Oh, Alice," Rosalind sighed. "I know we're in disagreement, but I could never do that."

"Good. Then you won't be angry when you read your letters."

Rosalind eyed the stack of correspondence piled on her desk.

"Alice, as a novelist, you should be aware that is not a transition designed to inspire feelings of calm and trust in your audience."

"Nonetheless, it's the only one I have. However, I also have some bread and jam left over from breakfast. Would you like some?" She didn't wait for Rosalind's answer but started cutting a fresh slice from the loaf. "And how does our Amelia in her new role of lady's maid?" she asked with studied casualness.

"Amelia is invaluable, and I believe she wrote to you."

"She did. Will you take a letter back when you go?"

"Of course."

While Alice fixed her bread and jam, Rosalind sorted through her own correspondence, breaking the seal on each letter and folding it open so she could see who had sent it. There were the usual bills to be dealt with, several missives from friends that could be set aside for later, one from Lady Preston, which would have to be dealt with very soon. There was also Sanderson's reply to her note from yesterday, as well as a letter from a Mrs. Heslop, beginning, *My Very Dear Miss Thorne* . . .

Rosalind held up the letter. "I take it this is the one I might be angry about?"

Alice shrugged.

She scanned the letter. "She says she has a house to let in Sloane Street that might suit my *particular* needs." Rosalind looked over the edge of the paper at Alice. "Why is this Mrs. Heslop writing to me?"

Alice shrugged again. "Perhaps you have friends in common? You know how quickly talk travels."

"Alice," said Rosalind sternly, "I've had a very trying morning."

"You look it. Have some jam." She handed Rosalind the fresh slice of bread on a napkin. "Tell me what's happened to make you late? Is it this business with the pearls?"

Rosalind looked down at the thick currant jam and good bread and told herself she should not allow Alice to distract her. But her breakfast had been interrupted, and there had so far been no time for luncheon. She gave in to her material needs and ate.

"Things are complicated with the Douglases," she told Alice. "The pearls are the least of it. I told you in my letter about this man Bryan Cantrell?"

"Yes, the late, unlamented abductor-turned-husband," said Alice. "I've a mind to resurrect him in my next story and kill him off again in some brutal and appropriate manner."

"You will not have to resurrect him," said Rosalind. "He has done so himself."

"Rosalind." Alice dusted her hands of imaginary crumbs. "You had best be planning to tell me all about this, immediately."

"I want to, but if I don't leave soon, I shall be late for Mr. Faulks."

Alice glanced at the mantel clock. "No, you won't."

"And why won't I?"

"Because he should be on his way here."

"Why?"

"Because I invited him. I still work for the Major, you know." "The Major" was the nickname for Algernon Phipps, the editor of the *London Chronicle*, the twice-weekly paper that published Alice's gossip columns. "He is determined that we should have the season's rumor mills churning ahead of every other paper in the city. And you know the most convenient way to hear what's worth hearing is to host our Mr. Faulks. Besides, it was ridiculous that you should meet with him separately, when we have this perfectly good parlor ready for all sorts of visitors. Indeed, Rosalind, one might almost think—"

Rosalind was never to know what one might think, because at that moment the doorbell rang. It took her an awkward moment to remember that Amelia was not there to answer. She went to the door herself and opened it to usher in Sanderson Faulks.

"Ah, Miss Thorne!" He bowed and doffed his pearl-gray hat. Mr. Sanderson Faulks was a confirmed dandy and always dressed to the height of fashion. Today that meant a wide-skirted gray coat with a nipped waist, and a striped scarf wound up to his chin. "How very good to see you. If you will give me but a moment . . ." He settled his walking stick into the stand and hung coat, muffler, and hat on the available pegs.

"Hello, Sanderson," said Alice as they walked into the parlor. "Do have some coffee." She held out a cup.

"Ah, bless you, my dear. I am quite frozen." He drank, looked at the liquid in the cup, and looked at Alice. Alice shrugged, and Sanderson sighed and pulled the cane-bottomed chair out from its corner, sat down, and stretched out his long legs.

"I suppose I ought to apologize for summoning you to a scene of so much chaos," said Alice. "Especially as I intend to make shameless use of you."

"Not at all," replied Sanderson easily. "This somewhat questionable coffee notwithstanding, I have been longing for a change of scene and subject matter. My ears are stuffed full of the *ton*'s latest obsession in painters, and you know how much I require variety in my conversation."

"I was not aware of any new obsession," said Rosalind.

"That, Miss Thorne, is because despite all my years of patient tutelage, you have remained obstinate in the matter of art and care only for your novels."

"Ahem!" coughed Alice.

Sanderson laid his hand over his breast and bowed slightly in silent apology.

Rosalind smiled and dropped her eyes demurely. "I beg your pardon. I never meant to wound you so, Mr. Faulks."

" 'Tis not so deep as a well nor so wide as a church door, but 'tis enough, 'twill serve," he said, quoting breezily. "But your letter indicated some urgency in my summons. Do tell me how I may be of assistance."

"Yes, Rosalind, do tell us why Sanderson is here," drawled Alice.

Sanderson made a wounded face. "I am devastated, Miss Littlefield. I did not mean to neglect the fact that it was you who invited me. I humbly beg your pardon." As if to illustrate his penitence, he poured some fresh coffee into Alice's cup.

"I will, but only because I want to know what's going on, as well," said Alice loftily.

Rosalind took a deep breath. "Alice knows this, Mr. Faulks, but I've a new commission from an old acquaintance, a Mrs. Douglas. She tells me her family has . . . lost or been robbed of a very valuable and distinctive pearl necklace. I have understood that on occasion, you may have dealings with persons who buy and sell unusual or valuable objects . . ."

"Ah! I understand. I am sure you've already put the matter in front of your inestimable Mr. Harkness, but you perhaps wish to pursue certain other avenues of inquiry?"

"Mr. Harkness is in Manchester. I did broach the subject with Mr. Tauton, but there are . . . complications."

"Oh?"

"Someone's returned from the dead," said Alice.

"Indeed?" murmured Mr. Faulks. "If that is the case, may I suggest, Miss Thorne, you should be sending for a priest?"

"Alice is teasing, but she's not entirely wrong."

Mr. Faulks set his coffee cup down and blotted his mouth. "Now I suspect you are teasing. What on earth has happened?"

Alice and Mr. Faulks shared a love of the dramatic as well as the absurd. They both listened avidly as Rosalind described Bryan Cantrell's return.

"When I saw them together, it occurred to me that if Nora had taken the pearls, this reappearance by Cantrell might have been planned," Rosalind said. "It would make an excellent excuse for her to leave the house without being much questioned, or examined."

"I don't understand," said Alice. "If the necklace is as distinctive as you say, how could they possible hope to sell it without being noticed?"

"Nothing could be easier," said Mr. Faulks. "One could dismantle it and sell the pearls to a jeweler a few at a time. Or simply take the lot across to Paris or Brussels and sell it, or them, there." Sanderson set his coffee cup aside and steepled his fingers under his sharp chin. "Have you considered that this was the initial plan? Cantrell reappears, and Miss Nora is thrown out of the house and leaves in tears, taking the pearls with her."

"I did think exactly that," said Rosalind. "No one could then wonder where she had gone or expect her to come back. But I do not think her shock or her regret was for show."

"Well, consider this," said Sanderson. "The initial plan was to leave and to take the pearls with them. But as you asked the crucial question, Miss Hodgeson conceived of a better scheme. One that would let her not only keep all the profits but also be rid of the erstwhile and presumably dissolute Mr. Cantrell. All she has to do is deny that he is her husband. He is thrown out of the house. She remains and may take the goods and be on her way whenever she pleases."

"No," Rosalind admitted slowly. "I confess, I had not considered that she might be turning on him."

"There may be honor among thieves, but I've yet to see it for myself." Mr. Faulks employed his most cynical drawl. "It could very well be that your Miss Hodgeson is engaging in what is colloquially known as the double cross."

But even as he said this, Rosalind remembered the tears in Nora's eyes. Nora Hodgeson did not strike Rosalind as the sort to cry because a plan had gone astray or because she had decided to tell a new lie.

But then again, Rosalind did not yet know Nora's true feelings about Bryan Cantrell. Love took many forms. Not all of them were consistent with happiness, or healthful for the individuals trapped in the coils. That did not make them any less real.

"I am, of course, entirely at your disposal," Sanderson told her. "I will make one or two small inquiries to begin with, and we shall proceed from there."

"The family is anxious to avoid all publicity, but I have been authorized to say that there is a finder's fee for the necklace."

"Well and good. That should loosen a few tongues. If you can describe this wayward item?"

Rosalind brought out her sketch. Mr. Faulks took up his quizzing glass and examined the drawing closely. For a moment, Rosalind feared he might make some remark on the quality of the sketching, but he only handed it back to her.

"Well, we must see what can be done. Now, I must beg you ladies will excuse me." He climbed to his feet. "A friend of mine has asked me to view some new and quite remarkable paintings he has an eye to purchasing."

"Remarkable?" said Rosalind.

"So I am led to believe. You have, of course, heard of Jacob Mayne?"

"I'm afraid not."

"Tsk-tsk, Miss Thorne. You are falling behind the times. Mr. Mayne is a hitherto undiscovered genius. The current exhibition of his paintings has taken the *ton* quite by storm. I'm surprised Miss Littlefield has not heard of it."

"Oh, I have," replied Alice. "I was hoping you could provide me the latest on-dit about the fuss."

"I would, but I have not yet formed an opinion. I hope to be able to this afternoon."

"Well, then, you must not be late, and you must return as soon as you are able," said Alice. "The Major is breathing down my neck to find *something* to create a stir, and I'm afraid these days Rosalind tells me things only in strictest confidence." She sighed dramatically.

"I will not fail you." Sanderson bowed. "But . . . perhaps, Miss Littlefield, you would do me the honor of waiting on me at Gunter's Tea Shop? I am sure after my appointment with Lord Langford, I shall be quite famished."

"Why, Mr. Faulks!" exclaimed Alice. "If I did not know better, I would take that as a reflection on my coffee making." He opened his mouth to protest, but Alice waved this away. "However, I forgive you and accept your invitation, especially if you promise me gossip with the cake."

"And please let me know if the pictures are suitable for viewing by gently bred young ladies," said Rosalind. "I am also charged with chaperoning the younger members of the Douglas household into the season."

"What is there you can't turn your capable hands to?" murmured Mr. Faulks. "Well, I shall surely write as soon as I have completed my reconnaissance." He bowed again. "Do not stir yourselves. I know my way."

"I think I had better go, as well." Rosalind scooped her letters up and, with some difficulty, stuffed the bundle into her reticule.

"Why the sudden rush?" asked Alice. "My coffee cannot have offended you."

"Of course not. But I have a call that must be made before the confidential hour. It's well past time I learned more about the Douglas family. For that, I will need a much more exclusive sort of gossip."

CHAPTER 17

Family Business

But she had never felt so strongly as now the disadvantages which much attend . . . so unsuitable a marriage, nor ever been so fully aware of the evils arising from so ill-judged a direction of talents . . .

Jane Austen, *Pride and Prejudice*

Nora had been sitting in the window for the better part of an hour when her father walked into the parlor.

She'd meant to sketch, but she had found herself unable to concentrate. Cantrell was out there. He was idling on the corner, watching who came and went, taking the measure of the house.

How many times had she idled alongside him? They had traveled like tinkers—spending a night here, a night there, and skipping out before their account could be called in. Cantrell's ear for language and her eye for detail had worked in concert as they crisscrossed the Continent, taking full advantage of the freedom and the chaos left behind by Napoleon's collapse. They might pass as aristocrats one day, vagabonds the next, even a soldier and his wife if Cantrell could steal a uniform. She'd dressed in breeches more than once, with her hair bundled underneath a hat, so that they'd looked like two anonymous loungers waiting for nothing in particular.

At first, their wandering had simply been a way to remain hidden until Cantrell judged the time was right to start putting the touch on her family. But then came the sickening realization that Douglas was not going to be convinced to pay up, and that Bethany would never beg for her husband to bring her sister back.

They had been together long enough by then that Nora believed Cantrell had come to depend on her. She thought now that her family had failed them, they could work together toward their own fortune and future.

That had been the first mistake. Well, perhaps the second.

But the next mistake, it seemed, had been to believe that when she did leave, he would shrug her off in his easy come, easy go way.

"Well, well. Here you are."

Papa wandered in, as if he had only noticed Nora sitting alone by chance. He strolled up to the window, his hands clasped behind him, and stared out into the street.

"What a perfectly foul day," he remarked.

Nora kept her attention on the street scene she'd been dissolutely working up. It wouldn't do for . . . much of anything, really. There was very little to it except some clumsy outlining and blobby shadows. She suddenly wanted to draw a big black *X* across the entire thing.

"I don't suppose you could spare a moment for your poor old father?"

Nora closed her sketchbook and returned her stick of charcoal to her box. She folded her hands over the book like a schoolgirl. "Are you going to ask me if I knew Cantrell was alive?"

"No. There's no point in it. You will lie to amuse yourself, if you choose."

"Where on earth could I have picked up such a revolting habit?" She blinked several times.

Papa appeared to ignore this. "Tell me, my dear, how much will it cost to convince you to leave?"

Nora felt the beginnings of a laugh bubbling beneath her rib cage. She almost wished Cantrell was with her to hear this. *Almost.* "You want to pay me to leave? You? Now?"

"Yes. Before Douglas is forced to throw you out."

"You mean before Sir Jasper decides to discard yet another heir?"

"Yes. I mean that exactly," he said.

She looked at him carefully to see if he'd been drinking. Probably, but not to the point where he was foxed.

"You surprise me," she said.

"I surprise myself," he admitted. "But needs must. What will it cost?"

"What makes you think you could possibly afford my price?"

"That's my affair."

Nora allowed herself a smile at this. "And why should I trust you to keep your word?"

"I could plead that I am your father and deserving of your trust. I could urge you to consider the feelings of your poor mother, who is in a state of considerable agitation over this disturbance. But I don't suppose that would do any good at all."

"And Mama's agitation will hardly lessen if I should vanish again," Nora reminded him. "As for the rest, I'm afraid I'm not so silly as to trust you, Papa."

"No, no, I thought not. I suppose that's my own fault."

"Yes, I suppose it is."

"Well, well," he murmured. "Perhaps I shall have to enlist Bethany to the cause, then, or have a word with this Miss Thorne she's acquired. Or I could speak with the great man himself. What do you think? Which would be easiest?"

Nora pressed her fingertips against her forehead. *Damn, Cantrell.* "I will tell you what I told Mariah . . ."

"Mariah?" Papa's brows arched. "What has she to do with this?"

Nora bit her tongue. "Do you think you're the only one who wishes I was elsewhere?" she said lightly, and watched him accept this. "I promise you that if I am allowed another fortnight, at most, then none of you will have to worry about me ever again."

"The problem, you see, is that I cannot trust you any more than you can trust me."

"No, I suppose not." Nora sighed bitterly. "What a disappointment I must be. Well, how about this for a bargain, then? If I am not gone by the end of the month, you may do as you please."

Finally, Papa turned from the window. Nora made herself meet his gaze. His eyes had gone pale and watery with age. He scrutinized her narrowly, as if wondering who this creature was in front of him, and how she had come to be his youngest daughter.

"This is not what I intended," he said. "For any of us."

"I'm sure." Nora reclaimed her charcoal and started darkening one of the shadows on her page. Papa watched her for a little, and when this produced no response, he wandered off.

Nora waited for a long moment. Then she got up and set her sketchbook aside. Surely a brief moment away from her post would not cause any harm. She needed to find Mariah.

Fortunately, she did not have to search very hard. When Mariah was not in her room, she was generally to be found in the library, and so it was now. She sat at the broad oak writing desk, frowning at a book open in front of her, scribbling in a notebook of her own.

Her head jerked up as Nora entered, and she slammed the notebook shut.

"I'm sorry," said Nora. "I didn't mean to startle you." She

braced herself. After what had happened this morning, she had no idea what Mariah was thinking or feeling. The truth was, Nora had welcomed Miss Thorne's instructions to sit in the front window to hold Cantrell's attention. It was the perfect excuse to avoid her sister.

"Did you want something?" Mariah laid her pen down and put the stopper back in the ink bottle.

"To tell you Papa just offered to pay me to leave the house."

"Did he? How enterprising." Her tone was dry, but Nora could tell she was genuinely surprised. "I wonder where he's gotten hold of that sort of money?"

"Do you know, earlier, I was making a joke for our oh-so-busy Miss Thorne, but now . . . Mariah, could Papa have stolen Bethany's pearls?"

Mariah's eyes narrowed. Nora could practically hear her thoughts rearranging themselves.

"That would mean he would have had to exert himself," Mariah said. "You know how he feels about that."

"I know how he usually feels, but could something have changed?"

"What?"

"I don't know. He's been in debt, and some of his creditors are less than honorable types. Can a loan have been called in?"

Mariah considered this. "It's possible. If we were back home, I might be able to find out, but as it is . . ." She waved toward the window and the London street beyond. "But if I was to guess, I'd say Papa's just afraid that if Douglas gets mad enough, he'll stop everybody's allowances and quite possibly remove access to his house, and his wine cellar."

"Yes, I suppose." But she couldn't believe it. Not yet.

Mariah sighed, as if already bored with her tedious sister. "What is it?"

"I was just thinking that Cantrell's a bit like Papa," she said. "At heart, he's lazy. Greedy, yes, but lazy. It doesn't matter to him what he does, as long as he can get somebody else to take care of the actual work."

A muscle twitched in Mariah's cheek. "Which is not exactly an argument for our dearest Papa becoming a thief."

"But Bethany's said all along that the box was left out on her dressing table. All anyone would have had to do was come along and pick it up. You know how it was that night. Mama was having one of her . . . spells, and Bethany went up to look after her. Papa could have seen her leaving and decided to take his chance. He might not even have been after the pearls at first. There's plenty in Bethany's case to choose from, including all sorts of things she never wears except on special occasions. He might have just gotten lucky."

"Why do you want Papa to be the thief?" asked Mariah.

"I don't," said Nora.

"Of course not." Mariah opened her notebook again and unstoppered the ink. "Was there something else?"

Irritated, Nora said, "Yes, actually, there was. What was all that nonsense at dinner last night about wanting to participate in the season?" Trying to get a rise out of Mariah was dangerous, but she couldn't stand this bitter calm.

"It's not nonsense," replied Mariah.

"But you hate parties and dances and all those absurdities."

"That is neither here nor there," Mariah told her primly. "If I am able to keep Miss Thorne busy with dresses and parties and excursions and all those absurdities, she will have less time to be nosing about the house and getting into places she shouldn't."

"Oh," said Nora, deflated. "I should have thought of that."

"Yes, you should. Of course, Cantrell's return will be a great help in that regard. We should now have enough going on to distract even such a prodigy of organization."

"Yes, she's already recruited me to her efforts. It seems Cantrell's watching the house. I'm supposed to be sitting in the window, showing him that I'm still at home."

"Be careful," said Mariah seriously. "I'm quite sure Miss Thorne suspects you're still working hand in glove with Cantrell."

Nora felt her brow crease. "Why would you think that?"

"Because it's very possible that you are."

The words dropped hard enough against Nora that she staggered. "Is that what you think?" But she already knew the answer. This was what Mariah had hidden under her calm. This was why she'd been so quick to usher Penelope out of the breakfast room, and why she hadn't come to find Nora, even though it had been hours since Cantrell had left.

"I am going to kill that man!" Nora muttered.

"Until today, I thought you had," said Mariah blandly.

All at once, the smell of dirt and blood assailed Nora from memory. Her knees shook and threatened to buckle. It was only sheer force of will that kept her upright.

Mariah couldn't even be bothered to look at her.

"You're serious," croaked Nora.

Mariah shrugged. "It was one possibility. You never did tell me how he died, just that he was dead."

"You really believed me capable—"

"I believed it possible," Mariah cut her off coldly. "You coming to me with your plan to commit a fraud worth thousands of pounds did not exactly convince me you were an innocent."

Exhaustion suddenly overwhelmed Nora. "All we need . . ."

"A fortnight at most. Yes, I know," said Mariah. "Tell me this. Is your . . . Cantrell a patient man?"

"He can be."

"Can we count on his patience now?"

A thousand memories flickered through Nora. She remembered sitting beside Cantrell for hours in a little café, waiting for a suitable victim to stroll past, and how he'd never once seemed bored or tired. But she also remembered how she had seen him lash out at strangers, at friends, at her.

Can we count on his patience now? Mariah's question repeated itself in her mind.

"I don't know," said Nora softly. "Truly, I do not know."

CHAPTER 18

Morning Calls

. . . it is very ungenerous in you to mention all that you knew.

Jane Austen, *Pride and Prejudice*

"I'm so delighted you decided to call, Miss Thorne." Lady Cowper passed Rosalind the delicate china cup and saucer. "It gives me the opportunity to thank you for the service you did for my brother and his family last year. Whatever I may think of my sister-in-law, I would not have her falsely accused. You prevented that from happening, and I am in your debt."

"I was honored to be able to render my assistance."

Lady Cowper was one of London's most influential and famous hostesses. Her comings and goings were regularly featured in the gossip columns, especially since she was one of the famed patronesses—the board of women who controlled access to Almack's and its exclusive Wednesday night balls.

Rosalind had met Lady Cowper through the auspices of Lady Jersey, the head of Almack's board. However, Rosalind had received permission to call only after she had assisted Lady Cowper's family with a matter that had begun in blackmail and ended in murder. Until today, she had not presumed on that invitation. She had felt she should save it for a time of need.

Lady Cowper smiled at Rosalind over the rim of her cup. "I hear from Lady Jersey that you continue with your various activities in conjunction with our London ladies."

"I am able to help from time to time," acknowledged Rosalind. "In fact, that is what brings me here today."

"Oh?"

Rosalind set her cup down and folded her hands, composing herself to business. "I have two young friends who are to be introduced into society this season. The first is a lovely girl, charming and accomplished, and her dowry is quite respectable. I expect she will have no troubles at all, given the proper introductions."

"She is to be congratulated," said Lady Cowper with studied blandness. "But the other?"

"Has a first-rate mind and is an accomplished musician, but has perhaps not had the chance to refine her social gifts as well as she might. I very much fear that if she is thrown straight into the ocean of balls and rout parties, she may very quickly drown."

"And who might these young ladies be?"

"Penelope Douglas and Mariah Hodgeson. Penelope is granddaughter to Sir Jasper Douglas."

Rosalind watched Lady Cowper's eyes flicker as she ran down the list of society names and personalities she carried in her keen and busy mind. All at once, the sharp light of understanding brightened her bland gaze.

"That would mean Miss Penelope is related to Mr. Gerald Douglas, Sir Jasper's newest heir?"

"She is his sister. Miss Hodgeson is his wife's sister."

"Well," said Lady Cowper, "as long as Mr. Douglas maintains Sir Jasper's favor, the pair of them are sure to be well dowered. That will certainly help things along."

Rosalind affected a small shrug. "I have heard there was some . . . trouble perhaps between the town and country branches of the Douglas family that might affect the girls' prospects."

"Oh, so you've got hold of that, have you?"

Again, Rosalind shrugged. "One cannot help but hear rumors."

Lady Cowper laughed. "Miss Thorne, spare us your modesty. Everyone knows that your ears are sharp as any vixen's, and that many of us are entirely dependent on your continued discretion and goodwill." She arched an eyebrow. "I trust I do not offend?"

"Certainly not," said Rosalind, because it was the only possible answer. "But I might ask if there is anything in particular I should be concerned about in connection with my protégés?"

"You mean was there scandal?" inquired Lady Cowper. "Indeed, there was, Huet Douglas, the first heir and uncle to your Mr. Gerald Douglas, was a bigamist."

Rosalind started at the word. It was common for a gentleman to keep a mistress or even two, but to marry them? That was not merely scandalous. It was criminal.

Lady Cowper nodded slowly. "And not just once. It's said our first heir had wives and children in London, Buckinghamshire, and Edinburgh, and, I believe, in Dublin, as well. Regardless of the details, the matter was severe enough that he fled to the Continent and died there. Apparently, the shock of it all brought on an apoplexy in Sir Jasper. He was still in his sickbed when he disinherited this unsatisfactory first heir in favor of Huet's son, Addison."

"Not Mr. Gerald Douglas?"

"Not yet," said Lady Cowper. "I knew the second heir slightly. Unfortunately, Addison Douglas did not possess the most durable sort of temperament, and he was much to be pitied, I think." She paused, clearly inviting Rosalind to think, as well. "I imagine he must have wondered about his own parentage and feared for his own legitimacy."

Rosalind felt sure that Lady Cowper was correct in this. An illegitimate person could not inherit an estate or title and was certain to be exiled from society. If Addison's legitimacy was at all in question, any other relative could sue over an inheritance, and the family's scandals might be laid bare before the inquiring public.

"The strain became too much," Lady Cowper went on. "Addison went out riding one day and simply failed to come home."

"How awful!"

"Yes." Lady Cowper frowned pensively at the tea things. "And that, for better or for worse, is how your Mr. Gerald Douglas—a member of the disregarded, underfinanced, and distinctly inferior branch of the family, and no one's choice— became Sir Jasper's heir number three and, so far, the only one not to bring on either scandal or tragedy."

So far, thought Rosalind. Now Mr. Douglas's excessive worries about Nora and her past made a great deal more sense. He had not expected this inheritance, but now that he had it, he wanted to keep it. So much so that he was willing to neglect his wife and family to make sure of his relationship with a demanding Sir Jasper.

Given Sir Jasper's reaction to his own son's behavior, a fresh scandal that involved marriage, or a lack of it, was the worst thing possible.

"Lady Cowper," said Rosalind, "if you were in my position, what advice would you give to the Douglas family regarding their girls?"

Lady Cowper considered this for a moment. "I would advise them to move quickly. Persons unused to the . . . particular demands of society and family can find that a fortune that came unexpectedly can leave the same way."

Rosalind nodded in understanding. Above and beyond Nora's past, and her present, there was the matter of these hidden families. It was Rosalind's experience that if there was money at stake, secret persons could become more willing to emerge from their obscurity.

Bryan Cantrell might prove to be only the first person demanding payment from Mr. Douglas.

"That we are still in the little season can help matters," said Rosalind. "I had envisioned a select and careful introduction for Miss Mariah Hodgeson, among company who can appreciate a woman of intellect. As I was considering matters, I remembered your family's connection with the Royal Institution and their board of patronesses . . ."

Unlike its sister establishment in scientific inquiry, the Royal Society, the Royal Institution actively encouraged women to attend its lectures and discussions. Several very prominent women served on a special board specifically to engage with society's hostesses on the Institution's behalf.

"We are thinking along similar lines," said Lady Cowper. "As it happens, there is a lecture at the Institution Thursday next, and I happen to know such lectures are usually followed by an informal supper party at Mary Sommerville's home. You know she wrote that book *Conversations in Chemistry*? Very popular among our more seriously minded ladies, so I am told." Lady Cowper smiled indulgently at the thought of such ladies. "I am quite certain I could arrange an invitation for you and your friend. You may try her out there. The world of scientific philanthropy is perhaps not so splendid as some others, but many of our best ladies subscribe to the Institution and its aims, and, of course, there are multiple connections between their board and that of Almack's. I could write to Lady Hippisley about tickets today, if that would suit?"

"It would suit exactly," said Rosalind, but wariness sparked in the back of her mind. It was not like Lady Cowper to make such a generous offer out of the goodness of her heart.

Lady Cowper smiled and leaned back in her chair, assuming a careless pose. "Do you know, Miss Thorne, before you called, I was planning to write to you. There's a trifling matter I hoped you might help me with."

"Oh?"

"Yes. Have you heard about this new painter Jacob Mayne?"

"As it happens, a friend of mine mentioned the name just this morning."

"Ah! Then you know what a sensation Lord Langford's exhibition of his work is causing?"

"Indeed," murmured Rosalind.

"Well, the man himself is quite dead—which is surely a shame," Lady Cowper added. "But his work is being represented by his spinster sister. That sister is now being absolutely *besieged* with invitations, all of which she has turned down. Not even those of us who are *personal* friends of Lord Langford have been able to so much as gain a glimpse of her. Indeed, Lord Langford himself hasn't seen her. He dealt only with *her* representative, a Mr. Sommerton."

Lady Cowper leaned forward. "My very dear, Miss Thorne, if I could only obtain an introduction to Miss Mayne, I could extend her an invitation of my own. Surely, Miss Mayne is a shy countrywoman and entirely unused to our *tonnish* ways. If she has any proper feeling, the idea of exhibiting herself in a grand gathering must *mortify* her, but this business of your protégés has given me a *perfect* idea. I would propose to her a small, intimate gathering—a luncheon, perhaps—with no more than a few very select friends, where she need feel no awkwardness at all for any country manners."

There was a greed in society for just that small bit of success that lifted one up above the others. Even the patronesses who together occupied the pinnacle of the *haut ton* were goaded by it. Perhaps especially them. As the first (and only) person to be introduced to Miss Mayne, Lady Cowper would become the sole gatekeeper between the "shy country-woman" and larger society. As such, she would be considered to have scored one of the first coups of the season.

Rosalind knew she must be very careful what she said next. Lady Cowper had just named access to this elusive Miss Mayne as the price of her assistance. If Rosalind offended or disappointed, the tickets and introductions for Mariah and Penelope might be entirely forgotten.

"I cannot say I am acquainted with Miss Mayne," Rosalind told her. "Nor do I know of anyone who is." Not even Sanderson Faulks had dropped her name.

"But surely, Miss Thorne, with your excellent and *varied* connections . . ."

"I will not make any promise when I am not sure of success." Rosalind looked her hostess directly in the eye. "I would never wish to disappoint you, Lady Cowper."

"But you will try?"

Rosalind paused. "I have some acquaintance with an interest in art and artists. I can ask if anything might be done, but—and I cannot say this forcefully enough, Lady Cowper—I am unable to promise I'll have better success than anyone else."

"But you *might*." Lady Cowper smiled. "And I will have the satisfaction of knowing that if you could not winkle Miss Mayne out of her shell, then no one else will be able to, either. And, of course, I know your character well enough to be sure you would never *dream* of giving her to anyone else while engaged to me."

It was a compliment, and a warning. Rosalind lowered her gaze humbly.

"Then it is settled," said Lady Cowper. "I will write to Lady Hippisley at once, and you will speak with your 'small acquaintance' on my behalf."

With their bargain sealed, Rosalind thanked Lady Cowper and took her leave. Once out in the street again, she drew in as deep a breath as her corset permitted. The idea of putting herself back into a cramped hackney was insupportable, so Rosalind simply turned her face toward the high street and started walking.

Perhaps by the time she reached Portsmouth Square, she would have some idea how on earth she was to meet yet one more new obligation.

CHAPTER 19

A Refreshing Turn Out of Doors

What are you doing? Are you out of your senses?

Jane Austen, *Pride and Prejudice*

Amelia met Morgan, Mrs. Douglas's lady's maid, by the simple expedient of knocking on the door and asking if there was any mending that she could help with. The sewing was the single biggest job for any maid, even in such an unconventional establishment as Miss Thorne and Miss Littlefield's. It was almost as much a constant as the cooking.

Now, Miss Thorne was not so bad. She was careful with her things, and not above taking care of some of the finer work herself. Miss Alice, on the other hand . . .

Miss Alice. Amelia paused for a moment at the small thrill that ran through her. Miss Alice was always in such a hurry, there was always something snagged or torn that must be set to rights.

Amelia couldn't believe it when Miss Alice had asked her to teach her to sew.

"It's an embarrassment that an independent person should not be able to care for their own clothes," Miss Alice had said as she showed Amelia the latest sagging skirt hem.

"You want looking after, that's what," Amelia had said.

"So I do," Miss Alice had said. "But that doesn't mean I shouldn't know how to look after myself."

So I do. And those big brown eyes had looked right into hers. Lord, she had such beautiful eyes. Amelia remembered how her heart had thumped. Miss Alice had meant it, too. She'd meant it the way Amelia wanted her to mean it.

But did it matter? That was the question. Amelia'd felt such things before. Not one of them had led to anything except another dismissal and another day of begging for a reference and another try at another registry office.

This time is different, she told herself. *Miss Alice and Miss Thorne are different.*

She'd seen it. Lived it, really—what with being sent out to spy on nefarious (a new word, one Miss Alice relished the use of), customers, like this Cantrell *person*. But some part of her could not bring herself to depend on it.

That, however, didn't mean she couldn't enjoy it while it lasted.

As it turned out, Morgan was a tiny, aged woman with white hair, a shuffling gait, and clouded eyes. It was clear that she was being kept on as a matter of duty and kindness. Mrs. Douglas, being a self-sufficient sort, clearly did not need as much assistance from her maid as some others might.

As Amelia helped thread Morgan's needles and pin a sagging ruffle straight, it became very clear that this old lady would no more have robbed from Mrs. Douglas than she would have robbed the King of England.

"A very fine lady, very kind," was Morgan's assessment of her employer. "Not great, not one for airs, but very kind. Just like my Lady Jasper." She touched the corner of her eye. "So much trouble. So many people after her all the time."

"Who's after her?" asked Amelia.

"Well, that mother of hers, for one, and the father. Each as bad as the other." Morgan leaned in close to her work and snipped a thread with her delicate scissors.

Seeing Morgan so willing to talk about her employer, Amelia asked a few curious questions about Mrs. Douglas's habits. In response, she was treated to a long list of her patience, her kindnesses, her rare maternal qualities. She didn't even have to ask about the pearls.

"You should have heard her the morning after!" said Morgan. "I was sure as sure I had lost my place, and at my age, who would have me? I'd be off to the workhouse before the day was out. But she sat me down, and she said, 'You've nothing to worry about, Morgan. I know you had nothing to do with this business, and my mind will not change on that point.'"

"So, what do you think did happen to the pearls?" asked Amelia as casually as she could. "They didn't go and swim back to their oysters, that's for certain!"

"Well, it's not for me to say," declared Morgan primly. "*I* am not one who goes gossiping about her betters. You'll have to look to Mrs. Hare for that!"

Amelia bowed her head, much chastened. Inside, she thought, *Thank you. I think I will.*

But there was something else to be done first. She knew it was risky, but she was not about to spend the entire day inside while Cantrell was sneaking about outside. She was going to have at least one more look at him to see what could be learned.

She had seen enough now to know that Miss Thorne found things out by talking, by writing letters and, most of all, by listening. Amelia had to admit, although it seemed to work amazingly well, it was a bit, well, *disappointing.* She wished it was more like Miss Alice wrote in her book—with chases and duels, and more excuses to swoon or run about the lawn in bare feet.

Well, maybe not the bare feet. Amelia shuddered. *When I become a young lady in a large house, I'll make sure to wear a stout pair of stockings to bed under with my flowing white nightgown.*

Amelia took her workbasket back to Miss Thorne's rooms and then took herself down the narrow, dark servants' stair.

Mrs. Hare was sitting in the servants' hall, writing in her housekeeping book.

"I'm just on my way to the post office," Amelia said as she breezed past. "Do you need anything while I'm out?"

"No, thank you, Amelia," Mrs. Hare replied. "Mind how you go, there's a good girl. I think we'll have more snow before too much longer."

"No need to worry about me." Just the same, Amelia was glad for her flannel-lined bonnet and the new mittens her sister had sent.

Muffled up to her nose, and with her basket slung over her arm, she climbed the stairs to the garden path. The side gate led to a rutted alleyway. Amelia gathered up her hems to keep them out of the piles of muck and slush and picked her way between the houses.

She reached the alley mouth. She paused and pressed herself close to the wall. Then, holding her breath, she peered around the corner.

Cantrell stood right at the entrance to the square, looking for all the world like he had every right to be there. Carriages and vans rolled over the cobbles. Barrow men and servants hurried up the walk. Cantrell let the whole world pass him on by. He didn't even seem to be feeling the cold.

Well, Amelia McGowan? She bit her lip. *There he is. Now what?*

No idea came. She was just about to give up the whole thing as ridiculous and walk right back into the house. But as she started to turn, she saw a woman wearing a servant's fluttering gray cloak hurry up the walk. Her black bonnet kept Amelia from seeing her face as she scuttled past the alley, and past Cantrell, who touched his hat to her. But as Cantrell straightened, a scrap of paper fluttered down in the woman's wake. Cantrell stooped and snatched it up the instant it touched the ground.

Amelia squeaked involuntarily and pressed her mittened hand over her mouth.

The woman was already around the corner and out of sight. Cantrell made no move at all to follow her.

While Amelia watched, Cantrell shook the paper open with one hand and read whatever was written there. In the next heartbeat, he was walking away in the opposite direction from the woman, swinging his stick and tucking that letter into his coat pocket.

What do I do? Amelia hesitated. She couldn't follow both of them. Miss Thorne would want to know where Cantrell went, but she'd also want to know who had dropped that note.

Could have been an accident? thought Amelia. But no. Cantrell had read the thing without even a smidge of hesitation and had walked off right afterward.

Amelia made her decision and took off running.

She reached the mouth of the square, and the high street. She stared about frantically for a moment before she caught sight of a gray cloak and a black bonnet bobbing along amid the passersby. Amelia snatched up her skirts and ran.

Her quarry was a quick one. Amelia was soon out of breath, trying to keep sight of that plain cloak and bonnet as they slipped in and out of a forest of backs and shoulders. Amelia stepped smartly and didn't pause to apologize as she elbowed a man carrying a clothespole, but at last she was able to draw level with her quarry.

Just hurry on past and then turn, like I've forgotten something . . .

But as she lengthened her stride, her toe stubbed hard

against a cobble, and she stumbled and fell against the cloaked woman.

"Watch yourself!" the woman cried, shoving Amelia off. "Oh! Amelia! For goodness sakes!"

It was Betsy.

"Oh, hullo!" Amelia hoped she sounded only normally out of breath. "I'm sorry for that. I didn't know you were going out, too. I would have asked to walk with you."

"Oh, yes, I just had a few errands for . . . for the house," Betsy said. "Where are you off to?"

Amelia remembered what she'd told Mrs. Hare just in time. "The post office."

"I'll walk with you, then. It's the apothecary's for me."

"For Mrs. Hodgeson?" asked Amelia. "Seems like she's a one who always needs her tinctures."

"Actually," said Betsy, "it's a secret, so you mustn't tell."

"The tinctures are a secret?"

"No, silly." Betsy slapped her arm playfully. "The drops is."

"Drops?"

"Eye drops. For Miss Penelope. Mr. Douglas has said she mustn't use any cosmetics at all, not even to brighten her eyes just the slightest bit. So, I fetch them for her. And very grateful she is, too." Betsy winked.

Amelia decided to do what Miss Alice would call *feigning ignorance*, and what her own mother would have called *playing dumb*. "Oh, well, it'll be nice for her to have a little something. This morning must have been a nasty shock."

"Too right it was," said Betsy. "I've never seen her so upset. Tragic it is. You know, it was her Mr. Cantrell was courting, until Miss Slyboots Hodgeson slipped between them."

"Not really?" said Amelia, making sure she sounded good and surprised.

"Sure as I'm standing here," said Betsy. "She's still in love, you mark my words."

That is news. "I can't believe that. Not after the way he's gone and treated Miss Nora . . ."

"Well, how should he treat a little hussy who went and threw herself at him? Wouldn't be at all surprised that it was her who talked him into running away from the first."

Amelia opened her mouth and closed it again, but she couldn't think of a thing to say.

"But I'm so glad we caught each other." Betsy pressed close beside her as they walked. "I've been dying to talk to you. It must be so exciting working for that Miss Thorne. Is she really a lady thief-taker?"

"It's nothing like that," said Amelia. "She just . . . helps out. If a lady's got trouble with a man, or someone's trying to cheat them, or their husband's up to no good, she helps them sort it out."

"Have you seen any dead bodies?" asked Betsy breathlessly. "Jimmy Smart says she's caught ever so many murderers!"

"Of course not!" replied Amelia primly. "Miss Thorne doesn't go out patrolling like the watch! Ladies with troubles come to her. Mostly, it's a lot of letters and visits. Not that different from a normal house, really." She could tell Betsy was disappointed, but the last thing Amelia wanted was that lot back at Portsmouth Square chewing over her Miss Thorne's business any more than they already were.

"Still . . ." Betsy leaned in. "I imagine you've done pretty well for yourself."

"I don't know what you mean," said Amelia loftily.

"Oh, come down off that high horse. All them fine ladies she helps out and the presents she gets doing it. I imagine they're *ever* so grateful, just like Miss Pen." To finish off, she dug Amelia in the ribs. "Bet they pass along a bit extra to be kept all up to date and all."

Which was quite enough, thank you. "Unlike *some* people, I don't take everything on offer."

"Well, more fool you," said Betsy. "We've all got to look out for ourselves, don't we? If they're willing to drop it, why shouldn't we be willing to catch it?"

"Which is all fine as far as it goes, until you're caught with what's dropped, and turned out for thieving."

"You're only caught if you're careless," said Betsy.

"Listen to you!" cried Amelia. "Next thing you'll be saying it was *you* who stole that necklace!"

To Amelia's shock, all Betsy did was sigh. "Don't I wish I had! You wouldn't see me hanging about belowstairs no more! I'd be on my way to Paris or maybe Rome. Someplace like that. I'd drink champagne and have a hundred silk dresses and a ring on every finger!" She sighed and stopped. "Aren't you going in?"

Amelia looked about her in confusion and then realized they were right in front of the post office.

"Oh! Right. Here's me. Well. I suppose I'll see you back at the house."

"I suppose you will," said Betsy with that same flippant carelessness.

Betsy smiled, and Amelia smiled, and she walked up the post office steps.

Now we'll see what you're really up to, Miss Betsy Chatterbox, she thought as she ducked behind one of the grand stone pillars. But when she peeked out, she blushed instantly.

Because Betsy was still standing down there, looking right at Amelia, her face all wreathed in smiles.

She waved and disappeared into the apothecary.

CHAPTER 20

Past Letters and Present Rumors

*She had even learnt to detect in the very
gentleness which had first delighted her, an affectation and a sameness to disgust and weary.*

Jane Austen, *Pride and Prejudice*

"**D**id I do right, miss?" asked Amelia uneasily when she'd finished her story. "Should I have followed Mr. Cantrell instead?"

"No, no, you did exactly right," Rosalind assured her. She had returned only half an hour ago from her calls, and her mind was still full of her conversation with Lady Cowper. "If Cantrell is receiving messages from someone in the house, it's not too far-fetched to suppose he will return. The runner will follow him then. Did Betsy give you any hint whom that note might have been from?" It was vital to know if Betsy was passing information to Cantrell herself or was acting for one of the family.

Amelia shook her head. "I tried every way I could think of to get her to say something, short of asking her outright. But it must have been Miss Penelope. I mean, she was already out getting Miss Pen's drops, and she did say she thinks Miss Pen is still in love with the man."

Rosalind remembered the incandescent fury on Pen's face as she delivered her stinging blow.

"Well, we shall see," said Rosalind. "But there is one more rumor I particularly want you to keep your ears open for."

"What's that, miss?"

Rosalind took a deep breath. "Nora has hinted that Mr. Douglas keeps a mistress."

"He'd hardly be the first," said Amelia. "Forgive my plain speaking."

"You are, of course, correct," agreed Rosalind. "But I would like to know if it is true, or if Nora is simply trying to stir up trouble."

"I'll see what I can find out," said Amelia.

"Thank you. Now, I will need you to take a note to Bow Street for me. We'll need to let Mr. Tauton know what you've seen."

With the note written, and Amelia duly dispatched to find a messenger, Rosalind got to her feet. She should find Bethany and let her know how matters had progressed.

But do I tell her about Betsy? Without knowing whom the note came from? Rosalind bit her lip.

Too many families were ready to suspect their servants the moment anything went wrong. Frequently, those suspicions were unfounded. But every now and then, there was a thief among the staff. Alice and George had told her stories of colleagues out and out bribing staff members in households belonging to people whose names ended up filling the gossip columns.

Such bribery was certainly something a man like Cantrell might stoop to. But a servant who was dismissed even on suspicion would have difficulty finding work again. Rosalind would not plunge another person into poverty without proof.

That note Betsy had dropped could just as easily have come from some member of the family.

And that does include Penelope.

The next obvious step was to confront Betsy with what she had done. But Betsy struck Rosalind as having a good amount of resolution. If confronted, she could simply deny any wrongdoing. Then she would be on her guard, and so would whoever she was working for.

Rosalind was still considering the various possibilities as she descended the stairs. As she arrived at the second-floor landing, the sound of piano music reached her. She paused, listening for a moment. It was a dark, rich melody, something written to fill concert halls and drown out the heart's distractions. Rosalind made a decision and followed the sound of the music to the blue sitting room.

The door was ajar. Through it, Rosalind saw Penelope sitting alone at the pianoforte, focused on the music.

Penelope, who might still be in love with Bryan Cantrell.

Penelope, who might even have enlisted a maid to send him a note.

Her back and shoulders were rigidly straight; her wrists precisely curved. Everything about her posture displayed that lifetime's worth of intensive physical training that was generally disguised by the term "good breeding."

It was odd. Penelope was the golden girl, the one beloved and sheltered by her brother, and the one Rosalind had ostensibly been brought to help. But Rosalind had spoken fewer words to Penelope than she had to anyone in the family.

It was past time to amend that oversight.

Rosalind stepped softly into the sitting room. Her motion must have caught Penelope's eye, because she jerked both hands away from the keyboard.

"Oh, Miss Thorne." She pressed a hand to her throat. "You startled me!"

"I'm sorry," said Rosalind. "I didn't want to interrupt. You play beautifully."

"Thank you." She ran a hand softly across the keys. "The music is one of the things I really do love about London. I only wish . . ." She stopped. "Well, there's no point in wishing, is there?"

"Wishes can be a beginning," said Rosalind.

"Not for me," replied Penelope bitterly. "Why did Cantrell have to come back now? Do you know how long it took Bethany to convince Gerald I should have any kind of season at all? Now he's talking about sending us home!"

"I believe your brother wants you to have some time to recover from your shock."

"You mean he's afraid I'll become ill, like I did last time, when Cantrell ran off with Nora." Penelope's words were clipped and bitter. "I was eating my heart out then, but I'm done with him, and he knows it!"

Rosalind paused for one heartbeat and then asked, "Who knows it?"

Penelope looked at her. Rosalind watched her expression shift from surprise to suspicion. "Gerald, of course."

"Of course," said Rosalind. "But for a moment, it sounded as if you meant Mr. Cantrell."

Penelope blanched. Rosalind cocked her head and watched the girl realize she'd been discovered.

"Don't tell," she whispered urgently. "Please don't. Gerald will never let me out of the house again."

Rosalind closed the door so they would not be accidentally overheard.

"You knew Mr. Cantrell was still alive?"

"No, no, I didn't. That is, not after Nora came back and told us all he'd died. I just . . ." She swallowed. "While they were away, he wrote to me."

Rosalind pressed her hand against the door to make sure it

was firmly shut. Then she moved to sit down on the stool beside the pianoforte.

"Will you tell me about it?" she asked softly.

Penelope was silent for a long moment. She sat very still, as a mannered girl was taught to do. All her feeling was in her eyes. They were tired and haunted and looked far older than they should.

"He and Nora had been gone only a year when the letters started," she said. "He told me how much he regretted his decision, how I was the one he truly loved. I always had been. But he got impatient and angry because I wouldn't accept his . . . proposals. He said . . . he said he wanted me so much he let his temper get the better of him. It was jealousy and anger that made him leave, nothing more." She bit her lip. "He wanted to know if any small piece of my heart was ready to forgive him for his weakness."

Rosalind waited.

"And then he asked for money," Penelope said. "He said his wife—" Her voice caught on the word. "He said Nora was spending everything he had. He wanted to leave her, but he couldn't afford it. If I could just send him even a little, he would be able to come back to me . . ."

"He did call Nora his wife?"

"Oh yes," said Penelope. "Yes, he did. I suppose I should have known he was lying about that, as well."

Rosalind was not surprised. Whether or not Nora and Cantrell had legally married, Nora could become a permanent excuse for him. If Penelope asked when he was coming back, he could simply blame Nora for any delay. If she asked him to run away with her, he could claim that he could not forsake his duty.

Nora would become the villain. Cantrell would remain the wounded knight

"The letters are what made me ill," Penelope whispered.

Rosalind nodded. Being hounded for money by the man who broke her heart would have certainly create a nervous strain. Having no one to confide in would make it worse.

"What stopped you?" Rosalind almost said, "What saved you?" but caught herself in time.

Penelope laid her hands lightly on the keyboard and tapped her fingertips against the keys, but not so firmly as to make any sound. "I think . . . I think I was waiting for him to make one declaration of love that was not followed by a plea for money."

Rosalind felt herself frown. "But why should he ask you for money? Do you have any of your own?" It was possible her late parents or some other relative had settled a sum on her.

"Oh, no. Well, not really. I have some pin money. But Gerald had been named Sir Jasper's heir by then, so I suppose Cantrell assumed I would have been given a share of any settlement, or that I could convince Gerald to give me something."

"So . . . these letters only started after Sir Jasper changed his will?"

"Yes. I remember. Gerald had just gotten back from London and signing the papers when the first one arrived."

"I see," said Rosalind. "How long did the letters continue?"

"To me, just some months."

"To you?" said Rosalind. "Was he writing to anyone else?"

Penelope nodded. "He wrote to my brother and to Bethany, as well. He begged them for money, just like he begged me. Well . . ." She stilled her fingers. "Not just like. He said different things. He said Nora was ill. Once, he even said Nora was expecting a baby. Nora wrote, too, mostly to Bethany, pleading for her to send even a little . . ." She stopped.

"How did you find out about this?" asked Rosalind. "Surely, Mr. Douglas didn't tell you."

A small, weak smile flickered across Penelope's pale face. "It was Mariah."

Rosalind felt her brows arch. Penelope's smile strengthened. "Oh, I know what you think. She's just angry and stubborn and, well, trivial. But she's not really. She's just . . . she's Mariah. She stole the letters. Some of them, anyway. Gerald and Bethany burnt most of them, I think. It was wrong of her, of course, but she wanted to show me what Cantrell really was, and what he . . . they were really doing."

Rosalind remembered Mariah at dinner, with her fierce decision and sharp, suspicious gaze. Then she remembered the way she'd managed to champion both Nora and Penelope when Cantrell had set the rest of the family back on their heels. Rosalind found she could well believe that Mariah would do whatever it took to help someone she had decided was hers to protect.

"Did you write Cantrell back?" asked Rosalind.

"Once," said Penelope. "Just to let him know I was done with him, and he could not use me to get to Douglas or Bethany."

"Did he continue to importune you?"

"For a while," said Penelope. "Of course, it all stopped just before Nora returned," Penelope went on. "Naturally, I assumed it was as she said—that he had died." Her face twisted like she was holding back tears. Rosalind touched her own sleeve to make sure she'd remembered to tuck a handkerchief there this morning. It might be needed.

"She should have told me!" cried Penelope angrily. "I wasted so much time feeling sorry for her. I believed she was another of his victims, that he forced her to write those letters and then left her destitute, but she was only out for what she could get from us!"

"It may not have been so simple," said Rosalind. "Some-

times people fall in over their heads. Especially when they believe they are being clever."

"Yes, that does sound very like Nora, doesn't it?" Penelope said bitterly. "Not that it matters. He's come back, and
he's ruining everything. Gerald's going to lock me in my
room! Mariah will see more of society than I will!"

"You do not know that."

"I do! He, Gerald, came to talk to me right after Cantrell
left. He stood there, telling me I did not have to come out. I
could wait. I could go home as soon as ever I liked, and that
I mustn't feel bad about it. There would be plenty of time
next year. Everything would be so much more settled by
then." She pressed her hands to her cheeks. "Except what
happens when something goes wrong next year? Or the year
after?" She lowered her hands and made a visible effort to
control herself. "Listen to me. I barely know you, and here I
am . . ." She shook her head. "Of course, I am an ungrateful
child, and selfish, as well. My brother only wants what's
right for me. It is his job to protect me, and he knows best."
The words were dutiful and correct, and devoid of all feeling.

"I know this is important to you," began Rosalind.

"Important," murmured Penelope. "Do you have any
idea? A girl without a husband is nothing. She's a child forever, dependent, pathetic, *useless*!" She blinked rapidly.

"That is not true."

"Maybe not for you," said Penelope. "You're different.
For the rest of us, life only starts when we're married. A husband means a house of one's one and servants who actually
follow orders. It means freedom." She swallowed. "I almost
threw that all away on Cantrell, and I *swore* I would not
make that mistake again. I would show Douglas how strong
I was, how well I behaved, and then I was sure he would forget, and he would let me go. And then when we came here,
when Bethany said she'd gotten you to help it, I believed it
would actually happen.

"Then I saw Cantrell," Penelope breathed. "And for a minute I forgot. For a minute all I could think was how I had missed being in the same room with him, seeing him smile, hearing him laugh . . ." She shook her head. "And then I got so angry that he could still work on me like that, and I betrayed myself. And Douglas saw, and now it's over."

"Not yet," said Rosalind. "There is still time." She paused, considering. "Penelope, would you like to attend a concert?"

Surprise took Penelope aback for a moment. "I . . . yes, of course."

"It happens that I've recently had a letter from a friend of mine," said Rosalind. "She's holding a musicale. Just an afternoon's entertainment for what friends of hers are in town for the little season. Nothing grand or formal."

"Oh, yes, I'd love that," said Penelope. "If, well, if Gerald agrees. May Mariah come, too?"

"If Mariah wants to attend, I'm sure I can obtain an invitation for her, as well."

"Thank you, Miss Thorne!" cried Penelope. "This will be marvelous!"

"It will not be entirely for relaxation," Rosalind reminded her. "Meredith, my friend, knows a number of society hostesses. It will be on you to make a good impression. If you do, it could lead to invitations to call. Since we are only in the little season, they will be only a few, but it will be a beginning."

"I understand perfectly! And you'll see what I can do. So will Gerald," she added. "So will everyone!"

Rosalind smiled. Hopefully, this event, and its possibilities, would distract Penelope from her despair while Mr. Tauton and his colleagues tracked Cantrell down.

But what then? Rosalind asked herself. And she found she had no answer.

CHAPTER 21

An Uncomfortable Conversation

We do not suffer by accident.

Jane Austen, *Pride and Prejudice*

That evening, Rosalind excused herself from dinner, pleading a slight headache. Instead, Amelia brought her supper on a tray. Rosalind dismissed her, saying she could very well serve herself. She very much enjoyed the ragout of mutton and winter vegetables but set aside the pudding and coffee for later. She expected to have a late night.

First, there were letters to be written. Alice must, of course, be brought up to the moment regarding the day's events. Meredith Burgoyne must be warned not only that Rosalind was attending her concert but also that she was bringing two young ladies with her, and, of course, a letter of thanks must be written to Lady Cowper.

Which brought Rosalind to the matter of how exactly to initiate inquiries regarding the mysterious Miss Mayne. Sanderson Faulks was the obvious first course. Rosalind, however, was hesitant to importune her friend on an additional matter after having commissioned him regarding the missing pearls. And, of course, it would never do to broadcast such inquiries across her general range of acquaintance. If word spread that she was looking for an introduction to Miss Mayne, she might very well defeat her own object.

Lady Cowper had mentioned an agent named Sommerton, but that name was unfamiliar to Rosalind. Lord Langford, however, might provide some opening. At least, his family might.

Rosalind was still puzzling over this when a soft knock sounded at her door. Having dismissed Amelia, Rosalind got up to open it herself and found Bethany waiting in the corridor.

"I hope I'm not disturbing you? I just wanted to see how you were."

"Not at all, Bethany. Please come in. I'm sorry to have missed dinner," Rosalind added as they both settled themselves beside the fire.

"You did not miss a great deal." Bethany sighed. "Father was somewhat subdued tonight. Mother was absent, but Douglas was home, which made for an agreeable change."

"I'm glad," said Rosalind. "I imagine you would like to hear how things stand regarding your business."

Bethany smiled in acknowledgment and hope. "Is there anything new?"

"If you mean any new answers, I'm afraid it is much too soon," Rosalind told her. "Inquiry regarding the pearls has been set in motion. Mr. Tauton, the Bow Street officer I contracted on your behalf, will set a runner to watch out for Mr. Cantrell."

"I wish that they may find him soon," said Bethany. "The idea that that . . . man is watching us is profoundly unsettling. I . . ." She shook herself. "Well, it does no good dwelling on it."

"You are right to be concerned," Rosalind told her. "This is deeply disquieting. Especially so soon after a theft."

"Yes." She knotted her fingers together. "I just . . . I don't want to sound hysterical."

It seemed to Rosalind what she really meant was, *I don't want to sound like my mother.*

"Concern about a real threat can hardly be considered hysteria," said Rosalind. "I hope your mother is no worse for these events?"

"Oh, no. At least, not really. She'd heard all about Cantrell, of course, and this threw her into spasms and was her reason for missing dinner." She gave Rosalind a sideways glance. "Please don't concern yourself. Mother's spasms are regular events and soon pass. Although, I suspect this time they came because she's also irritated with us."

"Why should that be?"

"We didn't run to her to ask what should be done," said Bethany. "I know it seems like a contradiction, but Mother very much believes herself the true manager of the household and everyone in it."

Rosalind returned a small smile. "I gathered as much when I first met her."

"Yes, I suppose you did." Bethany chuckled. "I think it allows her some compensation for no longer having her own establishment."

Rosalind remembered Lucinda's letter, where she said that the Hodgesons' house had been put up for let to cover some of the estate's debts. Such a loss would be difficult for anyone. However, to someone like Mrs. Hodgeson, who clearly liked to control—even dominate—any room she happened to be in, being dependent so on her daughter would be a severe blow.

"What did your mother have to say about Cantrell's return?" asked Rosalind.

Bethany waved her hand wearily. "A great deal of fluff and nonsense about how she knew it would happen."

"Surely she doesn't suggest she knew Cantrell was alive?" cried Rosalind.

"No, she doesn't go quite that far," said Bethany. "One thing you will learn about my mother is that she adjusts her recollection to fit current circumstances."

"Yes, I see."

"Well . . ." Bethany made to rise. "I should not keep you. I'm sure you're tired."

"Not in the least," said Rosalind again. "In fact, there was something I wanted to speak with you about."

"Yes?" Bethany settled back in her chair.

"It is my understanding that while Nora and Cantrell were absent from home, they wrote to you."

Bethany was clearly surprised by this, and it took her a moment to answer. "Not at first," she said. "I think it must have been at least a year before we heard from them. Cantrell wrote to Douglas, apologizing and claiming . . . claiming to have been overcome by a violent passion he could not control, and . . . well, more in that vein. He begged forgiveness."

"Did he ask for money?"

"Not at first, but that followed shortly afterward."

"And Nora?"

"She wrote to me," Bethany acknowledged. "In much the same vein, and for much the same reason. As it went on, the letters grew increasingly urgent. She even claimed at one point to be with child." Bethany's voice shook on these last words. "Is it strange that that's the lie I find so hard to forgive?"

"No," said Rosalind. "Not at all."

"Anyway, Douglas answered for us both with one letter, saying that no money would be forthcoming. There were a few more letters after that, pleading poverty and desperation, but they stopped eventually."

"You did not answer for yourself?"

"No," said Bethany. "I was too angry, and confused. And I must admit that at the time, I agreed with Douglas that Nora had put herself beyond the pale."

"What changed your mind?"

"Have you ever been parted from a sister, Miss Thorne?"

"Yes," said Rosalind. "I have. My sister Charlotte and I were separated for almost ten years before we reconciled."

Bethany looked surprised. "Then you know. There is a tie between sisters that is as tight as any bond between parent and child. That is why I had such need of you. I cannot reason objectively when it comes to my sister. I cannot tell which of her stories I should believe . . ." She swallowed. "I know only which ones I want to believe."

"I understand," said Rosalind.

Bethany regarded her for a moment. "I love them, Miss Thorne. All of them. I want them to have good lives. The same lives I want for my own children."

And there was the crux of it, Rosalind realized. Bethany's own children. She remembered being with Bethany in the nursery and seeing how she yearned to stay there, rather than go back downstairs to dine with her father and endure his endless slights and criticisms.

For herself, Bethany would accommodate; she would fix and smooth over. But for her children, and her sisters, she would fight. So she had called on Rosalind. The missing pearls were only the excuse. Her sisters, her family—they were the reason.

It was disquieting. Indeed, it was overwhelming. It was far more than Rosalind wanted to take on. She had known as much when she came here, but now the enormity of it all was settling in.

And yet she was not ready to leave.

I may regret this, she told herself. But she set that aside.

"I very much hope we will begin to make headway soon," said Rosalind. "In the meantime, did Penelope tell you that we've settled on an excellent possibility for her and Mariah's first outing?"

"Oh, yes. She mentioned a private concert?"

"At the home of a friend of mine, Mrs. Burgoyne," said Rosalind. "How was the news received?"

Bethany's mouth quirked up. "With tolerance. Douglas was dubious but did not openly object. Mariah agreed that it would be better than another afternoon shut up in the house."

"And how do you feel?" Rosalind asked her. "I do know I should have checked with you before I spoke to Pen . . ."

"Oh, I think it sounds like an excellent first step for them both," said Bethany. "And while Douglas is still ambivalent about Penelope having her season, he is ready to be convinced that a supervised outing cannot do any harm."

Douglas, who in his own way was trying to fight for his sister, whom he loved and whom he had failed. A failure that he refused to accept.

Rosalind remembered Penelope sitting at her pianoforte. *He stood there, telling me I did not have to come out. I could wait. I could go home as soon as ever I liked. . . .*

An idea occurred to her. "Bethany . . . how would it be if Nora came with us?"

Bethany stared at her. "Nora?"

"Yes. Sooner or later, she must be made known to the larger world." Fortunately, when Meredith said an event was informal, she generally meant it, and she and Rosalind had been friends for quite some time. Rosalind felt reasonably certain she could impose on her this once.

"But her past . . . the elopement . . . ," stammered Bethany.

"Could still be discovered, yes," said Rosalind. "And it probably will be. But ultimately, if the world sees Nora treated as a full and welcome member of the family, the scandal's effect will be lessened."

"You are saying we should brazen it out."

Rosalind nodded. "If we begin now, it is possible that the

worst of any scandal will have burnt out by the time Penelope begins to be seriously considered as a potential match for society's young men."

If the Hodgesons had appeared to be climbing the social ladder, considerations might be different. But Bethany and Douglas had no great ambitions to alarm the mamas of the *haut ton.* With a good dowry to buoy her, and her own accomplishments, Penelope could still have her hopes comfortably fulfilled, even as Nora's sister.

But Bethany was hesitating. "I don't think Douglas will agree to Nora accompanying Pen."

"Bethany," said Rosalind gently. "What Nora did was foolish, dangerous even, but does that mean she must pay for it with the rest of her life? Let her know you can forgive"

"Even with Cantrell watching the house?" said Bethany.

"Especially with Cantrell watching the house," said Rosalind. "If Nora continues to feel like an outcast in her own family, where will she turn next?"

In her private mind, Rosalind was not entirely sure Nora's elopement was entirely a girl's mistake. At least, not a mistake in the usual form. There was something more to the story. She was sure of it. But that did not change her opinions. Nora must be taken fully back into the family if the family, if Bethany, was to heal.

It certainly did not hurt matters that Rosalind's advocacy for Nora might just gain her a store of goodwill not only with Nora but with Mariah, too. Of all the family, it was Mariah who seemed to have the clearest view of her sisters' circumstances.

Bethany knotted her fingers together. "You are right, Rosalind. We cannot let Cantrell simply walk in to pluck Nora from us. And we cannot let her believe she has no choice but to go with him. I do believe Douglas will see the sense there." She paused, and unexpectedly, a small smile formed. "Do you remember what Mariah said last night at dinner? When she told us she wanted a season? She said she had as much right to consider the future as anyone else, and how was she to make any rational decision if all she'd done is sit in her room? The same could be said for Nora."

"Of course, it is for her to decide," said Rosalind. "I will freely admit, it is never easy to face out a scandal that you yourself have caused, but it can clear the storm more quickly. Also, if the worst is known now, there can be no surprises left for later."

"I had not thought of it that way," said Bethany. But now that she did, her expression seemed to lighten. There was, Rosalind knew, much comfort to be found in action. "Well, I should go let Nora know you'll secure her an additional invitation, if she wants it. Unless . . ." She hesitated. "You think it would be better coming from you?"

"No, I think you should tell her." If Bethany was to care for her whole family, she would need to discover for herself how to talk to her sister.

And Nora will have to discover how to talk to Bethany.

CHAPTER 22

The Invalid

*She was a woman of mean understanding, little
information and uncertain temper . . .*

Jane Austen, *Pride and Prejudice*

As soon as Bethany bid her good night, Rosalind retrieved the letter she'd written to Meredith. She added a postscript indicating that she might have a third young lady with her. She resealed the letter and returned it to the stack with the others.

She looked wistfully at her pudding, and at the most recent letter from Adam, which she had been saving for when she would have time to savor it. But that moment must now be postponed awhile longer.

She had a call to pay on Mrs. Hodgeson.

It never ceased to amaze Rosalind how often people settled within the same house managed to live entirely separate lives. Very often, they simply became slotted into roles as they were slotted into rooms, and neither was much examined, except in moments of crisis.

With the roles came assumptions. For example, it was assumed that a woman who believed absurdities about the health of her body would not accurately notice or discern what was happening around her.

Rosalind knew herself to be guilty of such dismissal, and she might have repeated this mistake with Mrs. Hodgeson but for one thing. Not only had Mrs. Hodgeson discovered the underlying reason for Rosalind's visit, but she also was not afraid to speak about it openly.

The maid, Gilpin, responded almost immediately to Rosalind's knock. She also made Rosalind wait in the corridor while she inquired whether her mistress would agree to be disturbed.

Her position on the threshold did not prevent Rosalind from hearing the reply.

"Miss Thorne? Well, at last! Yes, since she deigns to appear, let her come in!"

Gilpin returned, dropped a curtsy, and invited Rosalind to enter.

In general, Rosalind found the Portsmouth Square house comfortably airy. Mrs. Hodgeson's bedroom, however, was the exception. The fire blazed as if it was deepest midwinter instead of nearly spring, and the curtains were pulled shut. A carved maple whatnot cupboard looked as if it were doubling as an apothecary's counter. It was covered with bottles of various colors and sizes, a number of glasses, jars, several pitchers, and small basins—all testaments to Mrs. Hodgeson's efforts to maintain her health.

The lady herself reclined upon a sofa with no less than three pillows. More bottles waited on the table at her elbow, along with several magazines and a well-thumbed copy of *Boyle's Court and Country Guide*.

"Well!" Mrs. Hodgeson huffed as Rosalind made her curtsy and apologized for disturbing her so late. "At least you have decided to make an appearance. I trust you are pleased with yourself, Miss Thorne!"

"I'm sorry?" Rosalind blinked.

"Creating such a scene! Forcing Nora to tell shocking lies and worsening her position with our lord and master. Oh, yes," she added proudly. "I've heard everything, for all you may have tried to keep it from me!"

Rosalind had not been invited to sit. She realized, with some exasperated amusement, that Mrs. Hodgeson meant to keep her standing for this scold, like a naughty schoolgirl.

"A woman of your powers and your reputation!" Mrs. Hodgeson went on. "How could you even consider subjecting my girls to such an embarrassing display!"

She glared at Rosalind, and Rosalind made herself count three, to be certain that this pause was meant to provide her an opportunity to answer.

"I promise you, Mrs. Hodgeson, I did not mean to keep what occurred this morning a secret from you," Rosalind said. "I only thought it would be better if the details were relayed by Bethany."

"Well, you have that much delicacy of feeling." Mrs. Hodgeson sniffed. "But I do not forgive you for what you forced poor Nora to endure," she added. "My poor, poor wronged girl!" She buried her face in her handkerchief.

"Mrs. Hodgeson?" said Rosalind quietly.

"What!" she demanded into the linen folds.

"May I sit down?"

Without looking up, Mrs. Hodgeson pointed one long finger toward a tapestry chair. Rosalind sat and waited for the matron to finish wiping her eyes.

"Tell me, Mrs. Hodgeson," said Rosalind. "When Cantrell was staying with Douglas, did you have much contact with him?"

"You mean, did he make up to me as much as he did everyone else?" she sniffed. "You may be sure that he did, but he did not deceive *me*." She drew herself up once more in her attitude of triumph. "*I* knew him to be a plausible rascal!"

Rosalind did not bother to hide her attitude of surprise. Was it possible that, of all the family, Cantrell failed to deceive this overwrought and invalidish woman?

And yet it was conceivable that a woman who had built her life around an assumed persona might recognize another actor when she saw him.

"When you realized he was of deficient character, what did you do?" Rosalind asked.

"I am ashamed to admit to you, Miss Thorne, that at first, I did nothing. I believed him to be fixed on little Penelope. Poor thing! With only her brother to look out for her, and him all but throwing her in the path of that . . . creature! But what could I do? She was not *my* daughter. I, of course, warned Douglas, but would Douglas listen? He would not! And Bethany? Oh, she must stand by him and take his part in all things! My own daughter! But do I reproach her? I do not! Of course she must be loyal to her husband, but then! Oh then!" she wailed. "I heard from Mrs. Harding." Mrs. Harding was Lucinda's mother. "Nora went to her frequently, you know. They had a lovely gallery of pictures in their home, and Nora draws so exquisitely. But Mrs. Harding told me that one day, after she had sent Nora home, she happened to look out the window, and what did she see but *Cantrell* crossing the lawn to walk with Nora!"

"And it could not have been a coincidence? He may have simply been returning from his work at the bridge site."

"Certainly not! For that, he would have had to come from quite another direction. Of course, I asked Nora about it. She denied it even happened. The first lie, Miss Thorne! The first sign he had already interposed himself between mother and daughter!"

"What did you do then?" asked Rosalind.

"I did what any mother would! I remonstrated with him! I told him I knew his true nature and told him he had better leave at once, before I was forced to expose him publicly."

"What was his reply?"

"Oh, he's a blaggard, Miss Thorne," she said, her voice harsh with fury. "Without any conscience! Without any remorse. He *laughed* at me." Mrs. Hodgeson's voice trembled with the force of her outrage. "He called me . . . a silly biddy, and he patted my hand like I was a child! Then what did he do but go and tell Douglas all I had said, so that the two of them might laugh together! That you see, Miss Thorne, is why he ran off with Nora!" she concluded triumphantly.

Rosalind blinked. "I'm sorry, but I don't understand."

"He did it to injure me!" Mrs. Hodgeson spread her hands. "What greater wrong could he do me than to take away my best beloved daughter! He *knew* I would be pining away and unable to do *anything*! He knew my husband and son-in-law to both be unfeeling creatures who would be unwilling to mount any search. Oh! If only you knew what I suffered—what I do suffer!" She plied her handkerchief again. "I cannot eat! I cannot sleep! But a mother's heart is made to be broken! I forgive them, and no matter what they do to me, I will never desert them!" She blew her nose vigorously.

After this, they had to wait for Gilpin to take away the soiled linen and replaced it with fresh.

Once Gilpin withdrew, Rosalind asked, "Mrs. Hodgeson, did Nora write to you while she was gone?"

"How could she? With that monster watching over her every second? My poor girl." She pressed both hands against her breast. "What she must have suffered in her exile! I have begged her to share her travails with me, but she is still far too wounded to endure their repetition. It is that, you see, that makes her seem reckless and inconsiderate. Her frenetic manner is the mask behind which she hides her true feelings, her true *self*, even from her mother!"

This was an observation Rosalind found herself able to agree with. Nora did hide behind her bravado.

"But no more of this," said Mrs. Hodgeson abruptly. "What I want to hear from you, Miss Thorne, is what progress you make finding Bethany's missing necklace. Have you discovered the thief yet?"

"Not yet, ma'am, but I have hopes." Rosalind paused and made herself look down at her hands where they lay neatly folded in her lap. "Mrs. Hodgeson, when I first arrived, you said you could tell me the details of the disappearance."

"And so I could. If I chose," replied Mrs. Hodgeson grandly. "But surely Bethany has told you everything worth hearing."

Rosalind chose her next words carefully. It was plain that Mrs. Hodgeson now felt she had an advantage, and she intended to wield it.

"Bethany has told me everything she can. But in my experience, it is the people with the most sensitive dispositions who are best able to judge what is really happening in any large and busy household such as this."

At this, Mrs. Hodgeson's manner warmed considerably.

"Well, Miss Thorne, I see you do have some measure of understanding. Perhaps your reputation is not entirely undeserved."

Rosalind leaned forward. "Will you help me, Mrs. Hodgeson?"

"Help you? I shall do more than that. You see, I *know* who stole my dear Bethany's pearls."

Rosalind found she was not in the least surprised by this declaration. "Who is it?"

Mrs. Hodgeson looked toward the door; then she motioned for Rosalind to lean closer. "It was that *Morgan* creature."

Morgan? Rosalind sat back. The aged and frail lady's maid, kept on for the sake of kindness? And whom Amelia declared absolutely devoted to her mistress?

"She comes from Sir Jasper, you know," Mrs. Hodgeson

said. "He pretended to be appalled when he heard Bethany had no lady's maid, and sent a cuckoo to be nurtured in our bosom. It seems she waited on his wife. She's a *spy*." Mrs. Hodgeson sat back, waiting for Rosalind's exclamation.

"I had no idea," said Rosalind. She did, however, recall Amelia saying that Morgan had no particular affection for Mrs. Hodgeson.

"Well, it is not your fault." There was more than a hint of pity in Mrs. Hodgeson's tone now. "You do not have any *real* understanding of the ways of this house, and, of course, she's a careful, sneaking thing. But I tell you, Miss Thorne, Morgan took the necklace, and she delivered it straight to Sir Jasper!"

The surprise that overcame Rosalind's expression at this was entirely genuine.

"But why? I understood the necklace was a wedding present."

"Ah! You see, that's how clever he is! He had his spy steal the necklace and then tells Douglas that Nora must have done it so that he would insist that she be removed."

This speculation was startlingly close to one of the possibilities Nora had considered just that morning, before Cantrell's appearance. Except, of course, Nora suspected Douglas as the real thief.

"It's all his plan to divide our family," Mrs. Hodgeson went on. "We are to be moved out of the house one by one, until poor Bethany is left alone and defenseless with a man ruled entirely by the House of Jasper!"

Rosalind did not answer. On one level, it was entirely fantastical. On another . . .

But it all depended on Sir Jasper's nature, and on whether he was truly determined to separate his heir from his wife. But why would he be? Bethany was a countrywoman, it was true, but she was good and sensible and devoted to her fam-

ily. In the most mercenary sense, she had already proved herself the paragon of womanly virtue by providing the House
of Jasper, as Mrs. Hodgeson put it, with a male heir.

"Well, Miss Thorne?" Mrs. Hodgeson's expression grew
greedy. "Now that you know the truth, what will you do?
You will not tell Bethany, of course. She will not believe you.
She must be *shown* the truth."

That much was certainly correct. "I shall have to have
some sort of proof," Rosalind said. "However, now that I
know where to look, that should be easier to discover."

"Excellent. Now, you will come to me every day and tell
me what progress you have made. That way, I will be able to
advise you. Oh, if only I had my health!" She sighed. "But I
feel sure now we will be able to catch the creature napping,
and then Bethany would have no choice but to dismiss her.
What I wouldn't give to see Sir Jasper's face when his spy is
returned to him!"

She did not have the opportunity to embroider any further
on this theme. A knock on the door was followed by the appearance of Mr. Hodgeson. He swayed slightly as he crossed
to the sofa, and bowed unsteadily over his wife's hand. Rosalind smelled the distinct scent of port wine hanging about
him.

"There, my dear." He beamed at her myopically. "I've
come to say good night."

"Oh, you are so good, Mr. Hodgeson!"

Mr. Hodgeson leaned over his wife, a little unsteadily, and
planted a resounding kiss on her forehead. She beamed up at
him. The look he returned her was far more quizzical. He
turned slowly, as if only just becoming aware that Rosalind
was in the room.

"Miss Thorne," he said. "I beg your pardon. I did not see
you there." He bowed slowly and carefully.

"Good evening, Mr. Hodgeson. How are you?"

Mr. Hodgeson did not answer; instead he looked to his wife and then back to Rosalind. His cheeks, already flushed with drink, darkened yet further.

"I am well, Miss Thorne," he answered belatedly. "But my wife, you see, is not. I must ask you not to tire her."

"Oh, I am not in the least tired, Mr. Hodgeson," said Mrs. Hodgeson.

"Nonsense!" he replied stiffly. "You look exhausted. Gilpin! What do you mean letting your mistress sit up like this? Come, Miss Thorne, it is past time that we allowed Mrs. Hodgeson to retire."

Mr. Hodgeson might not be entirely sober, but neither was he going to brook any argument.

"I am sure Mr. Hodgeson is right." Rosalind got to her feet. "I wish you good night, Mrs. Hodgeson. I hope we may continue this conversation in the morning."

"Yes, yes, you may be sure that we will. I am *counting* on you!"

With this as her farewell, Rosalind found herself determinedly escorted to the door by Mr. Hodgeson.

Once the door was closed behind them, he reached out and gripped Rosalind's arm.

"What did she say?" he croaked.

"Mr. Hodgeson," said Rosalind coldly. "You will let go."

Mr. Hodgeson blinked at her. Then he loosened his grip.

"My, my apologies." He swallowed and rubbed his hands together. "But you must understand, my wife, she gets these . . . fancies in her head. She is very eager to exaggerate her own importance . . . her own vitality . . . you cannot countenance . . ." He wiped at his forehead.

"Thank you for your candor, Mr. Hodgeson," said Rosalind. "You may be sure I shall consider what you have told me very carefully."

"Thank you." He bowed again. "I . . . You will excuse me. I find I am very tired, as well." He turned and walked carefully down the corridor, his fingers trailing on the wainscoting, as if to guide him along.

Rosalind watched him until he disappeared into his rooms. Then she turned and walked slowly up the corridor to her own.

She thought of Mrs. Hodgeson's accusation of Morgan, and her declaration that Morgan was under orders from Sir Jasper. She thought about how Amelia had said there was discord belowstairs between those servants who had come from the country and those who had been supplied from Sir Jasper's household.

Discord between the staff from different households did not necessarily translate into such direct and dramatic sabotage. Neither did it rule such a thing out.

Then she thought of Mr. Hodgeson and his insistence that she pay no attention to his wife. He was drunk and plainly exasperated with his situation and his wife's invalid character.

But it was more than that.

Before this, Mr. Hodgeson had been angry. Now he was afraid.

CHAPTER 23

An Afternoon in Company

One cannot wonder that so very fine a young
man, with family, fortune, everything in his favor,
should think highly of himself.

Jane Austen, *Pride and Prejudice*

The next two days passed in relative quiet.
Rosalind took Mariah and Penelope to the establishment of one Mrs. Friske in Albemarle Street to order new dresses for the coming season. Mrs. Friske had been recommended by Hannah Littlefield. To Rosalind's relief and Mariah's surprise, Mrs. Friske spent a long time with the serious young woman, rationally discussing the properties of cloth and color, and the effects they created when properly combined. Measurements were taken. Pattern cards and fabrics were closely examined.

The rest of the afternoon was spent ransacking the young women's current wardrobes for the best choices to wear to Meredith Burgoyne's afternoon musicale.

Rosalind began to understand the rhythms of the house. Bethany spent her mornings in the nursery and much of the rest of the day dealing with household matters. Her "at home" times were attended by the same four ladies, all of them young wives she had met when she still lived in her parents' house.

Mrs. Hodgeson's main recreation was her drives. When she was not keeping estate abovestairs, she was out in the carriage, but seldom alone. Any one of her daughters or Penelope might be peremptorily summoned to drive with her, because, as she said, "I must have some companion, should my strength fail me. Servants are not to be relied upon, excepting my own Gilpin." Somewhat to Rosalind's surprise, the young women all went. Penelope reluctantly, Mariah sulkily, Nora with some hint of wry amusement. Bethany because it was her duty, and it kept the peace.

This habit very much helped explain how Mrs. Hodgeson remained so well informed about everyone's doings.

But she was not the only one who spent their days out and about. If Mr. Hodgeson was not in his apartments with his books and Mr. Douglas's port, he also absented himself from the house entirely. Apparently impervious to the weather, he would leave shortly before noon and not return until dinnertime. Not having a club or any acquaintance, he said, he walked or went to the coffeehouse to hear the news and perhaps to watch an auction or an argument.

As for Mr. Douglas, his travels abroad in the city took him to his club or the Royal Society or, of course, to Sir Jasper. Bethany had not been exaggerating. The Douglases' patron did indeed demand near daily attendance from his heir and would keep him closeted for hours.

Rosalind watched and waited and, of course, wrote her letters. She wrote to Lucinda, soliciting more details about the Hodgesons' estate and their troubles. She wrote to Mr. Prescott, her man of business, asking him to help illuminate her on the ways in which a distressed gentleman might acquire a loan if friends and bankers failed him.

She wrote her friend Cordelia Finch a chatty letter, and when she was finished with all the news she could share, she asked if Cordelia had lately heard anything from *her* friend Odetta Langford, and wasn't it her father who was having such a triumph with his showing of a new artist's work?

In the midst of all this, Rosalind found time to read the letter from Alice's Mrs. Heslop. It was, as she had suspected, an offer of a house she had ready to let. But somewhat more than that.

> *I know what it is, Miss Thorne, to be a woman who must move beyond the strictly domestic sphere in order to provide for those who depend on her. You may be certain that I should be happy to help provide a home to such a diligent and thoughtful woman as yourself. . . .*

Rosalind laid the letter aside. She wondered what Alice had said and what Mrs. Heslop had heard. This sort of flattery did not come from out of nowhere, and usually it had some aim behind it.

Rosalind had also received a note from Mr. Tauton, saying that the house was now being closely watched by a series of runners. So far, however, neither Cantrell nor any confederate had put in an appearance. Rosalind found herself wondering if she was mistaken and Cantrell would not return, after all. Perhaps the note that Betsy had let fall had contained all he required, for now at least.

Mr. Faulks had written, as well. He offered colorful and probably only slightly exaggerated descriptions of the establishments and persons he had approached regarding the pearls. He further assured her that word was circulating among "the relevant quarters" that a reward was to be offered for their safe return.

But so far, my dear Miss Thorne, I confess to utter defeat. The class of persons who might be interested in such a purchase or involved in facilitating the transaction is large, but not that large. Even if the pearls were sold some days or weeks ago, they would never have been forgotten or unrecognized. A pearl is not a diamond. It cannot be recut to disguise its origin. They must be sold whole and therefore must easily be recognized. I think we must reconcile ourselves to the possibility that if these pearls were sold, they were taken overseas.

If you wish, I can undertake to write to a few of my Continental acquaintances, but it will, I fear, be some time before I receive any answer.

Rosalind refolded the letter and laid it in her writing desk. She found she was not entirely surprised. Of course, she would write and accept Mr. Faulks's offer, but she did not now expect there to be any positive answer.

"This may be good news," she said to Bethany. "It may mean the thief is holding on to the necklace, and it may yet be recovered intact."

Each evening Rosalind made sure she looked in on Mrs. Hodgeson. Each evening she sat patiently through that lady's complaints, observations, and interrogations.

All the while, Rosalind contemplated the problem of Betsy. She had never before had to resort to out-and-out bribery of a servant to gain information, and she did not like to do it now. What could be sold to one person could be sold to many, and it was already clear that Betsy was ready to play the double agent. Previously, Rosalind would have found a way to create a bond of sympathy and asked innocent-seeming questions. But Betsy knew exactly what business Rosalind—and, by extension, Amelia—was engaged in, so that door was firmly closed.

Amelia did her best. She talked. She listened. She even, by her own description, engaged in a campaign of lurking. But all that gained her was a headache from eye strain. Betsy had closed up like a clam, and Rosalind, as of yet, had no firm idea how to safely open her again.

The fact that there did not seem to have been any more notes passed through her hands should have been reassuring, but it was not.

By the time Thursday arrived, Rosalind found herself looking forward to Meredith's musicale as something of a respite. It would be good to talk with a friend who had nothing to do with pearls, elopements, or family disputes.

At the appointed time, Rosalind was able to shepherd her charges to Meredith's house in Manchester Square in good time and good order. Bethany had loaned Nora a deep bronze tea dress that went well with her dark hair. Its vibrant color set her apart from her sisters in their pastels and signaled she was a mature woman. Cream gloves concealed the stains and calluses on her hands.

Mariah, unsurprisingly, had made difficulties. Rosalind had had to remind her three separate times that if she truly wished to give herself a chance in larger London society, she needed to make some small compromise with conventionality. Dark gray and navy blue would not answer for a young woman, especially in the afternoon. At last, they had settled on a simple day dress of pale blue, with a curved neckline that was just shy of daring, especially on a girl her age. A thinner girl could not have worn it, but as it was, it served to emphasize Mariah's swanlike neck and sloping shoulders.

"I shall probably catch cold," Mariah had sniffed as she looked at herself in the mirror.

"In that case, I shall prescribe tea with plenty of lemon

and honey," Rosalind had replied. "For now, I suggest a light shawl as a preventative."

Penelope had, of course, been the easiest. She had the good fortune to be one of those girls whom almost any gown would suit. Together, she and Rosalind had selected a simple white day dress with a fashionably high waist and a pink sash. The results were such that when they entered Meredith's grand salon, the assembled ladies and gentlemen all cast their inquisitive glances toward Rosalind's party and whispered asides.

"Who is that lovely girl?"

"That's Gerald Douglas's sister, Sir Jasper's heir. Very well settled, I hear, and just up from the country . . ."

"Fresh as a daisy, that girl. Do you know her? Who's that with her . . . ? Can you introduce me . . . ?

"Rosalind, my dear!" Meredith sailed forward to greet them. Meredith and Rosalind had been friends as girls, and she was one of the few who had not fallen away when Rosalind's father abandoned the family. "It's been an age! Introduce me to your protégés!"

Rosalind did. With quick eyes, Meredith measured each young woman up against the description Rosalind had given her.

"Miss Mariah!" said Meredith. "Rosalind's told me you have an interest in natural philosophy. Is this so?"

"Yes, some," said Mariah stiffly. Then she added, "I have not had the chance to study as much as I would like." It was a slightly sulky concession to the expectations of modesty, but it was something.

"I was just having the most *amusing* conversation with Mrs. Keene . . . Where can she have gotten to?" Meredith scanned her gathering. "Ah!" She pulled the startled Mariah up to a grand matron dressed all in burgundy and cream.

"Mrs. Keene! Do meet Miss Mariah Hodgeson. You must tell Miss Mariah about your visit to Lady Hippisley. It seems she's building her own laboratory at her home, if you can credit it!" she added to Mariah.

And so the round of introductions began—first to the matrons, and then to their daughters, and finally to those of their husbands, brothers, or sons who could be induced to come to an afternoon concert where there was no prospect of a good supper or cards.

With Mariah entirely absorbed by Mrs. Keene and her coterie, and Nora quietly occupying a place by the refreshment table, Rosalind was able to fade into the background and keep her eye on Penelope.

It was, Rosalind had to admit, one of the most impressive performances she'd ever seen on the part of a young girl at her first real party. Penelope's deportment was entirely correct. She kept her eyes downcast, lifting them only long enough to take fleeting glimpses of the room. When introduced, she smiled and spoke softly, but for the most part, she let the others do the talking. As a result, she soon had a ring of ladies, and the majority of the gentlemen, surrounding her.

"Well, my dear." Meredith stepped up close to Rosalind's side, so she could speak quietly. "Your little Miss Douglas has certainly charmed my company. I never thought to see you as chaperone, you know."

"It comes to us all, Meredith," murmured Rosalind. "Even to you one day."

"I daresay you are right. My nieces grow at an alarming rate. I hope they turn out half as well as this little one you've brought me today."

Rosalind smiled in polite acknowledgment. "I hate to ask, but I must do my duty. There seem to be a number of interested parties . . ." She made a circle with one finger to indicate the gentlemen gathering around Penelope.

"So I see," said Meredith. "And we've not even properly started yet. She'll be beating them off with a stick once the season is truly underway."

"Is there anyone we should be careful of?"

Meredith looked around. "Well, that depends. What do you intend for her?"

"What she intends for herself, a secure and comfortable establishment."

"You sound as if you don't approve."

"Do I? I hadn't meant to."

"Well, you know, not all of us can follow you and Alice into the wilds of independent womanhood. Some of us must have a home." Meredith paused. "Not that you don't have a home. Of course you do. I only meant . . ."

"I know what you meant," said Rosalind easily.

"I'd say most of the ones here today are pretty well fixed in terms of prospects. I'm not sure I'd wish Mrs. Grant on anyone as a mother-in-law." She nodded to a sour-faced woman dressed all in black and white. "There's been some rumors that Garling's father has had a disappointment with his shares, but I don't know how serious it is yet. Now, if she doesn't object to a man with a profession, Mrs. Sowerly's eldest is a fine prospect. He's going to inherit his father's practice and should do very well by it."

Rosalind nodded and listened with half an ear as her friend rattled off the names and their qualifications. Her gaze swept the room, and she located each of the girls. Mariah was talking animatedly with a bearded gentleman, who appeared to be listening with close attention. Nora was still at the refreshment table, nibbling a biscuit and watching the room with a hint of private amusement in her eyes. To Rosalind, she looked a bit like she was planning on picking pockets.

Hopefully, no one else sees that.

Penelope's ring of admirers was broken by a trio of severe-looking matrons and their several daughters.

"You'll have to excuse me, Meredith," said Rosalind. "I may need to rescue Pen."

The footman in plain livery opened the door. A dignified matron dressed in black strolled in on the arm of a tall, lean young man.

Rosalind's heart stopped dead.

The man was Cantrell.

CHAPTER 24

Riposte

*. . . he could think with pleasure of his own
importance, and, unshackled by business, occupy
himself solely in being civil to all the world.*

Jane Austen, *Pride and Prejudice*

"Rosalind," said Meredith. "You look quite faint. Whatever is it?"

"I can't explain now." She pressed her friend's hand. "I must get my girls away."

But it was too late. Cantrell had already seen them. While Rosalind watched, he excused himself from the dignified woman he had come in with and began to make his way over to where Nora stood.

Rosalind moved. She slid through the knots and bundles of people, her heart in her throat. She felt them turn to stare at her rudeness, but she could not afford to care. All that mattered was getting between Cantrell and the girls.

She missed the mark by inches. Nora saw him first and took a reflexive step back. Mariah was next. She swung about to face him, almost knocking the drink out of the hand of the bearded man.

Penelope, glancing between the matrons and their daughters, saw him last.

And fainted dead away.

"Pen!" Cantrell changed direction, swooping down toward her. Everyone turned. Everyone stared. Before he could reach Pen's side, Nora caught him by the shoulder and jerked him back.

"You keep away from her!" she shouted.

The assembly drew back in shock. Rosalind reached Penelope's side and dropped to her knees. She took the young woman's wrist and touched her forehead.

Meredith arrived on her heels.

"Oh dear, oh dear. The heat, of course," Meredith said to her milling guests. "Lennard! Winston! Help me with this young lady. The morning room will be much cooler. Aimes! We require some smelling salts!"

The footmen gently lifted Penelope and carried her away. Meredith followed closely.

"The poor child," Cantrell was saying to the woman he escorted and the room in general. "She's so delicate. I never meant . . ."

"You meant everything!" snapped Mariah.

Cantrell started. "Oh, no, Mariah. You are mistaken! I would never do anything to hurt poor Penelope."

The entirety of the room was riveted. There was no escaping the scene. No undoing the gossip that would shortly boil up to the surface.

No wiping the laughter from Cantrell's shining green eyes.

Rosalind felt a bright blaze of anger toward him, and the enormity of her own blunder.

"Mariah, Nora," she said. "You'd best go see to Pen."

Thankfully, the young women obeyed. At least Mariah did. When Nora did not show any sign of moving, she grabbed Nora by the hand and all but dragged her from the room. Nora cast one more murderous glare over her shoulder before she found her feet and hurried away with her sister.

Rosalind kept herself planted directly in Cantrell's path. She snapped open her fan, as if it could act as a shield. When Cantrell finally deigned to turn his gaze toward her, his handsome face was a study in concern.

"Please believe me, Miss Thorne," he pleaded. "If I had known that my arrival would have such an effect on poor Penelope, I should *never* have come."

"Campbell?" The matron he had escorted into the room sailed up beside him. "Who is that girl?"

Campbell? Rosalind arched one brow. Cantrell ignored her.

"She's someone I knew once in the country," he told the woman. Worse, he pitched his voice to carry. Rosalind felt the blood drain from her face. He wanted his story to be heard, and to be spread. "I'm afraid she cherished a schoolgirl affection for me, but I had thought . . ." He shook his head sadly. "Poor little thing!"

"And this?" The woman's voice quavered as she gestured toward Rosalind. She was a narrow woman with intelligent eyes. Her olive complexion had gone a little sallow with age. She wore a dress of black velvet with gray trim. A delicate lace cap covered her silver hair.

"Oh, I am so sorry," said Cantrell. "Mrs. Cecil Asherton, may I present Miss Rosalind Thorne?"

"*The* Miss Rosalind Thorne?" exclaimed Mrs. Asherton. "I am delighted! Campbell, you never told me you and she were acquainted!" She gave him a playful pat on his arm.

"We've met only recently," said Rosalind. "I had no idea he would be here."

"Oh, well, that's my doing," Mrs. Asherton told her. "My son was supposed to accompany me, you know, but he begged off at the last minute, and Campbell offered to escort me instead."

"Again, if I'd had any idea . . . ," said Cantrell earnestly.

"Yes, I'm sure," replied Rosalind. "Now I pray you will excuse me. I have to see to my friend."

"Yes, yes, of course. Poor girl," murmured Mrs. Asherton. "I do hope she will be all right."

So do I, thought Rosalind as she hurried from the room.

Meredith was waiting at the foot of the stairs.

"There you are," she said. "Your girls are just through there." She gestured toward the nearest door. "My dear Rosalind, I am so sorry. I have no idea who that Mr. Campbell is or how he was able to importune Mrs. Asherton into inviting him. Your Penelope will be fine in just a few minutes . . ."

"I must get them all home."

"I've already sent for your carriage. Once it's brought round, Winston will show you the way. I have to go back and see to my guests. You'll let me know . . ."

"As soon as I can," said Rosalind. She leaned close. "I beg you, tell anyone who asks that Penelope is suffering a slight indisposition from the heat, and do not let Mr. Campbell out of your sight until we are gone. I'll explain later."

Meredith squeezed her hand in promise and hurried back to the salon to attempt to calm her guests and salvage her party. Alone, Rosalind hurried to find her young charges.

It was obvious no one had planned on using the little morning room today. The drapes were still drawn, and no candles had been lit. Penelope stretched out on the sofa. Her eyes were open and glittering with tears. Mariah held a hand-kerchief to Penelope's head, her expression grim.

"How did Cantrell get here?" demanded Nora as soon as Rosalind shut the door. "Who told him we would be here? Did you know . . . !"

"Don't be ridiculous," said Mariah coldly. "If she'd known, she never would have brought us."

"He's never going to leave me alone," breathed Penelope.

"No, he isn't, is he, Nora?" The edge on Mariah's words could have cut stone.

Nora turned on Mariah, face filled with anger.

"Stop!" ordered Rosalind. Startled, they both turned toward her. "We must leave quickly," she told them all. "You can cut each other to pieces in the carriage if you like, but not before."

Her words and her tone startled the sisters into submission, which was fortunate, because just then the door opened and two maids appeared, carrying their bonnets and wraps.

"If you please, miss . . . ," the first maid began.

"Yes, thank you," said Rosalind, appalled at her own impatience. But she could not calm herself. She had to get them all out of here.

I never should have brought them. I should have known. He was watching. He had a spy in the house. What did I think would happen?

Not this. She had not realized he had already found another family to shelter him. She had assumed him to be hanging his hopes on whatever he could squeeze out of the Douglases. The maids were brisk and efficient. With some coaxing, Penelope was gotten to her feet, and all three young women were quickly bundled up. The footman, Winston, arrived to inform them that the carriage was ready. Mariah held Penelope's arm. Nora followed her sisters down the stairs, her face pale as death and just as implacable.

Once the driver closed them all into the carriage. Rosalind felt herself sag back against the squabs.

"Now," she said. "If you must argue, please do go ahead."

"Thank you for your kind permission," replied Mariah. "I'm so glad we needn't stand on ceremony."

"Stop it!" cried Penelope. "Just . . . stop."

"Goddamn the man!" Nora barked. "Why *now*?"

"Yes, why?" said Mariah. "I can't think."

"Mariah," returned Nora, "listen to Pen and stop, would you?"

"Yes, of course." She folded her hands in her lap. "I do beg your pardon."

"I can't stand it!" wailed Pen. "I'm going to smother and *die!*"

"You'll be all right," said Nora. "Just give yourself a minute."

"I will not be all right!" snapped Pen. "What's going to happen when my brother finds out!"

"He needn't find out," said Nora. "I'm certainly not going to tell him. Are you, Mariah?"

Mariah turned her face toward the carriage window.

"Miss Thorne?" said Nora.

"Silence may not answer," Rosalind said. "What will happen if he hears from another source?"

"Who do . . . You can't mean you're going to tell *Bethany?*" cried Nora.

Rosalind said nothing.

"Oh Lord, move over, Pen. It's my turn to faint. You cannot mean it, Miss Thorne. If you tell Bethany, she's sure to tell Douglas, and then—"

"Please, Miss Thorne," interrupted Penelope. Her voice was small and weak. She looked much younger than she had in Meredith's salon, surrounded by her admirers. "You can't tell my brother! It will be the end of everything."

Rosalind didn't answer. In truth, she didn't know what answer to give. It was Bethany who had engaged her to help find out what had happened to the pearls and to her family. She owed her a full account of what had happened this afternoon. At the same time, she needed these girls to trust her— all of them—if she was to find those answers.

What am I to do? This is my fault. I brought them out too soon. I should have made sure of Cantrell, first and foremost.

I should have set aside my concerns and confronted Betsy at once.

Rosalind pushed her self-pity aside. She looked at each of the young women with her, willing herself to see them clearly. Penelope, delicate enough to faint from shock, but knowing enough to put on one of the most adept social performances Rosalind had ever witnessed. Nora, disgraced, restless, and frightened.

Frightened. The word repeated itself in Rosalind's mind. Of course, she had reason to be frightened, with Cantrell appearing so suddenly.

Then there was Mariah. Bland, watchful, careful Mariah.

Why now? Nora had asked the same question Rosalind had been asking.

Yes, why? Mariah had answered. *I can't think.*

But Mariah didn't need to think, because it was very clear Mariah knew.

CHAPTER 25

The Gossip Belowstairs

How little did you tell me of what passed . . . !

Jane Austen, *Pride and Prejudice*

If there was one thing Amelia knew from her time in service, it was that everyone talked. Oh, the family might post what rules they pleased in the servants' hall, but nothing was going to stop the staff from talking about them that lived upstairs.

The question from the moment she had set foot in the house was how to get them to talk to *her*. Especially after that Mrs. Hodgeson went and gave the game away.

But there were two good ways to break through a silence, and Amelia was determined to use them both. The first was to make yourself useful. Over the past two days, she'd set about this with a will. She'd helped iron and fold the sheets and linens. She'd fetched, and she'd carried. She'd made no bones about helping haul pails of water or buckets of coal.

But mostly, she'd sat at the long table in the servants' hall, with the piles of mending, and plied her needle alongside Betsy and whoever else might come in for their turn. As soon as Miss Thorne had left with the young ladies for their musical, or music-*cale*, or whatever it might be, she'd immediately grabbed her workbasket and headed downstairs to join the others at the worktable.

The other way to loosen tongues, of course, was to talk. So, she did. Not that she gave away anything important, mind, but it was plain that plenty in the house were curious about Miss Thorne. So, Amelia decided that it would be all right to drop a few names, make a few hints, and add in a nod or two to the wise. And if a story or two were simply made up out of whole cloth, what was the harm?

In return for her little confidences and confections, Amelia heard about the staff's families and how they themselves had come to be in service. She heard that Mr. Dowdeswell had a sister who hadn't spoken to him in years, and how Mrs. Hare was left a widow at just eighteen, when her husband was killed by a stray shot during a hunting party.

She heard how Betsy had no plans to stay in service.

"Not me!" she said, leaning confidentially over the table-cloth she was mending. "One of these days, when I've saved my bit, you won't see me for dust!"

"Oh?" Amelia tried not to show any eagerness, but inside she was thinking about the note, and her talk about that note, and all Betsy had said about looking after oneself. "And just where will you go, then?"

But Betsy just gave her a saucy wink. "Never you mind," she said. "Let's just say there's a much better place waiting for me!"

"Oh, fudge!" said Mrs. Hare. "You couldn't hold on to tuppence if your life depended on it, you fool girl."

"Maybe I could. Maybe I couldn't," said Betsy loftily. "Maybe there's more than tuppence to be got."

"Where from? That's what I'd like to know!"

Betsy grinned. "I'll just bet you would."

Mrs. Hare reached out and gave her a hard rap on the wrist. "You go on like that, my girl, you'll end up in a world of trouble." She pointed one blunt finger at her. "Now, you just go take them fresh towels upstairs and help Rachael get the rooms done up."

Betsy pulled a face, and Mrs. Hare returned a glower. Betsy climbed to her feet.

"Yes, Mrs. Hare," she muttered, and stalked away.

Mrs. Hare shook her head and set about folding up the tablecloth Betsy had been working on.

"So, your Miss Thorne's taken charge of the young misses," she said. "I'm sure we all wish her luck with that. Heaven knows, someone's got to look out for them, especially now."

"Well, you know I shouldn't say," Amelia demurred. "But that's only a distraction, isn't it? She may look like she's playing chaperone, but you can be sure she's close on the track of them pearls." This was more than she should have properly said, but it put the conversation where Amelia wanted it to be.

"Oho?" Mrs. Hare raised her brows. "Got someone in mind, has she?"

Amelia shrugged and tucked and rolled a bit more of the hem she was working on so she could tack it down with close, careful stitches.

"What I can't work out is how they went missing in the first place," she said. "I mean, I know what Miss Thorne got told, about them just being left out and all, but it doesn't make no sense to me. How do you just forget the fortune that's been hanging round your neck all day?"

"Well, it wouldn't normally, would it? But the house was in such an uproar that night, I don't wonder half of us wouldn't forget where we put our own heads."

"Uproar? What happened? I mean, I know old Mrs. Hodgeson was poorly . . ."

"Poorly!" Mrs. Hare snorted. "I'd give her poorly if I had my way. Kicking up a fuss at the *king's funeral!*" She lowered her voice.

"No!" breathed Amelia.

Mrs. Hare nodded solemnly.

"Old Mrs. Hodgeson insisted on going with Mr. and Mrs. Douglas, didn't she? *And* that Mr. Hodgeson go with them. Well. It seems that their presence did not sit well with old Sir Jasper."

Amelia nodded. That she could readily believe, given what she'd heard about the old man.

"Now, I don't know exactly what happened, but I expect Mrs. Hodgeson was her usual self, and his nibs was not one to overlook her pushing and her fussing and declaring this, that, and the other, and he told her what he thought of her."

"He didn't!"

"He did. And it was such a set-down, it seems the old lady had one of her fits right there in the church!"

"Oh, my word!" cried Amelia.

"So, her and Mr. Hodgeson's back early, and that Gilpin's ordering everything her mistress needs, and Mr. Hodgeson's calling for brandy and dinner and I don't know what all, and the girls are fluttering about, and that's *before* Mr. and Mrs. Douglas get home. He's red in the face, and she's not much better. And the row they has! You could hear them through half the house!"

"But what about?"

"What wasn't it about? Him despairing about her family, her wanting to know why he won't stand up to the old man, him saying they all have to make sacrifices for the family's prosperity, her saying that don't mean selling their souls for the money . . ."

"Goodness," murmured Amelia.

"Well . . ." Mrs. Hare glanced over her shoulder. "In the middle of all this, Gilpin comes running down, saying her missus is in hysterics, and Mrs. Douglas, she goes up to see what she can do to help, and Mr. Douglas, he shuts himself up in his room, and somewhere in the night, the pearls is away with the fairies."

Amelia let herself be appropriately shocked by all of this. At the same time, she noticed Mr. Dowdeswell coming out of his pantry, with one of the ledger books under his arm.

"Well, I say it's all a shame," she announced.

Dowdeswell heard, and he stopped. To judge from his thunderous expression, he was getting ready to give her a dressing-down for running her idle tongue, never mind her hands were as busy as could be.

"I hope," he said ponderously, "you're not engaged in low gossip, my girl. I'd hate to have to tell your Miss Thorne you were up to any such while in our company."

"I should say not!" cried Amelia. "I was only going to remark that my Miss Thorne is acquainted with the *very* best families, and I have never heard of such carryings-on as these Hodgesons get up to."

At this dismissal of the Hodgesons, Dowdeswell's hackles lowered considerably.

"Well, it is not for me to say," he told her loftily, "but if I was to venture an opinion, I would tend to agree."

Amelia bent closer to her hem. "I don't say it argues against Mr. Douglas's judgment, but it wasn't as if he hadn't gotten a look at the mother before he married the daughter, is it? Or the father, either."

"Love, we are assured, is blind." But he didn't sound very certain of it.

Mrs. Hare rolled her eyes and humphed.

"That's as may be." Amelia held up her napkin to catch the light from the windows, so she could better see her handiwork. "But my own mother always said blood will tell."

Amelia's mother had never said any such thing, but a knowing light sparked in Mr. Dowdeswell's dark eyes.

"Your mother was a wise woman. Ah! It was a sad, sad

day for the family when we lost Mr. Addison. Such an unassuming young man. So very aware of his position, and ready
to be instructed by his elders!"

"Mr. Addison?" asked Amelia innocently.

"The current Mr. Douglas's cousin," said Mr. Dowdeswell. "The son of Mr. Huet Douglas. He was lost to us after
a riding accident."

"You mean he fell from his horse? Or was it a bad jump? I
worked in a house once where the son was forever trying to
jump over hedges and them things and went and broke his
neck! Horrible!"

"It was neither. He . . ." Mr. Dowdeswell dropped his
voice. "He vanished."

Amelia opened her eyes wide in shock.

Mr. Dowdeswell nodded solemnly. "No trace of him was
ever found. It was a bleak, bad time for Sir Jasper. For all of
us," he added heavily, and Amelia saw something suspiciously
like a tear glittering in his eye. Then he cleared his throat.
"Yes, well. You get on with your work now." He stalked away
and vanished into his pantry.

Mrs. Hare shook her head.

"Poor Dowdeswell. He loved his Mr. Addison like his
own. Won't hear a word said against him. Not healthy, that's
what I says."

"What do you mean?" asked Amelia.

"I mean you get too close to the family and you end up
selling off pieces of your soul, and for what?" she snorted.
"Do your job, but remember it is a job. No matter what
they"—she pointed to the ceiling—"may say, you ain't family, and you never will be. Just awful to see the way some will
fawn and fall in love with the ones that would pay them off
the minute things get tight."

"So, they was close, this Mr. Addison and Mr. Dowdeswell?"

"He'd like to think they were. That's why he spins them fairy stories. Trying to save the young master's reputation. That's what."

"You mean Mr. Addison didn't vanish?"

"Oh, he vanished, for certain. But it wasn't no accident. I made up his room afterward, didn't I? Didn't I find half a dozen shirts missing, and neckcloths and pantaloons? He didn't get in any accident. He scarpered."

"So you think he's still alive?"

"I don't think anything. But why wouldn't he? He didn't want the job. Sir Jasper's a hard taskmaster. And we've all seen how he treats Mr. Douglas. Why not just chuck it and go off somewhere?"

"Here." Amelia leaned forward. "There wasn't any funny business, was there?"

"What do you mean?"

"Well, I'd heard that Mr. Huet . . . he had something going on the side. In fact, he had a lot going."

Mrs. Hare looked over her shoulder. "And these are the people who have a nerve to go on about my Mrs. Douglas, when all she's ever done is try to look after her own."

"So there was something?"

"Well, as to Mr. Addison, I can't say for sure. But when your old da's got three or four other wives, and you're the only one who's supposed to be legitimate, only you ain't got no Ma, and she's supposed to have died bringing you into the world? Well, it wouldn't be human not to wonder if you was really any more legitimate than them others."

"But did he know, do you think? Could that be why he ran off? He didn't want to be found out as a . . . you know, a natural son?"

"Bless you! You probably read novels, don't you? Who was to find out? Who was to even look, once Sir Jasper had his say?"

"Why, all them other kids," said Amelia.

Mrs. Hare drew back. "Now, that's a nasty, suspicious thought." But there was more relish than anger in her voice. "But nothing to it, I daresay, or we'd have heard by now."

But then the bell rang, and the downstairs maid came into the hall, arguing with the second footman, and everyone had to be up and about and doing. Amelia found herself rather abruptly left to her mending and her thoughts.

And the fact that she'd have a deal to tell Miss Thorne when she got back.

CHAPTER 26

At Last, Enough

*Who should suffer but myself? It has been my
own doing, and I ought to feel it.*

Jane Austen, *Pride and Prejudice*

In the end, the question of whether Rosalind should tell
Bethany what had happened became a moot point. Unfortunately, the carriage ride did not last long enough for
Penelope to recover fully from her faint. The fact of the party
returning from the concert would have been enough to create
a stir in the Portsmouth Square house, but Penelope coming
home supported on Mariah's arm must necessarily cause an
uproar. And, of course, someone went running at once to
fetch Bethany.

Rosalind was helping to get Penelope settled on the sofa in
her sitting room when Bethany burst in.

"What on earth's happened!" she cried.

Nora had vanished into her own rooms. Mariah was laying a series of shawls over Penelope where she lay. Betsy slipped
into the room behind Bethany, carrying a basin of steaming
water.

Rosalind tried to catch the maid's eye and failed.

"Nothing happened, Bethany." Penelope pushed herself upright on the sofa. "I had a faint. That's all. Miss Thorne thought it better that we return home."

It was a smooth lie, and earnestly told. Bethany appeared ready to believe it.

Mariah laid down the last shawl. "Cantrell was at the concert."

"Mariah!" shrieked Penelope. "How could you!"

Betsy scuttled out of the room. Bethany gripped the back of the sofa. "Rosalind?"

"I am so sorry, Bethany," said Rosalind. "I did not realize how deeply he had already laid his plans."

"Don't tell my brother!" Penelope begged. "Please, please, he'll never let me out of the house again. You *know* he won't!"

"Perhaps he shouldn't," said Bethany. She pressed her hands against her cheeks. "But how! How could he know! It was all so last minute, we didn't even know Nora would be in attendance!"

"What's all this?"

Mrs. Hodgeson bustled through the open door, her handkerchief clutched in her bony hand. "Who is 'he'? What did 'he' know? Bethany?" She faced her eldest daughter.

Penelope buried her face in her hands. "I'm lost! Everything's lost!"

"Then you might show some resolution," muttered Mariah.

"But what *has happened*?" demanded Mrs. Hodgeson.

Bethany sighed. "It seems Cantrell somehow followed the girls to the concert."

"What!" cried Mrs. Hodgeson. "Miss Thorne? How can this be! What have you done!"

"He did not follow us," said Rosalind. "Not directly. He arrived with a Mrs. Asherton, who said he offered to escort her when her own son cried off—"

"And exactly who is this Mrs. Asherton?" demanded Mrs. Hodgeson, interrupting. "What kind of woman is she, to be walking about with such a man?" Mrs. Hodgeson drew herself upright, her entire stance becoming one of righteous indignation. "No good herself, I'll be bound! Probably dangling after him. Some young widow seduced by a pair of green eyes!"

"She said that Cantrell is a friend of her son's and agreed to escort her to the concert," replied Rosalind as calmly as she could. "There is no reason to believe that part of it is anything other than what it seems. But I have no doubt that Cantrell did so because somehow he knew Nora and Penelope would be there."

"Oh, poor dear Pen!" Mrs. Hodgeson wiped at her eyes with her kerchief. "Poor, frail, beautiful child! Oh, what you must have suffered!"

"You mustn't tax yourself, Mama," said Bethany. "It's not good for you. Perhaps you should go lie down?"

"How can I rest when that *person* is out there hounding us?" Mrs Hodgeson fluttered her handkerchief in the general direction of the windows. "And what, Miss Thorne, are you doing about it?"

Rosalind felt the words like a blow. It was of no help that she had been asking herself much the same question.

"The question becomes, How is he getting his information?" Rosalind could not help thinking of how quickly Betsy had left the room. "When we know that, we will better be able to counter him."

"Yes, well, with Sir Jasper having planted so many spies in this house, I'm sure none of our secrets are safe!" Mrs. Hodgeson sounded more angry than frightened at this thought. "However, now, since I see Penelope is so well attended, I shall go see my poor Norah." Mrs. Hodgeson sniffed. "She will be prostrate with fear!"

Rosalind thought this highly unlikely, but neither she nor

Bethany made any move to stop Mrs. Hodgeson as she bustled from the room.

Pen rolled onto her side, huddling underneath the shawls that had been laid over her.

"I'll stay with Pen," said Mariah. "You'd better go visit Nora, Bethany. I don't think she'll be in any mood to bear with Mama's ministrations, and you are better placed to tamp down the explosion."

"Yes," said Bethany. "I expect you're right. Rosalind?"

"Yes, of course."

Rosalind followed Bethany out into the corridor. Before they had gone more than a few steps, Bethany stopped and turned abruptly.

"Rosalind? You must tell me what really happened."

"Yes, of course. But we should talk in my room."

Bethany agreed. When they entered Rosalind's sitting room, Amelia was there, sitting beside the window and bent over some fresh mending.

"Amelia," said Rosalind. "I need you to go find Betsy at once and bring her here."

"Of course, miss." Amelia curtsied and hurried out.

"Betsy!" Bethany sank slowly into one of the chairs by the fire. "What has she to do with any of this?"

"I don't know yet," said Rosalind. "But I have reason to believe she may know something useful."

Bethany blinked, as if dazed, but she rallied quickly. "Well, never mind Betsy for now. Tell me what happened to Penelope!"

Slowly, carefully, she told her friend how they had arrived at Meredith's and how at first, everything had gone well. Penelope had shown every sign of some early conquests, and even Mariah had seemed to be enjoying the company.

And then Cantrell arrived, and Penelope swooned and Cantrell made certain those nearest him in the room room clearly heard his broad hints at her past infatuation.

"He knew, didn't he?" said Bethany. "That what he said would create talk?"

"Yes," said Rosalind. "The whole of it was on purpose. I am sorry, Bethany," she added. "I should have realized that he might have found out about the plan. But I did not expect him to have friends in town. At least not such that would intersect . . ." She stopped, unusually tongue-tied. "I underestimated him."

"We all did," said Bethany. "It is not your fault."

Rosalind was not entirely certain about that. Cantrell did not arrive at Meredith's by accident. He had known they would be there.

Someone had told him. He'd had time to plan. He'd known exactly what he was doing when he raised his voice and made sure the gathering knew that he'd met Penelope in the country and that she was sick with love for him.

Someone in the house had decided that instead of siding with their family, with their daughters or their sisters, they would take the side of the man who had his heart set on destroying them all.

But he had not been seen at the house since that first day. Neither had any confederate. That meant this someone also knew where he could be found.

She'd been here three days, and she'd failed to find his collaborator, just as she had failed to find the pearls or the thief or what secret tied Nora and Mariah so tightly together.

She had, in short, accomplished exactly nothing.

Rosalind felt her jaw tighten.

"Where is she!" roared a man's voice.

Rosalind and Bethany both jumped. Douglas was charging up the stairs, his face red with anger and exertion.

"Where is she!" he bellowed again as he reached the landing.

"Douglas!" Bethany ran to his side. "What is this? What's happened?"

"This!" Douglas thrust the note into Bethany's hands. "It was delivered while I was with Sir Jasper!"

Bethany read the paper. When she finished, she met her husband's infuriated gaze. She held the note out to Rosalind, who took it gingerly. Her heart hammered in her chest as she read.

> *Dear Sir,*
> *I've no wish to alarm you, but today I was attending a concert given by a Mrs. Burgoyne, and there I was witness to the most extraordinary scene and undignified scene involving your grandson's family. I thought you would wish to know.*

There was no signature and no direction.

"Now," said Douglas icily. "Where. Is. She?"

"There's no need for this uproar, Douglas." Nora walked in calmly through the door Douglas had left open behind him. "I am right here."

"Is this true?" He snatched the paper from Rosalind and thrust it at Nora.

Nora took the note and read it with an appearance of disinterest. But Rosalind saw her hand tremble.

"Cantrell wrote this," she said as she held the note out for Douglas. "Don't you know his hand?"

"But is it true?" demanded Douglas. "Did this . . . this scene happen?"

"It did," said Bethany. "And Cantrell was there to cause it."

"He was . . ." Douglas choked. "My God! Pen! He's after Pen!"

"Of course he isn't," said Nora tartly. "He's after me."

"Then he shall have you," said her brother-in-law, his voice heavy as stone. "Get out."

"Douglas!" cried Bethany.

"No, Bethany, it's all right," said Nora.

Where did she learn such self-command? wondered Rosalind. Nora even managed a hint of a smile.

"After such an event, it is only right that Mr. Douglas should be angry," Nora went on.

"Do not try any of your clever tricks with me!" Douglas sneered. "You will leave my house, at once, with . . ."

"No," said Bethany.

Douglas rounded on her. "*What?*"

Bethany did not so much as flinch. "I said no. Nora is my sister. If she leaves this house, I will go with her."

"No, Bethany," said Nora. "There's no need for that. I've outstayed my welcome. I'll go."

"Nora, you can't."

"I did before," said Nora easily. "Never you mind. I know how to take care of myself."

"I will not allow this! She is my sister!"

"In my house, under my roof—" began Douglas.

"Our house!" Bethany stabbed her finger toward the floor. "Our roof!"

"All you have is what's mine! You're lucky I don't throw all your ridiculous family into the gutter this instant!"

Bethany's hand fell to her side. She took a step backward. She seemed to Rosalind to shrink in on herself. All except her eyes. Her eyes blazed with fury and betrayal.

Douglas stood, chest heaving, hands trembling. "I'm sorry." He gasped out the words between gulps of air. "I didn't mean that. I didn't."

Bethany did not answer. Neither did she look away nor let her silent, stunned anger fade.

It was Nora who moved next. She walked up to her sister and whispered something in her ear. Bethany's whole body sagged, and Nora pressed her hand. Then she turned.

"Now then, Rosalind," she said briskly. "I think we'd better go."

Nora took Rosalind's arm. Rosalind was surprised enough that she let herself be steered away down the corridor and into Nora's bare room.

Nora shut the door. This seemed to be the limit of her composure, because she rested her head on the threshold.

"I never meant for this to happen," she said, her voice low and hard. "You must believe that. If I'd thought for one minute Cantrell would really come back, I never would have come within a thousand miles of my sisters. Any of them."

"I believe you," replied Rosalind.

Nora straightened and turned. "Thank you."

"Is there anywhere you can go?" Rosalind asked. She hoped that Bethany would convince Douglas to retract his demand for Nora to leave, but when she remembered the cold outrage in his voice, she was not sure. "Do you have friends who will help?"

"Yes, of course," said Nora with all her habitual concealing insouciance.

Rosalind just looked at her. Nora saw her open disbelief and shrugged.

"I'll be all right," she said, and gave a small laugh. "One thing about life with Cantrell. One learned to make do."

"You are welcome to stay at my house," Rosalind told her.

Nora drew back, startled. "Do you mean it?"

"It is small, and I will have to introduce you to my friend Alice Littlefield, who shares with me." Rosalind paused. "Actually, I think you two may well get on together."

This was the moment Amelia chose to make her reappearance. She hovered in the doorway and bobbed an uneasy curtsy.

"One moment please," said Rosalind as she crossed to her maid.

"She's not here, miss," whispered Amelia.

Rosalind swallowed her exclamation and arched her brows.

Amelia nodded vigorously. "Mrs. Hare said she was off on

an errand and nipped out before any could ask from who or where to."

Rosalind thought of Betsy hovering about Penelope and listening. This time she had to suppress a very strong desire to utter one of George Littlefield's more colorful curses.

"Some new disaster?" inquired Nora.

"Possibly," replied Rosalind blandly.

"Goodness," murmured Nora. "Well, in any case, I believe will take you up on your offer, Rosalind. Wandering around London all night is nowhere near as romantic as it sounds, especially in this weather."

Nora flashed one of her smiles full of bravado, but its edges were strained. *She's exhausted*, Rosalind thought. *This day is on the edge of being too much for her.*

It was a long moment before Nora spoke again, and this time Rosalind saw the struggle underneath her words.

"Why would you help me?"

"Because," said Rosalind, "I am hoping, eventually, you will trust me enough to tell me what you've been planning all this time."

She meant to add, *Then I may be able to finally help you.* But Nora had already turned away.

CHAPTER 27

A Morning Stroll

He did not leave his name, and till the next day it was only known that a gentleman had called on business.

Jane Austen, *Pride and Prejudice*

Johnny Wiggins supposed there must be worse things than keeping watch in the rain. In February. On what had to be the rawest afternoon of the year.

Mucking out stables, to take an example. In the rain. In February.

Digging ditches. In the rain. In February.

Come to that, any job was worse in the rain. In February.

Wiggins pulled his hat brim farther down and scowled at the terraced house across the way.

Not that he minded his job. Being a runner at Bow Street might mean being out in all weathers, but the pay was good, and the respect was better. His opinion was heard and valued in the pubs. Men bought him drinks. Sometimes they thought they'd get something for their generosity, and they might. If he was another man. If Wiggins was going to be bought, it wouldn't be for a mug of beer.

But might reconsider for a hot toddy or a swallow of good gin. Wiggins scowled at the sky and moved his barrow a bit closer to the wall.

The barrow full of rags had been his own idea. No one would question a rag-and-bone man loitering about a square such as this, especially not at such an early hour. Very few of these toffs would even look twice at him. If they did, they'd just think he was waiting on someone in one of the houses to collect their leavings for him. No one in their right mind would linger in this freezing damp, unless he had business.

And Wiggins had business, all right. His business was to keep watch on the house. So, that was what he did.

He watched the old lady and *her* maid head out for their daily drive. Unusual that. It was more her style to be shepherding one of the young ladies.

He watched the gentleman ride away in his new carriage, watched the old man stroll off on his constitutional.

Today, though, was a bit different. Today, a bit after one, a shaggy-looking fellow strolled into the square. He was hunched, unshaven, and bandy legged. *Porter,* Wiggins thought to himself.

The porter stationed himself at the corner and cast one eye at the iron-gray sky, spat, and folded his arms.

Now what are you waiting for, my good fellow?

Could be nothing, of course. Could be he hoped to pick up a job or two among the quality. Not likely in this neighborhood of fine houses. This sort would have their own footmen for the fetching and carrying. Still a harassed housekeeper might be of a mind to hire herself some help, if help were to be had.

All around them, the church bells began to peal the hour. The fellow spat again and straightened up.

Wiggins straightened, as well, and glanced toward the house he'd come to think of as his.

The fine carriage was being driven up to the front step. Wiggins couldn't see past it, but a glance between the wheels showed a whole flock of women's hemlines—cloaks and gowns and soft shoes. The girls were going out of an afternoon.

The porter spat as the carriage passed him. He settled down then, like he meant to wait forever.

As it happened, Porter and Wiggins alike had only a couple of hours to wait before the carriage returned. The flock of young misses and their guardian were helped out and hurried up the walk. Wiggins felt his brow scrunch up tight. He'd not expected them back until dark, at the earliest. *Something's gone wrong.*

Porter settled back on his heels, and Wiggins found himself wondering if he'd been expecting this.

Who are you? he wondered. *If you're looking for work, I'll eat my hat. You're already on a job. Same as me.*

The bells rang the quarter hour. Wiggins caught sight of motion in the alleyway beside the house. A minute later, a girl in a maid's cloak and bonnet, and with a lumpy bundle under her arm, scurried out and took off up the street like she feared something nasty might be nipping at her heels.

What're you about, then? Wiggins rubbed his chin.

Wiggins waited, but his blood was up. When the hour tolled again, and the house door opened once more. This time, it was the chaperone, Mr. Tauton's particular favorite, Miss Rosalind Thorne, who came down the steps. With her was one of the daughters of the house—the oldest of them, Wiggins thought. Between them, they carried a number of bandboxes and portmanteaux. Wiggins frowned again. What was this? What kind of family sent two women out into the street carrying their own bags?

Something had gone decidedly pear-shaped in that house. Even Porter was staring.

But Porter didn't move. Not even as the two women made for the mouth of the square and disappeared around the corner. Porter kept waiting, and Wiggins kept watching.

The bells rang the quarter hour. And the half. The light faded from watery gray to thick blue-black. Other houses on the square hung up their lanterns.

A shadow moved in the alleyway beside the house. Wiggins, tired and restless, straightened before he could stop himself. A male figure in a heavy wool coat and a battered broad-brimmed hat strode out from that narrow alley. He shouldered past a pair of women with their market baskets and came to a stop in front of the porter.

Wiggins's eyes narrowed. He was too far away to hear what was said, but it was a spirited conversation. Wool Coat was pointing at the street, probably telling the porter to go. Porter was holding up his hands, urging calm, trying to explain. Wool Coat jabbed a finger toward the street again. Porter retreated a few steps and spat in the gutter and slouched away, slowly, with many a long glance over his shoulder.

Wool Coat headed back to the house.

Now, this all might have nothing to do with Wiggins's business, but then again, it might. Wiggins did not trust his guts so much. They were chancy things and likely to get out of sorts after pickled beef or bad beer. But Porter had come with a purpose and just been shoved off. Now, it might be for the sake of preserving the peace and quiet of the neighborhood, but then again . . .

That was when a woman in a gray cloak and a broad black bonnet came scuttling out of that same narrow alleyway. She was either another servant, like the girl who'd left carrying her bundle, or someone who'd decided to dress as a servant for some little plan of their own. Whoever she was, she sighted on the porter's retreating back and set off after him. She moved at a steady pace, deliberate, but not so fast that she risked catching up.

Well, now, Johnny, me boy. This *is worth a look and see.*

Wiggins grabbed his barrow handles. He stepped into the street, drew a bead on the woman and the porter, and set out to follow them both.

Following a man through crowded streets was not such an easy job, especially at twilight. For preference, Wiggins would have had a partner for this job, but Mr. Townsend wasn't willing to spare another runner for what might well take all day and come to nothing.

So all on Johnny Wiggins again. His barrow wheel hit a pothole and jarred him up his arms. *Well, Wiggins, we'll show 'em all.*

It helped that the porter had no notion he was being followed by not one but two people. Miss Gray Cloak followed with a patience and skill that did her credit. It was no mean trick to track one raggedy man through this crowd. She was persistent, though, never getting too close, nor ever quite letting him get too far ahead.

Wiggins found himself worrying about the woman. Didn't she see how dark it had gotten? Any woman with a brain in her head knew the city could turn ugly after the sun went down.

Slowly, the neighborhood around them changed. The clean streets and smart houses gave way to older, sootier buildings that were crammed closer to each other and to the narrowing streets. The traffic and the people jostled together, and the noise got louder and more confused. Gin shops sprang up alongside the public houses. Crowds spilled out of both kinds, voices rising along with jugs and tankards.

Almost to Seven Dials. What business have we got here? Wiggins wondered.

Then, to Wiggins's surprise, Miss Gray Cloak changed her

tune. She gathered her hems and shouldered her way forward, then caught the porter by his sleeve. Wiggins put his barrow down, tugged down his hat brim.

The two of them talked. Porter pointed and then angled his hand and pointed again.

Giving directions.

The woman dropped some coins into his palm. The porter touched a finger to his forehead, pocketed the money, and strolled off, back in the direction from which he'd come.

For her part, the woman who'd just paid him off started up the side street.

Well now. What are we up to?

With a twinge, Wiggins abandoned his barrow. There wasn't a hope in the world that it would still be there when he got back, but needs must. This was a narrow street, and he might need to move sharpish before all was said and done. The barrow would only get in his way.

By herself, Miss Gray Cloak was easier to follow than the porter had been. She moved faster, to be sure, but her bonnet was far and away the best to be seen. All Wiggins needed to do was keep his eye fixed on its crown and brim as she bobbed and weaved among the washerwomen, basket men, and as wide an assortment of idlers as could fit themselves in between.

The house she stopped in front of was a ramshackle affair. From the looks of the roof and the half-timbered upper story, it had likely been there since this cobbled street was a dirt track. Still Wiggins had seen plenty worse. Evidently, the woman had, too, or maybe she'd finally realized the risk she was running. Several of the idlers on the street had taken note of her good cloak and the ribbons on her bonnet. Either way, she didn't hesitate a moment to climb the step and pound sharply on the door. The door opened, there was a pause, and the woman was taken inside.

"'Ere, you!" Wiggins hailed the nearest idler. "Wot's that house, then?"

The idler was a greasy man, and he gave the house a bleary eye. "'At's Mother Carey's. You need a room? It's cleaner than some."

"As it happens," said Wiggins. "Thanks."

The idler shrugged and nodded, and Wiggins took himself off. Instead of going to the front of "Mother Carey's," however, he veered around the side of the building. As he figured, there was a garden at the back, leastwise, that was what he guessed was behind the battered brick wall.

This was a risk, and maybe a fool's errand. But what choice did he have? It was move now or go back to standing about for God knows how long, waiting for a suspicious face to poke its nose out of that house.

No thank you. Done enough of that.

So it was over the wall for Johnny Wiggins. On the other side waited a weedy patch of green, with a slop yard and a chicken run. The birds clucked and squawked in their coop as he slipped past.

The kitchen window was dark, thankfully. Whatever servants drudged for this house, they were already gone for the day. Wiggins tried the kitchen door and found it open. There was, as he had hoped, a flight of stairs leading to the upstairs. He unknotted his neckcloth and mussed his hair and prepared a lie about being a cousin here to shift some furniture, should anybody ask.

Nobody did. He met no one going up the stairs, and when he got to the upper story, he saw that the four doors lining the corridor at the top of the stairs were all shut tight. But from the first of them, voices could be heard, clear as day.

"Liar!" bellowed a man.

"That's your specialty," replied a woman's cold voice.

Wiggins stole up beside the door and pressed his back against the wall.

"Well, if you think you can bribe me to go away quietly, you're most mistaken, my dear."

Thank the Good Lord for thin doors, thought Wiggins.

"Bribe you?" the woman sneered. "This is charity, Mr. Cantrell. It is clear you find yourself in straits. This will buy you out, if you move quickly. I can give you a name . . ."

"A name? A few bits and bobs? Oh, no, my dear, I came back for my wife, and I will accept nothing less."

"No." The word was cold, hard, and final.

"Well, now, you mustn't worry about any mistreatment." Wiggins could hear the wolfish grin in the fellow's—Cantrell's—voice. "There'll be no demands of that kind. I find that attraction has most definitely run its course. But that's a tidy little scheme being run on his lordship, and as it is the results of my patient tutelage, I figure I'm due my commission." He paused significantly. "You know all about commissions, do you not? I'm sure your Mr. Sommerton is demanding his. Does he know who he's really paying? I expect not," Cantrell answered himself. "Another reason you're going to keep quiet and do as I say."

"You think we're going to work for you?"

"I know you are," he answered. "And you'll keep quiet, too. You haven't seen half of what I can do to you if you don't behave. Oh," he said, his voice filled with fake solicitude, "now you've gone all pale. Have some wine."

"I want nothing from you."

"Just as well. It's very bad. But . . ." There was a pause. Wiggins suspected the man was drinking.

"Where did you hear about Sommerton?" asked the woman.

"Ah, now, you can't expect me to go giving away all my secrets," purred Cantrell. "Now, you'd better trot along home. These streets are hardly safe for a gentlewoman." He sneered the last word. "We'll call what you've brought a down payment. I'll let you know when I need more."

More silence. Wiggins conceived the idea that if he touched that door now, he'd be able to feel the burn of the woman's anger through it.

"Very well," she said.

"That's better." Cantrell was smiling. He was also moving toward the door. Wiggins could hear his boots on the bare boards. "I'll . . ."

But whatever Cantrell was going to do, Wiggins didn't hear it. He was already bolting down the back stairs.

Mr. Tauton would want to hear about this.

CHAPTER 28

The Houseguest

Their manner of living . . . was unsettled in the extreme.

Jane Austen, *Pride and Prejudice*

"Rosalind?" Alice hurried down the stairs as Rosalind and Nora shouldered their way into the narrow foyer of Little Russell Street. "What's happened?"

"Rather a lot, I'm afraid." Rosalind set the luggage down and stripped off her gloves. "Alice, this is . . ."

"Nora Hodgeson." Nora put down both portmanteau and bandbox and made her curtsy. "My apologies for the intrusion."

"Not at all," said Alice. "You're perfectly welcome. Rosalind?" Alice jerked her chin toward the parlor.

"Yes, of course," said Rosalind. The truth was she was abominably tired, but there was no putting Alice off. Not that she wanted to. Alice deserved an explanation.

She faced Nora. "I'll help you take your things up to the spare room. I'm afraid we are a little short of space . . ."

"Please don't worry," said Nora, with all her habitual

breezy cheer. "I assure you, compared to some of the places I've fetched up, this is positively palatial."

Ignoring Alice's glower, Rosalind helped carry Nora's luggage upstairs and left her to get settled in the back bedroom. Then she hurried back downstairs to meet Alice in the parlor.

That room had grown even more untidy since she'd last seen it. Looking at the plate with the shards of eggshell and scattered crumbs, Rosalind strongly suspected Alice had been feeding herself with boiled eggs and toasted muffins prepared on the parlor hearth.

Alice, however, was not about to give Rosalind a moment to comment on this.

"What on *earth* has happened?" she demanded. "You've never been one for bringing home strays before. And where's Amelia?"

"Nora has been thrown out of the house by her brother-in-law," said Rosalind. "She had nowhere to go. And Amelia is still at Portsmouth Square, trying to buttonhole a maid who has been playing spy."

"Oh dear," murmured Alice. "Things have gotten busy, haven't they?"

"I'm afraid so." Rosalind settled slowly into her chair. She pressed her palm against the desktop, as if she needed to be steadied. "It's this man, Bryan Cantrell," she said. "He found out . . . I don't yet know how . . ."

"But you suspect your missing maid?" inquired Alice.

"Yes," agreed Rosalind. "By whatever means, Cantrell found out Nora was to attend a concert with me and her sisters, and . . . he was there."

"Well," said Alice, "that can hardly be considered her fault. London society is not that large . . ."

"There was a scene, Alice," said Rosalind. "One of the girls fainted. Cantrell then proceeded to write an anonymous letter to Sir Jasper Douglas, who holds the family purse strings, saying there had been an unseemly commotion. Douglas's response was to throw Nora out."

"Oh," said Alice. "Oh dear."

"Yes, exactly," agreed Rosalind.

"Well, of course you couldn't let her wander the streets. But has she no friends of her own she can apply to?"

"Possibly, but . . . Alice, I don't want to let her go just yet."

"Ah. I thought this might not be pure charity."

"Yes." Rosalind felt her mouth tighten into a crooked, humorless smile. "It seems I have become the worst sort of mercenary."

Alice sighed. "Rosalind, you know that's not what I meant. Obviously, you think she can tell you something about these missing pearls. So, it's natural you should want to keep her nearby."

"That, and I'm positive there's more to her than meets the eye."

"Oh?"

"She's been planning something, and it is likely at least one of her sisters is her confederate. I had that feeling when I first met her, and Cantrell's behavior confirms it. He believes she's the key to some profit or advantage. Only I don't know what it is, or why he should think such a thing."

"Have you asked her?"

"There's been no time, and I am not sure she'll tell me the truth. The last time I broached the subject of her relationship with Cantrell, she was less than forthcoming."

"Rosalind," said Alice slowly. "Do we need to worry about this Cantrell fellow lurking about?"

"We might," Rosalind answered.

"I see. Well. I shall have to have George over to stay. We are going to be short on space indeed. Very short. Quite cramped, in fact. Dear me. What is to be done?" Alice tapped her chin.

Now it was Rosalind's turn to sigh.

"I read Mrs. Heslop's letter," she said.

"Did you? What did she have to say?"

Rosalind ignored this. "How ever did you meet her?"

"You're not the only one with connections about town, you know," replied Alice. "I mentioned to a friend that we were looking to move house. She mentioned me, and you, to her friend Mrs. Heslop. Apparently, she married a man, with a small pocketbook and small ambition. She and her sister bolster the family finances by furnishing and leasing out London houses. She's an admirer of yours, you know. Thinks you're an example to women of character."

"I will not move house because I have been flattered," said Rosalind.

"Well, I suppose we'll bed George down in front of the hearth," returned Alice. "He will not complain in the slightest."

"Alice," began Rosalind, "we cannot move house. Not now."

"Why not?"

"Because . . . because I'm about to lose my livelihood."

Alice opened her mouth to protest, but she looked at Rosalind and swallowed her words.

"I completely misread the situation," said Rosalind. The words spilled out of her, carried by frustration, fear, and weariness. "I have made no progress on any point. The girls placed in my charge will now be the subject of gossip, and me along with them. Whatever comes of business, my reputation is going to suffer." And when her reputation suffered, those ladies who wrote to her now would decide that she was not to be trusted, after all.

"Don't tell me you've given up," said Alice.

"I don't want to," said Rosalind. "But . . . Alice, I don't know if I can do this."

Alice reached out and took Rosalind's hand. They sat like that for a long moment, not speaking, just holding on to each other, asking for and offering the reassurance that came with a friend's touch.

"It's rather snuck up on both of us, hasn't it?" said Alice.

"I don't understand."

"The changes. This business of yours. At first, it looked like just . . . an extension of what you had done ever since you lost your mother. But it's strayed, step-by-step. And then, all at once, you stop and look back and . . ." She gestured vaguely around the crowded room. "Well, we've both come rather a long way, haven't we? And it's frightening when you realize there's no returning to what we once were."

"But why should it be so hard now?" Rosalind was ashamed at how petulant the question sounded. "I've known I could not return to my old life. Indeed, when I had the chance, I *chose* to keep what I had instead."

"That doesn't make it easy," said Alice. "Do you remember when George showed me our first flat? The one we could just barely afford? You held my hand the whole time. I thought I was going to faint."

"I remember your jokes about the savings on window curtains and coals," replied Rosalind.

"Because there was no window, and the flue was so filthy, it would not draw, and you had to find us curtains so that we could create something like privacy between the beds."

"You were so brave."

"I was so angry," Alice retorted. "And scared and sick. But I swore I would find my way out of the disaster. Not because I wanted to, but because there was no other choice. Now . . . do you know, Rosalind, sometimes I feel guilty at how well it's all gone."

"Guilty?"

Alice nodded. "My father died in despair and horror. George and I were left destitute, but now I consider myself better off than I ever could have been had I stayed in what some are pleased to call 'my right sphere.'"

"I have always admired you," said Rosalind. "I'm not sure

I could have had the energy or imagination to do what you have done."

"We each of us make our own way," said Alice. "And I know this. Whatever you may choose to do next, you will not let this *person* ruin the life you've built for yourself." Alice pressed her hand firmly. "You'll find out what happened and why, and then between us, we'll make sure the right people know everything they need to." She shook her hand briskly. "You should get upstairs and see how your guest is getting on." Alice stood. "And if we're to have houseguests, I'd better see if there's anything left in the pantry."

Alice was, as usual, right. She should get upstairs. If she was to solve this tangle, she needed to hear whatever Nora could be induced to tell her.

Rosalind set her own feelings and her own doubts aside and headed up the stairs.

CHAPTER 29

The Best-Laid Plans

*. . . what is the difference in matrimonial affairs
between the mercenary and the prudent motive?*

Jane Austen, *Pride and Prejudice*

Nora stood with her back to the open door. She lifted a
nightdress out of the portmanteau, shook it, and refolded it to slide under the thin pillow.

The sad truth of the matter was that the upstairs back
room really was little more than a cross between a storage
room and a sewing room. When Alice moved in, she had
taken the second bedroom, and, of course, Amelia had the
attic. There was a daybed in this room, but otherwise it was
a jumble of spare furnishings. For one of the few times in her
life, Rosalind found herself blushing for her housekeeping.

Even though she did not turn around, Nora seemed to feel
Rosalind's embarrassment.

"Don't worry in the slightest, Miss Thorne," she said as
she closed her portmanteau and tucked it away under the
bed. "I've slept in far worse."

"During your elopement?" Rosalind asked.

"Yes," Nora replied without hesitation or a trace of embarrassment. "We never did find that fortune we were after." She shook her head. "Waste no tears, Miss Thorne. I knew what I was doing."

"Then why did you do it?" asked Rosalind.

"I told you, Miss Thorne, my relationship . . ."

"Is now upending your sisters' lives," Rosalind reminded her. "Do you want Cantrell to ruin their future? To break the family? Or do you mean to hand yourself over to him, after all?"

"None of these," said Nora.

"I'm glad to hear it, and I'll be glad to help in whatever way I can, but there's nothing I can do without knowing the truth about Bryan Cantrell. And you."

Rosalind waited for Nora to protest. But the young woman lowered herself onto the edge of the bed. She rubbed her forehead. Rosalind felt a twinge of sympathy. She was tired, as well.

"What do you want to know?" asked Nora.

Everything. But that would not be a helpful comment. "Why did you elope with him?" asked Rosalind.

"How many reasons would you like?" said Nora glibly. "I eloped because I could. Because it seemed a better option than waiting for someone boring and respectable to decide to marry me. To save Penelope."

Rosalind's brows arched.

"Oh yes," said Nora. "She's a rather pathetic thing now, but she was worse then, if you can believe it. We were both sixteen, and Pen was a sheltered and beautiful hothouse rose. Cantrell was her brother's great friend and partner. She worshipped him."

"But you didn't?"

Nora smiled grimly. "It's tempting to say that I saw through him at once. But the truth was, he fascinated me. When he told me stories of his travels, he was a little salacious, a little infamous. I loved it. So, I admit I was jealous of the attention he paid Penelope. To make matters worse, I resented Douglas, and I resented Bethany for marrying a man who so obviously disdained the rest of us. Then Penelope told Mariah that Cantrell had asked her to run away with him, and Mariah told me, and I put two and two together."

"In what way?"

"I asked myself, Why should they run away? There was no need for it. Douglas was as firmly attached to Cantrell as Penelope was. He had to wait only a couple of years, three at the most, I'm sure, and Douglas would have given his consent gladly. So, I reasoned, there must have been something more to it. I knew Pen wasn't with child. So, Cantrell had to be after something or afraid of something. I put the idea to Mariah, and Mariah went to work on it." Nora paused. "She's very like you, you know, only not so well mannered. She was able to find out Cantrell had been living on credit since he got there, and at least one of the tradesmen was going to ask Douglas for payment. Once I knew that, the rest became obvious. Cantrell was planning to run away to avoid his creditors, and he was going to take Pen with him because Douglas would pay a ransom for her return."

"Was that when you offered to elope with him instead?" asked Rosalind.

"Yes," said Nora. "It was a blatant, mercenary proposition. I told him if he made off with me, there'd be far less fuss on the road, and no need for him to support a fainting flower of a girl. If his object was ransom, Bethany would make sure Douglas would pay for me just as readily as Penelope." She paused, her gaze distant as she watched the memories that flickered through her mind. "He agreed," Nora said finally. "And off we went."

Rosalind sat silent for a long moment.

"Now you're thinking of how to tell me I'm not welcome," said Nora.

"No," said Rosalind. "I am grateful for your honesty. What I can't understand is why Cantrell's agreed."

"He's a lazy man," Nora told her. "I recognized the type. The fact of the matter is he conducted himself rather like my father. They both have a tremendous willingness to disparage everyone around them, but no inclination to actually stir themselves to make anything better."

"Yes," said Rosalind. "My father was similar in that way."

"Really? Perhaps I shouldn't be surprised, considering that you are another of us who has decided to make her own way."

"Perhaps." Rosalind had no desire to continue on this particular track, so she changed the subject. "Where did you go after you left home?"

"London, at first. We were there for only a couple of weeks, though." Nora studied her hands for a moment.

Rosalind waited.

"Very soon after we arrived in the city, I realized I'd miscalculated. I'd assumed Cantrell would write to Douglas immediately or that I'd write to Bethany. But he said we needed to wait."

"Wait?"

"Yes. He said if we wrote immediately, they'd know we had eloped strictly for the money, and they—meaning Douglas, of course—would simply be furious. If we waited, Bethany would begin to miss me, and Douglas would be more ready to believe that ours had been an act of passion."

Rosalind nodded. As a piece of reasoning went, it was quite sound. "How did you plan to live until then?"

"I didn't plan. I had honestly thought our association would be over within a matter of weeks."

"You did not mean to stay with him?" This was a genuine surprise.

"No," said Nora. "Once I had my share of the ransom money, I planned to set myself up in the character of a young widow or some such. I'd hire a companion and travel and study painting, and not be plagued by sisters and parents and endless, endless expectations. I even told him those were my plans."

This, Rosalind realized, went a long way toward explaining why Cantrell would agree to Nora's proposition. If all went as planned, not only would he have money in hand, but he also wouldn't be left with the burden of a wife, much less a fragile one who might need attention and coaxing.

"How long until he made the first demand?"

"Almost a year. He wrote to Douglas. I wrote to Bethany."

Rosalind considered this. "Did you know about Sir Jasper and the inheritance?"

Nora shook her head. "How could we? We hadn't taken the precaution of making sure there was anyone in the village we could write to for news. And as for my family, we had only one answer to any of our letters, and that came from Douglas, declaring he would not be blackmailed. I had no idea that my family had become wealthy until I left Cantrell and returned home."

Rosalind felt certain Nora was speaking the truth, and yet it did not make any sense. Why would Cantrell bother to rob a man of only modest means? Before becoming Sir Jasper's heir, Douglas had had only modest means. Bethany had had no dowry at all. She knew that from when they were girls. Indeed, from what Rosalind had heard, Mr. Hodgeson had been sunk into debt for years.

So, where did Cantrell think the ransom money would come from?

It is that question of timing again. Rosalind frowned pensively. *It's a matter not just of what he has done but also of when he has done it.*

But Rosalind could make no sense out of the jumble of events laid before her. There was still something she did not know or did not see.

"What happened when Cantrell realized there would be no money forthcoming?" she asked.

"Well, to my surprise, he did *not* immediately drop me," said Nora. "I thought he might. But we'd . . . we'd taken a liking to each other. We had a similar sense of humor, I suppose. A way of looking at things, and people, that pleased us both. Also, Cantrell had taken me into his profession by then, and it turned out I was rather good at it."

"His profession as a swindler?" asked Rosalind.

"His favorite trick was to ingratiate himself to someone he'd just met and be invited for dinner or to stay. Once inside the house, he would, *we* would, learn what it held and decide what and how much we could remove. Then we would be gone, just like that."

"I see."

"Do you?"

Rosalind nodded. "It is not entirely an original scheme—to work one's way into a position of trust in a household and then rob the members. In the highest of circles, the robbery takes the form of a person moving in for an indeterminant amount of time and enjoying the host's hospitality for as long as one can manage."

"Yes, we certainly did that," said Nora. "Only when we left, we tended to make off with certain valuable objects. Or, if it was necessary, we'd go back for them." She gave Rosalind a sideways glance. "Now you're thinking of Bethany's pearls."

"Do you blame me?"

"Certainly not. But since you now know I am an experienced thief and a person who knows how to shift for herself, please do ask why on earth I would stay in the house after I had stolen the necklace."

"Yes," said Rosalind. "I had wondered about that, even before this."

"What will you do now?" Nora asked her.

Rosalind drew in a deep breath and pulled her thoughts back to the present. "I must go back to the Douglases' house. I need to speak with Bethany and with Mr. Douglas." *We need to find Betsy.* "After that, we shall see. It is very clear that Cantrell must be found and stopped before he ruins the family."

"Yes," said Nora. "Yes, it is clear." She smoothed down her skirts. "Well, I thank you for your hospitality. I trust I will not have to trespass on it for very long."

"You may stay as long as you need," said Rosalind. "Can I ask one other thing?"

Nora waved her hand, and Rosalind decided to take the gesture as assent. "Your mother says she knew from the first Cantrell was a scoundrel."

"She did, actually. Who would have thought it?" Nora shook her head in amazement. "She tried to warn Douglas and Bethany, and anyone else who would sit still. None of us listened, of course." Her brow furrowed. "I suppose I should have apologized to her. I wonder I never thought of it before now."

Silence fell. Rosalind contemplated the young woman in front of her. She believed Nora. But the part of her that was practical and much experienced also acknowledged that it was still possible that Nora and Cantrell were together in this scheme. Nora had the habits of thought required of a thief and a fraud. She understood the ways and means. With Betsy as a go-between, it would be the easiest thing in the world for Nora to let Cantrell know where she would be and when. She could have arranged the scene in the dining room and at the musicale.

Rosalind meant to ask Nora another question, but she heard the sound of the front-door bell being rung. Shortly afterward, the rumble of masculine voices rose from the foyer.

"Excuse me," said Rosalind. She did not wait for Nora's answer. Instead, she left her guest and started quickly down the narrow stairs.

Amelia stood in the tiny foyer, and so did Alice. Two men, obviously having just come in from the cold, stood with them.

One was Mr. Tauton.

The other Adam.

CHAPTER 30

Homecomings and Fresh Suspicions

*There was a something in her countenance which
made him listen with an apprehensive and
anxious attention . . .*

Jane Austen, *Pride and Prejudice*

Alifetime's worth of training and unyielding expectations kept Rosalind from running down the stairs. Neither did she throw herself into Adam's arms, allowing him to spin her around until they were both dizzy and laughing.

But she wanted to, with every fiber of her being. She wanted it so badly, it hurt her. Pain blossomed in the center of her chest as she walked decorously down the stairs to stand in front of him. She knew that the strength of her longing showed in her eyes as she made her curtsy. When he smiled in return and bowed over her hand, she saw that same longing reflected back in his gentle gaze.

"Welcome back, Mr. Harkness," she said.

"Thank you, Miss Thorne," he replied.

"Hullo, Miss Thorne," boomed Mr. Tauton. "They told us at the Douglases' house you would be here."

"Has something happened?" asked Alice.

"We've some news," said Mr. Tauton as he glanced up the stairs. Nora stood at the top landing, looking down on them all. "Whether it's good or bad has yet to be seen. But we've found your Mr. Cantrell."

"How?" Nora ran down the stairs. "Where is he?" She stopped beside Rosalind. "Who are you?"

"Miss Nora Hodgeson," said Rosalind, "this is Mr. Samuel Tauton and Mr. Adam Harkness. They are principal officers from the Bow Street Police Station."

"And I'm Alice Littlefield," said Alice to Mr. Tauton. "My brother George will be with us in short order. However, unless we all want to stand talking in the draft, may I suggest the dining room? I'm afraid we're quite out of room in the parlor."

While Nora, George, and the officers arranged themselves around the dining room table, Rosalind retreated to the kitchen to light the stove and put the kettle on. Alice joined her to assemble the tea set and open a tin that held the some slightly battered biscuits.

It was perhaps ridiculous to think of tea at such a time, but somehow the act of preparing it steadied Rosalind's nerves. Besides, some distance from Adam was an absolute necessity. Each time she looked at him, she seemed to lose her ability to think of anything except how far away he had been, how she had missed him, and how much she wanted to hear all that he had been doing. Yes, she had his letters, but she wanted to talk to him, to sit with him, to not let him go away again.

The worst part was, none of these feelings seemed to be put off by the usual firm declaration that she did not have any time for them.

Blessedly, Alice decided now was not the time for teasing or awkward remarks about how small the house was. Between them, they carried the tea and biscuits back into the dining room, so everyone might serve themselves. She wished she had more to give them. She wished it was a proper supper, but for the moment, this would have to do.

"Now," Rosalind said, as she claimed her own cup of tea, "what have you to tell us?"

Rosalind listened to Mr. Tauton describe Johnny Wiggins, the runner who'd been stationed to watch the house, and how he saw the "porter" warned off by a man who might have been a member of the household staff. Then he told them about the gray-cloaked woman who had followed the porter, and whom Wiggins had followed, all the way to Cantrell's boardinghouse.

Rosalind meant to watch Nora for her reactions to all this news, but her attention kept slipping to Adam. He looked tired and grim. Whatever had happened in Manchester had left him worn down. She imagined he wished he were comfortably settled in his mother's parlor, hearing his sister and two younger brothers tell him all their news. Instead, he was here.

He caught her gaze and gave one small shrug. He knew exactly what she was thinking, of course. He usually did. Rosalind shrugged in return and smiled.

"But who was this Miss Gray Cloak?" Nora demanded when Mr. Tauton had finished his recitation.

"That is what we were hoping you'd be able to tell us, Miss Hodgeson," said Adam. "Apparently, she offered Cantrell some payment to leave the family alone, which he refused. He said he wanted you to work for him." Adam spoke softly, but directly. "What is it you can do for Mr. Cantrell, Miss Hodgeson?"

"Much as I did for him before, I imagine," said Nora. "If your connections extend to the Continent, gentlemen, you may hear tell of a number of daring and successful house robberies. I was part of them." She lifted her chin. "There, you may arrest me if you please."

She wasn't lying, thought Rosalind. But neither was she telling the whole truth.

Adam saw it, as well. "It seems the last words our man heard the woman say to Cantrell were 'very well.' He took it as an assent to Cantrell's demands."

"Was it Mariah, Nora?" asked Rosalind abruptly.

"How on earth would I know?" Nora snapped back. "I was busy packing my things after being thrown out of the house. Ask this Mr. Wiggins who he saw."

"Miss Hodgeson, could Mr. Cantrell believe you would be ready to commit robbery for him?" asked Adam.

"He may believe it," said Nora. "But he'd be mistaken. I am finished with him. I *left* him! Years ago!"

Her tone was desperate and angry. She was frightened, Rosalind knew. Cantrell's hold over her was tighter than she'd realized.

They could force the issue. But that might only cause Nora to flee. Rosalind found she was not yet ready to take that risk.

But there was one question she needed answered.

"Why?"

"I beg your pardon?" snapped Nora.

"Why did you leave him? Did something happen?"

Nora bit her lip. Her hands rubbed together, as if she had suddenly touched something unpleasant.

Finally, she said, "He killed a man."

Rosalind shrank back reflexively.

Nora saw and gave a small chuckle. "Well, there it is. I've finally shocked you! I shall have to write this event in my diary."

"What happened?" asked Rosalind.

"We were going through a bad patch. We had them occasionally, but this was particularly severe. Two jobs in a row had gone badly, and the money was running very short. It was winter, we were cold and had not eaten in several days, and our landlord had informed us we were to be pitched out if we couldn't pay by morning, and he would keep our effects in payment for the rent we were in arrears.

"I was ready to go try my hand at picking pockets, or anything really," said Nora. "Cantrell had gone out on his own. He said to try to find a card game. He is, as you can imagine, a notable cheat. I stayed up waiting, nursing our little fire, and hoping. When he did come back . . . his face was bruised, and he was covered in blood." She closed her eyes. "There was a smell that clung to him. Copper and dirt and . . . I don't know . . ."

"Yes," said Rosalind. "I know that smell."

"He had a pocket book. It was as bloody as he was. He tossed it on the table. I remember the sound as it fell. I remember asking him what he'd done. 'What I had to,' he said. He dropped into the bed. He didn't even take off his shirt. Just wrapped himself in the quilt. I sat there for a little while and then bundled up what little I had and left." She rubbed her hands together again. "It seems I was not quite ready to try anything, after all."

Rosalind let her sit with her silence for a time. She tried to imagine how it had been for her—freezing, hungry, alone in a night when the wolf was not only at the door but across the threshold. Then her partner in her chosen life had come home and dropped the desperately needed money into her hands.

And yet in that moment, Nora had chosen to risk herself rather than take salvation that came at the cost of another person's life.

Probably it had not been so simple. Probably, there had been other, smaller failures and fights that had left their partnership, relationship—Rosalind was not even sure what to call it—vulnerable to this final blow.

But Nora's story told Rosalind something important. It said that Cantrell was capable of killing a man. Her thoughts drifted back to Amelia describing the conversation she'd had with Mrs. Hare and Mr. Dowdeswell about Addison Douglas, who had been Sir Jasper's heir. They not only had confirmed that Addison had vanished but also had elaborated on the details.

Now she found herself wondering if it was possible Cantrell had something to do with that, as well.

No. It cannot be. How would he have known? she asked herself. But the answer, or at least the next question, followed immediately. *How would he have known where Nora and Penelope were going to be this afternoon?*

It seemed that one of Mr. Cantrell's uncanny skills was finding such things out.

CHAPTER 31

Unlawful Acts

. . . you have been very sly, very reserved with me.

Jane Austen, *Pride and Prejudice*

"This was not the welcome I would have planned for you," said Rosalind.

"I never thought it was," Adam replied. "You could never be so . . . disorganized."

They sat close together, rocking through the crowded streets in the battered carriage Adam had brought from Bow Street. It was nearly noon. Rosalind had hoped to get underway much earlier than this, but Adam had first to attend Mr. Townsend at Bow Street and answer questions about how affairs in Manchester had been left. Judging by the tension in his jaw and his shoulders as he'd helped Rosalind into the carriage, it had not gone well.

Rosalind herself was not in the best of spirits. She had slept very little. Instead, she'd spent the night listening for movement from Nora's room and the young woman's step on the stair. Somewhat to her surprise, it had not come. Nora had still been with them when George Littlefield returned at the stroke of eight with a basketful of fresh buns, which he'd said were a gift from his wife, Hannah. Together, all the household had made themselves a good breakfast on the offerings.

Rosalind had written to Bethany, saying she intended to spend the night at Russell Square and return the next day with more news. She apologized for Amelia's continued presence in their house and said she hoped that it was not imposing too great a burden. She enclosed a note for Amelia, telling her to send immediate word about when Betsy had returned and what her errand had been.

But so far, no word had come.

But what she did do now was to strip off her woolen glove so she could take Adam's hand. Adam responded by pulling their clasped hands toward him and pressing an urgent kiss on her knuckles. Rosalind's breath caught. She touched his face, letting her fingers run down the line of his jaw. He had not shaved that morning. His stubble rasped against her unprotected fingertips.

Adam kissed her. He kissed her slowly, allowing them both to savoring the sweetness of the moment. They were together, unseen by the world. They could claim this small space of peace for themselves alone.

For a long time, that was all that mattered.

Eventually, the world must come back. Laughing, Rosalind and Adam helped each other smooth their hair. Rosalind straightened Adam's neckcloth. Adam settled her bonnet back into place and retied her ribbons.

He was blushing. So was she. Rosalind decided she did not care. Instead, she gave him one final peck on the cheek and then turned to peer through the carriage curtains to see where they were.

It was not the worst part of the town, but it was far from the best. The houses crowded close together. Their driver kept the horses at a walk so they could thread their way through the traffic of barrows, wagons, carts, and people. The crowds of idlers indicated a healthy crop of public houses and gin mills in the immediate vicinity. Men carrying poles draped with secondhand clothes or shoes or even birds in cages shouted at the passersby. Women shoved their barrows or lugged their baskets loaded with everything from apples to washing.

"Here!" Adam thumped on the roof of their carriage.

The driver pulled the team to a halt.

Adam regarded Rosalind. Clearly, he was contemplating asking if Rosalind would reconsider leaving the relative safety of the carriage. Perhaps he meant to reiterate that the neighborhood was not a good one, and that Bryan Cantrell was not to be trusted in any way.

Rosalind fixed her gaze on his. Adam returned his small, crooked smile, got out of the carriage, and helped Rosalind down.

"From what Tauton said, the place should be just down here." He nodded toward the mouth of a narrow lane. He also gave Rosalind his right arm.

The lane was no better, nor any worse, than its neighbors. The houses were old, mostly half-timbered, built cheek by jowl. The lane itself was filled with the city's smell and its ragged jumble of noises. In a highly unusual move, Adam had brought a stout stick with him. He carried it easily, and very visibly, in his left hand. It was no surprise that the people around them gave them both measuring glances, but no one ventured to approach.

As they came around the bend in the lane, Rosalind saw two people standing in front of a ramshackle gabled house. Rosalind put her hand on Adam's arm. He caught her signal at once and drew the pair of them aside, into the shadows of the nearest doorway.

Because the first of those two people was Bryan Cantrell.

Cantrell stood with a well-dressed young woman. Her finery was a little too bright, and her bonnet a little too overly decorated for strict good taste. She pressed her hands to her face. Cantrell rested both hands on her shoulders.

"Who is she?" breathed Adam.

But Rosalind just shook her head.

"How did you even know?" Cantrell was asking.

The girl lowered her hands. The edge of her bonnet hid her face and muffled her reply. Rosalind could not help herself. She started to move closer, but Adam held her back.

Betsy? wondered Rosalind. She wished desperately she could see the girl's face.

Cantrell straightened and ran both hands through his hair. Even from this distance, Rosalind could see he held himself crookedly, as if exhausted or drunk.

The girl dropped her face into her hands once more and wailed. The inhabitants of the street were watching the show with one eye, but without pausing in their activities of washing or bartering or hauling.

"No, no, don't do that!" cried Cantrell. "I'm sorry, Emma!"

Emma?

Cantrell dragged the girl to him in a rough embrace. "I don't—" A rattling van cut off his next words. Whatever they were, Emma was not satisfied with them. She jerked herself out of his arms.

"Emma!" pleaded Cantrell. "You must see this changes nothing between us!"

"Changes nothing?" she shot back. "Then why didn't you tell me about her?"

Adam pursed his lips in a silent whistle.

"Because it's none of your business!" Cantrell shouted. Then he seemed to re collect himself. "No, I'm sorry. But it isn't important. Our plans—"

"Yes, *our* plans!" snapped the woman, Emma, interrupting him. "The plans made by you and me, Barrett Campbell! And which did *not* include you getting yourself some little bit on the side!"

"I told you, this was not my fault! She followed me! If you would just listen, Emma!" Cantrell lurched toward her and grabbed both her hands. "All I did, all I am doing, I am doing for you. I swear it!"

"I don't believe you," replied Emma coldly. "I can't believe I wasted so much time on such a . . . a *scoundrel* as you! I am done!"

But as she made her dramatic retreat, the young woman, Emma, caught sight of Rosalind in the shadows and stopped.

"You're her, aren't you?" Emma said. Clearly, she saw how both Rosalind's and Adam's clothes marked them out as visitors to this neighborhood. "The other one."

"No," said Rosalind.

The way Emma twisted up her face said plainly she did not believe this. "Don't worry," she sneered. "He's all yours, for as long as you can keep him." With this, Emma hiked up her skirts and ran up the lane.

"Emma!" Cantrell bawled after her. But Emma had already vanished into the crowd. "Damn it! Emma!" Cantrell took several stumbling steps but then tripped on a cobble and staggered against the nearest house.

Reflex moved Rosalind toward him, but Adam tightened his hold on her arm.

Cantrell looked up.

"Oh," he said. "It's you. What on earth do you want?"

"I was hoping to speak with you," said Rosalind.

"Odd. I was hoping never to see you again." Cantrell pushed himself away from the wall and straightened his back, or at least he tried to. His face was pale, and despite the chill in the air, drops of perspiration stood out on his brow. His red and watery eyes took her measure, and her companion's. "Who's this?" he slurred.

"My name is Adam Harkness," Adam replied easily. "Knowing something of the neighborhood, I agreed to accompany Miss Thorne today."

"Well, unless you are all amused by standing here and freezing to death, you may as well come up."

The house was making some effort at respectability. The few windows had been freshly washed, and the narrow stairs had been recently scrubbed. The matting in the hall was worn, the boards were scuffed and splintered, but the whitewashing on the walls was reasonably fresh.

Cantrell climbed the stairs, leaning heavily on the rail. At the top, he led them down a dim hallway and pushed open a door. The room was dark, but of a reasonable size. The furnishings were old; the floor was bare. Despite this, the cloth on the table and the quilt on the bed were both clean. The remains of a luncheon of bread, cheese, and hothouse grapes lay on the table.

Cantrell went straight to the wine bottle that waited with the remains of the food, poured himself a large glass, and drank it down without pause. When he'd swallowed the last, he let out a gasp and set the glass down with a thump. Only then did he seem to remember he was not alone.

"Well." He dropped into the rush-bottomed chair beside the table. "What is it you want with me?"

Adam tilted his head toward Rosalind.

"Mr. Cantrell, I fear you are ill," she began.

Cantrell grinned, a sickly parody of the more charming expression he had used before. "You mean you fear I'm stinking drunk." He poured another glass of wine. "Not to worry, madam. It will take much more than one bottle of bad red to set me back on my heels." He gulped the wine again and belched and pressed the heel of his hand against his side. "Now, who sent you? My darling sister-in-law or my charming wife?"

"Neither," said Rosalind. "I came on my own volition."

"What for?" Cantrell refilled his glass, or tried to. The last of the wine dribbled slowly out of the bottle. "You can't think I stole those blasted pearls. They were gone well before I darkened the sacred Douglas doorstep."

"How did you know about the pearls?" asked Adam.

Cantrell raised an unsteady hand and tapped his nose. "That's my secret, Mr. . . . Harking. Harken." He giggled, but it turned to a groan, and he pressed his hand against his side again. "Hark! Hark! The dogs do bark!" He giggled again but then shook his head heavily. "Believe me, I wish I did have them. It'd be so much simpler than dealing with these everlasting *females*!" He sneered the final word and drank his wine, glowering at Rosalind.

"I will not take any more of your time than necessary, Mr. Cantrell," said Rosalind. "I am here simply to ask what you want."

"What do I want?" His breath came in short pants. His hand dug harder into his side. "I want what's mine by right! I want that little chit to give me what I'm due, and she will." He pointed one long finger at Rosalind. "She will, and the grand Douglas will get to watch!"

"Cantrell, I think you'd better lie down," said Adam. "You're not well."

Cantrell climbed to his feet, but his knees quickly collapsed. Before Rosalind could move, Adam had caught Cantrell by the shoulders and heaved him onto the bed.

Rosalind pulled off her gloves and clasped Cantrell's hand. "Cold as ice."

Cantrell gave a foul belch. "I don't need your . . . your . . . inter . . . inter . . ."

Rosalind ignored his attempt at protest and laid her hand across his brow and then his chest. "His head, too. His heart is going mad. He needs a doctor."

"I know a man," said Adam. "I'll send the driver." He

ducked out of the room, slamming the door hard behind himself.

Rosalind grabbed the quilt that had been folded over the foot of the bed, and spread it across Cantrell. His face had gone white as paper. His mouth had turned an ugly mottled red and blue.

Rosalind looked around the room for some resource to help her. There was no water in the basin. No grate where she could light a fire. The room's only warmth came from the chimney. A greatcoat hung on a peg by the door. Rosalind grabbed that and laid it over the quilt.

"Damn you," croaked Cantrell. "Damn you all. Leave a man in peace, can't you?"

"No," said Rosalind. She stripped off her own coat and laid it over the other.

"Won't do you any good," he breathed. "I got her. Dead to rights, I got her. Them. All of them . . . I know . . ."

Cantrell coughed so hard, he choked. He rolled onto his side; his hand crept out from under the coverings, "Oh Christ," he croaked, and his eyes squeezed shut. "It hurts."

Rosalind grasped his hand. He squeezed her fingers, but his grip was feeble and fluttering.

Footsteps pounded up the stairs. Startled, Rosalind turned.

Adam barged back into the room.

Cantrell's hand slid out of Rosalind's. His eyes rolled open.

Bryan Cantrell was dead.

CHAPTER 32

A Friend in Need

You know not what you are about.

Jane Austen, *Pride and Prejudice*

Rosalind straightened and backed away. There was no logic to the movement; it was purely reflexive. Adam caught her reaching hand and squeezed it tight for a brief moment before he pushed past her. He rolled Cantrell onto his back, then held his face close—feeling for the other man's breath against his cheek, Rosalind supposed. He clasped a limp hand. Then Adam laid his hand over Cantrell's eyelids and drew them gently closed. He stood back from the lifeless body. He also took Rosalind's arm and turned her away, wrapping her in a one-armed embrace as he did.

They stayed just like that, with Adam as a shield between her and the dead man. Rosalind let herself luxuriate in the solid warmth of his presence, but only for a moment. Then she swallowed her shock ruthlessly and pushed gently away.

"Adam, what could have happened?"

Adam shook his head. "Under other circumstances, I'd say the man was taken in his illness. Perhaps it was the bad wine he complained of. Or perhaps he'd been ill for some days."

"But under these circumstances?" prompted Rosalind.

"I think it best we send for the coroner," said Adam.

"Yes," Rosalind agreed. "He's threatened at least one woman, clearly wronged another, and knew more than he said about the theft of a valuable set of pearls. I find I cannot believe the fact that he is now lying dead is simple coincidence."

"Fisher"—this was their driver—"should be back shortly. We'll hear what the doctor has to say and then send for Sir David if needs be." Sir David Royce was the coroner for the City of London. "There's something odd about his mouth," Adam went on. "It looks swollen, maybe bruised."

"Yes, I was noticing the same thing," said Rosalind. "I wonder, perhaps—"

The sound of light, quick footsteps on the stairs cut off Rosalind's wondering. The door swung back, and a tall, slender young man entered, pulling off his hat as he did.

"Campbell!" he cried. "What do you mean—" Then he saw Rosalind and Adam and froze. "Who the devil are you?"

Adam stepped toward the newcomer, clearly meaning to block his view of what lay on the bed. But it was too late. The man had already seen past them both.

"My God!" He tossed his hat and stick carelessly aside and leaned over his friend. "Campbell!"

There was no answer. Likewise, there was no mistaking that the person on the bed was no more.

"I'm sorry, sir," said Adam.

The man straightened up, visibly shaking. He wiped his hand across his face. "But . . . but I just spoke with him! He told me how things were looking up for him! That he might finally be out of his difficulties. He . . ." The young man swayed on his feet.

"You should sit down." Rosalind pushed the rush-bottomed chair toward him.

"Yes, thank you." The young man eased himself into the chair. He pulled a handkerchief from his pocket and wiped his face. "Not very manly of me, is it?" He gave a small laugh.

"Don't be too hard on yourself," said Adam. "You've had a shock. Here." He pulled a silver flask out of his coat and handed it across to the young man.

The young man took the flask gratefully and drank. "Asherton," he said when he swallowed. "My name. I mean, I'm Thaddeus Asherton."

"Asherton!" exclaimed Rosalind. "Are you related to Mrs. Cecil Asherton?"

"She's my mother." Asherton squinted at Rosalind, presumably trying to reconcile her obvious respectability with these less than respectable surroundings. "D'ye know her?"

"We've met." Rosalind looked at him again. Yes, she could see the relationship between this man and the matron she'd spoken to at Meredith's concert. It was there in the shape of his face and the angle of his gray eyes. "I am so sorry to meet her son under such circumstances."

"Such circumstances, ha!" Asherton passed his hand in front of his eyes. "My God! I thought he'd live to be a hundred! What can have happened?" He wiped his eyes. "Who are you? Are you family? He said he was estranged from his but . . ."

"This is Miss Rosalind Thorne," said Adam. "And my name is Harkness. We had some business with Mr. . . . Campbell. May I ask what brought you here, sir?"

"I'm . . . I was a friend. He . . . I . . . Lord . . ." He rubbed at his face again. "We shouldn't be sitting here talking like this. We must . . . do something. But I don't know what . . ." He looked at them pleadingly.

"Does Mr. Campbell have any family?" asked Rosalind. "They should be told."

"No, no one. No one he was on speaking terms with, anyway. That is . . . oh my Lord . . . Emma," he breathed. "Some-one will have to tell Emma."

Adam kept his face admirably calm.

"Emma?" prompted Rosalind.

"Yes. Emma Lelyveld, the young lady he was seeing." He took another swig from the flask. "He intended to marry her."

You must see this changes nothing between us! Campbell had said.

"She'll be heartbroken," Mr. Asherton was saying. "She was devoted to him. You could see it whenever they were to-gether."

Our plans! she'd shouted. *Which did not include you get-ting yourself some little bit on the side!*

"I should . . . Yes, I should go to her." This resolution seemed to steady Mr. Asherton, and he pushed himself to his feet.

Rosalind glanced at Adam, a question in her eyes. Adam nodded his understanding.

"Indeed, you should, sir," he said. "And Miss Thorne should not stay here. I've sent my driver for the doctor, but I saw a livery on the corner. Would you walk her down and see to it she has good conveyance?" He pulled some coins from his pocket.

Mr. Asherton waved this away. "No need, no need. I'll drive her myself. The least I can do, isn't it? You're quite right. A lady—an acquaintance of Mother's!—shouldn't be in a place like this." His brow creased, and she knew he was wondering how a lady had come to be here in the first place. Thankfully, the discretion of good manners kept him from asking. Instead, he offered her his arm. "Miss Thorne?"

It was a wrench to leave Adam in this moment. She badly wanted to stay beside him. She told herself it was because they needed to sort through the things in the flat, to find out if there was any hint here as to what exactly had brought on Bryan Cantrell's untimely death. However, Rosalind also knew that Adam, with all his experience, was perfectly well equipped for the task. She would be of much more use coaxing Mr. Asherton into telling her what he knew about the man Cantrell-Campbell. Asherton was, after all, the first person she'd met—not counting the brief encounter with Miss Emma Lelyveld—who had known the man outside of his long and sordid acquaintance with the Hodgeson family.

Once again, her deportment training came to her aid. Her face gave away nothing; neither did her voice. "Thank you, Mr. Asherton. That is very kind of you." She took the arm he offered and let Mr. Asherton steer her away.

Each step that took her away from Adam tugged hard at her spirits, but she did not let herself look back.

Mr. Asherton was a courtly gentleman who obviously took pride in his manners. He led Rosalind gently down the stairs and held the door, then immediately took her arm again to steer her firmly through the crowds in the narrow street.

"Had you known Mr. Campbell for long?" Rosalind asked him.

"Not long. A year or so," said Mr. Asherton. "A funny story there, but . . . not necessarily one for a lady," he added. "But he pulled me out of a bit of a scrape, and we've been . . . had been . . . friends ever since. He stayed with me often when he was in town."

"But not this time?"

"No. Well, he did for a while, but then he declared he had some business across town, and left. Just for a few days, he said. My God! If I'd known he'd fetch up in such a place . . ." Asherton glanced warily about them. "What possible business could he have had down here?"

Rosalind bowed her head, as if acknowledging how needless this tragedy was. "When did he leave you?"

"Oh, no more than a couple days ago. It was quite the surprise, let me tell you. One minute, all things are quite as usual, and the next, he's saying he won't sponge off me any longer. I told him it was no bother at all, which, of course, it wasn't, but he answered that things were looking up."

"In what way?"

"With his suit, you know."

"Suit?"

Asherton's brows shot up. "You don't know about his suit?"

"I did not know Mr. Campbell well," Rosalind told him. "He was friends with a friend of mine."

"Oh, I see." Mr. Asherton steered her around a particularly sprawling mud puddle. "Well, shouldn't be talking—confidences between friends and all that—but I suppose it can't matter now." He sighed. "You see, Campbell was due an inheritance, but the thing had gotten tangled up in the courts. There was a cousin—or something—and an improperly dated will, and . . . well, it was a d . . . terrible mess. Used up all his resources trying to fight for his rights, poor fellow."

"How awful," murmured Rosalind. "But you said it was looking up?"

"That's what he said. He said he should soon have what he was owed. Just a matter of days, he said. It was wonderful, really. I'd never seen him so pleased. Claire was overjoyed. She was sure that he and Emma would finally be able to get married."

"I'm sorry," said Rosalind. "Who is Claire?"

"Claire Lelyveld. She and Emma are cousins. Dear little thing." His expression grew wistful. "She's an orphan, you know, all alone in the world, you know, except for Emma. And neither of them with a bean to their names until they get married. Family just handed her over to this horrid old aunt as a chaperone because they didn't want to be bothered." He sighed gustily. "It's not at all fair, when she's such a good, such a lovely . . ." But he re-collected himself and stopped.

"Claire will be quite devastated, as well. She and Campbell got on like a house on fire!"

They'd reached the livery stables. Like Mr. Cantrell's rooms, the ramshackle buildings seemed to be doing their best in bad circumstances.

"Don't mind the looks of the place," he told Rosalind. "I quizzed them closely when I arrived. Thought I'd be staying longer, you see. They know what they're about here. Wouldn't have trusted them with my cattle otherwise, you may be sure."

Indeed, the stablemen were all but falling over themselves to see that Rosalind had a comfortable chair and a cup of (very bad) tea against the chill while the horses were harnessed. When the carriage was brought round, it proved to be what gentlemen called a "high-flyer"—a light racing vehicle much more suited for summer than winter. Asherton blushed as he helped her up and tucked the rug around her knees. "So sorry, Miss Thorne. Didn't expect to be driving a lady out today, you see. I'll let the sides down, and you'll be quite snug."

"I'm sure I will be perfectly comfortable." Rosalind smiled and hoped she sounded like she meant it.

"Where should I take you?" he asked.

A number of rapid calculations flickered quickly through Rosalind's mind. "Little Russell Street," she said. "Do you know it?"

"I do." Mr. Asherton hopped up on the driver's seat and took the reins from the stableman. "We'll have you home in a trice!"

Asherton was a good driver, and she had the feeling he was taking extra care for her sake. However, as Rosalind had anticipated, it was a cold, damp ride, even with the folding top raised and the curtains tightly closed. She drew the rug up to her collar, kept her hands well tucked in, and gritted her teeth to stop them chattering.

The chill eating into her hands reminded her fiercely of how cold Cantrell's hand had felt. In her mind, Rosalind heard the echo of his dying words.

I got her. Dead to rights, I got her. I know. . . .

Who is the "her"? Rosalind wondered. *Nora? Bethany? Penelope perhaps? Betsy or this Emma? Some other woman altogether?*

Cantrell had known about the missing pearls. Someone from the house had talked to him. But was it that theft that had convinced him he had this unnamed female "dead to rights"? Or was it some other affair entirely? How many schemes did he have running? How many houses had he connived his way into?

Houses and hearts? Perhaps Emma had discovered that Cantrell was supposed to be married to another woman? Or perhaps Lady Cowper's revelations about bigamy among the Douglas family were coloring her interpretation of this other argument.

Rosalind sighed and shivered under her thick rug. Every way she turned the tangle of their affairs, she seemed to find some new thread she had not anticipated or accounted for.

The streets around her had grown familiar. Rosalind chaffed her arms briskly and tried to set her unquiet thoughts aside. She needed to pull herself together, because her house would not be empty. Alice would be there, and George.

And Nora.

Mr. Asherton turned the horses down Little Russell Street and stopped in front of her door. Rosalind made herself smile. She wanted to run inside immediately, but there was one other thing she needed.

"Mr. Asherton, may I trouble you for Miss Lelyveld's address? I know my friend would like to send her a note of condolence."

"Oh, that's damned . . . sorry . . . That's very good of you, I'm sure." Mr. Asherton pulled a pencil and notebook from his coat pocket and scribbled down the street number. "There you are." He tore out the leaf and handed it to her.

"Thank you, Mr. Asherton. And my condolences to you, as well."

"Thank you, Miss Thorne, and thank you for . . . Well, you've done marvelously, having had such a dreadful shock in such a place." He helped her down from the carriage. "I'm very glad to have met you."

She held out her hand, which he took and bowed over. She presented him with a polite smile. She walked up to the door, being sure not to show any sign of distress or hurry, and let herself inside.

As soon as the door closed, Rosalind darted into the parlor. "Alice!" she called. "Where's Nora?"

And she thought, *Please, please, please let her still be here.*

CHAPTER 33

The Cause

. . . your first duty is, to take a view of the body of the deceased, wherein you will be careful to observe, if there be any marks of violence thereon . . .

John Impey, *The Office and Duty of Coroners*

When Rosalind left on Asherton's arm, Adam stayed by the door, listening until the sound of their footsteps from the stairs faded. Only then did he let his shoulders slump and let his mouth release the curses that had been clogging his throat.

Adam was not normally given to useless expressions of anger, but this once his reserve failed him. After the cock-up in Manchester, he'd hoped to find himself with some breathing space to try to decide what to do next. Instead, what he had found was Sam Tauton sitting on his mother's doorstep, with the news that Rosalind was smack in the middle of a family tangle that just happened to involve the theft of thousands of pounds worth of jewelry.

And now a most untimely death.

At least Rosalind was safe. At least he'd been able to talk with her a little, to hold her hand, to see the warmth in her

260 Darcie Wilde

eyes that waited just for him. It was not enough. But it would have to do for now.

Adam made himself turn away from the door. Moving with determination, he returned to the bed to strip both coat and quilt off Cantrell's corpse. He looked long and hard at the dead man. There was definitely something wrong about his mouth. Even as the last of the color was rapidly draining from him, he could see the rough reddish blisters standing out against his lips.

Adam filed this away in his memory. Then, moving carefully, he searched the dead man's pockets. He found a few coins, a ring of keys, and a small clasp knife. The watch was cheap and flashy, as was the chain. He wore no rings or seals.

Adam sorted through the keys. One he judged to be to the front door of the house, with another to the room itself. But there was a third—a plain brass key smaller than the others.

To a trunk, maybe? He'd seen nothing like that yet, but even in a room this bare, there'd be plenty of space for surprises.

Adam left Cantrell's few possessions on the table. He looked over the remains of the meal and lifted up the cloth that had been crumpled in the basket. Underneath it, he found a torn label. Probably it had been tied to the basket handle.

FOR MY LOVE, WITH MY LOVE.

And that was all. Nonetheless, Adam laid it beside the rest of the belongings and set to work searching the rest of the room.

It did not take long. There was little to find beyond the battered furnishings and the remains of the meal. There was one portmanteau with a change of linen. A hat and coat and battered walking stick. A pair of boots.

Either Cantrell did not own much or he was not planning to stay here long.

Or both.

There was no trace of any woman's hand in the place. There was no trunk, either, or any notes or letters. Adam pulled open every drawer, ran his hands over the mantel, looked through the spindly wardrobe.

What he did find was a smear of black ash at the bottom of the dry washbasin. Adam muttered a curse of frustration. Something had been burned, and it had left no helpful trace behind.

Adam returned to the bed with its grim occupant. Steeling himself, he reached under the pillow. He felt nothing between the pillowcase and the mattress ticking. Then, just so he could say he'd been thorough about the business, he shoved his hand under the mattress.

His fingertips brushed paper.

Adam stretched and muttered another curse for good measure. After a moment's shuffling and scrabbling, he pulled out a flat brown-paper package tied in plain twine.

"And what have we here?"

Adam slit the twine with his own knife and folded the paper back. Inside the package were three pictures. Two were colored sketches. Adam knew little of art, but he was struck by how much the artist was able to make of a few simple lines. The third was a painting of a young woman asleep beside the hearth in a country kitchen.

Adam frowned. Wiggins had said the woman he'd seen leaving the Douglases' house yesterday had been carrying a package wrapped in brown paper. This, then, would seem to be that package. But what to make of its contents? Had they been stolen? Wiggins had said the woman had brought some kind of payment, with the hope of being able to buy Cantrell off. Were these valuable? Adam squinted at them again and then shrugged and wrapped them back up. That answer would have to come from others.

He heard footsteps thundering up the stairs and went to open the door. Fisher, the driver who'd come with him from Bow Street, pushed open the door for a portly, balding man. He showed no dismay at his surroundings but plumped his bag down on the table and strode over to the bed.

"God rest him," he murmured. "I'm sorry for your loss, sir."

"The loss isn't mine," said Adam. "My name's Harkness. I'm from the Bow Street Police Station."

"Yes, your man told me this was Bow Street business. Name's Piggot," said the man. "Ethan Piggot, surgeon." The man pulled a large red kerchief from his pocket and wiped his perspiring face. "What was it, then? A quarrel?"

"I'm hoping you can tell me," said Adam. "He was sound enough when last seen, but today he collapsed suddenly and died within the space of a few minutes."

"Mmm, did he now?" Piggot rubbed his chin. "Could be any of a thousand things. My advice is to comfort his family and bury him quick."

Adam took a deep breath. "Could you have a look at him, sir? It's possible all is not as it should be."

Piggot tucked his kerchief away. "Probably nothing to see. Seldom is in cases of sudden collapse. But if you insist."

Despite his reluctance, Piggot immediately assumed a businesslike demeanor. For a moment, he stared hard at the corpse, as if he could make it yield its secrets by force of will. Then he rolled up his shirtsleeves. He peeled back one of Cantrell's eyelids and then the other. He frowned. He prodded at the blisters on the dead man's lips and then—with no sign of squeamishness at all—pried open his mouth, peered inside, and even took a deep sniff.

Piggot pulled a face and straightened up. He spied the empty wine bottle on the table and grabbed it up. For a minute, Adam thought the man wanted a drink, but he simply sniffed at the bottle. And pulled another disgusted face.

"Well." He took up the cork and shoved it deep down the bottle's neck. "There's your answer, and a nasty one it is, too."

"What is it?"

"Poison," said Piggot firmly. "Belladonna, and plenty of it. Thought so when I saw the rash round his mouth. It was in the wine. You can't mistake the smell, but you have to know it, you see." He shoved the bottle toward Adam. "I think, Mr. Harkness of Bow Street, your next port of call better be with the coroner. There's been murder done."

CHAPTER 34

An Instance of Poor Timing

*. . . what is the difference in matrimonial affairs
between the mercenary and the prudent motive?*

Jane Austen, *Pride and Prejudice*

The parlor was empty. Rosalind stood in the middle of the
clutter, her own shout ringing in her ears.

"Alice?" she called again.

Alice pushed her way in through the door from the dining
room. She was drying her hands on a towel. George followed
behind her, his shirtsleeves rolled up to his elbows. The Littlefields had kept house together for a number of years, and
George made no fuss about helping his sister with the domestic duties.

"Rosalind! What on earth—" began Alice.

Rosalind cut her off. "Has there been any message from
Amelia yet?"

"No, none. What—"

But Rosalind interrupted again. "Where is Nora?"

"Up in her room," said Alice. "She asked me for ink and
paper. She said she had letters to write. Rosalind, what's happened?"

"Bryan Cantrell is dead," said Rosalind. "He collapsed
and he died while Adam and I were talking with him."

"I'll go get her," said George. He nipped out into the foyer and raced up the stairs. Both Alice and Rosalind watched the stairs with a growing sense of foreboding as they listened to his footsteps overhead.

In a moment, he reappeared, alone, with a piece of paper in his hand.

"She's scarpered," he said grimly. He handed Rosalind the paper. On it, Nora had scrawled:

> *Gone to visit a friend. Will return soon.*
> *N.*

"Oh, that little *idiot*." Alice stamped her foot. "I should have *known*! I knew it was far too quiet up there!"

"She can't have been gone more than an hour," said George.

"Yes, but gone where?" shot back Alice. "She could be halfway out of the city by now."

"I'll go see if she took her bag." Rosalind started toward the door.

"Rosalind, wait." George nodded toward the window. Outside, Nora Hodgeson was striding up the street. Everything about her signaled extreme frustration. Despite this, Rosalind felt a rush of relief.

As Nora let herself in, Alice hurried into the foyer to meet her. Rosalind heard their voices through the door but could not hear what was said. But in the next heartbeat, the parlor door burst open, and Nora ran in, with Alice close behind.

"What is this?" Nora demanded. "Alice says Cantrell is *dead*?"

"I'm afraid he is," said Rosalind.

Nora stared for one heartbeat. In the next, she clapped both hands across her mouth. She bent forward, her shoulders shuddering and eyes squeezed shut. An odd choking noise forced itself out between her fingers.

She was laughing.

Rosalind had seen shock before in its various forms, and she recognized it now. She threw her arm around Nora's shoulders and steered her to the chair at Alice's writing table. George, who was as familiar as Rosalind with this sort of nervous response, pulled a seldom touched decanter off the mantel. Alice held out a coffee cup so he could pour in a healthy measure and passed the drink to Nora.

Nora gulped down the entire dose without batting an eye and pressed the back of her hand against her mouth. Rosalind laid a hand on Nora's shoulder.

"It's all right," breathed Nora. "I'm all right. I just . . . good God," she whispered. "Good God, can it be true?"

"I was there," said Rosalind. "I'm sorry."

"Yes, yes, you would be," murmured Nora. "Maybe I will be, too, eventually. I did care, once. It was never love exactly, but it was sympathy, a kind of partnership. I thought. I believed." She closed her eyes. "How did it happen?"

"He was already quite ill when we arrived, and in a matter of minutes, he simply ceased to breathe," said Rosalind. "There was no time to do anything for him."

Nora shivered hard. "Well, I suppose I should be grateful it was quick." She looked at her empty cup. "Or is that wicked?"

"It's all right," said Alice. "You don't need to understand what you feel all at once."

Nora smiled weakly. George poured a bit more of the brandy into her cup.

"Nora," said Rosalind, "before Cantrell's collapse, we saw him arguing with a young woman, a Miss Emma Lelyveld."

Nora shook her head. "I've never heard of her."

"She seemed to have heard of you. She was extremely angry at Cantrell for taking up with another woman. Apparently, she thought Cantrell was going to marry her."

"How do you know this?"

THE SECRET OF THE LOST PEARLS 267

"A friend of Cantrell's arrived shortly after he died, and told us."

Nora's face twisted up tightly, and for a moment Rosalind thought she was going to start laughing again. "A friend he was living with, perhaps?"

As soon as she said it, Rosalind understood. So did Alice.

"Oh my *Lord*!" Alice exclaimed. "He was doing it again, wasn't he? Exactly what he did to the Douglases? Makes friends, moves in, importunes a young girl—"

"It's the game he goes back to when there's nothing better on offer," said Nora.

"So you were just one of many?" asked Rosalind.

Nora gave her a wry smile. "I like to think I was at least a little special. He, after all, did not abandon me for someone else. Quite the reverse."

Rosalind nodded, but inside her thoughts turned. Nora might be right that Cantrell knew there was something special about her. Why else would he keep her with him after all hope of ransom payments was gone? Nora had said it was because they had some fellow feeling, and obviously, she was a useful partner in his schemes. But that didn't feel like enough. Not for the sort of man Cantrell had proved himself to be.

"So," said Nora. "What is to be done now?"

George and Alice both looked to Rosalind.

"I must return to Portsmouth Square," Rosalind told them all. "I'll need to give them the news there. And . . . well, what happens afterward depends on what, if anything, Amelia has found out and, of course, what Mr. Harkness discovers."

"Yes, I wondered where he and that other fellow had got themselves to," said Nora.

"Before I left, a doctor had been sent for. Mr. Harkness needed to wait for him, and to search the rooms to see if there was any sign of who had been there."

"You think he was killed, don't you?" asked Nora warily.

"I think it is possible."

"And so, of course, you think it is possible I killed him?"

"Did you?" asked Rosalind.

"No," said Nora at once. "I may have wanted to, but no."

"Then where did you get off to just now?" Alice asked.

"And why not tell us?" added George. "I would have gone with you."

"Yes, I know," said Nora. "And that's exactly why I didn't tell you. I needed to see this person alone."

"What for?" demanded Alice.

Nora very clearly bit back her initial reply. "I am owed some money, and I attempted to collect it. I regret to say I was not successful." She rubbed her mottled hands together.

"You're welcome to stay here as long as you need to," Rosalind said. She also ignored Alice's exasperated glance.

"Where your Littlefields can keep an eye on me?" Nora smiled, but no one else did. She sighed exasperatedly. "Please, don't worry. Mr. Sommerton may have disappointed me for the moment, but I'm not going to run."

It seemed to Rosalind that the words "not yet" remained unsaid. But what truly caught her attention was the name Sommerton. It sounded familiar, but she could not remember where she had heard it. But it had been recently, that she was sure of.

"I should go," said Rosalind. "I'll send a note as soon as I know anything more. If Mr. Harkness comes here, will you let him know where I've gone?"

George promised they would. Rosalind took up her gloves and left the room, but Alice followed her. When they reached the foyer, her friend put a hand on Rosalind's sleeve.

"Rosalind, I don't like this," Alice said frankly. "You sound far too much on edge. You don't need to leave this minute. It might be better to wait until you know more about what happened. I mean, I know this all looks very odd, but it might be simple bad luck."

But Rosalind shook her head. "I cannot believe that. Even if I did not need to let Bethany know what happened, I've left Amelia with the Douglases for too long. I have to find out if Betsy's returned, and if she has, I need to find some way to get her to talk to me." *To bribe her if necessary.* "And there is still this matter of the pearls."

Alice pressed her mouth into a thin, straight line. "I'm beginning to dislike this Portsmouth Square house, for your sake."

"Oh, so am I," said Rosalind. "So am I."

But as she was drawing on her gloves and trying to rally her thoughts, a knock sounded at the front door. Rosalind looked at Alice, and Alice raised her brows.

Rosalind opened the door. A ragged boy stood on the stoop. He was tousled, grubby, and thoroughly pink in the face from running.

"I've a letter for Miss Rosalind Thorne." He dug deep in his jacket pocket and, after a couple of tries, yanked out the object in question.

Rosalind gave the boy sixpence and took the thoroughly crumpled note. Her name was written across the front in Adam's strong hand.

I've sent for Sir David, she read when she opened it. *Cantrell was poisoned, most likely with belladonna.*

There was a little more. A detail or two. A request that Rosalind meet him at Bow Street, and that she bring Sanderson Faulks, if he could be found.

But Rosalind's mind could not seem to focus on any lines beyond the first.

Cantrell was poisoned, most likely with belladonna.

"Is there any answer?" asked the boy. "I was told to wait for an answer."

"Yes," said Rosalind. "You may tell the gentleman who gave you this, I will meet him at his place of work. He'll know what is meant."

"Yes, miss." The boy bounded down the stairs and sprinted off down the street.

Rosalind closed the door and turned Alice.

"Rosalind, what is it?" asked Alice. "It's from Adam, isn't it? Does he say . . . ?"

"Cantrell was murdered," Rosalind said, finishing for her. "Poisoned. With belladonna."

"Well, you suspected there was foul play."

"Yes," agreed Rosalind. "The problem is the means."

"I don't understand," said Alice.

Rosalind glanced toward the parlor door. It remained shut. Nonetheless, she lowered her voice to make sure she would not be overheard.

"You remember I told you the Douglases' upstairs maid, Betsy, delivered a message to Cantrell?"

Alice nodded.

"That same day, Betsy was commissioned to buy some eye drops at the apothecary, for brightening a lady's eyes."

"Oh." Alice, of course, knew as well as Rosalind that the formula for such drops frequently included a quantity of belladonna. "But who were they purchased for . . . ?"

"Penelope Douglas," said Rosalind. "And as of yesterday afternoon, Betsy had gone missing."

CHAPTER 35

Some Evidence and Argument

*Coroners are very ancient officers at common law
. . . and may now bind to the peace any person
who makes an affray in their presence.*

John Impey, *The Office and Duty of Coroners*

It was quite some time before Rosalind managed to track down Mr. Faulks. He was not in his rooms, and his man there did not know which of his four or five clubs he intended to dine at that afternoon. Fortunately, George had agreed to come with her, leaving Alice with Nora. Rosalind could hardly be seen parading through Pall Mall and St. James's, inquiring after a rather notorious dandy.

But such restraints of etiquette and custom did not apply to George. He was able to enter where he chose and make inquiries on Rosalind's behalf. As Mr. Faulks was known to associate with all manner of persons as part of his various business matters, one newspaperman in an immaculately mended coat and worn half boots did not arouse too much curiosity.

In the end, they discovered Mr. Faulks at White's, a club

whose members were known for their love of all manner of betting and gaming.

"I trust we do not interrupt something urgent, Mr. Faulks," said Rosalind as Sanderson climbed into the hired carriage.

"Not at all, Miss Thorne. I had already completed my business, and, of course, I am always ready to assist you and your Mr. Harkness. May I know why I am required?"

"I wish I could tell you," said Rosalind. "I've had only one hasty note from Mr. Harkness. I can tell you a man has been killed."

"Goodness," murmured Sanderson. "Is it over these famous pearls of yours?"

"It is possible," said Rosalind. "But I think it more likely it is either love or money."

Sanderson's brows arched. As the driver took them through the streets at as brisk a trot as could be managed in London's evening traffic, Rosalind told Sanderson, and George, about finding Cantrell, and about what had happened afterward.

By the time she was finished, the cab had pulled up in front of Bow Street. Sanderson climbed out and helped Rosalind down. George leapt down behind them, very much intent on joining them inside. There was no question that whatever he learned would quickly end up in the headlines of the *Chronicle*.

"George . . . ," began Rosalind.

"Oh, come, Rosalind, be reasonable," said George. "Murder? The theft of a priceless pearl necklace? The Major will have my head if I don't follow this through."

"I was speaking in confidence," she reminded him.

George looked unusually rebellious. Rosalind felt her patience wilt, but she remembered that George and Hannah were expecting their first child in a matter of months. Impending fatherhood could make a man especially anxious for the security of his pocket and position.

"If you will agree to wait just a few days, I will make sure you have the full story," she said. "And it should extend to several new pieces for Alice and the gossip columns."

"All right," said George reluctantly. "But if another paper gets hold of the story first, all agreements are off."

Rosalind agreed to this stipulation, and she further reminded George that if he took himself over to the Brown Bear for a drink, he'd surely pick up some very interesting tidbits of news there. George brightened considerably at this and strolled off in search of beer and talk. That left Sanderson to escort Rosalind into the police station.

Members of the dandy set prided themselves on an appearance of unflappability, but this was a quality Mr. Faulks genuinely possessed. He strolled through the unruly crowd that filled Bow Street's lobby and did not so much as turn a hair. When a flashily dressed merchant trod on the toes of his flawless Hessian boots, Sanderson merely nudged the man with the head of his walking stick and murmured, "Have a care, my good sir!"

"I somehow feel I should apologize . . . ," said Rosalind.

"My dear Miss Thorne, whatever for?" Sanderson replied, an arch smile playing about his lips. "I shall be able to dine out on this experience for months!"

At last, they were able to spot Adam. He took them from the lobby through the wardroom, where the patrols assembled before being assigned their various routes for the day or night, to the patrol room.

The patrol room was the base of operations for Bow Street's eight principal officers. To Rosalind, it always felt like a combination of shipping office and circulating library. Large maps of London and Westminster had been tacked to the walls. The shelves were filled with bound volumes of newspaper clippings. Papers from across the length and breadth of England hung on racks or were stacked on the tables. Among them were issues of Bow Street's own paper, the *Hue & Cry*. Circulated among the police offices of London and its outskirts, this singular publication was mostly given over to details of crimes and descriptions of stolen property that was either missing or had been discovered in pawnshops or other questionable places. Doubtlessly, Mr. Tauton had placed a description of the lost Douglas pearls in its pages.

A long table stretched down the center of the room. To one side stood Sir David Royce, the coroner for the City of London. Beside him waited Mr. Tauton and, somewhat to Rosalind's consternation, Mr. John Townsend.

John Townsend was the chief among Bow Street's principal officers. According to Adam, he had made his initial fame disrupting a gang of Irish saboteurs that had made their nest in London. He was a straight, proud, portly man who was deeply proud of his relationship with the former Prince of Wales, the man who was shortly to be crowned King George IV.

The look he turned on Sanderson and Rosalind as she made her curtsy was less than welcoming. The glower he spared for Adam was hardly any better.

Sir David, however, bowed to them both. "Miss Thorne, thank you so much for coming."

"I hope I can be of some assistance, Sir David," she replied. She also introduced Sanderson, who swept off his hat and bowed to both him and Mr. Townsend.

"Mr. Townsend, I am honored," Sanderson announced. "One hears so much about your excellent work in protecting our king and our city. It is a delight to be able to give you my thanks in person. I recognize the gratitude of a person such as myself may mean very little to you, but the opportunity, sir, means a great deal to me."

"Only doing my duty, sir, only my duty!" replied Mr. Townsend. At the same time, his chest puffed out noticeably.

"You are too modest, I'm sure," murmured Sanderson.

Mr. Townsend bowed in acknowledgment of this compliment and then turned to Adam. "Harkness, you may take Miss Thorne to wait in my office."

"If you've no objection, Mr. Townsend, I was hoping Miss Thorne might stay," said Sir David. "She has been closely involved in this affair for some days now. She may have information that could prove most valuable."

"Sir David, I respect your office, and your experience, but I must protest at putting any reliance on the hearsay of an untutored female."

Sir David smiled blandly. "I would hardly call Miss Thorne untutored, sir. I recognize it is irregular, but I ask you to indulge me in this matter."

The two men stared at each other. Sanderson passed his hand over his mouth. Rosalind suspected he was hiding a smile. She prepared herself to wait patiently while these two men sorted the matter of her presence and her usefulness out between them.

It was no real contest, of course. Any violent death, whether murder or accident, was the province of the coroner, and his authority was absolute. If Sir David did not deem it necessary, Bow Street might not even have a hand in the investigation.

"It is, of course, your decision, Sir David," said Mr. Townsend reluctantly. "But you must excuse me while I speak to Mr. Harkness on an internal matter. Mr. Tauton will see to whatever else you may require. Harkness?"

If Rosalind did not know Adam so well, she might entirely have missed the stubborn set of his jaw. But all he said was, "You will excuse me?" before he followed Mr. Townsend into his private office.

The door shut. Firmly.

Sir David shook his head. Mr. Tauton rubbed his finger across his upper lip.

"Well," said Sanderson, "I, for one, do not wish to interrupt the obviously very important business of this place a moment longer than necessary. How may I be of assistance, gentlemen?" He looked from Sir David to Mr. Tauton.

"Well, Mr. Faulks," said Sir David. "I imagine Miss Thorne has told you something about this man Bryan Cantrell?"

Sanderson bowed his head in acknowledgment.

"When Harkness and Miss Thorne found him, he was in a run-down flat, with very little in it by way of personal possessions. The remains of a meal and a bottle of wine were on the table. Mr. Harkness found this label. We presume it was from the food basket."

A folded paper lay on the table, alongside a stack of closely written pages. Mr. Tauton opened the paper, pulled out a torn label, and handed it to Rosalind.

FOR MY LOVE, WITH MY LOVE.

"The landlady of the boardinghouse—calls herself Mother Carey—says she saw no one, just the basket, but she knew who it would be for."

Of course she would. Rosalind could picture Cantrell reading the label with his charming grin and his bright eyes lit up. Who did he think it had come from? Rosalind knew of three immediate possibilities, and probably there were others.

"Do you recognize the hand, Miss Thorne?" asked Mr. Tauton.

Rosalind took the label and examined it closely. The handwriting was thin and uneven, as if the message had been dashed off in a hurry. The tails on the *y*'s were very straight and long, almost as if they were to underscore the other words.

"No, I don't know it." Rosalind handed the label back to Mr. Tauton.

"Ah, well, worth a try," he said.

"Now, in addition to the basket, there was a peculiar package found with the body," said Sir David. "Mr. Faulks, Mr. Harkness suggested you might be able to give us an opinion of the contents."

Mr. Tauton took a flat package from the top of one of the wooden filing cabinets, set it on the long table in front of Sanderson, and unwrapped it.

Inside were three pictures. The first was a landscape done in charcoal and crayon, both well rendered and richly shaded. The second item was an oil painting on an unframed canvas. It depicted the kitchen of a country house. A young woman had fallen asleep beside the hearth, her head thrown back and her skirts rucked up to her knees. Her suspiciously clean bare feet were planted in front of her. The third picture was nothing more than a sketch on paper. It was of a milkmaid who had fallen asleep under a hedgerow; her peasant blouse had slipped off one shoulder.

Rosalind's heart thumped once, hard. She had seen this sketch before.

But even more surprising was Sanderson's reaction. He seemed transfixed. He raised his quizzing glass to his eye and bent over the pictures until his nose practically touched the surface.

At last, Sanderson lifted his head. "How did this philistine, Cantrell, get hold of these?" he demanded.

"Are they good, then?" asked Sir David.

"Good!" Now Sanderson stared at Sir David through his glass. "If I am correct, they're worth more than the contents of this entire room. At least at the moment." He twirled the glass thoughtfully. "I will need to consult with some colleagues to be certain, of course."

"But what are they?" asked Rosalind.

"You will recall I told you that the world of art is all aflutter with a new painter?"

Rosalind paused. "Yes. Jacob Mayne?"

"Mayne?" Sir David echoed, surprised. "I was planning to take Lady David to his exhibition at the week's end. It is causing quite the sensation. These are his work, then?"

"I believe so." Sanderson took up the charcoal sketch. "And if they are, these three works represent as much as four hundred pounds in value. If they went to auction, it might be even more, given the current frenzy in the market." He took the sketch to the window and held it up to the light. "But I think they are his. I'd have to check with Sommerton to be absolutely sure . . ."

The name stung Rosalind. "Sommerton?"

"Yes, Richard Sommerton," said Sanderson. "He is representing Miss Mayne in the matter of her brother's work." He paused, clearly noticing Rosalind's disconcerted expression. "Have I said something wrong?"

"No," said Rosalind. "No. I am just . . . reminded of something."

She was reminded of Lady Cowper mentioning that name. And Nora Hodgeson.

Reminded of Nora's sketches in her room, and her hands, stained with faded color. Reminded of her saying how she wished to go to Paris and to Rome to study painting, and how Lucinda said Nora had spent hours in their home, copying the paintings there.

Reminded of the sketch of the sleeping shepherdess she had seen in Nora's room.

And how Nora had learned so much about how to tell an engaging lie.

And, despite everything, how close she remained to Mariah and Penelope.

Oh, those girls. Rosalind let out a long breath. *Those foolish, foolish girls.*

"Thank you, Mr. Faulks," said Sir David. "Now, Miss Thorne, I understand you are as well informed as anyone about the victim. If you would please share what you've learned?"

Sanderson pulled out a chair for Rosalind, and she and the men sat down. She took a moment to gather her wits and told the men how Bethany had come to her with her problem of the stolen pearls, and how Bryan Cantrell had burst into the dining room and then appeared at Meredith's concert.

She told them how Betsy had passed Cantrell a note while he watched the house, and how Betsy had since disappeared.

She repeated what Nora had told her about Cantrell's career as a thief and swindler, how he had kept watch over the Portsmouth Square house, and how she and Adam had come upon him in the street, arguing with Miss Emma Lelyveld.

All the time she was talking, Rosalind was aware of John Townsend's voice rumbling through the door of his office. She could not understand the words, but the tone was preemptory and angry. Every so often, she heard Adam make some brief reply.

Rosalind forced herself to keep her attention on Sir David and Mr. Tauton and her story. Sanderson lounged in his chair, apparently relaxed, even drowsy. But Rosalind knew he was attending closely to every word.

Just as she was relating her conversation with Thaddeus Asherton, Mr. Townsend's door opened once again, and Adam walked out. His face was a perfect stoic mask, but the set of his shoulders and the careful way he moved told Rosalind he was brimming with anger.

He closed the office door with exquisite care and came to join them at the table.

Mr. Tauton gave Adam a speaking glance as he sat, but said nothing.

"Thank you, Miss Thorne," Sir David said instead. "That is all very clear. It may be you will be called on to repeat it all for my clerk so we may have it entered into evidence."

"You'll be opening an inquest, then, Sir David?" said Mr. Tauton.

"Without question. Mr. Harkness, I'd like you to be on hand to assist matters?"

"I'd be only too glad," Adam answered. "However, I am not certain I will find myself at liberty to do so."

Sir David did not seem at all troubled by this. "I will make my request to Mr. Townsend personally. I am sure he will make no objection." Adam looked skeptical but made no further remark. "In fact, I'll go speak with him now. Perhaps, Mr. Tauton, if you'll accompany me to help fill in the details, we can release Mr. Faulks back to his own business, and I think, Mr. Harkness, we may trust you to see Miss Thorne safely to her destination."

They each said their farewells, and Adam ushered Rosalind and Sanderson out of the station and through the gate and into the afternoon bustle.

"Sanderson," said Rosalind, "I'm going to ask you to hold all of this in confidence. If word gets out . . . it might prove highly disruptive."

"Will it?" said Sanderson. "Because a dead scoundrel has gotten hold of some valuable paintings?"

"Yes, well, there's rather more to it."

"You amaze me," he said blandly. "I shall remain as silent as the grave. However, just at this moment, Miss Thorne, you must excuse me. I have business of my own yet to be accomplished today. Mr. Harkness, I trust I may leave her in your care? Excellent. Do not hesitate to call on me whenever you have need." He bowed over her hand and sauntered away up Bow Street, as if nothing in the world could ever disturb him.

Rosalind wished she could feel the same.

CHAPTER 36

An Unsettled Reunion

*. . . his affection was not the work of a day, but
had stood the test of many months' suspense . . .*

Jane Austen, *Pride and Prejudice*

"I know it's still cold," said Adam to Rosalind. "But
I would you mind very much if we walked a ways?"

"Certainly not," she replied. "I feel certain the fresh air
would do me good."

He offered her an arm, and they set off. It was late in the
afternoon, and twilight would soon settle in. The streets
around the station were busy, but they walked together easily, comfortable in the anonymity of the eternal London
crowd. They soon both comfortably adjusted stride, attitude,
and attention to allow for the presence of the other.

They had also both long been in the habit of walking to
settle their thoughts. Rosalind keenly felt Adam's need to do
so now. As much as her own mind was caught up in the whirl
of trouble that surrounded Bethany's family, she was deeply
concerned about Adam and what had passed just now between him and Mr. Townsend. Since he'd returned from

Manchester, she had felt that there was some unresolved tension in him. She felt it again now.

But she did not press him. He would tell her when he was ready. For this moment, being together was enough.

"I imagine," said Adam at last, "you heard some of what passed between me and Mr. Townsend."

"Nothing distinct," said Rosalind. "But I'm afraid it would take a much thicker door to conceal his general displeasure."

Adam's smile was wry, and brief.

"What happened?" Rosalind asked.

"It was this business out in Manchester," he said. "I think I told you, it had been suggested that the culprits were some men from one of the manufactories."

"Yes," said Rosalind. "Specifically, some men who had agitated for higher wages."

"And better housing," said Adam. "They'd all been fired recently for having the temerity to ask but had not gone quietly."

"I take it you did not think they were your shopbreakers?"

"I knew they were not. And I did not arrest them."

Rosalind consider this. "Were you told to arrest them?"

"I was," replied Adam. "And even though we were quickly able to clap hold of the real thieves, it was made quite clear that the city's officials wanted us to arrest their troublemakers, as well, and use the robberies as the excuse. That is what was behind my early departure," he said ruefully. "I'm afraid I simply turned tail and ran."

"Rather than arrest men for crimes they did not commit?" murmured Rosalind. "How cowardly of you."

"Yes, well, as a result of that cowardice, Townsend is less than happy with me. I do not exhibit myself well, he says. I am known to make trouble, and now I am disobedient."

"But . . . I thought you were in his good graces. Especially after his royal patron spoke in your favor." Only a few months ago, Adam had been singled out by the Prince of Wales—now King George—for special duties and special praise.

"And that, I'm afraid, is my true failing," said Adam. "His Majesty also wanted the workers arrested."

"His . . . ," gasped Rosalind. "I don't understand."

"It's because of the Peterloo Massacre," Adam said.

Rosalind fell silent.

The tragedy had occurred only a few months ago. The press and pamphlets had been filled with the horror of it for weeks. Rosalind and the Littlefields had sat in George and Hannah's front room, poring over the various accounts. George had run out to buy new editions of the papers as they came out, and had brought copies of the *Chronicle* still wet from the presses. A rally had been held for the cause of voting reform at St. Peter's Field. Thousands were believed to have shown up in support of the cause. The local authorities had become alarmed at the size of the crowd and had asked for the cavalry be called in.

Fifteen people had died when the soldiers charged the crowd.

And now that she was reminded of it, Rosalind remembered that this had all happened in the center of Manchester.

"Were they afraid of another mob?" she asked.

"Yes," said Adam. "Perhaps not over voting reform, but over wages and working conditions . . . The subject doesn't matter. It's the possibility of a mob that worries His Majesty and Mr. Townsend. He . . . they are adamant that even the possibility of such an event must be snuffed out before it can begin." Adam steered her around a market woman who was retrieving the apples that had spilled from her basket. "So, it seems, when I was sent to Manchester, my real task was to provide the excuse to arrest these men before they could rally another mob to their cause. Whatever it might turn out to be. And now I am informed—at length—that apprehending the actual thieves is not considered an adequate substitute."

There was no answer to this. Rosalind did not even try to find one. She pressed her hand against his arm, and they walked on. The world moved around them. The horses and carriages and vans clattered past. The afternoon was cooling, and the clouds were lowering, turning the day a steel, watery gray.

"So, now comes the question," said Adam. "What do I do? Make my apologies and accept that I must do as I'm told, even when . . . ?" He didn't finish.

"What do you want to do?" Rosalind asked.

"I don't know. I wish I did. This is what I know, Rosalind." He swept his free hand out. Rosalind understood that gesture to encompass all his worth as an officer, first in the highway patrol and now at Bow Street. "I am good at my profession, and I believe I have done good in it. But of late . . ." He shook his head. "I fear that the law looks more to stability than to justice. I knew this," he whispered. "I know this," he said. He sighed sharply. "And yet if I turn away from Bow Street, how do I support my mother, my sister and her family, my younger brothers . . ." He turned again. "You."

Rosalind felt her throat close. They had not yet talked of marriage. She was not ready for it, was not in any way certain that was the path that she wanted to take, even with Adam.

She recovered as quickly as she could, but he saw her hesitation. "I'm sorry," he said. "I shouldn't have . . . It is far too soon, of course, and we have never talked . . ."

Rosalind folded her hands over his. "I can wait," she said. "*We* can wait until you have made your decision, and afterward if necessary." She gave him a small smile. "It's not as if I'm pining away for want of occupation."

"Yes, this business at Portsmouth Square." They stopped on a corner to wait for a van to rattle past. "It sounds as if

I'm not the only one who finds themselves in a complicated situation."

"No," agreed Rosalind. "And it seems the longer I stare at it, the more confusing it all becomes."

"What's confusing you?"

"The timing of Cantrell's actions," she told him. "We know him to have been a mercenary and a swindler. But he took up with Douglas when Douglas had no money. He kept Nora with him when there was no expectation of money. Why? I don't know. I don't even know who he is, not really."

"And you think this is important?"

"Yes, I do. I've told Bethany—Mrs. Douglas—it is important to know the whole truth. Which it is, for her sisters, and me," she added.

"Why?"

"Because the revelation of Cantrell's true motives and his identity will clear their names. As things stand, their conduct is suspect, and their chances in society are much damaged. Without the full story."

"Without it the *haut ton* believes what it chooses about them." Adam paused. "And about you."

"Yes," said Rosalind. "I admit that part of my motivation now is entirely self-serving."

They walked on in silence, stepping over puddles, avoiding their fellow pedestrians.

"Tell me the story again," said Adam. "About this inheritance and how Cantrell came to foist himself on the Douglases."

"It was the other way around," said Rosalind. "Cantrell came first. The inheritance came afterward, which is exactly what confuses me."

"Tell me," Adam urged her.

So Rosalind did. Adam listened silently. He made no interruption. But when Rosalind finally fell silent, his question entirely surprised her.

"How long has it been since anyone has seen Addison Douglas?"

"Over a year, certainly."

"What search was made for him?"

"I am ashamed to say I don't know." In fact, she had not asked, or thought of it much. Her attention had been entirely focused on what had happened afterward.

"And Cantrell was with the Douglases before Addison vanished, but after Addison became Sir Jasper's heir?"

"Yes," said Rosalind. Her gaze met Adam's. "What is it you're thinking?"

"I'm thinking that one of the mistakes people make about swindlers is not realizing how long and how patiently they work before they spring their traps."

"You think Cantrell somehow knew Douglas stood to inherit after Addison?"

"It's possible. It would make some sense."

"But how? These are not prominent people. There business is not published in the papers or talked over at dinner parties."

"I don't know," admitted Adam. "A chance word dropped in a club? Men tend to talk about the fortunes and families of those they know. Perhaps Cantrell was friends with Addison Douglas. You say he made a habit of ingratiating himself to people who might be useful. Have you spoken to any of Addison's friends?"

"Only to Lady Cowper, who said she knew him slightly," said Rosalind. "She said that Addison did not have a strong temperament, and, of course, Sir Jasper is a demanding patron." Rosalind paused. Had she been too quick to accept this assessment? Indeed, had she been so focused on Cantrell and Nora, she had not stopped to consider how deeply Addison's fate might still be linked to that of the family at Portsmouth Square?

"Lady Cowper seemed to think Addison had simply run

away," said Rosalind. "That or . . ." She let the sentence trail away.

Adam quirked his brows.

"That he may have killed himself."

"There's another possibility," said Adam.

"Yes," agreed Rosalind. "That Cantrell may have killed him to bring his friend that much closer to the Douglas fortune."

"Cantrell may even have come to the Douglases with that plan in mind," said Adam. "He could have ingratiated himself there and wooed young Miss Penelope, with the plan that this Addison would soon be out of the way, leaving Douglas free to inherit."

"If that's the case, why didn't he stay to the finish?" asked Rosalind. "Why run off?"

"To make it look better," said Adam. "Or perhaps he thought Douglas was getting cold feet about the plan and would need an extra incentive to part with the money once he had it."

Rosalind was silent, letting this new, bleak possibility settle into her mind. "But Nora said they were abroad when Sir Jasper changed his mind and his will."

"Do we know when Addison went missing? Or how long he was gone before Sir Jasper changed his will?"

"I do not," admitted Rosalind.

"Have you spoken with Sir Jasper about any of this?"

"No," said Rosalind. "I've wanted to, but he does not visit the house, and I could find no excuse to go to him." She mustered a teasing tone. "You make me feel quite neglectful."

"Then I apologize. This business has more layers than almost any I've run across. One person cannot be expected to dig through them all. And as I do have an excuse to see Sir Jasper, I will use it."

They had reached Portsmouth Square. Rosalind looked up at the house and saw the lantern had already been hung beside the door and half the windows glowed with welcoming candlelight.

From where she stood, it was impossible to tell that anything at all was wrong.

"I expect Sir Jasper will not be pleased to see you," said Rosalind.

"I imagine he will be less pleased to be called before the coroner's court," replied Adam with a small smile. "Of course, this all may be nothing but my suspicious mind. It may be that Cantrell is guilty of nothing but taking what he could get when he could, and there was no larger design." Adam paused for a moment and then reached into his coat pocket. "There's one other thing. We found these when we searched him."

He brought out a ring of keys. "This small one seems to be to a trunk or a box," he said. "But I found nothing in his rooms."

"Mr. Asherton said Cantrell was staying with him. Perhaps the trunk is still with him." Her heart and her thoughts quickened. "Can you let me keep this? While you are quizzing Sir Jasper, I will speak with the Ashertons and see what may be learned there."

"I think that's an excellent idea. But what about these paintings that your Mr. Faulks says are so valuable?"

"Will you let me keep my counsel on those for now?" said Rosalind. "I want to be sure I know what I'm talking about before I say anything, but I strongly suspect that Mr. Cantrell was not the only person engaged in a fraud."

"Very well." Adam took the key ring, slipped the brass key off, and laid it in Rosalind's palm. "You work at this tangle on your end, and I will work on mine, and with luck, we will meet again in the middle."

Rosalind closed her fingers over the key. "This will not make more trouble for you with Mr. Townsend?"

"Not immediately. Sir David has determined that I should help him in his inquiries, and Townsend cannot be seen to go against the coroner. Afterward"—the corner of his mouth curled—"afterward, we shall see."

She touched his sleeve, and he turned on her a look of warmth and trust that took away the last of her breath. But they could do no more and separated there.

For now, Rosalind reminded herself. *Only for now.*

But for now, she must drag her thoughts away from Adam and what turn his future might take. Rosalind hurried through the entrance of the square, trying to bring some order to nerve and thought.

When she'd left Little Russell Street, she had been wondering whether it was Penelope who might have killed Bryan Cantrell.

Now she must wonder the same about Nora.

And Mariah.

CHAPTER 37

Unfortunate News

Murder is defined to be, when a person of sound memory and discretion unlawfully killeth any reasonable creature in being and under the king's peace, with malice aforethought . .

John Impey, *The Office and Duty of Coroners*

The house was quiet when Rosalind arrived. The footman opened the door for her. A maid whose name she did not know took her coat and bonnet. When she asked, she was informed that Mrs. Douglas was in her writing room. Rosalind thanked the girl and asked her to send for Amelia to meet her in her rooms.

Unfortunately, Bethany was not alone in the lavender-and-white room. Penelope sat with her at a prettily painted worktable. They leaned close together, caught up in some earnest conversation. But when Rosalind entered, they both broke off at once.

"Rosalind!" cried Bethany. "Thank goodness. We were wondering what could be happening to keep you away so long. How is Nora?"

"Nora is perfectly fine," said Rosalind. "My friends George and Alice Littlefield are with her."

"But something's happened," said Penelope. "Or you wouldn't have been gone so long. We thought perhaps you'd found Betsy."

"She has not returned?" asked Rosalind.

"No," said Bethany. "And Mrs. Hare says her things are gone from her room. Probably she has just decided to leave. Mrs. Hare says she was never very happy in service. But to leave without giving notice, and with everything so unsettled . . ."

And about to become more so. Rosalind considered asking to speak with Penelope in private but quickly discarded this idea. She felt it important that Bethany be present when Penelope heard her news. She wanted to see what the girl's reaction was.

Rosalind closed the room's door and then returned to stand beside the table.

"I'm sorry," she began. "I have to tell you, Bryan Cantrell is dead."

Penelope's first reaction was to clutch at Bethany's hand. For a moment, Rosalind was afraid she would faint again.

"How . . . ?" Penelope stammered. "How could you know this?"

"I was there," said Rosalind.

"There?" Penelope's voice rose to a shriek.

"Penelope, calm yourself," said Bethany mechanically. Her own complexion had turned a sickly gray, and shock warred with horror in her expression.

Penelope was not in any mood to be calmed. Instead, she lurched to her feet.

"How could you be with . . . *him* at such a time?" she demanded of Rosalind.

"The runners from Bow Street had discovered where he

lived," said Rosalind. She was not ready to reveal all the details of that business yet. "I had gone to confront him and, hopefully, to persuade him to leave you all alone."

Penelope swallowed, but her color was improving rapidly. In fact, her skin was becoming flushed.

"And he really is dead?" Penelope asked softly. "This is not another lie?"

"It is not," said Rosalind. "He is dead. It is possible he was poisoned."

Penelope took a step back, and another. Bethany rose, probably thinking the girl might collapse and need support. But Penelope swallowed and drew herself up.

"I think . . ." She stopped and began again. "I think I will go to my room. I think . . . if anyone asks, I am quite well. It is only a slight . . ." She did not seem able to finish. She gulped down a breath of air and another.

"Pen, sit down," urged Bethany.

But Penelope wasn't listening. Instead, she threw open the door and, as a result, nearly collided with Mrs. Hodgeson. This proved to be one shock too many for the young woman. She took one look at her mother-in-law and burst into tears. That good woman was so startled, she stepped backward, giving Pen room to brush past and hurry away.

"Penelope!" Mrs. Hodgeson cried over her shoulder. "What on earth is the matter with her now, Bethany? Miss Thorne! I heard that you had returned. What news?" She settled shakily onto the sofa. "Have you found . . . ?" She paused and took their faces in, her own eyes opened so wide they were almost round.

It was Bethany who answered. "Cantrell is dead, Mama."

"Dead?" Mrs. Hodgeson repeated. "He cannot be dead. He was just . . ." She waved her hand. "He was just here. We just saw him."

"Nonetheless," said Rosalind, "he is dead."

"But . . . ," she stammered. "But it was an illness, surely. I saw it in him when he came to us so suddenly. I knew he was not well. And who could be surprised? A man with his dissipated habits may be carried off by illness or some disorder of the blood at any minute."

"Mama," said Bethany, "Rosalind says he was poisoned."

"Impossible," announced Mrs. Hodgeson. "Who could even know such a thing?"

"It seems that the poison was belladonna, which leaves a detectible trace on its victim," said Rosalind. She spoke to Bethany, watching her face, but Bethany showed no additional surprise or agitation.

Mrs. Hodgeson pressed her handkerchief to her mouth. "Oh my ... oh my ...," she stammered. "Oh, my poor dear Nora!" she burst out finally. "I must go to her at once! I must ..." She heaved herself to her feet. "Gilpin. I need Gilpin. I must get dressed. I must go to her ..."

"Mama, please!" said Bethany. "Nora is well looked after by Miss Thorne's friends, I'm sure."

"And how am I to leave my daughter to the care of strangers at such a time?" demanded Mrs. Hodgeson.

"But I need you here!" cried Bethany desperately.

"Penelope is gravely overwrought," said Rosalind. "She will need all our support."

Mrs. Hodgeson froze in place. "Yes, yes," she murmured. "To be sure. I shall go see that the poor girl is settled. But you will not keep me from my Nora!" She pulled her wrapper more closely about her bony frame and tottered from the room.

"I'm not sure that was the best idea," said Bethany. "Poor Pen!"

"Mariah will help her," said Rosalind. "I'm sure she's already on her way."

"Yes, I imagine." Bethany's hand stole to her throat. "Rosalind ... what you said ... belladonna ..." She stopped and visibly shuddered as she tried to pull herself together. "Who could be responsible ... ?"

Rosalind shook her head. "I don't know."

Bethany's eyes strayed to the door. Rosalind knew what she was thinking. Someone in the house. One of her family.

"I believe Cantrell had other schemes underway," said Rosalind. "There is no evidence it was someone from this house." Except for the note. Except for the purchase of the substance that killed him, and Penelope's anger and her fear that this man would ruin all her hopes and dreams.

Except for the fact that Betsy had gone missing.

Except for the story the runner John Wiggins had told about how a man in a wool coat who had remonstrated with the person Cantrell sent to wait nearby for . . . something. And how a woman in a servant's cloak and bonnet and carrying a package had run from this house straight to Cantrell.

And except for how Nora had told her family Cantrell was dead, and concealed the fact that she had known him to be alive.

So many questions had swirled around the man himself in life, never mind in death. Including what he might have had to do with the disappearance of Addison Douglas, the event that thrust a fortune into Gerald Douglas's hands.

"I must tell Douglas." Bethany started for the door and then stopped. "Oh, no, he'll be gone by now. There's a—"

As if summoned by the sound of his name, the door opened and Douglas stepped into the room.

"What is there to tell me?" Douglas asked his wife. He was dressed to go out, in greatcoat and boots, and carried his gloves in his hand.

"Oh!" exclaimed Bethany. "I thought you'd gone."

"I was just about to leave. The carriage is waiting." He pointed over his shoulder. "But Mrs. Hare told me there'd been some outcry." His gaze flickered to Rosalind. "What's happened this time?"

"Bryan Cantrell is dead," said Bethany.

Douglas's face went blank from surprise, but only for a single heartbeat. "Well, thank God for that, then."

"Douglas!" cried Bethany.

"What am I supposed to say?" he snapped. "Surely, I am not expected to make any show of grief after all he has done to us?"

"I don't know." Bethany threw up her hands. "I don't know anything."

Douglas looked like he wanted to shout, but he suppressed the urge. Instead, he took Bethany's hand. "I'm sorry," he said. "This has been a most unsettled time. We've all felt it." Bethany looked up into her husband's eyes. He nodded and pressed her hand. "But don't you see, Bethany? With Cantrell dead, it's over. It's done. We can begin again."

Bethany wanted to believe him. Rosalind could see the struggle in her features. But in the end, she could not. "Rosalind?" she asked.

Douglas turned to her, as well. She could see in his eyes what he wanted her to say.

"I'm sorry," said Rosalind. "I truly wish it was over, but it is not."

"Why not?" Douglas demanded. "The man is dead, and that closes every account."

"Cantrell was poisoned," she said. "There must be an inquest. Questions will have to be asked about the disturbance he caused here, the threats he made."

"But that's all Nora's business," said Douglas. "And she no long resides here."

"It is not only Nora's business," Rosalind reminded him.

Douglas threw up his hands and uttered a censorious oath. "I'm sorry," he said immediately to Bethany. "I'm sorry. I am not . . . I cannot . . ." He stopped. "Miss Thorne, would you excuse us please?"

Rosalind looked to Bethany, who gave the barest hint of a nod. "Certainly."

She left the room. Standing in the corridor, she fought back the most uncivilized urge to put an ear to the door.

Now is not the time for eavesdropping, she told herself firmly. But she still hesitated. She urgently needed to speak to Amelia and hear what had been happening in the house since she left. At the same time, she needed to speak with Mariah.

Rosalind made her choice and strode down the corridor to the main stairway.

I must find Mariah.

And it must be quickly, before Mariah had time to absorb what had happened to Cantrell, and to concoct the next lie.

CHAPTER 38

Between a Husband and Wife

*There was a something in her countenance which
made him listen with an apprehensive and
anxious attention.*

Jane Austen, *Pride and Prejudice*

Alone with her husband, Bethany tried to clear her mind.
She tried, as she knew she should, to set her emotions
aside and speak rationally.

She tried not to think how many times she'd had to make
this same attempt, and not just with Douglas. There had
been all the years before she'd even met him—all the times
when she'd had to listen to her father's drawling recitations
on the defects of yet another tenant who'd decided to try
their luck in the city rather than stay and struggle on their
farm, or to her mother's declarations of another new malady
and the distillation of another new remedy, which would require yet another lengthy bout of rest and quiet.

Bethany knew she must manage. She must not be upset or
tired or neglectful. She must remain rational and dispassion-
ate, direct the servants, answer the creditors, and coax her

sisters. She must not ask to be excused, because without her, nothing would ever be done.

Bethany must not ever cry.

When she'd married Douglas, it seemed she'd finally found a partner. He was not afraid of work. He did not find the possibility that things could be made better with actual effort a ridiculous idea.

And he loved her. And he loved their children.

At least he had.

"Bethany," he said. She could tell he had already reached some decision. That was his way. His mind worked so fast, sometimes it was difficult to keep up. Once, those quicksilver thoughts had been about cross bracing and curves and elegance of design, all things she'd never even stopped to consider before she met him. Now . . . well, now it was other things.

"I think you should go back to Hertfordshire," said Douglas. "This business of a season, it's pointless now. Pen will only be overwhelmed."

"You're sending us away," Bethany said dully.

"No! Of course not. I'm just suggesting that you go, just until things settle down here. It's been too much. You need the time as much as any of the girls."

Bethany drew in another deep breath. *I must be rational. I must be reasonable. I must see he wants only what's best.* "And you?" she inquired.

"I have business to attend to, Beth. I'll have to stay."

"With Sir Jasper?"

"Possibly. If he invites me, I won't be able to refuse."

Calm. Rational. Reasonable. Not bitter. Not regretful. "Well, I owe Mama an apology."

"I don't . . ."

"It is all happening exactly as she said." Bethany wrapped her arms around herself. She was cold. She should have put on a shawl. She should have been sensible. "She said we are to be separated from you so that Sir Jasper may have you to himself without the encumbrance of a country wife."

"That's not what's happening!"

"Isn't it?"

"No, Beth! You're my wife! It's my duty to *protect* you! And provide for you!"

"Perhaps I don't want to be protected." There. She'd said it. Calmly. Rationally.

Douglas looked at her like she'd suddenly begun to speak Latin. "Then what do you want?"

What do I want? The question echoed in her mind. She remembered Rosalind had posed it to her back when all this began. *Back when I began this thing.* Sitting in the crowded little parlor, so afraid of what Sir Jasper might discover to drive her husband further away. So afraid of what Nora might have done that would make it impossible to allow her to stay.

What do I want? It seemed an impossible question. Except it was not. Not really.

"I want you," she said. "I miss you, Gerald."

"Miss me?" he echoed. "But I'm right here!"

"No, you're not." She rubbed her arms, trying to smooth down the goose bumps. "You're with Sir Jasper, and the money. You spend all day planning how to keep him happy today, and you'll do the same tomorrow, and the next day and the one after that, and all the long, wasted days until he dies." She was trembling now, trying to hold back the full force of her feeling. "And by then you'll have the money, but you'll have forgotten who you *are.*"

Be rational.

But that wasn't what she wanted. She didn't want to present reasons. She wanted Gerald to feel what she felt. She wanted him to know how much she hurt.

"When I married you, you were a builder, Gerald," she said, and her voice shook. "You wanted to bridge the world and bring whole kingdom together with the work of your hands. Now you're a vulture!" Her voice rose to a shout. "Your only work is sitting in a corner, waiting for an old man to die!"

He was staring at her now. Horrified. "Is that what you think of me?" he whispered.

"Yes," she said. Then, "No. I think you're trapped, Gerald." His name came out as half a sob. "Trapped by the wealth we've been given, and what's being dangled in front of us."

He was breathing hard now, his empty hands tightening and releasing. He'd never used to do that. This gesture was only since he'd become Sir Jasper's heir, since he'd stopped drawing and surveying and planning. Stopped being the engineer and builder she'd married.

She caught those hands now and held them, willing him to be still.

"Do you remember that dinner party where we met?" she asked him. "You spent an entire half hour telling me all about new construction techniques, and how it was now possible to use iron instead of wood, and how important it all was . . ." She smiled and felt the tears prickling behind her eyes.

Gerald looked down at her hands holding his. "I thought you were bored."

"Well, it was hardly romantic, but it was *new*. Ambitious. I'd never met anyone who planned things on the sheer scale you did. And you were filled with such energy. That was what I fell in love with. That energy. That ambition. That is why I'll never forgive Cantrell."

"I don't understand."

"When he took Nora, when he threatened Pen, he robbed you of that energy. Instead of reaching out to fulfill your own ambition, all your attention turned to trying to protect us.

We were all walled up behind the money, behind impossible expectations and the knowledge of our own inadequacy."

Douglas drew his hands away slowly. He crossed the room, moving to the windows. He stared out at the gardens, all wrapped in burlap for the winter. Bethany stayed where she was, her heart pounding frantically.

I've said too much. I've lost him for good. The useless country wife with the ridiculous family . . .

"I remember that party," said Douglas softly. He turned then, and she lifted her eyes to his face, and what she saw there stopped her breath. "But even more, I remember when I first saw you. You were walking up the lane in the sunshine. I stopped and I stared. Just . . . stared, like a schoolboy." He gestured helplessly. "You seemed so alive. So bright. Like you'd been drinking in the sunlight, and now it was shining through your eyes and your fingertips and the ends of your hair . . . I suppose I must have known about you before that." His mouth twisted into a wondering smile. "But I'd never really *seen* you before. I fell in love that very instant.

"And it's not your inadequacy that walls us in, Beth. It's mine. It was always mine." He hung his head. "And it's too late to change."

"I don't believe that," she said sharply.

"I gave away every other choice when I let Cantrell into the house. I let him charm me and sway me. What business do I have trying to make my own way in the world when I was ready to surrender my own judgment to the first plausible rascal who came along?"

"You made a mistake, Gerald. We all did."

"You have no idea, Beth—"

"Then *tell* me!" she cried. "Stop protecting and hiding and putting up walls and trust me!"

He looked at her shocked, tired, mouth agape. "I do trust you."

"Then act like it!"

"Beth." He breathed her name, a sound like a prayer. He was reaching for her, but she could not move. Her legs were trembling too badly; her heart would not slow down enough to allow her to breathe properly.

Gerald saw, and he seemed to understand. He walked toward her, until he stood so close, she could feel the warmth of his skin.

"I wish you had told me how you felt."

She swallowed. She lifted a hand and laid it on his chest, right where she could feel how his heart beat as frantically as hers.

"I wish I had, too," she told him. "But I didn't know how. I've never known how. I'm not Nora, you see. All I know how to do is patch things up and keep them going. That's always been my part."

He took her in his arms. He kissed her forehead and her mouth. "I'm sorry, Beth. Truly, I am. I've been an ass. Worse. A frightened, witless fool. And I've let you down so badly." His voice broke on the last word.

Bethany wrapped her arms about him, and he pulled her close. They held each other, and she rested her forehead against his broad shoulder. She remembered she had embraced him like this when he asked her to marry him, and again when she told him she was carrying their first child.

She remembered the man she had married because she liked and admired him, and then she had grown to love him and then had feared she had lost him.

She saw that man now looking down at her, with an expression of wonder in his eyes. "Do you believe it's that simple? We just choose again?"

"It is that simple, and that difficult. I'm not afraid, Gerald."

He hesitated again, remembering something, hearing some voice in his mind.

"But Pen has to have a dowry. And Gerry . . ."

"Will make his own way in the world," said Bethany. "Like his father always planned."

"But Pen?"

"What future does she have if we sell our souls to buy it?"

His eyes searched hers, and Bethany felt another stab of fear. She'd said too much, been too dramatic, nearly hysterical . . .

But he just nodded. "Yes," he said. "Very well, we'll . . ." He stopped, and then, to Bethany's surprise, he laughed.

"What is it?"

"I was about to say we'll cross that bridge when we come to it, and it just struck me as funny." He chuckled again, and she laughed with him, and soon they were both guffawing with laughter for no reason at all.

When finally the laughter faded, he took her hand in both of his, and he kissed it. "Oh, Beth. You don't know what you've done for me. I've been . . ." He swallowed. "I've been caught in such a coil. You will have to be patient with me, Beth. It will be a long time before I can . . . learn to speak again about everything."

"We will have all the time we need," she told him.

His small wondering smile flickered across his features. "I will go and see Sir Jasper. I'll break with him. If he does not accept me, and my wife and my family, then I want nothing from him. Because you're right. I have been a vulture." He took a deep breath. "No more of that now."

"Should I wait up for you?" she asked softly.

Douglas reached out and brushed a stray lock of hair from her forehead. "I will go in the morning. Tonight, Beth, I think I would much rather stay with you."

CHAPTER 39

Mariah

Unfeeling, selfish girl!
Jane Austen, *Pride and Prejudice*

Rosalind had guessed correctly. When she left the room where Bethany and Douglas had made themselves private, she found Mariah was already with Penelope. The two girls sat together on the divan that had been positioned in front of the fire in Penelope's room. Mariah held Penelope's hands, while Mrs. Hodgeson fluttered around the room.

"And you must have the lavender and yarrow, and Gilpin will make you one of my special tisanes. It is my own recipe and quite infallible for calming nerves!"

"Miss Thorne," said Mariah as Rosalind entered. "I believe we were expecting you."

Mrs. Hodgeson froze. "Miss Thorne!" she cried. "I thought you were with Bethany."

"I was." Rosalind breezed past the matron. "Penelope? How are you?"

Penelope lifted her tearstained face. But though she tried to speak, no words came out. She buried her face against Mariah's shoulder and burst into a fresh storm of tears.

Mariah, slowly, stiffly, brought her arm up to encircle the girl's shoulders.

"There!" cried Mrs. Hodgeson. "You see what you've done? Gilpin!" She dashed out the door. "Gilpin!"

"Pen," said Mariah. "That's enough. Stop it."

"I can't!"

Mariah pushed her sister-in-law backward, so Penelope had to look her in the face. "You *must*, Pen. I need you to be calm. There are things that need to be done, and I cannot stay here to be your handkerchief."

Penelope screwed her face up tight. She swallowed all her remaining tears in one hard gulp. "Yes," she gasped. "Yes, all right. I'll try."

Mariah nodded once and rose to her feet. "I've rung for tea. Don't let Mother and Gilpin pour any of their ridiculous potions down your throat." She walked straight out the door. "Miss Thorne? Are you coming?"

Rosalind had little choice but to follow. But as she did, she let her gaze sweep across Penelope's dressing table, looking for any bottle that might contain the eye drops Betsy had been sent to purchase.

She saw nothing.

In the corridor, the noise of Mrs. Hodgeson upbraiding Gilpin, and the world in general, was clearly audible. Mariah glided past her mother's door without so much as an eyeblink. When they reached her own rooms, Mariah took a key from her apron pocket and unlocked the door.

Mariah's sitting room was part library, part workroom. The shelves were filled with books. The desk was covered with papers, scissors, ink bottles, and glue pots, all of which combined to leave an acrid tang to the air. The fire was nothing but a few coals. Mariah made no move to poke them up. She waved Rosalind to the window seat, but she stationed herself in front of her desk. It was almost as if she meant to protect it from Rosalind's view.

"I assume you've told Nora about Cantrell," Mariah said without preamble. "How did she receive the news?"

"She seemed to take it well, all things considered," replied Rosalind. She remained standing.

"Will you . . ." Mariah folded her arms tightly around herself. "Will you tell her I'm sorry?"

"You can tell her yourself. You would be welcome at any time."

"Thank you. I may do so. Later."

Rosalind contemplated the young woman in front of her. She saw again how hardened and self-contained Mariah had made herself. Despite this, she was clearly attached to her pretty sister-in-law and to Nora. She was very like Bethany, Rosalind realized. She wanted to protect the ones she cared about, and to make things right. She believed there was no one else as willing or capable.

But Bethany had learned to cover her labors with patience and good humor. Mariah had never managed that trick.

"I don't like your look, Miss Thorne," said Mariah. "What can you be thinking?"

"I'm thinking that you should know that after Cantrell died, a search was made of his flat," said Rosalind. "No money was found, or any jewelry. But there was a package containing three pictures. I was reliably informed that they were all the work of a person called Jacob Mayne." Unease flickered deep in Mariah's eyes. "He's a painter who is currently causing quite the sensation among the London art world."

"Is he?" Mariah sounded thoroughly bored by the idea. "How nice for him."

"Yes," agreed Rosalind. "Unfortunately, he's dead. I am given to understand that all his affairs are being managed by a spinster sister."

"Do you suspect her of Cantrell's murder?" asked Mariah.

"Because otherwise I don't see how this could possibly be of interest to me."

"The remarkable thing about this sister is that no one seems to have ever met her. I was even asked to run her to earth by an acquaintance—Lady Cowper. She desperately wants to invite Miss Mayne to lunch."

"I am sure Miss Mayne will be delighted to accept when you find her."

"I should hope so," said Rosalind. "But Lady Cowper told me the only person in London who has ever even laid eyes on her is the agent acting for her."

Mariah was silent. A dark flush began to creep up her throat.

"Nora is Jacob Mayne, is she not?" said Rosalind.

Mariah lifted her chin. "How on earth do you suppose that?"

"Nora draws constantly. I recognized one of the sketches found in Cantrell's flat, although I did not remember at the time where I'd seen it. Besides that, her hands are quite stained from her work. I noticed when I first met her. And then she let fall the name of Sommerton as someone who owed her money."

Mariah's jaw worked silently back and forth for a long, slow moment.

"The stains come from mixing the colors," said Mariah finally. "I warned her she should take more care." She paused, and her lips pressed into a rare, thin smile. "Just as I warned her you would be dangerous."

"How did you come to be part of the scheme?" asked Rosalind.

The corner of Mariah's smile twitched. "She came to me perhaps a month after her reappearance. She told me she had no intention of staying in our sister's house. Then she told me something of the life she had lived with Cantrell. She said she'd come up with a scheme that would bring her in an independent income. She told me that the easiest kind of person to fool was a collector. One of Cantrell's favorite games, she said, was to pick up some painting in a pawnshop and pass it off as something rare and priceless." She eyed Rosalind. "But you do not appear surprised."

"I'm familiar with the scheme," said Rosalind blandly. "It's a very old one."

"Yes. Well. Cantrell was never terribly original. Nora had always been good at drawing and painting. It is her one real accomplishment, after telling lies, of course," she added. "So, it wasn't really very difficult to put the plan together. We would invent a dead genius with a tragic story and a desperate sister. All that was needed was time and space to create a store of pictures."

"Where did you go?"

"My father's estate has quite a number of unused cottages on it. He has not had great luck in keeping tenants, even during what I am assured are very hard times. Being unwilling to put any kind of check on his steward and his gamekeeper while they bled the estate dry probably has something to do with it," she added. "It was a simple matter to set Nora up in one. Our parents had never been much troubled to ask what we did with our days, and Bethany was occupied with her house and baby, and the other tenants couldn't be bothered to wonder what we were up to. They had enough worries of their own.

"When we had enough paintings, I contrived to get Bethany to take me with her on a jaunt to London. I spent much of my time in the circulating libraries and bookshops and managed to assemble a list of salesmen and gallery owners, whom I later wrote to in my character of the grieving sister."

"So, you are Miss Mayne?"

"On paper, I am. In person, Nora is."

"Why?"

"Because she's prettier," Mariah said frankly. "It's always easier to convince a man you are a helpless innocent when you're pretty."

"Why did you agree to help her?" asked Rosalind.

"Because she promised that this time she'd take me with her when she left," said Mariah. "And, frankly, because it offered some relief from the boredom of my sister's house."

Rosalind nodded. Mariah had believed her character and her figure—neither of which conformed to the strict expectations for young women—would make marriage difficult, if not impossible. She would remain stranded with her family forever. It was natural that she should be angry, and that she should be torn between her feelings of love and abandonment. It was natural, as well, that she should try to find her own way out.

"Now I have a question for you, Miss Thorne," said Mariah briskly. "How did you come to connect me to Jacob Mayne?"

"You were seen taking those pictures to Mr. Cantrell."

Mariah stared silently at her. Her face was an expressionless mask. "Seen?" she croaked finally.

"Yes. The Bow Street Runner who was set to watch the house saw you leave. Or, rather, he saw someone dressed as a servant leave and follow a man who had been watching the house. The circumstance aroused his curiosity, and he followed them both. He waited outside the door and heard you arguing with Cantrell."

Slowly, and with great and careful dignity, Mariah walked around her desk and sat in the wooden chair. It was as if she needed the desk as a shield between herself and Rosalind.

"And now you mean to remind me that the day I took the pictures to him, the day he was heard to be blackmailing me and my sister, was the day before he died."

"Yes," said Rosalind.

Mariah looked at her desk. She closed one of the books

and stoppered the open ink bottle. She began laying the various scissors, rulers, and protractors in their boxes.

"Am I to be arrested?" Mariah spoke dispassionately. Rosalind could only guess at what was happening inside her.

"Not yet," said Rosalind.

"Is Nora?"

"The coroner has only just begun his inquiries," said Rosalind. "There is still a great deal of evidence to be gathered."

"But we are in danger."

"Possibly. However, you can help yourselves."

Mariah's eyes narrowed suspiciously. "How?"

"May I see something you've written?"

The question obviously took Mariah by surprise. She continued to stare at Rosalind, as if the answer might appear in the air between them. At last, however, she swept her gaze across her crowded desk, selected a book of extracts, and held it out.

"No," said Rosalind. "I'll need something less formal. A letter, perhaps?"

Mariah sighed impatiently but obliged. She riffled through a stack of papers, pulled out a paper, and shoved it across the desk toward Rosalind.

Rosalind picked up the page. It was an inquiry to a bookseller about a series of bound lectures from Sir Humphrey Davies. Rosalind scanned the page.

"Thank you," she said as she handed it back.

"Will you tell me why you needed to see something informal I had written?" asked Mariah.

"Cantrell was poisoned with belladonna," said Rosalind. "It was administered in a bottle of wine that came to him in a basket of food. There was a label on the basket."

"Ah," said Mariah. "You wanted to see if my handwriting matched that on the label."

"Yes," said Rosalind simply.

"I could have disguised it."

"Possibly," agreed Rosalind. "But if you had, you probably would not be mentioning the fact now."

"Perhaps I am very clever."

"You are very clever, but you are not, I think, overconfident."

Mariah paused, lost in thought for a moment. Then she opened a drawer and pulled out a folded paper. She held this out to Rosalind, who took it from her.

"What's this?" Rosalind asked.

"It's from Nora."

Rosalind unfolded the paper. It was a brief note, just to say that she would be gone until late evening, because she wanted to stop at an additional gallery, and Mariah mustn't worry.

Rosalind touched the *y*'s in *gallery* and *worry*. Neither one had the long, dramatic tails she'd noticed on the basket's label. The *e*'s were likewise much narrower, and the *w* was much broader.

She folded the paper again. "This is not the same writing as on the label."

Mariah's shoulders sagged in simple, plain relief. "Thank you," she said.

"Mariah, I need to speak plainly. This is helpful"—she held up the paper—"but it will not keep you and Nora out of danger. There will be many more questions, and my word carries only limited weight with some of those who will be involved. I strongly urge you to be patient and not to do anything rash, like trying to run away."

"How could I run?" Mariah leaned across the desk and plucked the note out of Rosalind's fingers. "I have no friends and no resources . . ." She stopped and gave a grim chuckle. "Oh, you're thinking of the pearls."

"Yes. I am."

"Well, I don't have them." Mariah dropped the note back

in her drawer and closed it. "I wish that I did, because I would run. Probably before tomorrow morning."

"Do you know who took them?"

"No," she said. Then something seemed to occur to her. "At least, I don't think that I do. Yet." She folded her hands on the blotter, looking very like a schoolmistress. "Is there anything else?"

"Yes. Do you know why Betsy has run away?"

For a moment, Rosalind was sure Mariah meant to put her off. But she changed her mind and simply shrugged. "I'm sorry, but I don't know that, either. I admit, I thought she might be up to something, and I wasted a little time watching her, but . . ." She shook her head. "I never caught her doing anything more sinister than sneaking a drink of Douglas's sherry." She smiled again, but very briefly. "Now, tell me, Miss Thorne. What do you mean to do? About Nora and me and our . . . private business?"

Rosalind considered this. "Many of us find we must assume some role to navigate our lives. Some find that role assigned to them—the beauty, the spinster, the wicked girl."

"The useful woman?" inquired Mariah.

"The sensible sister," added Rosalind. "But if one person can take on a role that they choose for themselves, why should they be blamed for it?" She looked Mariah in the eye. "I was brought here to find a missing necklace. I am staying to help a friend and, if I can, help discover who decided to take a man's life. The identity of someone who has happened to paint a set of very popular pictures is none of my affair."

Mariah studied her, looking for some trace of a lie or even hesitation.

"I imagine," said Mariah, "you'll have a different answer if it is proved that one or the other of us killed Cantrell."

"Yes," said Rosalind.

Mariah nodded once. "Well, then, I suppose we must hope that does not happen."

CHAPTER 40

Sir Jasper

*. . . obstinacy is the real defect of his character
after all.*

Jane Austen, *Pride and Prejudice*

Adam was perfectly aware that seven o'clock on a February evening was not the proper hour to be calling on a gentleman.

Not that any such hour existed for a Bow Street officer, especially one sent as an emissary from the coroner. But Adam was restless. The events in Manchester would not stop eating at him. He did not particularly mind the dressing-down from Townsend. He had received numerous such lectures before. Townsend had made it his mission to elevate Bow Street's standing in the eyes of the aristocracy, Parliament and, of course, the Crown. According to Townsend, however, Adam continually failed to bring himself up to scratch. He might have a string of notable successes behind him, and a certain fame in the press, but he did not do well at a dinner party, and neither did he care for a crush. He cared for his work, for his family, for his fellow officers. And for Rosalind.

Oh, very much for Rosalind.

But he also cared, he found, for that odd, elusive, and far too malleable thing known as honor. Because of that, he did not care for the tactics of thief-takers—the ones who worked hand in glove with thieves to steal valuable items and then "find" them in order to claim the reward. He also did not care for those who told tales against their neighbors for revenge. Or because they wanted some particular group of troublemakers gone.

But as long as he stayed with Bow Street, there were orders to be followed, whether he liked them or not. He must do as he was told, or he must leave and find some other profession.

This hard truth had occupied Adam's mind more or less fully since he left Manchester. So, he found the business of Bryan Cantrell to be something of a relief. While he was occupied with helping sort out this tangled problem—with its vanished necklace, missing maid, and dead scoundrel—he could put off other worries, and other decisions.

That was why he chose to visit Sir Jasper at once. If his mind stayed busy, he would not fall back into that unfamiliar, uncomfortable gloom.

Had Sir Jasper been an ordinary London resident—a "cit"—it would have been next to impossible to find him without at least knowing which neighborhood he resided in.

Fortunately, however, Sir Jasper had a title and money to back it and, as such, was eligible to be listed in *Boyle's Court and Country Guide*. Bow Street kept a copy of this handy book for just such emergencies. Sold mostly to tourists and curiosity seekers, it listed "fashionable" personages by name and told which street they lived in.

According to the guide, Sir Jasper Douglas resided in Upper Wimpole Street. Adam had spent much of his Bow Street career building a map of London in his head. So, once he knew the street, he had no trouble discovering the house.

That house proved to be old and sprawling, and easily the largest on its block. When Adam presented himself at the

door with his warrant from Sir David, he was met by a footman in full livery, including powdered wig and gold braid.
The footman showed him into a vaulted entrance hall, which
might have done service as a cathedral. There Adam was left
to cool his heels while the tall case clock chimed the half hour
and the three-quarters. When the footman finally reappeared, it was only to hand Adam off to a comrade in arms
who was identically dressed, except for an extra row of braid
on his sleeves.

This man took Adam up a staircase broad enough to have
graced a Covent Garden theater. But what truly struck Adam
was the silence. All around him was evidence of enormous
wealth, the kind that came from generations of accumula-
tion, but the only human sound he could hear was his own
breathing.

On the second floor, the footman led him down a long carpeted gallery and then through a maze of dark paneled
rooms, each one progressively lower, darker, and warmer
than the last. Adam had the unaccountable feeling of being
taken deep underground.

The footman opened what Adam sincerely hoped would
be the final door, stood aside, and bowed. Adam walked past
him into the darkened chamber. The velvet drapes were
closed. A single lamp on the table and the low fire were all
the light allowed.

"Well?" barked a rough voice from the shadows. "What
do you mean by this intrusion, sir?"

Adam blinked his eyes hard, trying to adjust to the twilight.

"Well?" barked the voice again. "What's your business?"

Sir Jasper Douglas sat in a heavily carved chair by the fire,
wrapped in a scarlet dressing gown. Probably he had once
been a large man, but age and illness had shriveled him. His
sallow, spotted skin hung loosely from his bones; and his
right eye drooped; and his right hand was withered. Adam

remembered what Rosalind had said about the man. He had suffered an apoplexy when he learned about his son's outside families. Clearly, that had brought on a stroke. Adam found himself wondering if he could even walk without assistance.

Despite his physical limitation, it was immediately clear that Sir Jasper retained all his wits. As Adam made his bow, the man glowered at him balefully through his good eye.

"Forgive me for intruding, Sir Jasper," Adam said. "My name is—"

"My man already told me your name," Sir Jasper cut him off. "You're one of them runner fellows, from Bow Street. I ask again, sir, what is your business here?"

"I have some questions about Addison Douglas."

"Then you have wasted your time," announced Sir Jasper. "I know nothing about him."

"And yet I believe he is your grandson, and that you had named him your heir for a time?"

Sir Jasper jerked his right hand to wave this away. "And would to God I never had. He was weak, sir. Weak and worthless."

"In what way?" asked Adam.

"What do you mean?"

Adam shrugged. "A man can be afflicted by many kinds of weakness. Drink may weaken him, or illness, accident, or vice."

Sir Jasper barked a laugh. "Drink! Vice! That I could have dealt with. Addison was a traitor to his heritage! Not that I would expect a man of your kind or class to understand the duty that family imposes."

Adam thought of his mother, who had worked every day to see her children through life with strength, pride, and assurance. If she were standing in front of Sir Jasper just then, her reply might bring on another stroke.

"I understand Addison's father also lost your favor," said Adam.

Sir Jasper pounded the chair arm with his left hand. "These are private affairs! What business do you or any other grubby thief-taker have prying into them?"

Adam felt a muscle in his cheek twitch. "A man has been murdered, sir. He was connected to your family."

"Not *my* family," said Sir Jasper firmly. "Perhaps you mean that country chit Gerald married. Her family has all manner of bends and breakages."

"You do not approve of Mr. Gerald Douglas's marriage?"

"No, I do not. I do not apologize for this. But his father was an obstinate man, and he removed himself from his family, and the family must now live with the consequences of his decisions. However, I do not have to see them or concern myself with their doings. My work is to counter their influence on my heir and make him understand his duty and his place!"

Adam felt the house's silence press heavily against him. He heard the crackle of the fire and the ticking of the gilded clock on the mantel, but nothing else. This man, who spoke so forcefully about family, had none near him.

"Sir Jasper," said Adam, "I do not wish to open old wounds, but I am charged with gathering evidence regarding a breach of the king's peace. Your grandson Addison Douglas may have some important information. Do you know where he is?"

"No, I do not, and what's more, I do not care!"

"It is my understanding he vanished some years ago. What search was made for him?"

"None!"

Adam folded his hands behind him and waited.

Sir Jasper's eyes sank deep into his lined face. He hunched his bony shoulders. His hands trembled. Adam glanced about the room, looking for the bellpull, in case he needed to summon help.

"He stood there," croaked Sir Jasper at last. "He stood there in front of me and told me to my face that he did not want my money. That he felt sorry for all his father's half-breed brats and would rather the fortune be shared out among them."

Adam nodded once. Rosalind had told him that Huet Douglas, Addison's father, the original heir, was a bigamist and had been forced to flee the country. She'd said there were at least three women who believed they were Huet's legal wife, and an unknown number of children who could claim him as their father, if he would acknowledge them.

It seemed that even though Huet, and Sir Jasper, did not wish to acknowledge them, Addison Douglas did.

"What did you do when Addison told you he did not want the money?"

"I told him he was ungrateful, as well as a fool. Did he think I was going to enrich a pack of mongrel children gotten on the sly by my worthless son? Then I told him if he didn't want to live up to his position, I didn't want him, and he could get out. And he did." The man struggled to straighten himself up. "No you, sir, with your middle-class morality, I suppose you will tell me I did wrong."

Adam ignored this. "Did you ever hear from him again?"

"Once. He wrote to me to renounce his fortune once and for all. Ha! As if I hadn't already excised him from my will. Didn't even have the nerve to face me again," he added with grim satisfaction.

"He wrote you?" said Adam. "Did you keep the letter?"

"What manner of question is that?"

Adam bit back his first reply. He was not yet ready to be thrown out. "There may be useful information in it."

"Useful to whom?" sneered Sir Jasper.

"To myself," replied Adam. "To Sir David Royce, the coroner, and to you, sir, as it may help discover Mr. Addison's whereabouts."

"Have I not made it clear I do not care where he is?"

"It is possible one day you might."

Sir Jasper's whole body trembled, and for a moment he

could not speak. He was, Adam realized, overwhelmed by outrage and old grief. Adam wondered how many personal losses the man had suffered. What had happened to his parents? Did he have brothers and sisters? There must have been a wife once, but he had seen no sign of her in the house. His younger son had broken with him. His eldest had left him alone and ashamed.

How many bitter memories had this old man collected in place of living family?

"I did not keep the letter," Sir Jasper said finally. "It was burnt."

Adam considered the man in front of him. He considered the lost Addison Douglas and Gerald Douglas, whom Rosalind had described as tired and trapped, and who had been hunted and haunted by a swindler who somehow seemed to know his fortunes before he himself did.

He also considered that Addison Douglas, whatever his fate, had had more honor than sense. If he had kept his mouth shut until Sir Jasper died, he could have taken the inheritance and done as he pleased.

He considered Bryan Cantrell and his many schemes.

"Sir Jasper," said Adam, "I have one more question for you, and then I hope I shall be able to leave you to your privacy."

"Well, then, for the love of God, ask it!"

"If I was to describe a man to you, a tall, lean man with dark hair and unusually bright green eyes, would that recall any person to mind?"

Adam could tell the man meant to bite his head off again, but then slowly his expression softened into thoughtfulness.

"Do you mean Benjamin Case?"

Maybe I do. "Who was Mr. Case?"

"My confidential secretary, at least he was for a while. Huet brought him to me, when . . . when I thought I could still trust him, and when my eyesight started to go. All those years in the tropical sun in India, and now I'm condemned to sit in the dark." He laughed mirthlessly. "I remember he was very keen, had excellent manners, worked like the devil. I liked him," added Sir Jasper stiffly. "When . . . when I discovered Huet's crimes, he was a support, a comfort unlooked for. He—" Sir Jasper coughed and shook his head. "Well. I remember those eyes of his."

"Where is Mr. Case now?" Adam asked.

"Took a posting overseas. I haven't heard from him in an age or more. What do you mean by bringing him up?"

Adam looked at the old man slumped in his chair, alone in this dim and sweltering room. "A matter of a character reference that was misplaced," he lied. "But you have cleared that up."

"The devil if I know how," barked Sir Jasper. "Now, sir, as you promised . . ."

Adam bowed. "Thank you for your time, Sir Jasper."

The old man grunted and waved him away. Adam went.

Outside, darkness had well and truly fallen. The street was filled with carriages. Footmen and linkboys ran ahead with lanterns and torches to shepherd the occupants to their homes or their entertainments. The shouts and the clop of horses' hooves clattered past, carried by the thin, damp wind.

Adam turned up his coat collar and started walking.

So Huet Douglas brought Sir Jasper a secretary named Benjamin Case. And now it seems we have one more alias for Bryan Cantrell, and one more house he snuck himself into. God knows how many more we will discover before this business is done.

But one thing was now very clear. Bryan Cantrell, or Campbell or Case, had known a great deal about Sir Jasper's private business. Including his private shame.

And he'd known that Addison Douglas had become Sir Jasper's heir.

Then, when Case, or Campbell, or Cantrell moved on from Sir Jasper's employ, and he'd just so happened to fetch up at Gerald Douglas's house in Hertfordshire.

Adam did not often withhold his thoughts or suspicions from Rosalind. He respected her intelligence and resolution far too much. But this once, he'd kept back a theory. For one thing, it had been rank speculation. For another, it had been clear she already had a mounting stack of her own suspicions to wrestle with.

But his talk with Sir Jasper had just turned Adam's speculation into a possibility.

Because Bryan Cantrell had known how Sir Jasper was planning to leave his money before he made friends with Gerald Douglas.

Gerald Douglas, according to Rosalind, was a man with ambition and responsibilities, but without money.

What if the charming and plausible Bryan Cantrell had convinced Gerald Douglas that he had a better right to Sir Jasper's fortune than weak, generous, conscience-stricken Cousin Addison?

CHAPTER 41

Discovered

How little did you tell me of what passed . . . !
Jane Austen, *Pride and Prejudice*

When Rosalind returned to her rooms after her conversation with Mariah, she found Amelia waiting anxiously for her.

"What is it, Amelia?" she asked. "Is it Betsy?"

"I wish it was," answered Amelia. "But there's been no sign of her, and when Mrs. Hare went to look in her room, she said Betsy'd cleared right out. She thinks she's run off with some man."

Such things did happen. Service was a hard life, and more than one girl had been known to leave abruptly for what might look like greener pastures, especially when promises of love and adventure were attached.

"Is that what you think?" Rosalind asked.

"If she did a runner, it wasn't for love," said Amelia firmly. "She's looking to make her fortune, or at least a few bob. She as much as told me she was picking up the extra for all her little favors, like dropping that note. *And* she was going on about not staying in service all her life, *and* having a better place waiting for her!" Amelia concluded triumphantly.

Rosalind bit her lip. *I was too slow. I should have spoken to her at once.* She had wanted to know if Betsy was Cantrell's confederate inside the house or only the go-between for someone else, but Rosalind had not wanted to accuse the girl of conspiring with Cantrell, or anyone else, without definite proof. Now it was too late. Betsy was gone, and she had a city to hide in. Assuming she hadn't already decided to leave London.

What will I do now? But even as she thought this, an idea surfaced.

"Has her room been cleaned yet?"

Amelia's brow furrowed. "I don't know, miss."

"Can you show me where it is? Perhaps she's left behind something that will tell us who she was doing those favors for."

Amelia's eyes lit up at the prospect of a search. "You just follow me, miss."

The doorway to the servants' stairs waited at the far end of the corridor. They had not yet gotten halfway down the hall when a voice hailed them.

"Miss Thorne!"

It was Mr. Hodgeson. He was coming toward them from the opposite end of the corridor, probably having just climbed the main staircase. Rosalind had no choice but to stop and turn to acknowledge him. She was not entirely sure what Amelia muttered under her breath, but it was probably something very rude, and she felt certain she agreed with the sentiment.

"Mr. Hodgeson," said Rosalind. "What can I do for you?"

He planted himself in front of her. His face was a bright pink, but whether the color came from the effort of climbing stairs or something else, Rosalind could not tell.

"I understand our Nora now finds herself a widow." The amount of cheer in his voice was disturbing.

"If you mean that Mr. Cantrell has died, that is true."

"Well, well. If there was ever a man destined for a bad end, surely it was him." Mr. Hodgeson looked at her owlishly over the rims of his spectacles. "Do they say what happened? Or perhaps I should ask, Can *you* say what happened? Hmm?"

"It was poison, Mr. Hodgeson."

Mr. Hodgeson opened his mouth and then closed it. "Well, well," he said again. "That surprises me. I assumed it would be hooligans and a blow to the head or a stabbing. Yes. A stabbing would have suited him quite well." He chuckled to himself.

Rosalind found herself wondering how much Mr. Hodgeson had already had to drink this evening, but in the dim corridor, it was difficult to tell.

"And is there any sign who did the deed?" he asked lightly. "Another spurned woman? Or a spurned moneylender perhaps?" he added. "With such fellows, I imagine it comes down to one or the other."

"If any such thing has been found, I don't know of it," said Rosalind. At the same time, she thought of the brass key in her reticule, and the box, or trunk or case, that was hopefully waiting at the Ashertons.

"Well, well," said Mr. Hodgeson yet again. "I suppose I should not detain you, Miss Thorne. You look as though you have business."

"Thank you." Rosalind hurried away, with Amelia in her wake. But when they reached the door to the servants' stair, Rosalind turned. Mr. Hodgeson had not moved.

He was watching them.

But there was nothing she could do. To turn back now would seem strange. She had to follow Amelia into the narrow, dark stairway and let the door close.

Despite that, she could still feel Mr. Hodgeson's bleary gaze on the back of her neck as they climbed.

In any London house, the servants' quarters were generally found on the very top floor. The women would be housed on one corridor, and the men on another, usually with stout doors between them.

The maids' hallway was deserted, of course. Dinner may have passed for the family, but the boudoir fires needed to be lit, the beds turned down, nightclothes laid out, drinks and tea fetched, and people helped off with their daytime clothes, which must then be inspected and folded away or taken downstairs for cleaning and repair. It would be hours before any member of the staff would be able to seek their beds.

Amelia opened the third door on the right. "In here, miss," she said. "Betsy shared with Susan. She's the parlormaid. Betsy's is the bed by the window."

The chamber was Spartan, but it was not cold, like some Rosalind had seen. Both beds had colorful quilts and a pair of good, if faded, rugs beside them. There was an etching of a country church in a sunlit field on the wall, a pretty painted lamp, a tatted doily on the dresser, and a couple of recent magazines on the shared nightstand.

A cap and apron had been tossed carelessly onto Betsy's bed. A brief inspection of the dresser showed that the top two drawers had been cleaned out, with only a torn handkerchief left behind.

Rosalind looked under the pillow and inside the case. There was nothing.

Probably there's nothing to find, thought Rosalind, brimming with frustration. *Betsy is a sharp girl. If there was anything, she would have taken it with her.*

"Look under the bed, Amelia," she said, determined to be thorough. She picked up one of the magazines and leafed through its pages, hoping that some letter or note might have been tucked in there.

Amelia stretched out flat on her belly and wriggled her way underneath the low iron bedstead. She sneezed.

"Bless—" began Rosalind, but she froze before she could finish. Footsteps were thudding up the stairs and stomping down the hallway.

Amelia must have heard, as well, because she squeaked and scrambled out from under the bed just as a thunderous Mrs. Hare appeared in the doorway.

"Was there something you wanted, Miss Thorne?" The housekeeper folded her formidable arms and thrust out her chin.

Rosalind was so shocked, her first thought was to ask what on earth the woman was doing up here. She should be supervising the maids who were getting the family's rooms ready for bedtime.

Thankfully, Rosalind found she had enough presence of mind to swallow this first, startled response.

"I beg your pardon, Mrs. Hare," she said. "I thought if I could have a look at Betsy's quarters, I might be able to discover something that would help tell us where she'd gone. As I did not want to disturb any of the staff, I asked Amelia to bring me up here."

Amelia climbed to her feet, eyes downcast and expression entirely contrite. Rosalind noted she also had both hands clenched tight behind her back.

Neither Mrs. Hare's expression nor her stance softened the least bit.

"Now, I'm sure, Miss Thorne, that we are all very glad you're here to support Mrs. Douglas in her time of troubles," she said, without meaning a word of it. "But I'd thank you if you was to apply to *me* for leave to look about my girls' rooms, *if* any such was to need doing. Just because they are in service does not mean they are not entitled to their little bit of privacy."

"You are right of course, Mrs. Hare," said Rosalind humbly. "I have overstepped, and I do apologize."

"Humph. Yes. Well. I'm sure we all make our mistakes, and I don't know but things are done differently in some other houses. *Howsomeever*, as I told the mister when I caught *him* up here, 'In *this* house, *my* girls will not be—' "

"I'm sorry, Mrs. Hare," Rosalind interrupted. "You told the mister? Do you mean Mr. Douglas?"

"Heavens no!" cried Mrs. Hare. "He's no time for such foolishness. I mean the other. Mr. Hodgeson!"

Rosalind had to work not to stare. "I'm sorry, but you cannot mean you found Mr. Hodgeson in Betsy's rooms."

Mrs. Hare drew back, evidently realizing she'd said too much. In the same moment, Rosalind realized how the house-keeper had come to be upstairs at just this time.

"Mrs. Hare, this is very important," said Rosalind. "It may have to do with why Betsy left. She could be in trouble."

Mrs. Hare's full mouth pursed up tight in disapproval. "I did warn that girl. I does my best with them, Miss Thorne, but sometimes there's one who will not listen."

"Of that I have no doubt, Mrs. Hare," said Rosalind. "None of this can be laid at your door. But I must know, Was there ever any other member of the family up here when they should not have been?"

Mrs. Hare did not answer right away. Rosalind knew the housekeeper was ticking through an entire series of private calculations. Rosalind could not blame her. Mrs. Hare's position was no more secure than that of any other member of the staff. If she said the wrong thing or trusted the wrong person, she could find herself turned away without references.

At last, Mrs. Hare shook her head. "Not that I saw. It was only Mr. Hodgeson. He said he'd gotten lost. He may have been . . ." She cleared her throat. "He may have had a bit too much to drink."

Rosalind nodded. Inside, she wondered, *How do I ask this next question?* "Did Betsy seem . . . particularly favored by anyone? I know that she occasionally ran errands for Miss Penelope. Was there anyone else?"

This, it seemed, was going too far for Mrs. Hare. She drew herself up to her full height. "You'll forgive me, Miss Thorne. I still have my work to do." She stepped aside, very clearly signaling that Rosalind should make her way back downstairs, where she belonged.

"Yes, of course," said Rosalind. "Do forgive me for taking up so much of your time. Amelia?"

Amelia bobbed a small curtsy and walked out, head still bowed, hands still clenched tight, but now in front of her. Rosalind said nothing; she just followed Amelia down the stairs, down the now-empty corridor, and into their rooms.

Rosalind shut the door and turned the key.

Amelia faced her, eyes shining. She held up her closed hand, turned it over, and opened her fingers.

Cradled in the center of her palm lay a single black pearl.

CHAPTER 42

Disappointments and Discoveries

Affectation of candor is common enough. One meets it everywhere.

Jane Austen, *Pride and Prejudice*

"This was under the bed?" Rosalind plucked the pearl from Amelia's hand.

"Way at the back," she said. "I just barely caught the glimmer."

Rosalind took the pearl over to the lamp and held it close. The light caught on its rough curves and showed the faint, irregular swirl of its coloring.

"Is it real?" asked Amelia eagerly.

"I think it is." She closed her hand tight around it. "Well done, Amelia."

"Thank you, miss!" She spread her skirts and curtsied broadly like an actress taking her bow. "Now what do we do?"

That is an excellent question. But it was only one of a dozen that swirled through Rosalind's thoughts.

"Should I go fetch Mrs. Douglas?" said Amelia. "Or will you send for Mr. Harkness? If Betsy's gone and scarpered with the pearls . . ."

"No. Not yet. We don't know how this"—she held the pearl up between thumb and forefinger—"came to be in Betsy's room. She may be the thief. It looks very bad. But if she took the necklace, why did she stay in the house for so long?" She remembered Nora asking her a similar question. "The necklace was taken nearly a fortnight before Bethany even came to me. That's a long time to keep hold of something so large and valuable, especially while the house is being turned upside down. The intelligent thing would be to vanish right after the theft. After all, if she was ready to steal such a thing, she must have had some idea where to sell it, so hanging about would have done her no good."

Unless she'd been planning to sell it to Cantrell, and she's running now because he's dead. Rosalind frowned. Cantrell had known about the pearls. He had been in communication with someone in the house. As Adam had reminded her, swindlers frequently worked far longer to set up their schemes than their victims realized.

But that didn't make sense, either. If Cantrell knew he'd soon have the pearls in hand, why would he bother with Nora? Or Pen? Could he possibly have been that reckless?

"But if Betsy didn't take the necklace, how did the pearl get under her bed?" asked Amelia.

"Perhaps she was holding the necklace for someone else," said Rosalind. "Or perhaps someone hid the pearls in her room, so that if they were discovered, she would be blamed."

Amelia's eyes went wide. "You're thinking about Mr. Hodgeson, then, ain't you? Mrs. Hare said she caught him nosing around where he'd no business . . ."

Rosalind nodded. "And Nora suspected him. She thought he might still have creditors to whom he owed money."

"He should be in his rooms by now," Amelia told her. "I mean, if you wanted to ask him something. Jimmy Smart—he's the footman—he says Old Hodgeson . . ." She stopped and started again. "Mr. Hodgeson always goes straight to his room after dinner, usually with a book and a bottle."

"We'll need to find him quickly, then." Men who were worse for drink might talk a great deal, but it was much harder to make any sense of it or to sort out the difference between truth and dreams.

Rosalind pulled her handkerchief from her sleeve and quickly knotted the pearl inside it. It was a schoolgirl solution, but the best one she had right now. She tucked it back in so that the lump was on the inside of her wrist.

Mr. Hodgeson's rooms proved to be right next door to Mrs. Hodgeson's. But Rosalind was still surprised to see Gilpin answer the door, and even more so to see that Mrs. Hodgeson stood in the middle of the moss-green room. Newspapers and periodicals waited on the table beside the wingback chair, along with an empty glass and decanter.

"Miss Thorne." Mrs. Hodgeson fluttered her handkerchief, dabbing her brow and her cheeks. "Whatever is the matter?"

"I was hoping to speak to Mr. Hodgeson."

"You will have to wait," she said. "My husband is not well. I've just been seeing to him."

"I hope it is nothing serious," said Rosalind.

"We all may hope," replied Mrs. Hodgeson dolefully. "Mr. Hodgeson, despite my urgings, cares nothing for his health. He will go out at all hours in all weathers, as you have seen. Well, now all those chickens have come home to roost." She shook her head heavily. "And, of course, it is left entirely to me"—she patted her chest with a nervous hand—"to tend him. But never mind that!"

"I'm so sorry to hear he is unwell," said Rosalind, although she felt certain that the empty glass and decanter had a great deal to do with his ailment.

But he had been speaking clearly to her less than an hour

ago, she reminded herself. Perhaps something was wrong. Or perhaps . . .

Rosalind's gaze slid over Mrs. Hodgeson's shoulder. In her mind's eye she saw Betsy's empty room, her discarded cap and apron. She became very aware of where her knotted handkerchief with its precious secret pressed against her wrist.

"Should I go find Bethany for you?" Rosalind asked. "Perhaps Mr. Hodgeson may need a doctor . . . ?"

"Doctors!" sneered Mrs. Hodgeson. "Wretched men in fancy waistcoats who know more about bleeding a person's pocket than they ever did about medicine! No." She lifted her chin proudly. "I will care for my husband. I know exactly what he needs. He is in bed now, with one of my special compresses. It never fails him. He shall be perfectly well in the morning."

Suspicion prickled down Rosalind's neck. "Nonetheless, I think someone should see him."

"You go too far, Miss Thorne!" Mrs. Hodgeson stamped one foot like an affronted schoolgirl. "I have cared for my husband for twenty years! He is ill, but he will recover, and I will not have him disturbed." Her chin quivered. "No! Under no circumstances!"

"Mrs. Hodgeson . . . ," began Rosalind. "I must ask—"

"What is this racket?" roared a man's voice. The door to the boudoir flew open, and Mr. Hodgeson stood there, leaning heavily against the threshold. "Can't a man have some peace in his own rooms!" He glowered at his wife, and then he saw Rosalind. "Well. It's you. What are you doing here?"

Mrs. Hodgeson ran to him at once. "She heard you were ill, my dear, and came to see if there was anything she could do. As if my care of you was not enough!" huffed Mrs. Hodgeson.

"Yes, well, you may be sure, Miss Thorne, I've had quite

enough of a number of things." He looked down at his fussing, fluttering wife. "Now, you may take yourself off."

Mrs. Hodgeson's glower confirmed this. Gilpin opened the door.

Rosalind curtsied her apology and did as she was told, with Amelia right behind.

"Which is what I get for being too suspicious," breathed Rosalind.

Amelia shrugged. "Even you can't be right every time, miss. Although ..." The mischievous light appeared in her eyes again. Rosalind arched her brows. Amelia jerked her head toward the closed door.

Mrs. Hodgeson's closed door. Rosalind looked over her shoulder. Slowly, questioning the move even as she made it, she reached out and tried the handle.

It was locked.

She shook her head and turned away, then took herself down the hall toward her own rooms before anyone could see her loitering. Amelia quickly caught up with her.

"Do you want me to see if I can find the key?"

Rosalind glanced up the hallway. "No," she murmured. "There's too much chance we will be seen. We'll attack the problem of Mrs. and Mrs. Hodgeson tomorrow," she said. "By then, we should have more information in hand."

"Seems to me we have a deal already," said Amelia. "The pearl, Betsy's gone, Mr. Hodgeson's lurking about ..."

"But it's all disconnected. The pearl was in Betsy's room. But if we say anything now, it will just be assumed she stole the necklace, and no one will look any further."

"But what about Old Hodgeson lurking and all ...?" whispered Amelia urgently.

"Mr. Hodgeson is a discontented and drunken man," Rosalind reminded her softly. They should not be talking out here. She hurried toward her own door. "If he's thought to be following a pretty and mercenary maid around, what are they going to assume he's after?"

"Oh." Amelia flushed.

"Miss Thorne?" A new voice interrupted them.

Penelope. Rosalind suppressed a groan and pasted a calm smile on her face.

"I heard you talking," Penelope said. "Is everything all right? Has . . . has something else happened?"

"Not at all." Rosalind felt a pang of guilt for her impatience. The girl looked wan and at least as tired as Rosalind felt. "I was just coming to find you, actually," she lied. "I wanted to see how you were doing."

"Oh, well. Do come in." Penelope drifted back inside her room, leaving the door open for Rosalind and Amelia to follow. She sat down in the exact center of her divan.

"Mrs. Hodgeson made me one of her special tisanes." Pen lifted a pewter mug off the round table and looked at its contents dubiously. "She says she's coming back to see if I've drunk it."

"Allow me, miss?" said Amelia helpfully. Penelope handed her the tankard, and Amelia bustled away into the boudoir. A moment later, they heard the sound of something being emptied out, probably into the commode. A moment later, she reappeared with the tankard in her hand.

"There," she said. "Fresh water. Now you can tell her you drank everything you were given."

The corner of Pen's mouth curled up. "Thank you, Amelia."

Amelia bobbed a curtsy, then withdrew to the corner.

"How are you feeling?" Rosalind asked.

Penelope took a long swallow of water and then shivered. "I don't know. One minute I think I'm fine, and the next I want to burst into tears. It feels like I'm losing my mind!" She clutched her tankard tightly and shivered again.

"You're not losing your mind," said Rosalind firmly. "I have seen this exact thing many times. It's a perfectly natural reaction to such shattering events. You will be all right, but it will take a little time."

"Do you promise?"

"No," said Rosalind. "But I believe."

Penelope smiled. It was a soft, small smile, but it was real. "Then I suppose that will have to do."

"Penelope," said Rosalind gently, "I have a question I need to ask you. This is going to seem very odd . . ."

Penelope gave a small hiccough of a laugh. "Right now, everything seems odd, so I suppose one more question can't make it any worse."

"I am given to understand that Betsy recently went on an errand for you."

"What?" Her brow furrowed. "Oh. The drops. I'd forgotten. Yes. I'd been feeling tired, you see, and I didn't want Gerald to think I was taking ill. I thought if my eyes were brighter, I'd look healthier."

"Where are they?"

"On my vanity." Penelope gestured vaguely toward the mirrored table. "I only used them once. I didn't like them. They made everything blurry."

Rosalind went over to the dressing table. It was remarkably free of clutter for a young lady's table. There was only one bottle of scent and a few pots of cream among the brushes, combs, hand mirrors, and boxes of hairpins.

There was no bottle of drops.

Rosalind looked over her shoulder. Pen was staring at the fire.

"Oh yes," said Rosalind. "Here they are."

"Why do you care about my drops?" Pen did not look away from the flames.

"It's not important," said Rosalind. "An idea I had. I should leave and let you get some rest."

Pen looked into the tankard, took another swallow of water, and then set it aside. "I am extremely tired."

"I'll just ring for the maid." Rosalind crossed to the bell-pull.

"Thank you." Pen looked up at her. "Miss Thorne?"

"Yes?" Rosalind turned toward her.

"What's going to become of us?"

"That's going to be up to you," answered Rosalind.

"Is that something else you believe?" She sounded impatient.

"Yes." Rosalind took Pen's hand. The girl lifted her bright amber eyes and met Rosalind's gaze. "I know it is very bad now, but I also know that it is possible to recover from far worse than this." She hesitated. "And even if the future does not look like what one initially hoped for, that does not mean it cannot be a good and a happy one."

"Is that what happened to you?" Penelope asked. "You recovered from a bad time?"

"Yes."

The corner of Pen's mouth twitched. Her fingers squeezed Rosalind's. "Thank you, Miss Thorne."

Rosalind rang the bell and urged her to get some rest and left her there. She passed the maid in the corridor as she made her way to her room, with Amelia right behind.

She closed the door behind them with a sigh of gratitude.

"Well, miss?" said Amelia. "What do we do now?"

Rosalind leaned backward until her head and shoulders rested against the door.

What do we do now? She repeated the question to herself. *Now that we know the eye drops are gone, like the necklace and like Betsy?*

Penelope had openly and artlessly admitted to asking Betsy to buy the drops for her. They doubtlessly contained belladonna, which was the poison that had killed Cantrell.

And the bottle was missing, but Pen hadn't known that. She had showed no surprise at all when Rosalind pretended to have found them, and had exhibited only mild curiosity at

Rosalind's interest. If she'd had anything to do with Cantrell's poisoning, she never would have been so indifferent. Penelope was not Mariah or Nora. Penelope's feelings ran strong, and she had not yet learned to hide them. At least, not that well.

What do we do now?

"We send a note to Bow Street for Mr. Harkness," she said. "With luck, he'll be able to meet me at Little Russell Street tomorrow morning, and I can show him what we found." She touched the lump in her sleeve from the knotted handkerchief and the pearl. "In the meantime, we'll do what we can to make sure we don't lose anyone or anything else."

CHAPTER 43

Breakfast and Fresh Beginnings

. . . I could very easily forgive his pride, if he had not mortified mine.

Jane Austen, *Pride and Prejudice*

The first thing Rosalind did when she awoke the next morning was to send Amelia to see if the post had arrived yet.

It had been a long night. She and Amelia had slept in shifts, one of them always keeping awake to watch the door and listen for the telltale sounds of footsteps on the carpet.

Amelia had even prowled the house twice, ready with a story that Miss Thorne needed something in the middle of the night. But there had been no sign of any untoward movement. Amelia had even sworn she heard snorting from Mr. Hodgeson's room.

Now that she was looking at events by the light of day, Rosalind was almost ready to believe she had overreacted when she thought Mr. Hodgeson might have bolted.

Almost.

When Amelia returned with the post, Rosalind read over

the letters from Lucinda and Mr. Prescott, while an impatient Amelia tried to help her get dressed. Lucinda's letter was full of village gossip about Mr. Hodgeson's estate and the predations of his steward and his gamekeeper, both of whom had been summarily dismissed by Mr. Douglas. Mr. Prescott's was bland and painfully detailed, and all about how any gentleman might procure a loan of any amount if he did not care about the character of the lender, and if he was sure he was able to pay the interest, which was likely to be very high.

> *And, if you will pardon me for pointing out such a harsh reality, such men will not be content with condemning a man to prison for their failure to pay.*
> *I trust that no friend of yours finds themselves in debt to such men.*

"Hold still, miss!" ordered Amelia for the twelfth time.

"I'm sorry." Rosalind put her letters down. "But I must go find Mr. Douglas."

"You'll not do so looking like a rag doll." Amelia twisted Rosalind's hair tight and ruthlessly shoved three pins in place.

Rosalind gritted her teeth and reminded herself that this would go much faster if she held still. The moment Amelia lifted her hands away from her head, Rosalind sprang to her feet and rushed out the door and down to the breakfast room at a pace that would have done Nora proud. She barely remembered to slow down to a proper and decorous walk before she reached the door.

The first thing she saw in the breakfast room was Douglas and Bethany at the table together, a rack of toast and a pot of tea between them. Rosalind hoped she kept her surprise hidden.

"Oh, Rosalind, good morning," said Bethany brightly.

"Good morning," replied Rosalind. "Good morning, Mr. Douglas."

"Good morning, Miss Thorne," he replied. "Will you have some tea?"

"Thank you," said Rosalind. "I think I will take coffee this morning instead. It was a long night." She took up a plate and began filling it with the ragout of root vegetables and several slices of ham. She had missed dinner the night before and was quite ravenous.

"I'm sorry to hear it," said Douglas as Rosalind took her seat at the table. "I am glad you've come down. I feel I owe you an apology."

"An apology?" repeated Rosalind.

"Yes. I have not been . . . I have not been as patient or forthcoming these past couple of days as I should have, and I am sorry."

As Rosalind sliced her ham, she looked across to Bethany. Bethany only arched her brows over the rim of her cup. Rosalind expelled a long breath. Clearly, something had changed between Bethany and her husband, and that change, it would seem, was for the better.

"It has not been an easy time for anyone," said Rosalind. "And I'm afraid it will not be over for a little while yet." She thought of the pearl knotted in her handkerchief. She thought of Betsy's empty room, and Mr. Hodgeson staring after her and Amelia as they climbed the stairs.

"Have you found something new?" asked Bethany. "Something about Betsy? I must tell you, Mrs. Hare was most upset that you were caught in her room. She had more than a few words for me this morning."

"Yes, I'm not surprised," said Rosalind. "That was a mistake of mine, and I apologize for it. But no, I have not found anything definite. I hope, however, to have a different answer later today." She paused. "Mr. Douglas, may I ask you a question? I'm afraid it's a personal one. About money."

He waved his half-empty cup, giving her permission. "What is it?"

"When you took over Mr. Hodgeson's estate . . . was there any sign that he had ever made use of a moneylender?"

"A private moneylender you mean?"

"Yes. Someone who might not go to the courts to collect a debt."

Douglas reached for the pot and refilled his cup. Then he refilled Bethany's. "His accounts were a hideous mess," he said. "I am not exaggerating to say it took me months to sort them out, but I saw nothing like that. Bethany?" Douglas looked to his wife. "Do you know anything?"

"No. I'm afraid not," said Bethany. "I did sometimes try to understand the estate accounts, but as you say, it was a hideous mess, and it was made clear to me, several times, that if I thought I could have anything to do with money, I was terribly silly." She pulled a wry face. "What's this about, Rosalind?"

Rosalind took a deep breath. "I'm trying to discover if Cantrell kept in touch with anyone in the house before he made his return."

"But we all thought he was dead," said Bethany. "Who would have . . . who could have . . . ?"

Rosalind chose her next words with care. "There is some evidence that Cantrell was receiving information from inside the house."

Douglas's expression grew thunderous. "From who?"

"I don't know," said Rosalind. "But it occurred to me that if Cantrell knew something about Mr. Hodgeson's money troubles, he could have been blackmailing him."

"Rosalind," said Bethany, "you cannot be thinking that *Papa* had reason to murder Cantrell."

"That's not a jump I'm ready to make," Rosalind told her. "I am saying that Cantrell had a confederate in the house. Someone who was passing him information about the movements of the family. That would be how Cantrell knew we were going to Meredith's concert."

Douglas's hand shook where it lay on the table. For a moment, Rosalind thought he was going to shout, but he did not.

"So, when you suspected there was a spy in the house, you looked for weak links in the family chain, and you came up with William," Douglas said.

"I hate . . ." Bethany stopped and took a swallow of tea. "I hate to say this, but it's . . . it's not outside the realm of possibility."

"I'm sorry to have to speak this way," said Rosalind.

"No, no," Douglas sighed. He took another swallow of tea, and Rosalind suspected he wished it was something much stronger. "You've not even hit on the best reason to suspect him."

"What is that?"

"He hates me," said Douglas flatly. "When I married Beth, he came and asked me for money. He told me the estate was in trouble, and it had become 'quite a bother' . . . I think those are the words he used. When I wouldn't simply give him what he wanted on the grounds that he was my father-in-law, he got very angry."

Rosalind looked to Bethany, who nodded. "I see."

"Then I told him that the only way I *would* help him was if he handed me over the management of the estate. And I made him sign a paper to that effect." Douglas's fingers curled into a fist. "I think that was the last straw. He went away for three days and did not speak to me. Then he came back, rather the worse for wear, and dropped the paper on my desk." Douglas looked down at his own hand and saw how it had clenched. Slowly, he straightened his fingers out. "Since then, we've barely been on speaking terms. If he could do me an injury, he would." He paused and then added, "I suppose that sounds arrogant. Once again, I am making the entire matter about myself."

"No," said Rosalind. "From what I know of Mr. Hodgeson, it is entirely possible you are correct."

Douglas glanced at the tall case clock that stood in the corner. "And from what I know of him, I suspect he will not be able to speak coherently until noon, at least. And I have some urgent business of my own this morning. When that is finished, I will go speak with my solicitors. They may know something more. When I return this afternoon, I will see if Hodgeson can be convinced to talk with me."

"Thank you," said Rosalind.

Douglas got to his feet. He took Bethany's hand and kissed it. "I will be home this afternoon," he assured her. "Miss Thorne." He bowed over her hand and strode out of the room.

Rosalind arched her brows at Bethany. Bethany blushed like a schoolgirl.

"It seems you have had a reconciliation," said Rosalind.

"We are trying," said Bethany. "I'm under no illusions that this change will be permanent, or that things will be easy, but we are trying." She paused. "I knew he was angry with himself over what happened with Cantrell, but I didn't realize quite how badly wounded he still was. When we were talking last night, he told me he gave away every other choice when he let Cantrell into the house, and that he had no business trying to make his own way in the world when he was ready to surrender his judgment to the first plausible rascal who came along."

"Perhaps now he'll find some peace."

"Yes," murmured Bethany. "Yes, whatever happens next, Cantrell can do no more damage to us." Her gaze went distant for a moment, but then she shook herself. "Now, tell me, what is your agenda for today?"

Rosalind looked at the clock. "I have to meet with one of the Bow Street officers, and after that . . . after that I hope very much I will be able to bring back, if not good news, at least useful news." She paused.

"Good," said Bethany firmly. "Let us hope we will soon be able to put an end to this whole awful business."

"I think we may," said Rosalind. *I only wish I was more certain what kind of ending it will be.*

CHAPTER 44

Due Suspicions

. . . what becomes of the moral, if our comfort
springs from a breach of promise?

Jane Austen, *Pride and Prejudice*

When Rosalind arrived at Little Russell Street, she found Alice sitting in the parlor with tea and a toasted muffin, pouring over the latest issue of the *London Daily*.

"Rosalind!" She jumped up, sending a small shower of crumbs everywhere. "You look awful!"

"Thank you," Rosalind said. "I'm glad to see you, too."

"You know what I mean. Sit down. I'd toast you a muffin, but George ate them all." Alice took up the pot and poured out a fresh cup of tea.

"I've had my breakfast." Rosalind took cup Alice handed her and drank thirstily. "Where's Nora?"

"Still asleep, poor thing." Alice refilled her own cup. "She's still feeling the effects of last night."

Rosalind eyed her friend. "Last night?"

"We stayed up rather late," said Alice breezily. "I may have treated us to a bottle of wine. Don't be angry," she added quickly.

"I'm not," said Rosalind. "You probably did her a favor by limiting her desire to be out and about today. Although I'm surprised you're not worse for the wear yourself."

"You shouldn't be. I'm sure she's led a most dissolute life, but I am equally sure she has never been taken up as the pet mascot of a group of newspapermen." Alice grinned. "One quickly learns how to pace oneself."

"Does George know about this particular skill of yours?"

"No." Alice glared suspiciously at her. "And you are not going to tell him."

"I would not dream of it," replied Rosalind solemnly.

"So, what have you to tell us?" asked Alice eagerly.

"I want to wait for Adam," said Rosalind.

"Well, you will not have to wait long." Alice jerked her chin toward the window. Outside, Adam was striding up the street.

Smiling, Rosalind went to the door. Adam entered, taking off his hat as he did so. Rosalind held out her hand for him to take and kiss. Then he looked into her eyes, asking a silent question. She answered by kissing his mouth.

It was by no means a long kiss. She had not lost that much of her propriety. Alice was likely to spring up from her seat at any moment, and Nora might decide to wake up and come downstairs.

But it did happen, and it was very sweet, and when she pulled away, Adam gave her his devastating smile and touched the corner of her mouth tenderly. Rosalind's knees turned weak as water.

"My goodness!" called Alice from the parlor. "*Whatever* can be keeping them?"

"I'm going to do her an injury," muttered Rosalind.

"Please not where I can see," said Adam. "It would be embarrassing to have to arrest you."

Rosalind took Adam into the parlor, glowered at Alice,

and resumed her seat. Alice poured a third cup of tea and held it out to Adam, smiling sweetly.

"Where's George?" asked Adam.

"He left early. Apparently, he's chasing down a new story, something he heard at the Brown Bear." Alice drank her own tea. "Do you know, I think I'm not going to miss being a reporter. We novelists get to sleep in as late as we choose." She turned to Rosalind. "Now, Rosalind, your Mr. Harkness is here. You can talk. What have you found out?"

Rosalind set her cup down and pulled her handkerchief from her sleeve. She undid the knot and unfolded the cloth to show her prize.

Alice gasped. "Is that a pearl?"

Rosalind nodded. "Amelia found it in Betsy's—she's the maid who vanished—it was under the bed in her room."

Adam took the pearl carefully in his fingers. He rolled it back and forth, testing the texture of it, just as Rosalind had done. Just as carefully, he laid it back down in the center of her handkerchief.

"Tell me," he said.

So, Rosalind told them about her conversation with Mariah, and how she had confirmed that Nora and Mariah between them had invented Jacob Mayne.

"Oh, I can't wait to hear what Sanderson will have to say!" cried Alice.

"I'm sure not all of it will be printable," said Rosalind.

She told them how they had gone to search Betsy's room and been spied by Mr. Hodgeson, and how their search of the room had been interrupted by Mrs. Hare. How Amelia had discovered the pearl.

Then Rosalind took a deep breath and reminded herself that to err was indeed human, and she told them about her suspicion that Mr. Hodgeson had run away, but she had been mistaken. Neither member of her audience seemed inclined to laugh, which was a relief. Then she told them about Pen and her missing eye drops.

When she finally finished, they all sat silently for a long moment, each turning over their own thoughts.

It was Alice who spoke first.

"Well. I cannot believe this Betsy person is the thief. I don't know why she's gone, but no maid who has been around for longer than five minutes would be fool enough to steal such a thing. Why, if she was caught, even with that one pearl, she could be hanged!" English law stipulated that the theft of any property worth more than five pounds could be answered with a death sentence.

"Amelia did say Betsy was a mercenary girl, but this"— Rosalind held up the pearl—"notwithstanding, I have a hard time believing she stole the entire necklace."

"On her own, probably not," said Adam. "But she might have stolen it for someone else."

That was not a comfortable thought. Rosalind felt Mr. Hodgeson's gaze on the back of her neck. Could he have convinced Betsy to take the pearls? Perhaps he had meant to pass it off as a joke, or perhaps he had played on her greed?

It was possible, but it remained a terrible risk. Rosalind knotted her handkerchief around the pearl again.

"Did you see Sir Jasper?" Rosalind asked Adam before her thoughts could fall into an unprofitable spiral. "What did he say?"

Adam swirled his tea for a moment before he drank. "A great deal," said Adam. "But what was important was that we were right. Cantrell—or whatever his real name may turn out to be—was definitely working his own scheme well before he slipped into Gerald Douglas's good graces."

Rosalind listened with her heart in her throat as Adam described his meeting with Sir Jasper. He described how that ruined man coldly dismissed first Huet and then Addison.

And then he told them how Bryan Cantrell, as Benjamin Case, had become a member of Sir Jasper's household.

Alice uttered a most unladylike oath. "He went to Sir Jasper's *first?*"

"So it seems," said Adam. "And once he knew that the will had been rewritten in Addison's favor, that's when he went to Douglas."

Alice frowned "Why not go to Addison?"

"Perhaps he did," breathed Rosalind.

Alice's brows shot up. "You think Cantrell killed Addison?"

"It's possible," said Rosalind. "Nora told me he did kill a man, probably over a game of cards. It's why she left him."

"There's another possibility," said Adam. "That he conspired with Douglas."

Alice's jaw dropped "You can't be serious."

Adam did not answer this.

Rosalind regarded him. She let her thoughts travel over everything that had been said. Could it be that Douglas had made some sort of bargain with Cantrell? Douglas was an ambitious man. He was in need of money, not only for himself and his business plans, but to save his father-in-law from debtors' prison.

He told me he gave away every other choice when he let Cantrell into the house, Bethany had said. *And that he had no business trying to make his own way in the world when he was ready to surrender his judgment to the first plausible rascal who came along.*

She imagined Cantrell in his character as Douglas's friend. She imagined them sitting together late at night. A suggestion would be made, first with a laugh and then more earnestly. The wine would be passed back and forth, details of how to accomplish the thing would be considered and rejected, and it would all be passed off as a joke. But the idea would come back around, and then around again, until at last, it did not sound so mad, after all

One stranger would vanish. It could well be an accident, or perhaps he had simply no longer wanted to be found. Cantrell could persuade him life would be easier that way. Then one letter to an old man, rejecting a burdensome inheritance, and the thing would be done. All the money would simply land in Douglas's lap, and all the problems would be solved.

He was ready to surrender his judgment to the first plausible rascal who came along.

"But if the plan was murder, what on earth was all this business with the elopement?" cried Alice.

"To provide a covering story," said Adam. "Cantrell had to be sure no one would look at him too closely, let alone connect him to Sir Jasper. But if he elopes, everyone sees that. No one will think of him as having killed a man or stolen an inheritance. Besides, Douglas is the one who would have the motivation to kill Addison, not Cantrell."

"No," said Rosalind. "Douglas would never have agreed to any plan that would end in Cantrell eloping with Penelope."

"Cantrell didn't elope with Penelope," said Adam. "He eloped with Nora."

"But it doesn't make sense!" cried Alice. "If it's as you say, and he had conspired with Douglas, why would he come back from the grave and only bother with Nora?"

"Look at it this way," said Adam. "Cantrell elopes with Nora and flees the country. They wait. A year later, he hears from his spy in the house that the will has been changed and Douglas is now Sir Jasper's heir. That's when the letters begin. The ransom demands are cover for the payment they agreed on."

"But Douglas didn't pay," Rosalind reminded him.

"Douglas decided not to go through with it. Perhaps Sir Jasper did not settle as much money on him as he thought.

Perhaps the debts on the estate are larger than he believed. Perhaps he just decided he would gamble that between Cantrell's debts and the possibility of being taken up for murder, Cantrell simply wouldn't dare come back to England. Then, of course, Nora returns home and tells everyone he's dead, and Douglas thinks he's in the clear."

"But what part do the pearls play?" asked Rosalind.

"They may not play any part in this. They might be a coincidence or . . ." Adam paused. "Payment."

"I don't understand," said Rosalind.

"Cantrell may have written secretly to Douglas. If he has a confederate in the house, that would not be difficult. Cantrell reminds him of their deal and says he's coming to collect. Douglas offers him the pearls. Betsy is used for a go-between. It is her job to hand over the pearls, take her payment, and vanish. Only Cantrell dies before she can deliver them."

"So where is she—are they—now?" prompted Alice.

Adam shook his head. "I don't know."

"What about Nora and her paintings?" asked Rosalind. "Why bother with her?"

"That could be down to simple greed. Or he might have wanted revenge for her leaving him."

Rosalind drummed her fingers restlessly on her desktop. Could it have happened that way? It made for a complex scheme, but none of it was impossible. And the way Adam had told it, the timing of Cantrell's actions finally made sense.

But it's all disconnected. She had said as much to Amelia, and she felt it again now. They had a set of circumstances, with few facts and less proof to hold them together. Indeed, most of what they had was lost: lost pearls, lost Betsy, lost Addison Douglas. How were they to be certain of anything?

It was Adam who answered that unspoken question.

"We need to know what Cantrell has left behind. If Douglas put even one piece of incriminating evidence in Cantrell's hands, I am certain Cantrell will have kept it."

Rosalind set her cup down. "In that case, I had better not waste any more time. I need to call on Mrs. Asherton."

"Do you want me to come with you?" asked Adam.

Rosalind smiled. "Let me try first. Mrs. Asherton struck me as a very proper lady. I'm afraid a Bow Street officer might put her back up."

Adam bowed. "Then I leave it in your hands, Miss Thorne."

CHAPTER 45

A Mother's Concerns

... angry people are not always wise ...

Jane Austen, *Pride and Prejudice*

Mrs. Hodgeson knocked briskly on her daughter's door. Really, the girl should know better than to keep her waiting. It was most injurious to her health.

At last Mariah opened the door. "Oh. Mama," she said, with that *deplorable* lack of spirit she could sometimes show.

"Mariah, I have been waiting for you for at least twenty minutes. You agreed to accompany me in the carriage this morning!"

"You decided that I should," said Mariah peevishly. "I never agreed."

Mrs. Hodgeson sighed. "Don't be difficult, girl. Come along."

"Perhaps I am busy."

"What business could you have that is more important than assisting your mother? And," she added, "do not jut your chin out in that stubborn way. It is most unattractive."

Thankfully, Mariah did not choose to make any more trouble. There was, of course, all the usual fuss with bonnets and coats, and that little parlormaid, Susan, *would* bring the wrong shawl. Oh, how she missed Betsy! Mr. Hodgeson might roll his eyes, but the girl had seemed to have such a superior understanding. It was a shame she should have run off so abruptly.

Well, we all have our little trials to bear, Mrs. Hodgeson thought piously as she let herself be handed into the closed carriage. Then, of course, there must be rugs and hot bricks, and Mariah would make such faces. Well, she was young yet. She would understand the importance of warmth and of comfort later.

The truth was, she found these carriage rides horribly fatiguing, and the girls could be so troublesome, but how else was she to talk without being overheard? With half the staff being Sir Jasper's spies, not one confidential word could be uttered in the house. Especially not now, when matters were reaching such a crisis. Her heart had been in absolute palpitations for days.

It does not matter. I will be strong. For my family, I must be.

"Now then, Mariah," said Mrs. Hodgeson as the carriage started forward. "It is time you and I had a little talk."

"Why?"

"Don't be tiresome, please. I cannot bear it." She extracted her handkerchief from her reticule and pressed it against her temple. She should have brought her lavender water. Should she go back for it? No. She would be strong. "It's about Miss Thorne."

"Is it? I thought you were one of her admirers."

"Yes, yes." She waved her hand vigorously, as if to shoo all previous impressions away. "She is very clever and highly placed, and when it was simply a matter of the missing pearls, well, that was one thing. But now it is more than that."

"I don't understand." Mariah frowned.

She shouldn't, thought Mrs. Hodgeson. She'd have wrinkles before she was twenty-five. Not that with Mariah it mattered as much. *Oh, what did I do to have such a plain daughter?*

"Mariah," she said gently, "I wonder that you have not realized it yet. Miss Thorne means to make mischief for Nora! I'm sure she does!"

For once, the girl looked genuinely confused. "But she's invited Nora to stay at her house."

"The better to spy on her! Don't you see? She has decided to prove that Nora killed Cantrell!"

"Nora did not kill Cantrell." Mariah's answer was cold, flat, and definite.

"I know that, you wretched girl!" cried Mrs. Hodgeson. "But the Thorne woman has decided that she has. The question is, What will we do about it?"

"Why do you think I can do anything? Bethany brought her here. Bethany's the one who has to get rid of her."

"Bethany's frightened."

"Of what?"

Mrs. Hodgeson leaned forward and whispered, "Douglas."

"Bethany has not shown any sign of being frightened of Douglas."

"That was before. Now everything's changed. She's prepared to sacrifice her sister!"

"Why?" began Mariah. "You think *Douglas* killed Cantrell?"

"Who has more to lose than Douglas? You will recall the note that was written to Sir Jasper, about poor Pen at the concert? It puts Douglas's position with Sir Jasper in the worst kind of danger!" The carriage jolted across a missing cobble, and Mrs. Hodgeson squeaked and clutched at Mariah's hand.

Mariah drew her hand back. "If Cantrell was killed to save the money, any one of us might have done it."

"It's not only the money, of course. It's Penelope."

Mariah fell silent. Finally, she seemed to be hearing what was said.

Mrs. Hodgeson pressed ahead. "Oh, the man may have the hardest heart in the world, and he may have coldly ripped the estate from your dear papa's hands, but even I must acknowledge he loves his sister and will do anything to protect her. Anything!"

Mariah turned her face toward the window. She meant to hide what she was thinking, but Mrs. Hodgeson saw how tightly she laced her fingers together.

"If Douglas killed Cantrell, what will prevent Miss Thorne from finding that out?" Mariah asked.

"Can we be sure she will look past her own nose and her own interests? Mariah, I found out . . . the woman is working! For *money*," she sneered.

"That is hardly surprising."

"Oh, my girl, you do not understand!" cried Mrs. Hodgeson. "We've sheltered you from this sort of vulgarity, but consider. She is expecting a fee from *Bethany*. Do you think she will recover any answers that Bethany disapproves of? Of course not! Her fee depends precisely on how much she pleases those who pay her!"

"The lady thief-taker," Mariah breathed.

"Exactly!" said Mrs. Hodgeson triumphantly. "I do not pretend that poor Bethany is anything but torn. Indeed, I'm sure her heart bleeds, but she is a mother now, and her first concern is for her children. Therefore, she must protect their father. It would be unnatural of her to do otherwise. But I am also a mother, and I cannot stand by and watch my daughter—my daughter who has already been so cruelly wronged and *defamed* by that woman!—being led to the gallows!"

Mariah swallowed.

"I know you love your sister." Mrs. Hodgeson's heart

swelled as she spoke. "I know she broke your heart when she ran away, as she did her loving mama's! But I see the two of you together, protecting one another, consoling one another."

Mariah looked away.

Mrs. Hodgeson went on. "Yes, I know, I am an invalidish old woman, as silly as any of the girls I mothered, but I do have eyes. You will not let Nora down when she needs you."

Mariah looked down at her own hands. Mrs. Hodgeson held her breath. She knew her daughter was thinking hard. The girl was not as inscrutable as she believed. No child was to a doting parent. The secret was to pay *attention*. It was true, however, that she held herself very close indeed, especially now.

The girl must see the way of it. She *must* understand!

"Well, Mama," said Mariah finally. "You need have no worries. You see, I have already demonstrated to her that Nora is innocent."

"Mariah!" Mrs. Hodgeson cried. "Dearest girl! But how . . . !"

"It seems it was a matter of handwriting. I showed her a letter Nora had written, and one I had, and it seemed to satisfy her."

It was a shame the girl would not stop wearing those silly spectacles, Mrs. Hodgeson thought. Her eyes could be quite lovely.

"Oh, my child. How wonderful!" She pressed her handkerchief to her mouth. "But can we be sure? Truly?"

Mariah lifted her gaze. "I promise," she said. "If anything else needs to be done, I will see to it."

Mrs. Hodgeson seized her daughter's hand and squeezed it. "I knew that I could rely on you!"

Mariah smiled briefly. "Mama?"

"Yes, my dear?"

"That lavender water you gave to Pen? She said it worked wonders on her headache."

"Of course it did! It's my own recipe!" Really, the poor girl should not grimace so, Mrs. Hodgeson thought. It made her look *quite* haggard.

"Do you think you could let me have a bottle when we get home? My head is splitting."

CHAPTER 46

What Is Left Behind

You do not know what he really is . . .

Jane Austen, *Pride and Prejudice*

"Mrs. Asherton. Thank you for seeing me."

Mrs. Asherton's home was very like the woman herself, neat and unpretentious, but tending somewhat toward an abundance of frills. When Rosalind was shown into the sitting room, Mrs. Asherton set aside her fancywork, instructed the maid to run for an extra cup, and invited Rosalind to make herself comfortable.

"I do apologize for disturbing you so early," said Rosalind as she settled onto the round-backed chair. Etiquette stipulated that a "morning" call could not be made before eleven o'clock, and it was barely ten. But this once, Rosalind did not find herself able to disguise her business under the strict niceties of the social call.

"Oh, you are not disturbing me in the least, Miss Thorne," replied Mrs. Asherton politely. "I am delighted to have you here. Tell me, how does your little protégé? Penelope, was it?"

"She is quite well, thank you, and much recovered."

The maid arrived with the tea, and Mrs. Asherton poured Rosalind the requisite cup and offered the choice of milk or lemon biscuit as an accompaniment. Once Rosalind had sipped and nibbled and complimented Mrs. Asherton's cook, she was able to set the cup down.

"Mrs. Asherton, I feel I am being remiss in not offering you condolences on your recent loss."

"Oh, yes, poor Mr. Campbell!" Mrs. Asherton shook her head sadly. "You are very kind. He was my son's friend, of course, but he had become very dear to all of us. He was devastated to see he had caused young Penelope such distress, you know. He assured me that had he known she would be there, he never would have agreed to accompany me."

"Then he told you about their . . . past association?"

"Oh, yes, he explained everything." Mrs. Asherton leaned forward to speak confidentially. "And she is not in the least to be blamed, I'm sure. What girl could fail to cherish a tendre for such a man? His eyes alone must . . . must have . . . worked excessively on such an impressionable imagination."

Rosalind found she could picture exactly how Cantrell would have looked as he spun this tale for Mrs. Asherton—his words would be gentle, and those green eyes distant and regretful.

"I imagine his Emma must be quite heartbroken," said Rosalind.

"Little Claire tells us she does nothing but sit in her room and cry." Mrs. Asherton sighed and clasped her hands together. "Oh, I wish Thaddeus had not had to be the one to break it to her. She's such a dear young creature! We were almost as fond of her as we were of Campbell." She sighed again. "But, Miss Thorne, what I fail to understand is how you came to be with him at the fatal moment. Thad told me all about it, of course, but he could not understand it, either."

"As a matter of fact, Mrs. Asherton, it is the same reason that brings me to you today."

"I'm afraid I don't quite understand."

Rosalind folded her hands, and let her gaze fall, indicating she was about to speak on a delicate and slightly uncomfortable matter. "I'm afraid my protégé may have written some letters, imprudent, girlish letters . . ." She paused meaningfully. "After what happened, Mr. Campbell contacted the family, offering to return them. It fell to me to go collect them. That's what I was attempting to do when . . ." Rosalind shuddered delicately.

"Oh!" Mrs. Asherton pressed her hand against her mouth. "Oh my dear! Oh, *now* I understand! How awful that must have been for you!"

Rosalind agreed that it was. "The problem is that when his things were gone through at those dreary rooms, no letters were found, but since I knew he was staying with you, I was wondering if he'd left anything behind. A box or . . ."

"Oh! Oh, yes. His trunk is still in his room. He'd left us only a few days before, you see, and hadn't sent for it yet." She glanced away. "I suppose we should have gone through it already, but I honestly couldn't bring myself to do it. It probably seems ridiculous to you, Miss Thorne, but I've been so reluctant to search through his things it. He was only a guest, however attached I may have been to him. It just seemed . . . indelicate."

"I do understand," said Rosalind. "It is difficult to know what to do at these times."

"Well, perhaps your coming is a favor unlooked for," said Mrs. Asherton brightly. "This is a task I have put off shamefully. I know Mr. Campbell was at odds with his family, but I've felt they should be told. Only he never gave us any hint where they could be found. I'm sure there's something in his trunk that will let us know how to proceed. And, of course, if your protégé's letters are there, you shall have them."

"Thank you, Mrs. Asherton," said Rosalind. "You are very kind."

"Well, I will tell you, Miss Thorne . . ." A light glimmered in Mrs. Asherton's eye. "When I was young, I received a similar kindness, without which, I fear, things would have been much different for all of us!"

She smiled and Rosalind smiled, and they both finished their tea.

The rooms that had been set aside for "Mr. Campbell" were in the north wing of the house. They were well paneled with dark wood and furnished with sturdy and comfortable armchairs, tables, thick rugs, and pleasing ornaments. Under Mrs. Asherton's direction, the footman brought a stout steamer trunk out of the boudoir.

The item had clearly seen much use. Its brass bindings were badly scratched. Mud and water had stained its leather sides. The footman rattled the latches.

"Locked, I'm afraid, ma'am," he declared.

"Oh dear," murmured Mrs. Asherton. "I'm sorry, Miss Thorne. I didn't stop to think . . ."

Rosalind tilted her head, as if considering the problem. "Perhaps Mr. Can . . . Campbell left a spare key?" she suggested. "I know many people do. Perhaps on the mantel . . . ?"

This caused an immediate search. Rosalind had previously noted a carved box on the table, among the decanters. Putting her back to Mrs. Asherton, Rosalind slipped the trunk key from her glove.

"Here it is!" she cried, holding the key aloft.

"Ah, excellent, Miss Thorne!" returned Mrs. Asherton.

Rosalind handed the key to the footman, who unlocked the trunk and opened it wide. As with most trunks made for long voyages, it had a series of drawers built into one half. Rosalind opened them in order and discovered that the third drawer held several bundles of letters, all tied with plain twine, many with foreign stamps, and all with different directions.

"Goodness." Mrs. Asherton picked up a bundle. "He did travel extensively, did he not? You know the girl's hand, I suppose?"

"Not as well as I should," admitted Rosalind. "And several of these could have been written by young ladies . . ."

"Oh dear," murmured Mrs. Asherton, flicking through the bundle she held. "And some of them may be relations or, I imagine, his lawyers or his bankers." Because, of course, a young gentleman like Mr. Campbell would have affairs that required letters to be written. "Some in here might even be from Emma," Mrs. Asherton sighed. "I suppose they must all be gone through." Her tone and her expression showed how little she looked forward to the task.

"Mrs. Asherton," said Rosalind carefully, "if you like, and if you think it would be appropriate, I can manage this correspondence."

"Are you certain you want to?" asked Mrs. Asherton. "It would not cause your friends any discomfort?"

Rosalind looked her directly in the eye. "I abhor keeping secrets," she said. "But there are times when discretion is a kindness. Do you not agree?"

The matron returned her direct gaze. "Yes, especially when matters of young indiscretion may be involved." She placed her bundle of letters into Rosalind's hands.

"How would it be if I took possession of the trunk?" suggested Rosalind. "Then, when I find from these"—she held up the letters—"where his family is to be found, I can simply have it sent on, and I need not bother your house again."

"Oh, I am sure it's no trouble," said Mrs. Asherton. "But I

would be happy to leave this matter in your hands. I know it is a far more, well, trivial matter than you are accustomed to being consulted about. But if you are willing . . ."

Rosalind smiled. "You may be sure, Mrs. Asherton, this is exactly the sort of matter I am consulted about."

There was some additional polite hesitation, but in the end, they closed the trunk and Mrs. Asherton's footman carried the trunk down to the waiting carriage, where the driver secured it to the luggage rack.

CHAPTER 47

Contents and Conclusions

*The arrival of letters was the first grand object of
every morning's impatience.*

Jane Austen, *Pride and Prejudice*

"Rosalind!" cried Alice as Adam and the cabdriver between them hefted Cantrell's trunk into the foyer.
"This is really too much! I don't mind a stray girl, and I can
live with George snoring on the sofa for a time, but where on
earth do you intend to put that?"

"In the dining room," she said to Alice and the men. "And
it's only temporary."

"Humph! I'll believe it when I see it."

"It's Cantrell's trunk," Rosalind told her. "And it's got his
letters in it."

"Oh, well . . . !" said Alice, much mollified. "That's all together different. I hope you're not going to try to keep this to
yourself."

"I wouldn't dream of it," said Rosalind. "Is Nora not
awake yet?" asked Rosalind.

"Not yet, and yes, I did look in on her," added Alice. "She
is there."

Rosalind felt a rush of relief and hoped it did not show too badly.

Once she had paid off the driver, Rosalind unlocked the trunk. Adam helped push it open.

"I suggest we divide and conquer." Rosalind pulled out the third drawer, where the letters waited. "Alice and I can look through the letters and, Adam, you can search through the remainder of the property."

"As you wish." Adam—proving he was not immune to dramatic flourish—took off his coat and rolled up his shirt-sleeves. Rosalind found she had to look away. She also noted the room had grown unaccountably warm.

Recalling herself to the business of the moment, Rosalind handed Alice a bundle of Cantrell's correspondence and took one for herself.

"What exactly are we looking for?" said Alice.

"Anything that connects Cantrell to Gerald Douglas," said Adam as he pulled the first drawer out from the trunk and set it on the table.

"Or anyone else in the family." Rosalind undid the twine on her bundle and began sorting through the letters.

They all became very busy at once. Adam removed Cantrell's varied belongings from the trunk—his shaving kit, cuff links, stockings, breeches, neckcloths, all the detritus of a man's life—and examined each item carefully. Rosalind and Alice, meantime, set about separating the letters into stacks, each according to the various names to whom they'd been directed.

Soon, they found themselves with half a dozen different piles.

"This one's to a Mr. Collier," muttered Alice.

"And this one is to Mr. Carter," said Rosalind, adding it to the assigned pile. A scraping noise caught her ear, and she looked over at Adam. He was head and shoulders inside the trunk. "What are you doing?"

"There's something been sewn up under the lining here."
He pulled a clasp knife from his pocket and flicked open the
blade. "I can see the outline . . ."

Rosalind craned her neck to see what he was doing, but
his back and shoulders blocked her view. After a moment
and some muffled exclamations, Adam straightened up. In
his hand, he held a man's pocket book.

"What's in it?" asked Alice eagerly.

Adam flipped the book open and rifled through its contents. "These look like . . . promissory notes," he said. He extracted one and read it over quickly. "It seems in addition to
all his other schemes, our Mr. Cantrell was playing go-
between for a moneylender." He paused, reading again. "I
know the man he's using. He's no one I'd want to do business
with."

"And that's not all we've got," said Alice. "Look, Rosalind." Alice held up a letter. "This is addressed to Huet
Douglas."

This letter was older and more yellowed than the others.
The seal was crumbling, but it hadn't been broken, as it
would have been if the letter had ever been read.

"It was sent back . . ." Rosalind cracked the ancient seal
and flipped open the page and read. Adam and Alice both
crowded behind her.

The letter was written in a woman's spidery hand, and the
ink was badly faded. But Rosalind was able to read:

> *My Dearest:*
> *You cannot be so cruel as to leave me without any an-*
> *swer. What have I ever done except trust to your good-*
> *ness and honor, and where have I ever put my faith*
> *except in your love for me and our children?*
> *We are on the edge of desperation here. I've had to*
> *bring Barney home from school because I can no longer*
> *pay the fees, and we are threatened by the bailiffs.*

> *I have your letter saying Sir Jasper will not consent to any advance, but, Huet, you must try harder! You know there is nowhere else for us to turn.*
> *Your affectionate,*
> *Elaine Douglas*

The *Douglas* had been underlined.

"Rosalind . . . ," said Alice slowly. "Didn't Lady Cowper tell you that Huet Douglas was a bigamist?"

"She did," Rosalind agreed. She seemed unable to tear her eyes away from the heartbroken letter.

"And that there were multiple wives, and children?"

"Yes."

"You don't suppose . . . ," said Alice slowly.

"I do, Alice," said Rosalind. "I suppose it very much."

"I admit, I had wondered about Cantrell's origins," said Adam as he tucked the pocket book into his jacket where it hung on the back of the chair. He took the letter. "It makes sense, especially as a spark for revenge."

"What does?" Nora—yawning, her hair mussed, and her dress less fresh than it should have been—came into the dining room. She squinted at the trunk. "What on earth have you been doing?"

"You may want to sit down, Nora," advised Alice. "I'll get you some tea."

"I don't want any." Nora reached for the nearest stack of letters. "What is all this?"

"The trunk belonged to Bryan Cantrell," said Rosalind. "So does this." She took Elaine's letter from Adam and passed it to Nora.

Nora read, her lips moving soundlessly as she scanned the words. "I don't understand," she said.

"You know that Huet Douglas was the person Sir Jasper first named as his heir?" said Rosalind.

"Yes, of course," said Nora. "Then it was Addison."

"Did anyone tell you why Huet was disinherited?"

"Only that there was some scandal . . ." Nora's face went momentarily blank. Then she held up the letter. "This," she said. "This is the scandal?"

"Apparently, Huet had several families," said Alice.

"You think this Elaine was Cantrell's mother? That he was one of Huet's sons?" Nora asked.

"And that he knew that the father who had failed to answer this letter was destined to be a rich man. But, of course, without his father's acknowledgment, none of that wealth would ever come to him." Rosalind shook her head.

"But Sir Jasper's ideas about family and heritage are . . . inflexible," said Adam. "Huet had to know that if his outside families were discovered, his father would disinherit him immediately."

"But you said Huet recommended Cantrell as a private secretary for Sir Jasper," said Alice. "Why would he do that?"

"As a compromise?" suggested Rosalind. "It would be a way to provide for his son without having to openly acknowledge him."

"He would hardly be the first man to do so." Adam's face was grim, indicating what he thought about such nice sensibilities. "But given his mother's unanswered letter, I think it more likely that Cantrell sought out his father and prevailed on him to give him some kind of help. Perhaps they even thought Cantrell could charm the old man into giving up his prejudices. Or that was what Huet thought was meant to happen."

"What do you mean?" asked Alice.

"I've been thinking about this," said Adam. "One thing we don't yet know is *how* Sir Jasper found out about Huet's bigamy."

"Do you think Cantrell told him?" cried Nora.

"He certainly would have been in a perfect position to . . ." Rosalind hesitated, looking for the right words.

"Just happen to let something slip?" suggested Alice.

Rosalind nodded.

"He planned to revenge himself on the entire family," said Adam. "Beginning to end, and if we've guessed right, he made a very neat job of it. He felled both Sir Jasper and Huet with a single blow and then plotted to use Gerald Douglas against Addison."

"And then used all of us against Gerald," said Nora wearily.

"So it would seem," breathed Rosalind.

Nora stared at the letter. Slowly, gently, she folded it up once more and laid it on the table. She pushed it away, as if she could no longer bear to have it near her.

"And I thought myself so clever," she said. "I thought I was the one who convinced him to go along with *my* scheme. But he already had a plan in place when he came to us." She shook her head. "And I fell for it, just like everyone else."

"But *why*?" demanded Alice. "Why go through all this . . . this nonsense? If he wanted revenge, why not just kill Sir Jasper? Or Huet?"

"Because killing Huet wouldn't accomplish anything," said Adam. "Cantrell wanted the money, which Sir Jasper controlled, and simply killing the old man might throw suspicion on the household staff."

"Servants are always the first ones suspected," observed Alice.

"Cantrell wanted to make sure his tracks were well and truly covered," finished Adam.

"And it wouldn't have been as much fun," said Nora.

"Fun?" Rosalind felt her brow furrow.

Nora nodded. "Oh, yes. He loved his little games. Came near to getting us caught a few times, but that made it all the more exciting."

A swindler works longer and harder than anyone realizes. Rosalind stared at the letters. In her mind, she rearranged the events in their proper order.

As a young man, Cantrell had grown angry at his careless, selfish father and determined he would get revenge.

He lied and he plotted and he convinced that father to do something for him. His father, perhaps out of guilt or fear of exposure, got the son a position in Sir Jasper's house.

Then he exposed his father. Possibly even through a series of poison-pen letters to Sir Jasper, like the one he'd written after the ill-fated concert.

Then the son went to insinuate himself into the household of the third heir. Oh, Addison meant to be kind and to divide the money among the families. But that would not do. What good was a twelfth or fourteenth or smaller share when he could have half?

Especially after he discovered that the Hodgeson family was filled with all manner of possibilities for causing his latest enemy humiliation and ruin.

Rosalind could picture the gleam in Cantrell's eyes as he baited his hooks for Mr. Hodgeson, for Pen, and for Nora.

He was patient. He waited. He carefully considered which victim to make immediate use of and which to save for later.

Rosalind looked up at Adam, her question all in her eyes. *Does this remove suspicion from Gerald Douglas?*

She saw his grim answer.

No.

None of this exonerated Gerald Douglas, not of Addison's murder or of Cantrell's. Cantrell still could have convinced Douglas to take part in his schemes. Douglas could still have killed Cantrell to save himself, his sister, and the rest of his family. Not to mention preserve his inheritance.

"Damn the man!" cried Nora, as if she'd heard Rosalind's thoughts. She swept one arm across the table, scattering the letters, the stockings, and the cuff links.

Rosalind put a hand on Nora's shoulder. She did not look up, but neither did she push Rosalind away.

That was when the doorbell rang.

"Oh, for heaven's sake," muttered Alice. She left to answer the door.

"I can't think why I'm so angry," said Nora to Rosalind and Adam. "It can't make any real difference. Not now."

"No," said Rosalind. "But it doesn't have to."

Nora pressed her fingertips against her eyes.

"Rosalind." Alice came back into the room, carrying a note. "It's from Portsmouth Square. The man said he'd wait for a reply."

Rosalind quickly broke the seal and read:

> *Come quickly. Papa has vanished.*
> *Bethany*

Rosalind read the note again.

"What is it?" said Adam.

"We need to return to Portsmouth Square at once." Rosalind's voice rasped in her throat.

"What?" said Nora with false gaiety. "Has someone else vanished?"

"Your father," said Rosalind.

But it was more than that. Rosalind's throat closed around her breath. She touched the paper, tracing her fingertips along the long, slashing tails that underscored both *y*'s.

Oh, Bethany. No.

CHAPTER 48

The Flight

. . . I shall be the last person to confess it.

Jane Austen, *Pride and Prejudice*

Nora insisted on coming with them.

Rosalind wished desperately there was some way to put her off, but there was none, so Rosalind, Adam, and Nora all climbed into the hired cab together. Alice stayed behind to continue going through the trunk.

"Just in case anything else turns up," she'd said.

Every inch of the jouncing, rattling ride, Rosalind remained aware of the note from Bethany lying in her reticule.

She wanted to tell Adam what she'd read, and what she'd seen. She wanted to hear any alternative possibilities. There was something he had not said to her, as well. It was written all over his face. But they both remained silent. Nora might affect an air of unconcern, but Rosalind could not bring herself to speculate about whether her older sister might have murdered her lover within earshot of the young woman.

When they reached Portsmouth Square, Nora jumped from the cab without waiting to be helped, grabbed her hems, and ran. She ran up the walk, burst through the doors, ran past the footman and straight into the morning room.

Bethany and Douglas were both there, standing in front of Mrs. Hodgeson. Mariah was there, as well, standing in the corner like a waiting maid. In fact, Gilpin was right beside her, looking distinctly uncomfortable.

"Nora!" exclaimed Bethany. "You're home!"

"Yes, of course," said Nora lightly as she breezed across the room. "I wasn't going to miss the fun . . ." She stopped and actually looked a little ashamed as she took her sister's hands. "I'm sorry, Bethany. It's a bad habit. Pay no attention to me. I came home because I couldn't stay away anymore."

Bethany gave a small cry and hugged her sister hard.

Douglas faced Adam.

"Mr. Gerald Douglas, this is Mr. Adam Harkness, from Bow Street," Rosalind introduced them.

"Bow Street!" cried Mrs. Hodgeson, half starting from her chair. "What has Bow Street to do with this? Your father has only gone for one of his walks! He'll be back for dinner. This fuss is all too ridiculous!"

"But, Mama!" said Bethany. "He's taken his bag! His shirts are gone, as well, and his purse!"

At this, Mrs. Hodgeson's confidence trembled and wavered and broke.

"Oh! Oh!" She buried her face in her handkerchief. "He's abandoned me! Oh! What have I done to deserve this!"

Mariah turned her face away.

Bethany patted her mother's shoulders. "I'm sure it's not because of you, Mama . . . !"

"It is! It is! He's tired of me! I've grown old! He's run off with that girl! I know he has!"

Bethany sighed, exasperated. Rosalind watched as she heaved her sobbing mother to her feet and walked her to her waiting maid.

Bethany, she thought toward her friend. *Bethany, what have you done?*

Doubt clawed at the back of Rosalind's mind. She was missing something, or had lost something. Bethany watched as Gilpin led her mother out of the room and closed the door after her.

What have you done? thought Rosalind again.

"Thank you for coming, Mr. Harkness," Douglas was saying to Adam. "I wish I thought you could do some good here. I . . ." He hesitated. "I imagine Miss Thorne has told you about our various troubles?"

"I've been informed, yes." Adam took off his hat and tucked it under his arm. He had already assumed the easy dignity that came over him when he was about his duties. "Can you tell me when your father-in-law was last seen?"

"It was only an hour or two ago," Douglas said. "We wouldn't have thought anything of it. As Mrs. Hodgeson said, he frequently takes long walks about the city. But the maid noticed the missing shirts and the missing bag."

"Did he take a carriage? Or a horse?"

"He may have hired a cab," said Bethany. "But if he did, he went to a stand or to a stable, because our footman said he did not ask one of the servants to fetch one."

Rosalind fixed her eyes on Adam. It was easier than looking to Bethany and wondering.

The worst thing was Rosalind knew Bethany could have killed Cantrell. She could have taken Penelope's drops. She could have discovered where Cantrell lived and taken the poison to him. And she would have good reason to do it. After all, it had always been Bethany's job to fix her family's problems.

"You'll forgive me," Adam said to Bethany. "But I've been told that your father is not a terribly energetic man."

It was Nora who answered. "You mean, is he lazy? Yes.

He is. And he drinks, but he's never done anything like this. I admit, I wondered if maybe . . ." She stopped. "I don't think I've ever felt so sick about being right."

"Nora, please." Bethany slumped onto the sofa. Douglas sat beside her and took her hand.

Rosalind swallowed.

Adam nodded once. He also pulled out his pocket watch and checked the time. "It's possible I will be able to find him, but I'll have to leave at once."

"You're serious," said Douglas.

"I am. You must excuse me now, though."

"Of course," said Bethany.

"I'll walk you out," said Rosalind.

When they reached the entrance hall, she touched his arm. "Where are you going?"

He put his hat on and tugged the brim down. "I don't like to say here. I may be wrong, about a number of things." He paused. "Will you stay here, or do you want to go back to Little Russell Street?"

"I'll stay," she said. "There's a decision to be made, and some questions I still need to ask."

Adam searched her eyes for a long moment. Rosalind let him look his fill. She was afraid, yes, but not for herself. Not now.

"Very well," he said. "I wish I had time to talk, but you can put yourself at ease about Douglas."

"I know," she said.

"I thought you might." Adam took her hand and pressed it. "I shouldn't be more than two hours."

"If you are, I'm going to send Mr. Tauton after you."

"It would serve me right if you did." He smiled but then turned on his heel and left her there.

Rosalind waited until the door closed behind him. Suddenly, she felt very small, and very alone. She found she very much did not want to walk back into the morning room, to face Bethany and smile and feel the weight inside her.

Bethany had killed Cantrell. The note offered proof. Rosalind could not deny it, but neither could she bring herself to believe it.

"Miss Thorne!" Amelia's voice cut across her thoughts. Startled, Rosalind jerked around to see her maid racing down the stairs "There's been such a to-do . . ." She stopped as she saw Rosalind's face. "Are you all right, miss?"

"No," whispered Rosalind. "No, I don't believe I am."

CHAPTER 49

The Wayward Parent

He has been accused of many faults at different times, but this is the true one.

Jane Austen, *Pride and Prejudice*

Adam liked to think he had strong nerves, but by the time they reached the Red Rover Carriage House, he was very glad to be back on firm cobblestones. The cabdriver was a bored, restless young man. As soon as Adam had informed him he was on Bow Street's business, the young driver had demonstrated his willingness to risk his neck, and his horses, and his passenger, driving hell-for-leather between the vans and wagons.

Adam was very glad to pay the young madman off.

The Red Rover had served as a terminus for the Dover stage for at least two hundred years. It was a venerable half-timbered building, and its cobbled yard brimmed with people. Just now, the massive stagecoach was being loaded up with luggage. Would-be passengers swarmed around it, arguing with the driver, the ostlers, and each other.

Adam shoved his way politely but firmly to the driver. The

man responded to his inquiry by checking his waybill and pointing to the carriage house. Adam thanked him and ducked inside the crowded public room. There he shouldered his way to the bar. He shouted into the barman's ear. The barman bustled away and shouted at the landlord. The landlord returned and shouted at Adam, pointing at a gentleman dressed in a wool coat and broad hat who sat at a corner table, with a large glass and a large bottle for company. His valise sat on his feet.

Adam thanked the landlord, handed him a couple of shillings, and made his way to Mr. Hodgeson's table.

"You should not leave your bag so, sir." As he spoke, Adam snatched the valise neatly off the man's feet. Hodgeson made to jump up, but Adam sat down across from him and put the valise on the table.

"Mr. Hodgeson," he said. "My name is Harkness."

"Well, well." Hodgeson grabbed the bag out of Adam's hand and hugged it to him. "I'd invite you to sit, but you already have. Should I call for another glass? You may not want it, though. The stuff is all very bad." Despite this declaration, he took another large swallow from the glass. He did not let go of the valise.

"Your family is looking for you," Adam told him.

Mr. Hodgeson regarded him coolly. "I must be frank. You do not look like any relation of mine."

"I'm from Bow Street, Mr. Hodgeson."

"Well, well." Mr. Hodgeson blinked. "That took less time than I would have thought. How did you find me?"

"You are not experienced at hiding. You needed to leave the country, so you would naturally book a seat on the Dover stage. Which leaves from this door in . . ." Adam looked to the clock and the chalkboard that hung together over the bar. "A quarter hour, more or less. I was a little surprised you're not already on board."

"I had no desire to join the scrum," said Hodgeson. "And I found that I had need to fortify myself before I left forever." He drained his glass. "So, am I to be arrested?"

"Not unless it becomes necessary," said Adam. "Where's your maid, Betsy?"

"I neither know nor care where that ingrate has gotten to," he said loftily.

"But she was to meet you here?"

"Yes, and I paid for her room, and for her time. And what does she do but take my money and leave the . . . my possessions in the care of that . . . person behind the bar and go on her merry way!"

So, that was it. A fortune in pearls had been sitting underneath a bar in a carriage house, all because a young woman had decided that a bird in the hand was worth more than the possibility of a noose round her neck.

Betsy, Adam decided, was a smart girl.

"How much did you owe Mr. Cantrell?" asked Adam curiously.

Hodgeson shrugged. "Does it even matter? More than I could repay."

"How did you come to be in debt to him?"

"Eh? Oh, very easily. My girl married a mean, suspicious, impatient man. He talked of taking away the land, of leasing out the house, a thousand details. I knew if I had just a little extra, I could fob him off. Things would settle down again. They always had. Yardley, my steward, would see to everything."

Privately, Adam wondered how long Yardley had been cheating this sad man.

"Cantrell told me he knew a man in London who would be happy to loan me the money. Easy as that. I signed a paper, and the money was there. I gave it to Yardley, to pay the bills."

"Where is Yardley now?"

Hodgeson raised his glass and took a long drink. "God knows," he said as he set the glass back down. "I do not."

"So he took the money and scarpered."

"Scarpered? Interesting word, but I think I grasp your meaning. Yes. He scarpered."

"What did Cantrell do?"

"He laughed and told me not to worry. He said we'd all be in the pink again."

"How soon after that did he run off with Nora?"

Hodgeson shrugged.

"And no one wrote to you asking for the money?"

"No. No one. I thought I'd had a lucky escape. Surely this London fellow was after Cantrell for repayment. Of course, I now had no way to keep Douglas from running roughshod over my affairs, but at least he was willing to take care of the whole business, and I found myself with remarkably little inconvenience." He chuckled, as if he'd finally gotten the joke. "To tell you the truth, Mr. Harkness, it was a very comfortable arrangement."

"When did Cantrell start writing to you again?"

"Not long ago. Some weeks. He said he had returned to England and was in need of funds. I told him I had none. He reminded me he held a paper with my signature and a promise of payment."

"So you stole the pearls to buy him off."

Hodgeson raised his glass in salute. "And so I stole the pearls."

"Where are they?"

Mr. Hodgeson reached into his coat. He took out a lumpy package wrapped in brown paper and tied with plain twine and tossed it onto the table. "I suppose I should be glad the landlord here is more honest than he looks."

Adam took the package up and stowed it in his pocket. He wanted to look, badly. But assuming the man in front of him was telling the truth, he hardly wanted to display thousands of pounds worth of gemstones in a posting house. He'd already spotted several likely thieves, and they were just now paying too much attention to this little exchange.

"Time to be getting on, Mr. Hodgeson."

"Yes, I expect it is."

The man did not resist as Adam led him into the mud-spattered yard. Adam caught one of the ostlers by the sleeve and sent him running for a cab.

"Why didn't you give the pearls to Cantrell?" he asked as they waited for the man to carry out his commission.

"Well, it's very strange. I found, once I had them, that I didn't want to give them up so quickly. I thought, 'William, my boy, here is ready money in your hand. Here is a chance for the thing you've never had.'"

"Freedom?"

"Just so. Why shouldn't I simply leave? I don't need much. I could live out all my days in solitary comfort. No more reminders of my . . . previous mistakes . . . need trouble me. So, I put Cantrell off. I told him there were delays in getting the money. I blamed Douglas. That was very convenient. Then . . . well, then it turned out that our Nora had more energy and imagination than anyone gave her credit for. Although, I didn't know it at the time."

"But you knew something had changed," said Adam.

"Certainly I did. Suddenly, Cantrell was saying he would not pursue the debt. All he wanted was information. He wanted to know about Nora's doings. When she was leaving the house and where she was going, those sorts of things." He shrugged. "I obliged."

"You were willing to set that man on your daughter's heels?"

"It seemed better than to have him on mine," said Hodgeson. "Besides, I thought they were married."

"Except she said she was not."

"She lies," he said, as easily as if they were talking about the weather. "She has always done so. She ran away with the blaggard. Was I the one to protect her from the consequences of her own silliness?"

"You are her father."

"So I am." He arched his brows in an expression of bemusement. "And it's hardly been a bed of roses."

Adam felt his jaw tighten. "When did you decide to kill him?" he asked.

For the first time, Hodgeson seemed genuinely confused. "Eh? Kill him? I didn't kill him. Far too much trouble for me. Besides, I didn't need to. I was leaving."

CHAPTER 50

The Nature of Sacrifice

*The unlawfulness arises from the killing without
warrant or excuse . . . it may be by poisoning,
striking, starving or drowning and a thousand
other forms . . .*

John Impey, *The Office and Duty of Coroners*

Once Rosalind was safely enclosed in her own rooms, Amelia hurried forward to take her coat and bonnet. Rosalind sat heavily on the dressing table's chair and opened her reticule. She removed the note and frowned at it.

> *Come quickly. Papa has vanished.*
> *Bethany*

"Is there anything you need, miss?" asked Amelia.
Yes.
She needed a different conclusion than the one she'd reached. Rosalind ran her finger along the written lines, as if the texture of the paper could reveal something, anything, that she had missed.

There was no question in her mind that this handwriting was the same as she had seen on the label found in Cantrell's room.

But despite that, something was wrong. Rosalind lifted her eyes to the mirror and looked at her reflection. The woman who looked back at her from between the forest of bottles was a solemn, lost creature, and more than a little frightened. Rosalind felt sorry for her. But she felt angry, as well. That fear would help no one. Not Bethany, not Nora, Mariah, or Penelope.

Still, something was wrong. She felt it. Slowly, an idea surfaced in Rosalind's mind.

"Amelia?" she said. "I need my writing desk!"

"Yes, miss."

But as she turned away, a flash of color caught her eye, and Rosalind turned back. She glowered at the bottles on the table. She knew most of them quite well, as she'd brought them here with her. The only additions supplied by the staff here were an extra bottle of toilet water and a pot of night cream.

And now a dark blue bottle, which Rosalind was certain had not been there this morning.

Slowly, Rosalind reached out and picked the bottle up. A paper label was tied around its neck. It read:

LAVENDER AND YARROW WATER
FOR HEADACHE, VERTIGO, ENNUI, AND VAPOROUS
SENTIMENTS

Rosalind started to her feet. "Amelia! Where did this come from?"

Amelia set the writing desk down on the table beside the window and came to look. "Miss Mariah brought that for you. She said you'd asked for it. It's one of Mrs. Hodgeson's recipes, although I'm not sure I'd trust anything that woman brewed up, and I'm positive you've never had whatsis . . . vaporous sentiment?" Her brows knit. "What even are . . ."

Rosalind wasn't listening. She thrust the bottle into Amelia's hands and darted over to the table so quickly, she almost fell against it. She threw open her desk and sorted frantically through the letters inside. There. She had kept it—the letter Bethany had written her, the one where she agreed to Mr. Prescott's terms and said again how glad she would be to have Rosalind come to stay.

With trembling hands, Rosalind smoothed that letter out. She laid it beside the note she'd gotten summoning her back to Portsmouth Square because Mr. Hodgeson had vanished.

She set the bottle next to them. And stared at them all.

Rosalind closed her eyes and let out a very long breath.

"Miss?" said Amelia cautiously. "Is something wrong?"

"Yes." Rosalind opened her eyes again. "And no."

Because the handwriting on the urgent note did not match the handwriting in the polite letter. But it did match the writing on the bottle's label.

Bethany's name had been signed to the note, but Bethany had not written it.

It all made a terrible kind of sense.

Cantrell—Barnard Douglas—had wanted revenge. He had wanted to destroy Sir Jasper and all his line. Getting rid of Addison Douglas had been a simple matter, a slight impediment to the real goal of robbing Huet's family. For his scheme, Cantrell needed Gerald Douglas, and Gerald could be robbed and ruined by slow degrees using his wife's flawed family.

So, Cantrell had set the hooks to catch them all. He'd lied, and he'd charmed and seduced. He'd caught Douglas and Penelope and Nora and Mr. Hodgeson.

But not Mrs. Hodgeson.

Mrs. Hodgeson had recognized the man calling himself

Cantrell for the scoundrel he was. She had tried to warn a son-in-law who would not listen.

She loved her daughters. She insisted she was the one to save the family.

She distrusted doctors and brewed her own remedies and recipes to recoup her health.

She had a copy of *Boyle's Court and Country Guide* in her room. Rosalind had seen it there. She could have looked up the Ashertons address at any time. With one visit, and a plausible story, she could have discovered Cantrell's whereabouts from the trusting Mrs. Asherton or her well-meaning son. She could have purchased that luncheon and the bottle of wine.

She would have saved her indolent husband. She would have saved her daughters, and herself.

And it had worked, until Mariah had decided it was enough. Because Mariah was too like her mother and her older sister. Too strong. Too protective.

But Mariah had also been too unwilling to hide what she knew.

Rosalind straightened and turned. She smoothed down her skirts. "I need to speak with Mrs. Hodgeson."

The walk down the hallway felt unreal. She knocked on Mrs. Hodgeson's door, just as if paying another one of her after-dinner visits. Gilpin showed no surprise or concern when she opened the door.

Thankfully, Mrs. Hodgeson was alone. She reclined on her sofa. As Rosalind came to stand beside her, Mrs. Hodgeson removed the compress that covered her eyes.

"Is something wrong, Miss Thorne?" she asked.

"Will you ask Gilpin to excuse us please?" asked Rosalind.

"Never," said Mrs. Hodgeson. "I need her by me. My husband, Miss Thorne, has deserted me. I cannot . . . I will not!"

"You do not want Gilpin to hear what I have to say to you

just now," said Rosalind. "Unless she already knows what you have done."

There was an odd ringing in her ears. Rosalind couldn't fathom where it had come from, but it was making it very hard to think.

Mrs. Hodgeson pulled herself upright. She stared into Rosalind's face. Rosalind had no notion what she saw there, but she said, "Gilpin, leave us."

"But, madam—"

Mrs. Hobson waved her hand fiercely. Gilpin lifted her nose, curtsied, and took herself off into the boudoir. She shut the door like an exclamation point.

"Now, then, Miss Thorne," Mrs. Hodgeson sniffed. "What is it I am meant to have done?"

"You took a basket of food to Cantrell," said Rosalind. "You included a bottle of wine that you had poisoned. You were careful not to be seen. You wrote on a label." She felt oddly breathless. "You wrote on a label, 'For my love, with my love,' so he would think it was from the girl he was courting and not question it."

"I don't know what you're talking about." She fluttered her handkerchief. "You should be the one lying down."

"You murdered Bryan Cantrell," said Rosalind. "And before I have to alert the house to the fact, I'd like to know why."

Mrs. Hodgeson stared at her, disbelief and outrage filling her watery eyes. Rosalind watched her considering whether to break down in tears. And watched her discard the idea.

"He could never refuse a meal or a drink," she said. "I was sure that had not changed. And I was right." For a moment, her face showed her triumph, but the expression dissolved into a pious anger.

"Why, Mrs. Hodgeson?"

"Who else was going to? It was quite obvious the man was never going to leave us alone of his own accord. I had to protect my daughters!" She pressed her trembling hands against her face. "I never meant for him to die! I only meant for him to become ill. It was to gain time, for Nora!" She lifted her face. "I knew, you see, that she planned to leave us. I could not like it. What mother could? But with Douglas so unkind, with no home of our own, where we could give her shelter, how could I urge her to stay?"

"I don't believe you, Mrs. Hodgeson."

"I beg your pardon?" she cried.

"I don't believe you," repeated Rosalind. "You said it yourself. You knew Cantrell would never leave you alone of his own accord. You knew from the first you would have to kill him."

"You may believe what you like. I can only say that I am sure no one will believe *you!*"

"Then I may say what I wish," said Rosalind. "And neither of us will have anything to fear."

"You may certainly not say what you wish!" Mrs. Hodgeson heaved herself to her feet. "I see your game, Miss Thorne!" She waved her handkerchief between them. "You think to extract payment so you will not go about repeating your lies! You wormed your way into my Bethany's confidence, and *this* was your plan all along!"

Rosalind drew herself up to her full height. "You may insult me as you please, Mrs. Hodgeson. It will change nothing." She turned. She should go. She should find Bethany. . . .

But Mrs. Hodgeson scuttled forward and slipped into her path.

"Now, please, please, Miss Thorne," she said, the words breathlessly tumbling out of her. "Of course I know that I did wrong, but it was an accident! Nothing more! I told you! I only wanted to make him ill!"

Rosalind made no answer.

Mrs. Hodgeson shot out one bony hand and grabbed her wrist. "If you are concerned about your fees, Miss Thorne, I will pay them."

Rosalind was not prepared for the stab of anger this sent through her, and it took her a moment before she was able to be sure of her voice. "Please let go of me, Mrs. Hodgeson."

Slowly, Mrs. Hodgeson lifted her hand away. "Please," she whispered. "I only wanted to save my family."

"I know," said Rosalind. "And that's the real tragedy."

Rosalind went to the boudoir door and opened it. Gilpin was still standing there, ready as ever. Rosalind wondered idly how much she had overheard. Tears stood in her dark eyes.

Probably a great deal.

"Gilpin," she said, "your mistress needs you."

Gilpin curtsied. "Yes, miss."

Rosalind made her way down the stairs carefully. Her feet did not seem to feel the floor properly, and her balance was . . . off. She stood at the foot of the stairs and tried to think.

Where do I go next?

The decision was made for her. The library door opened. Mariah met her gaze, and recognition flashed behind her eyes.

"You've spoken to Mama?" Mariah asked softly.

"Yes," said Rosalind. "Why did you put that bottle in my room?"

"She tried to tell me that you were going to blame Cantrell's death on Nora. I realized she must have . . ." Mariah's chin trembled. "I tried to tell myself she did it to protecting us, and Pen and . . . and I found her reasoning was quite flawed." She looked away. "You will tell Bethany and Douglas?"

"Yes," said Rosalind. "But why did you not tell them yourself?"

"Quite frankly, I was not sure they'd believe me," she replied. The words contained much of her familiar acid. "And because, Miss Thorne, of all the people in this house, it seems you are the one I trust the most."

They faced each other in silence for a long moment.

"What will you do?" Rosalind asked.

"I believe I had better find Penelope. I think when she hears out what's happening, she will take the news rather ill."

"I'll tell Nora where you are."

Rosalind walked slowly down the stairs. She met the parlor-maid and was told that Mr. and Mrs. Douglas were still in the morning room with Miss Hodgeson.

This report proved to be correct. When Rosalind opened the doors, Douglas, Bethany, and Nora all turned to face her.

"What is it, Rosalind?" asked Bethany.

Rosalind drew in a deep breath and searched for a place to begin. But she had no time to speak. In the next moment, the doors opened behind her, and the footman entered.

"Mrs. Douglas?" he said. "I . . . You are requested up-stairs."

Bethany rose to her feet. "What's happened?"

But Rosalind saw the servant's expression, and she knew.

I was too late, she thought. She closed her eyes as Bethany rushed past her, followed closely by Douglas.

Rosalind opened her eyes again and found she was facing Nora.

"What is it!" Nora demanded.

"Your mama," said Rosalind.

Nora started, and Nora stared. Rosalind watched as awful understanding blossomed in the young woman's eyes. She held her arms open, and Nora fell into them and wept.

EPILOGUE

But above all, above respect and esteem, there
was a motive within her of goodwill which could
not be overlooked. It was gratitude ...

Jane Austen, *Pride and Prejudice*

It was four weeks later, and the season had just begun. Rosalind sat beside Nora Hodgeson in a lovely light equipage pulled by a pair of very smart, steady horses, who made light work of the intricacies of London traffic.

Nora wore unadorned black, including a black coat and bonnet. Her hair had been pulled back into a simple bundle of curls.

It had been a difficult month for the family. Mrs. Hodgeson's death, which had come after she'd spoken with Rosalind, was officially ruled heart failure by the coroner. At the same time, Gerald Douglas declined to press any charge of theft against his father-in-law and sent the bag of pearls to Sterne and Fiske to be restrung according to the original plan.

Mr. Hodgeson did not survive his wife by more than a fortnight. But whether it was due to the shock of his wife's death or the shock of finding himself forgiven by his son-in-law, no one could say.

The work of arranging the funerals and all the attendant business of preparing the house and family for mourning came as something of a relief to Bethany, because it did not leave her with overmuch time to think or to grieve over what her parents had become. That would come later, Rosalind knew, but she trusted that Bethany and Douglas would see each other through.

Douglas spent one very long day closeted with Sir Jasper and left the encounter grim, determined, and—to everyone's surprise—not one farthing poorer. It seemed that while Sir Jasper's family feeling was much wounded by Douglas's plain speaking, it would not allow him to leave his monies and lands to some anonymous charity.

Rosalind promised that next year she would be proud to chaperone Penelope through the full season. She further offered that once their mourning period was over, she would be able to introduce Bethany to some friends with whom she was sure both Bethany and Douglas would get along very well.

Which left Nora and Mariah. Rosalind watched Nora fuss with her bonnet ribbons.

"I have not yet asked you your plans for the future."

"I have determined I shall go to the Continent," replied Nora. "As I had originally planned when this whole sad adventure began. Only this time I will not have to lie when I say that I am a young widow." She smiled, but the expression was a little wan.

"What of Mariah? Does she go with you?"

"Surprisingly not. At least not yet. It seems she's fallen rather deeply in with this Mrs. Keene and her friends. This shared obsession with chemistry and prisms and rational philosophies has produced a significant bond." She shook her head. "Well, we shall all see what happens, I suppose. But don't worry. I shall be quite proper in my travels. Gilpin comes with me."

Rosalind arched her brows, but all she said was, "May I write to you?"

"I should like that. I'll let you know where to direct your letters as soon as I am sure." Nora paused. "Rosalind, I . . . I have a question."

"What is it?"

"Do you think . . . what happened, what my mother did? Was it my fault? Because . . ."

"No," said Rosalind. "She made her choices. She decided to do as she did, without reference to anyone else."

"Yes. That is true." Nora tugged at her bonnet ribbons again. "Do you know, I wonder sometimes what I would have done if she had told me her plans." For a moment, she looked troubled, but as she was still Nora, it was only for a moment. "But then I remind myself I have many better things to do." The carriage slowed. "Ah, I believe we are arrived."

The driver opened the door and let down the steps. Rosalind climbed out and turned. Nora stepped out slowly, tentatively. She had, Rosalind saw, perched a pince-nez on her nose.

"Goodness me," she said as she took in the breadth of Lady Cowper's house. She said it again as the livery footman bowed to her in the arched doorways. And again as Lady Cowper came forward to meet her in the grand entry hall.

"Lady Cowper," said Rosalind. "May I introduce you to Miss Leonora Mayne?"

"How do you *do*, Miss Mayne!" Lady Cowper curtsied grandly. "Thank you so much for calling!"

"Oh, erm, yes." Nora bobbed a schoolgirl's curtsy in answer. "And I, that is, I must apologize for being so long to answer your ladyship's kind invitation!" Nora did not seem to be able to make herself speak above a whisper. "I am . . . I am not used to such company. That so many people have become so *taken* with my brother's work, well, it has been so overwhelming!"

"Yes, I do understand. Now, you must come with me. My friends are so eager to meet you, and afterward we shall have such a lovely luncheon! I do hope you are fond of salmon!"

She looped her arm through Nora's, but Nora hesitated. "Oh, ah, does Miss Thorne not dine with us?"

"I'm sorry, Miss Mayne, but I believe I told you I have an appointment," said Rosalind. "However, I know Lady Cowper will take very good care of you."

"Indeed I shall. Why, Miss Mayne, you shall be my *treasure*."

Still chatting, Lady Cowper led her treasure away.

"And here . . . !" Mrs. Heslop threw open the door to the front parlor. "Is where you shall meet your ladies, Miss Thorne!"

After she'd left Lady Cowper, Rosalind had taken the borrowed carriage to collect Adam and Alice at Little Russell Street, and from there they had all driven to meet Mrs. Heslop at her Orchard Street home.

Now Rosalind, followed closely by Alice and Adam, walked into a beautifully appointed room. It faced south, so the light was excellent, and the cheerful gold wallpaper made it seem soaked in sunshine. The bowed windows overlooked the quiet square. The carpets were quite new, and a cheerful fire burned in the hearth, proving that the chimney drew beautifully.

Rosalind turned in place, looking at the colors, the light, and the view of the square. She reminded herself they had not yet inspected the attics, much less the cellar. She was not entirely sure she liked the situation of the dining room, and as for the kitchen . . .

"Well?" Mrs. Heslop said to her brightly. "What do you think, Miss Thorne?"

Rosalind looked around the large, airy room. She felt the calculations clatter through her thoughts—so much for rent, so much more for coals, provisions, linens. So much more. Another maid to come in days, a cook at the very least, another bed . . .

She looked at Alice and at Adam.

She felt herself smile.

"It's perfect."